THE KISHI

Tales From Esowon

ANTOINE BANDELE

Edited By

JOSIAH DAVIS

Publisher: Bandele Books
Interior Design: Vellum
Editor: Josiah Davis
Cover Artist: Sutthiwat Dekachamphu
Cover Design: Mariah Sinclair
Cartographer: Maria Gandolfo | RenflowerGrapx
Character Art: Vivian A. Friedel

ISBN: 978-0-9998483-3-3

Paperback, Second Edition | March 5, 2020

CONTENTS

The Kishi is the first book in the *Tales from Esowon*, a series of standalone novels introducing the world of Esowon, its many regions, and the characters who occupy it.

For suggested and chronological reading order visit antoinebandele.com/esowon-timeline

If you enjoy this story and are interested in the rest of its world you can join Antoine Bandele's e-mail alerts list. He'll send you notifications for new book releases, exclusive updates, and behind-the-page content.

Visit this link:
antoinebandele.com/stay-in-touch

Special Thanks to my
Alpha, Beta, and Proof Readers!

Seth Hansen
Yolanda Bevans
Andrea S.U.
Avinoam Land
Richard Smith
Jesse Garrard
Debashish Das

And to my Kickstarter Backers!

Roban Sky Athens
William Anderson
William Bailey
Callan Brown
Casey Brown
Matthew Brown
Joel Butler
Rory Christian
Steve Cubias
Ricardo Elliott II
Ruben Garcia
Roy Kim
Reece Kimpton
Miki Marsala
Henry Mayper
Thomas Davis
Megan Fisher
Francois Fourre

Jesse Garrard
AJ Howard
Camille Lofters
Jessie Marston
Von Dexter Montegut II
Vidal Pierce
Kam Reed
Nekia Renee
Michael Scott
Christopher Spenceley
Ben Spencer
Storrs Start
Mireya Torres
Monica Torres
Andrea S.U.
Hawk Zindell

PRONUNCIATION GUIDE

Characters

A·ma·na - ə'mä'nä
Ay·o - ī'ō
E·me·ka - ə'me'kä
E·si - e'sē
I·ken·na - ē'ken'nä
I·man·i - ē'mä'nē
I·me - ē'mā
Mo·sai - mō'sī
Nan·ga - nän'gä
Nee·ma - nī'mä
Ny·a - nī'ä
O·ba - ō'bä
U·zo·ma - ü'zō'mä
Ye·mi - yeə'mē
Ko·jo - kō'jō
Kwa·chi - kwä'chē
Ye·ji·de - yeə'gē'dā

Terms & Titles

Kor - cor
Kor'de - cor'dā

Locations

Ba·jok - bä'jōk
E·so·won - e'sō'wän
Go·lah - go'läh
N·yo·ka - nī'yō'kä
Ya·se·ti - yə'se'tē

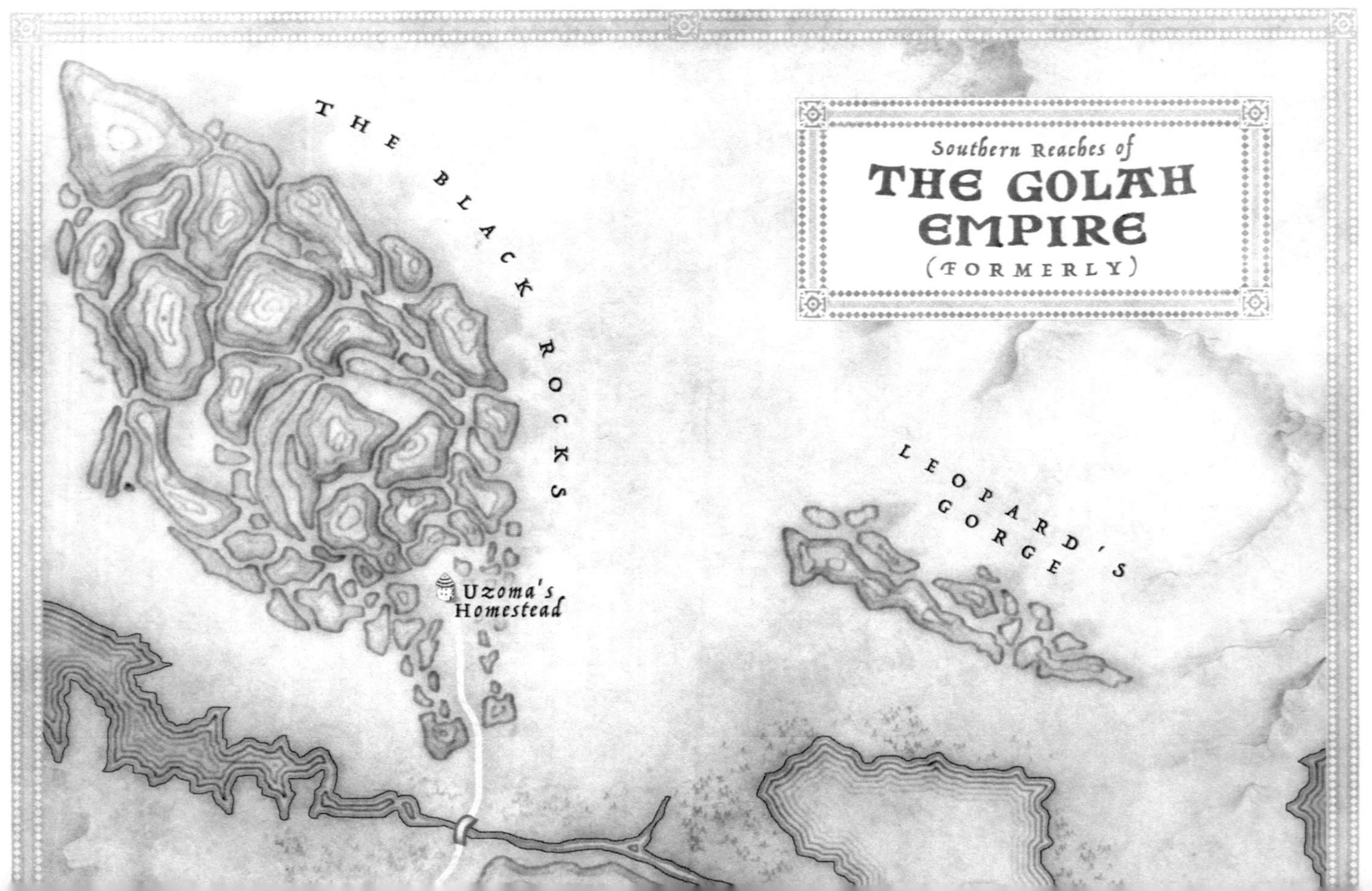
Southern Reaches of
THE GOLAH EMPIRE
(FORMERLY)
THE BLACK ROCKS
LEOPARD'S GORGE
Uzoma's Homestead

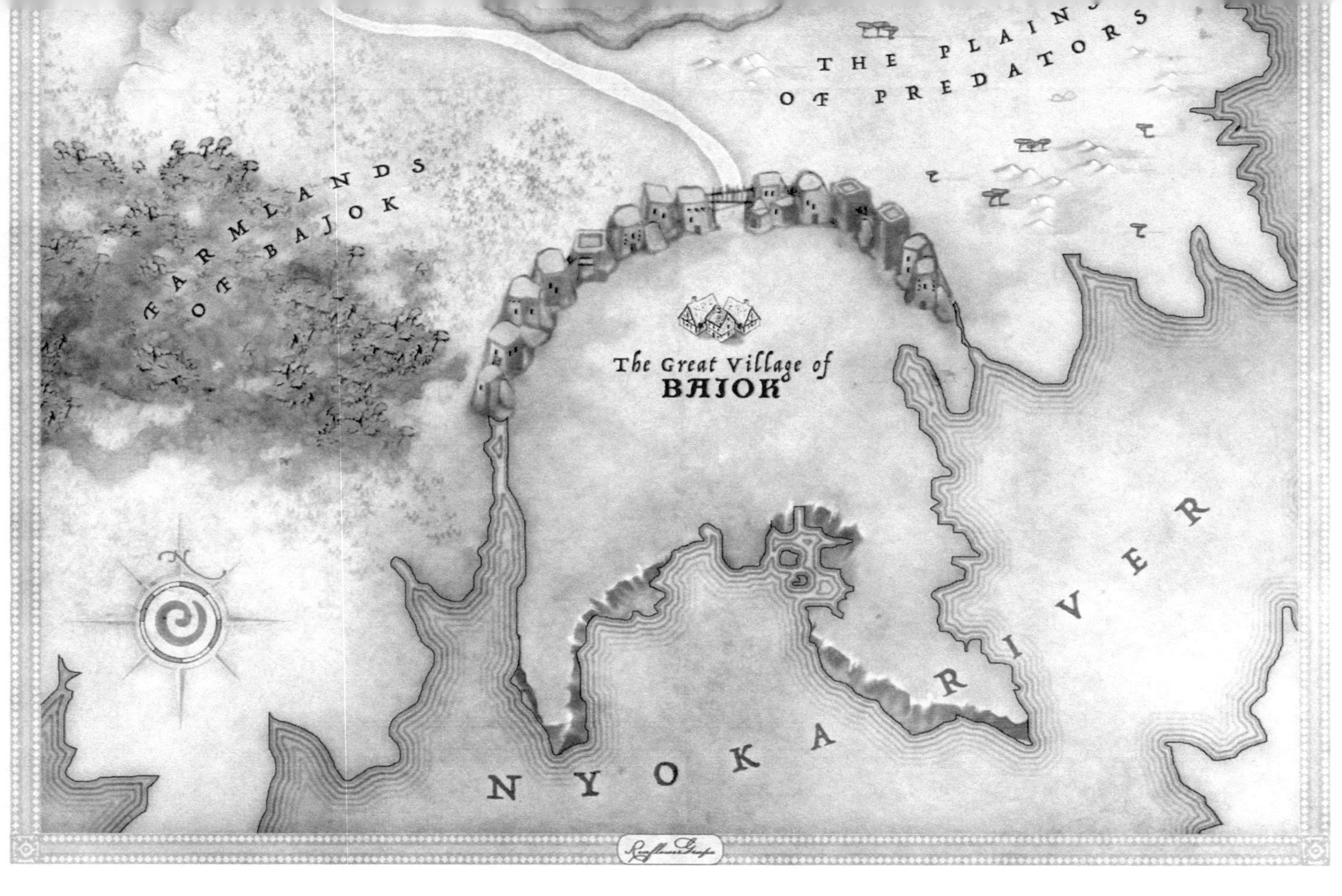
THE PLAIN
OF PREDATORS
FARMLANDS
OF BAJOK
The Great Village of
BAJOK
NYOKA RIVER
N

To my mother,
who nurtured my creativity.

To my father,
who molded my disposition.

Like spirits of Bajok,
you lead me down a better path.

"Be wary of handsome men,"
To us our mother once said.
"Don't forget Ife who was lost to the rocks.
In love with a man's charm and flowing locs.
But tricked she was, deceived right and proper.
Oh yes, that man was a real heart stopper.
No man at all was he, but a demon sharp and sly.
Behind his head hid a beast. No one heard her cry."

— THE LEGEND OF THE KISHI

CHAPTER 1

THE MAN WITH NO NAME

Everything about him was perfect.

He danced like a leopard, and sang like a nightingale. Though sweat dripped down his muscles, he smelled as fresh as fruit. He was well-mannered and considerate to man, woman, and child alike. Everyone loved him. And that laugh! So infectious. It lit up the surrounding space, casting a perfect aura around his head. This man truly had no flaws.

Yet Imani did not know what he looked like, nor did she know his name.

It had been several hours since the festival had begun. The village celebrated a visiting nation—the Ya-Seti, if Imani had heard the soldiers correctly. She'd lost all sense of time. It felt like only a few moments since she had sneaked away from home, slipping out her window, her mother and father none the wiser. Imani thought she had woken them when she crushed the bean plants underfoot. She had cursed at herself, tiptoeing around the other plants as she walked the never-ending farmland.

Imani had never been to the Great Village of Bajok, at least never to its central festival grounds. Her father only let her go to the outskirts to trade their harvest every so often.

"No need to intermingle with this sort," her father had said one day at the market. "This village is becoming more and more … ambitious. Look at that hut there; it's twice, no, three times as big as ours. What's the need for it?"

It didn't matter to Imani. All she cared about was what the village would have in store for *her*. The Great Village stood atop a small plateau, surrounded by a mud wall five times as tall as a man stood. Her father was right—the huts were grand, even more so at the village's central grounds. Some of the huts stacked one on top of the other, rising high. The Great Village dwarfed her family's farm at least ten times over.

The festival's sights and sounds overtook Imani. There was a drum circle, in which men fought while holding hands in some strange ritual. Their faces were bloody from the combat. Women laughed as they twisted and turned to the beat of the drums. They all wore long blue skirts with white tops.

Imani knew their tops represented the glow of the two moons and that the blue bottoms signified the rivers and oceans. As the women danced, they looked like tiny moons shifting the waters of the world.

The villagers were beautiful, all of them. It seemed like they all had eyes of golden brown, and their skin was flawless. Perhaps it was the energy in the village that made them so beautiful. Each woman wore a wide smile, and the men's laughter was alluring.

"It's amazing, isn't it?" her friend said when she found Imani in the throng of villagers. Like Imani, Yejide wore a blue skirt with a white top.

"It doesn't look this big from the markets." Imani didn't want to take her eyes off any of it, but the sight of Yejide's teeth made her wince. "Did you use the licorice root like I told you to?"

Yejide stopped smiling, covering her mouth. "I was so excited I forgot."

"Here, take this." Imani offered Yejide her own root from her skirt.

"Thanks," Yejide said as she cleaned her teeth. White teeth didn't matter much out in the farmlands—at least, not most of the time. It was an honest mistake. But if Imani were to blend in with the villagers, she couldn't have her friend walking about with yellowed teeth.

A man in a large mask pounded the ground in front of Imani as Yejide used the root discreetly. At first, the man stomped slowly. Imani scrunched up her face as though she smelled a nasty odor. She'd had many suitors before, and no man had yet impressed her. But something about the way this man moved caught her attention. He rolled his hips in a rhythmic circle. The reflection of the festival fires flickered atop his chest as he held out a hand. Imani could not take her eyes off that gyration; it was ... hypnotic.

"Thank you," Yejide cut in. "But we are dancing together."

In truth, neither of them had been dancing. Yejide tried a simple two-step to sell her lie, but that did not deter the man. Nor did it deter Imani.

Imani took the man's hand and mimicked his tempo. They danced atop the soft ground. Imani's heart pounded under her breast, and her breath quickened, though from the dancing or from the man, she couldn't decide.

Yejide would not be left out and went to find a man of her own, pulling an eager participant from the crowd. She and her new partner danced in circles around one another. But Imani took no notice, her attention locked on her own cohort.

"Feel the rhythm of the sister spirits. Let your arms take up your skirt and move them like the moons shift the waters," the man said.

Imani lifted her blue skirt; she at least got that part right. The custom of these festivals was to wear such things. Yejide did the same with her partner, mimicking Imani. Both did their best not to attract the wrong attention. A pair of farm girls had to look like regular villagers.

But Imani couldn't get the dance right. Her partner, however, was perfect. His moves represented the spirits of the earth. He stomped the ground as though to call the elemental spirit Himself. Imani watched him, letting the man's own dancing spirit fill her.

"That's it. Relax. Follow the drums; they will guide your feet." He gave her a full smile—it was all she could see through the hole of his ceremonial mask. His teeth were straight and as white as the moons. Imani hopped and skipped like the waves of the ocean.

"You see that? You're a natural." The man stomped his feet again. Thump, thump. "Now turn around me."

Imani did as he asked. Like the other women, she twisted around him like water crashing around a rock. The singers in the drum circle sang their hymn.

This is Esowon; this is Esowon.
Water over rocks, this is how it starts.
Water's the hands of the painter.
Rock's the canvas of the artist.

"You're not from the village, are you?" The man turned on his heel and clapped twice.

"That obvious?" Imani's cheeks went red.

He shrugged while holding the tempo of the drums. Imani bit her lip; he never missed a beat.

"Strictly, I'm of Bajok, but I serve as a farmhand."

"Your beauty is wasted on the beans," the man said, voice muffled by his mask.

Imani blushed. She turned away, feeling silly. What had come over her?

"You don't have to be bashful." The man pulled her chin back up with his finger. His touch was gentle. "Come, drink with me."

The man guided Imani by the small of her back. Yejide looked over her partner's shoulder, keeping a close eye on Imani. When Imani met her friend's eyes, the stupor she'd felt during the dance left her.

"Wait, I can't," she said. "My friend—"

"Can join us if she likes." The man flashed a smile. He waved a hand at Yejide and her dancing partner. Yejide waved her skinny arm back, beaming as she skipped toward them.

"I was offering your friend a drink if you wanted to join—"

"We'd love to! Right?" Yejide turned a hawk-like gaze toward her partner, who shrugged.

The group drifted from the drum circle, where others still danced, kicking up the soft dirt in a whirlwind. To Imani, the dust clouds and the fluttering blue dresses reminded her of the stories her mother had told her.

"This is how the world was created by the Gods," her mother had told a young Imani while dancing at their farm. Her movements had been like magic.

As they moved toward the drinks, the man kept the beat of the drum with his steps. When they approached the jugs of wine, his sweat had already dried.

"Have you had our palm wine before?" He grabbed a jug.

"My father only lets me have some on our first harvest." Imani clutched her wrist. Why was she so nervous?

"You can have as much as you'd like here." He turned to the man watching over the wine. "Isn't that right, friend?"

"Fine by me. The Chief says we can drink our fill today," the wine man said, swaying dizzily. He'd already had his own taste.

Yejide was slow to drink, but her partner took a generous swig from the large jug.

"It's so … sour," Yejide said with pinched eyes.

Imani drank as much as she could until it burned her throat. "What is all this?" She pointed toward the festivities.

"You see there?" The man nodded toward the far end of the festival grounds. "That's our Great-Chief and the Kor of Ya-Seti."

"The Kor?" Imani tried to follow the man's gaze.

"The ruler of the Ya-Seti. And the Kor'de is his ruling-wife. They come far from the east, almost to the Sapphire Seas."

That's a long way to travel, Imani thought. Through the mass of the villagers' waving hands and turning bodies, she found where the royal men sat. The Great-Chief was there, wearing his ceremonial mask of war. She'd never seen him so close before. He was the primary reason for their prosperity. He was tall and broad-shouldered, a warrior through and through, the strongest of all the men in their village.

Next to him sat an impossibly old-looking man. His skin was wizened beyond belief, hair grayer than a sheep's. Yet he wore a golden crown twice as tall as his head, and glistening around its brim were two silver snakes. A gold sash sat atop the elaborate white silks that stretched from his torso down to his heels.

Next to the pair were two war elephants, also decked in gold. One had gold chains falling from its tusks; the other, an entirely gold mask. Each elephant carried a cart on its back, in which a trio of archers was perched.

"I didn't know there was so much gold in the entire world," Yejide said, her mouth wide in disbelief.

"It's a big show, really. They want to make a good impression on the Chief. And we want to make a good impression on them—is the drink too sour? I can get you another." The man pointed at Imani's drink. She blushed and took another sip. Already her skin tingled from the wine.

"You see, they want to marry off their daughter to the Great-Chief's first son. This is all a show of respect."

Imani looked at the young woman sitting next to the visiting Kor. She was gorgeous with her long neck and smooth skin. Like her father, she wore long white silks, but her head was draped with a silver headpiece.

"She's the bride to be, I assume?" Imani nodded to the woman. "She's beautiful."

"For a Ya-Seti. The best women are right here in Bajok."

Imani blushed again—she needed to stop doing that. Yejide was looking at her with raised eyebrows.

Before Imani could give her friend a look back, a small girl brushed against her leg. She was crying.

"What's wrong?" Imani knelt.

"The boys won't let me play with them," the girl sobbed.

"Don't worry; we'll play with you," the man said before Imani could respond.

He swung the small girl atop his shoulders and danced again. The girl squealed with joy, holding on to the man's mask.

Imani smiled. Watching him dance with the girl warmed her heart. Something unnatural within her made her want to join him. She downed the rest of her wine and trotted up to them, taking the man's hand and holding on tight.

"Well, come on, let's go." Yejide grabbed her partner's wrist.

After a few dances, the little girl ran off to her mother and brothers with a beaming smile. Imani and the man went along with her to where her family was sharing peanut soup and *fufu*. The little girl gave the man most of hers, and the man gave his share to Imani. The dish would have been too hot for her if the fufu had not absorbed most of the spicy soup.

Yejide still danced with the other villagers. Imani was not sure how she had lost her friend, but she pushed the thought to the back of her mind, her attention locked on the man.

She smiled as he told jokes to the family. Even though he laughed at his own jokes, she couldn't help but chuckle herself. Her sides were hurting when the village shaman cleared the drum circle.

"Brothers and Sisters of Bajok!" the shaman bellowed with a staff in his right hand. The village went silent. He wore a large headpiece made of palm and twine. A jeweled crystal covered one of his eyes, and his shoulders were draped in straw. One of his shoulders was plastered with a small ceremonial mask. Imani couldn't tell what the face was, but she assumed it represented Deh'ala, the Gatekeeper spirit. Besides that, the shaman wore nothing else save for straw that covered his manhood and ankles. His body was painted bright blue with a few white streaks across his face.

"Let us welcome our brothers and sisters from the far lands of Ya-Seti!" The audience tapped their chests lightly, but the shaman shook his head. "That will not do. How will the spirits know of this union with such silent tongues? I say again, let us welcome our family from Ya-Seti!"

This time, the crowd pounded their chests so hard Imani could feel them through the ground. She joined in on the gesture, driven by the sheer energy emanating from the village. With the last round of cheers, wisps of smoke swirled from the fires surrounding the drum circle.

The shaman waved a hand, and the drummers of the circle came to his side. For a moment, it was silent as the crowd waited for the shaman's next move. He placed his hand in the soft dirt below, lifting it as though he were holding a newborn child aloft. He clasped his hands together and shook the sand. The drummers thumped on their hides, keeping the shaman's beat. This was important if they were to manifest the spirit—both shaman and drum had to be in unison. He turned in circles, shouting in the language of the Old Spirits. Imani could only make out some of the names, such as Deh'ala.

After a few moments, the shaman cast the sand, pinch by pinch, into the fire pits surrounding him and his drum circle. Each fire went out the moment earth touched it. For what felt like an eternity, everything was dark. Only the stars lit the village circle. The shaman, the drum circle, the entire village, and its visitors remained still and silent.

And then, fire and rock surged twenty paces in the air.

It was stark white and bright as day—like no fire Imani had ever seen. Spirits shot out from these white flames. Imani couldn't put the names to the shapes, but she felt their power within the circle. A few strides away, a woman shouted in joy. A few yards from that, a frail elder jumped up and stomped the ground like a newborn zebra.

"Spirits of Bajok! You have blessed us with your presence here! Is it assumed this marriage paints itself in Ula's stars?"

Imani turned to the man she'd spent all this time with, but he was no longer there. The little girl and her family remained, enamored with the sights that flickered before them. But where had the man gone? She didn't even know his name, or even worse, what he looked like. She stood, and another brilliant light flashed above the shaman.

"Ula! Great Spirit of the Cosmos," the shaman began as a great wisp in the shape of a woman floated down in front of him. "Please, will the First Son of Bajok and our new sister of Ya-Seti join us!"

From the grand stage, the bride and groom-to-be stepped down to join the shaman and the spirits. A villager handed the Ya-Seti Princess a ceremonial mask. The First Son wore a large black mask with white markings, not unlike the man Imani had enjoyed her night with. Like the Great-Chief, the First Son also wore an elaborate headpiece—though less prominent, of course. The Princess now wore a large white mask with holes for her eyes. The markings on her mask were swirls like small suns.

"Please, young ones, sit among our spirits and ancestors." The shaman waved an inviting hand to the surrounding space. They sat next to him without protest. "Please, Great and Powerful Ula, tell us if this is the right path for these two young souls!"

The spirits shifted and coiled around the pair, some passing straight through them. Goosebumps protruded from their skin. Imani swore she could feel them, too, as though the judgement of the spirits did not pass only through the would-be Chief and his future wife, but through the entire village. Were the spirits asking if the village approved of this marriage, as well? Imani knew nothing of the Great-Chief, his son, or these foreign Ya-Seti. She would have to entrust the decision to the spirits and ancestors.

The marriage spirit called Ula spoke. The voice was unlike anything Imani had ever heard. It was neither human nor animal; it was … alien. But the shaman, a vessel between the spirits and the mortals, translated.

"*The man. The woman,*" the shaman began in a distorted voice. His eyes were stark white, and the jeweled crystal shone violet. "*Match, they could be. But this village still carries dark spirits and unnatural demons.*"

"Tell us where these demons are, and we will cast them away!" the shaman proclaimed in his own voice again. It was strange how the shaman could go from speaking in the spirit's voice to his own so quickly.

"*These demons are difficult to see. Neither mortals nor spirits. Our vision does not see them clearly. Be wary, Children of Bajok.*"

The Great-Chief stepped forward. "Impossible; we rid our village of those vile beasts ages ago!" Because he didn't have his mask on, his red, flushed face could be seen openly.

"Our Chief speaks the truth. We have no—" said the shaman.

"*Something dark remains!*" the spirit shouted. "*This marriage cannot be claimed.*"

And then the white plumes crashed back into the fire pits. For a moment, the village was sheltered in darkness. Bajok and Ya-Seti alike were hushed. Slowly, the fires rose again to light the drum circle. The villagers of Bajok all looked to their Chief, who was still red-faced. The few Ya-Seti looked to their Kor. He remained unmoved.

"The Ya-Seti are demons!" one woman shouted from across the circle.

One of the foreigners shouted back in a language Imani could not understand.

"Leave! We don't want you here!" another villager cursed.

Another Ya-Seti, a handmaiden by the looks of her, clenched a fist and scowled.

"Silence!" the Great-Chief bellowed. "This is not how we treat our brothers and sisters from the east. These dark spirits remain our own. The Ya-Seti have nothing to do with it."

The Great-Chief looked to each person from his village, the powerful eyes of a father. There was a reason he was their leader. "It was my belief these demons were gone, and we've yet to see evidence they have returned."

"What about those dead girls?" one villager said.

"Those were animal attacks!"

"The spirits don't say that!"

"The spirits didn't say anything at all!"

Imani looked for the man again. What was his damned name? The shaman raised his staff, then struck it against the earth. The dirt cracked. Dust rose and fell.

"You dare speak against the Great-Chief?" he shouted. His blue skin lit up as he spoke.

The clamoring voices settled.

"If these demons have returned, it is my obligation to destroy them again," the Chief continued. He pointed his large finger at the villager who had shouted out of turn. "Those girls died to animal attacks."

Silence.

"I trust that the people of Bajok will keep us safe during this time," said the Ya-Seti bride-to-be. "In my homelands, we are often tested like this. Not by our ancestors, or our spirits, but by the elements and our own enemies. My father, our Kor, has taught us that men should be given the chance to prove themselves before we cry out against them. Are these festivals not held to cleanse the village of such evil spirits?"

"They are," said the Great-Chief. "And thank you, young Shanaki. Already I can see you will prosper within our great village."

"All due credit to my Kor-father." She gestured to the old man gracefully who returned her nod slowly.

"So, should we not continue this cleanse?" Shanaki asked.

"Indeed, we should! Drummers!" The shaman gestured to them.

Once again, they pounded their hides and sang beautiful melodies. But it wasn't enough. Though the village went back to eating, drinking, and dancing, the feeling wasn't the same. There was an air of darkness.

Imani looked for the man again but couldn't find him anywhere. She turned to the young girl she had played with earlier.

"Have you seen the man I was with?" Imani asked kindly.

The little girl shook her head, braids flying to and fro. Imani kept looking. He was no longer in the dance circle. None of the men in masks were him; they didn't dance as smoothly as he had.

She returned to the man serving the palm wine, but he had not seen her suitor either. Imani even went over to the fighting circle, but he wasn't there.

For a moment, Imani thought she'd never find him again. Maybe he had been a figment of her imagination. But no, he had played with the girl, and the wine server remembered him well enough. And Yejide! She had stepped between them before they'd parted ways.

Maybe she'd made a bad impression. Perhaps he was off with another beautiful girl, dancing and sharing fruit with her instead.

"Does your father know you're here?" a voice behind her said. Imani frowned. It was Nanga.

"That's really none of your concern." She turned around to face him. He was a Bajok warrior with broad shoulders and a chiseled body—but a terrible attitude.

"Seeing as my job is to protect Bajok with my life, I would say it is my business." Nanga crossed his arms, his spear clutched in one hand. "I won't tell your father if you give me a smile."

Imani scoffed. "You are ever the charmer. It's a wonder you haven't married."

Nanga only smiled. This was the type of man Imani had hoped to avoid, the kind of suitor that made her cringe. She needed to find a way out.

"Thank you, Nanga. I was looking all over for her." That voice ... It was the man! That graceful man. Before she turned, she knew it was him. He smelled of sweet desert flowers just as before. But how could he? He had been dancing and sweating all night.

He still wore that mask, though. She'd have to fix that as soon as she could.

"I was speaking to her first," Nanga interjected.

"Shouldn't you be on the northern edges of the village?" the man asked. Nanga dropped his head. Something was wrong. Nanga never backed down so easily.

Nanga's frown twisted further down his mouth. Imani felt something in the air. It was intangible, but it ran through her like a dark cloud. "Yes, I guess I should go back to my post." Nanga turned on his heel and left.

"Sorry about all that," the man said, touching Imani's shoulder. The sensations she'd felt before evaporated. The man felt so warm, so ... right.

"Let's leave here, now." Imani took his hand and started away from the festival grounds.

"Imani!" It was Yejide. She had lost her partner. "What are you doing?"

Imani stopped. The man took a polite step away, though he stood close enough to listen.

"We were supposed to leave together." Yejide's eyes were sharp but hurt. "What's wrong with you?"

"Nothing at all," Imani said, though she had a hard time keeping her balance.

"You're never like this," Yejide said. She stepped in closer to whisper to Imani. "What's so special about this one?—Well, I get it: nice body, kind, affectionate, and his face—Wait, we've not even seen his face! We don't even know who he is! It's like the story of Ife..."

"Well, I guess I'll find out," Imani answered.

"By yourself?"

"What's so wrong with that?"

"Your father would not approve." Yejide crossed her tiny arms.

"Good thing he's not here," Imani shot back. "Your father wouldn't approve of you being here, either."

"It's a bad idea, Imani, that's all I'm saying. Something feels wrong about that man." Yejide stole a glance at him. He waited patiently, tapping his feet to the beat of the drum like he had no care in the world.

"Well, I have a good feeling about him. I can't explain it." Imani turned to the man. She couldn't wait anymore. She needed to be with him now. But why? Yejide was right; he was a bit *too* perfect.

What's wrong with that? Imani thought. That's what they were looking for in the first place, right? *Yejide is just jealous.*

"Just trust me, okay?"

"No!" Yejide shouted, tugging at Imani's arm. "We're leaving."

"Let go of me!" Imani pushed back. "You can't keep me from him! Just because no man wants your skin-and-bones doesn't mean I can't have any fun."

Yejide's eyes watered. They had been friends for years, and Imani had never raised her voice at Yejide. Everything felt wrong, yet the man felt so right. What was happening to her?

"Is everything okay?" said the man. When he placed his hand on Imani's back, she forgot all about her worry and how she had hurt Yejide.

"Let's go." Imani grabbed the man again.

"Are you sure everything is fine?" he asked, looking over his shoulder to the now crying Yejide.

"Everything is perfect," Imani said. "Hurry, before someone else stops us."

It did not take long for Imani and the man to cross the outskirts of the village. The sounds of the drums went from loud thumps to indistinct pats. Imani stopped near a riverbed.

"Any farther and the beasts of the night will find us." The man chuckled.

"I'm with you; you'll protect us," Imani answered.

"You haven't even seen me fight."

"I don't have to." Imani still clutched his hand. "Why do you cover your face?"

The man's laughter subsided.

"Are you…" Imani whispered.

"Ugly? Disfigured? Both? No, I'm just—"

"Let me see your face."

"I shouldn't. I'm trying to be good."

"Good is for the priests and the shaman. I want to see your face."

The man shook his head at first. But after a short while, he agreed. He turned away from Imani as he removed his mask. His head was covered with well-maintained locs that flowed down his shoulders—though the sides of his head were bare.

Slowly, the man showed his face, the light of the moons shimmering atop his dark skin. Imani was first taken by his eyes. They were a golden brown, like the other villagers, but they were … moving? No, they couldn't be. The inside of eyes didn't move. But they were more beautiful than any sunrise Imani had ever seen.

The man's skin was too smooth to be real, no blemishes, no wrinkles, not even the dark shadow men had around their cheeks. His nose was a perfectly round shape and his lips …

That smile. His perfect teeth lit up brighter than the moons. Imani thought she heard music, but there was no music at all. She could still see the lights of the village in the distance, but the music was too far away to hear. No, this music came from him. It was that infectious laugh again. It was almost like a song.

Imani could have sworn she'd seen his face before. She just couldn't place it.

"I've seen you on the plains before ... what's your name?"

The man answered, but Imani couldn't hear the response. His beauty confounded her mind. She was drunk on more than palm wine.

Before she knew it, the man's lips were on her neck, softly pecking. He moved his mouth down, lifting her shirt, his tongue lightly brushing her navel. Imani's eyes rolled into the back of her head. She'd felt nothing like this before.

Imani touched the man's face and pressed it against her own, tasting his sweet mouth, tracing his lips with her own. She let him touch her throbbing breasts as he kissed her harder and harder. Imani didn't mind. She wanted him to bite, wanted him to let her bleed. Imani's hands went to the back of the man's hair, but she felt something odd.

Where she expected to find smooth and soft skin was a growing lump. She could have sworn she felt—no it couldn't be—a nose? A snout, even?

The man's kisses were too hard now; his gentle love bites were more than painful.

"Slow down." Imani pushed him with her free hand.

But he wouldn't stop. He pressed his jaw harder against her throat. Her hand on the back of his head was being engulfed by —teeth?

"What is this?" Imani's heart pounded harder. Before she could pull her hand away, there was a crunch. Pain shot down Imani's arm. It didn't make sense—the back of the man's head had bitten Imani's hand. Yet the pain was real. Imani screamed but was silenced by the crunch of her own neck.

Then she fell.

The young woman looked to her hand that was no longer there, replaced now with a bloody stub. She tried to scream again, but she had no throat. Terror filled her now. The man towered above her—no, not a man, a beast. A dark spirit. A demon.

The man was now on all fours, but his joints were impossibly crooked and bending backward. The back of his head was no longer his back but his front. Peeking through the part in his locs was the face of a hyena, cackling and laughing; the same laugh that had sounded so beautiful just moments ago. Its mouth was matted with blood, and it was salivating.

The last thing Imani saw was a bloody maw enveloping her face.

CHAPTER 2

THE VILLAGE OF BAJOK

Travelers from Guela had told Amana that the Nyoka River was too treacherous to navigate at night. But when he was told that his destination was so close, he could not wait. In truth, it was not so bad. It had been an hour since the sun had fallen below the horizon, and the crocodiles seemed docile enough—perhaps filled with their fair share of wildebeest.

It had been a few years since Amana had taken up the practice of the Junga monks, but he had only learned a sliver of their teachings. His sole education came from the Scroll of the Balanced Five—or *Boiэm*, as the mountain monks called it. It advised nothing against impatient thought or action, as far as Amana could recall. Maybe a different tenet of the Junga monks made such a claim. But all Amana had was the Scroll of the Five. He had to continue, had to find the Great Elder Uzoma.

Legend had it that the man had faced impossible odds to save the small village of Bajok. He had been impossibly outnumbered, yet still came out on top. Some said Uzoma was the perfect warrior, the best in a century. Others said the Elder might be a demigod, with hidden powers only he was privy to. Amana didn't know what to believe, but he knew that this legend was the key to his enlightenment.

The river current carried him freely, and the crocodiles were well down the river. Amana stopped rowing and pulled out a small scroll. Etched at the top were the words "Boism: The Balanced Five." He read it over twice. The only tenets that stuck out were the ones listed under "Acts of War" and "Words of War." These creeds of war had gotten him into trouble on his travels plenty of times. But he was sure the Great Elder Uzoma could help him there.

Amana tucked the scroll back into his pack and continued rowing. Beyond a sharp bend in the river, Amana spotted what he presumed was the village of Bajok. Even at this distance, there were faint sounds of a festival. Who or what was being celebrated, Amana didn't know. One villager in Guela had mentioned something about a Great Nation caravanning through the lands. "A Great Nation of golden elephants," he had said to Amana in a broken accent.

After a half hour, Amana reached the river port where other boats were docked. Amana tied off his own longboat, securing it to a post lodged in the mud. Would that really hold? He hoped so; the festival called to him.

Though the night air was chilled, Amana did not bother wrapping his cloak tight against his skin. He relied on his long hair and beard for warmth. In line with the teachings of the Junga, he had not cut his hair since he had started the practice. There were monks in the east—Amana had seen himself—whose hair was longer than they were tall and whose beards stretched to their bellies.

"No farther, stranger," said a voice in the dark. A man stepped from the shadows. It was a local warrior, dressed in padded armor and wrapped in a red tunic, a sword hanging from his waist. The weapon's small hilt and teardrop blade threw Amana off. It hadn't come from the region. After the fall of the Golah

Empire, many of its city-states had broken down into scattered villages like Bajok. This warrior must have won it off of someone farther north.

Amana's suspicions were solidified by the warrior's neck piece. It was almost certainly decorated with human teeth—a custom of Bajok.

Amana sucked his own teeth. He hadn't checked to see if he was alone. It had been a while since he had to sneak into an event.

"You one of them foreigners?" said the man in his thick Bajok accent. It was his best attempt at the Mother Tongue.

"Ah, yes ..." Amana trailed off. He hunched over and rubbed the backs of his hands, taking on the persona of a humble priest.

"Why you so late?" asked the warrior.

"I fell behind ..."

"Why you no dressed like them?"

"Well, you see ..." Amana pulled the scrolls from his bag. "I'm one of the priests. I am a pious man."

"Who's Pious?" said the man. One of his eyes was bigger than the other.

"No, no, there's no Pious. I am a man of religion, of virtue." Amana hoped whatever visiting nation was here followed some form of religion, though it didn't seem to matter. The warrior would have been too dim-witted to know himself. "Go ahead." Amana handed him his scroll. "Read it for yourself."

The warrior snatched the scroll from Amana's hand and pressed the parchment close to his nose, squinting his eyes. "What do these lines say?"

"They say I'm a man of my word." Amana flashed his best smile. The warrior raised an eyebrow. "I'm unarmed if that's the issue." Amana lifted his traveling cloak, turning around for the warrior.

"All right, then." The warrior shoved the scroll back into Amana's hands. Amana relaxed his shoulders. *That was easy enough.*

"One of your people should know you." The warrior grabbed Amana by the collar, pulling him into the festival grounds.

When they arrived at the village's main courtyard, Amana's eyebrows rose. The festival was lavish. Had this been a few years prior, Amana would've seen the event as more than a celebration.

The festival was a prime target for plundering.

The two war elephants standing near the festival stage could fetch a good price by themselves. And the jewelry around their tusks and heads could buy him a decent ship. The archers sitting atop the elephants were lethargic, likely from a long day of traveling. With just a dozen good men, hell, even with a handful of decent men, Amana could—

No, that was not why he was here. He could not return to that life or to that mentality. Not after what happened. He was here to find Elder Uzoma, not steal from a wealthy nation. But he had to get rid of his new friend first.

"Rafiki!" Amana shouted to one of the archers. It didn't matter if that was his name or not, Amana only needed his attention. The archer didn't move his head, but he let his eyes drift down. "Tell this man you know me!"

Amana's voice didn't pierce through the drum circle's thumping beat. That's what he had been hoping for. The archer broke his statue-like gaze to lean over his perch, cupping his hand over his ear.

"You see, my friend," Amana said to the warrior with a friendly smile. "I'm with them."

The warrior loosened his grip around Amana's cloak. That was all Amana needed. Just as the warrior was shouting "You know this man?" Amana smashed the side of his fist into the warrior's wrists. The man's skin was thicker than Amana expected, but his punch was strong enough to make his escape.

He dipped into a group of dancers. The women were dressed in white tops with flowing blue bottoms. Some of the men only wore a cloth around their middle with no shirt. Most of these men sported large ceremonial masks. As Amana shouldered through the crowd, he removed his cloak.

"Stop that man!" the warrior shouted in his native tongue, or at least that's what Amana thought. Some of the men stopped stomping the ground, looking for anyone with a guilty face. Amana threw out another name.

"It's Enu again!" he shouted, hidden in the crowd. "He's made away with the palm wine!"

"Enu?" one man whipped his head from left to right.

"Not again; where is he?" said another.

The group of men around Amana pushed into his pursuer. With the Bajok warrior distracted, Amana slipped away into the drum circle.

"Can I borrow this?" Amana attempted the local tongue, pointing to a wooden bowl filled with white paste. The drummer didn't understand Amana's words, but he understood what the foreigner wanted to do. He smiled and nodded. Amana did his best with the time he had, painting his face like the other men.

For such a small village, there were far more people than Amana had expected. It was packed shoulder to shoulder. The women danced circles around each other while the men looked for partners to share the night with. It would be easy to lose himself in the crowd. But he didn't know where the guard was.

Amana sat near the drum circle, bobbing his head to the beat. His best option was to stay still and observe. He had lost track of the warrior, so he couldn't be sure he was safe.

The people of Bajok looked different from those in Guela, though the villages were only leagues apart. Where the villagers of Guela had rounder faces, many of the villagers here had sharp jaws and high cheekbones. Most of the men looked related to one another, a common trait in smaller villages like these. The family bloodlines ran strong here. Many of the women had inhuman, golden eyes, usually a carryover from animal shape-shifters. This village likely teemed with deep, ancestral magic. But where was Elder Uzoma?

A laughing man wobbled in front of Amana. Amana asked where the elder might be, trying his accent with a new villager. But the man did not answer, holding up a large jug of wine, waving it left and right, then shoving it in Amana's face. Amana tried the next villager that passed him, but his accent was too heavy to understand.

Maybe Amana would have better luck with the visiting nation. Perhaps he'd pay "Rafiki" another visit.

Now that he was settled, he got a better look at the soldiers. They wore deep-blue armor, with streaks of gold across their torsos. Their armor and bows were finely made, a quality that could only be likened to one Great Nation Amana knew of: the Ya-Seti. What were they doing in a place like this?

His answer sat on the stage, where a beautiful Ya-Seti woman crossed her legs atop a simple Bajok throne. This was a marriage festival. And these villagers were going all out to impress their guests.

A marriage proposal of this nature could only mean one thing: This was a marriage of magic. Either this bride-to-be or the groom of this village were mystics who possessed magical abilities. Amana had seen it before. One great Kingdom married into another smaller one for the benefit of heirs who'd one day rule with powerful magic. From what Amana could tell, the magic in this village was stronger than what the Ya-Seti had, at least as a collective.

It all added up. Almost all the women had the golden eyes attributed to shape-shifters. And now that he thought of it, when he had hit the warrior, his skin had been tougher than normal. Where Amana could usually feel the impression of bone, there were only layers of skin. The warrior likely had enhanced, stronger skin.

Magic in the east was a dying thing, even here in the west, to a lesser extent. Gone were the days of mystics who could manipulate mountains and hordes of armies, the foundation for most Great Nations throughout history. The Ya-Seti must have been desperate if they'd traveled all this way. Stranger still, they seemed to be marrying their daughter off to this village. What could the Ya-Seti gain from such a small faction? Whatever the case, the Ya-Seti would speak the Mother Tongue. One of them might help him.

Confident he'd lost the warrior in the thick of the festival, Amana stood up to find one of the Ya-Seti. He only made it a few steps before a circle of men caught his attention. Two men within the circle danced around each other, yet both had bloody noses and swollen eyes. On closer examination, Amana realized the men were not dancing. They were fighting.

Fascinatingly, they mostly fought with their feet instead of their hands. Odd. He'd never considered using his feet in combat—at least not as artfully as they seemed to be using them. Nothing could beat a good one-two knuckle slug.

But Amana had to admit there was a beauty to the fighting style, both a dance and a bout. One fighter changed direction in an instant, shifting his weight from one foot to the next, lulling his opponent into a trance, wiggling his hips like a serpent.

Amana glimpsed at what the fighter intended next. It was his gift of short-sight, as commoners called it. From birth, Amana had been blessed with little flashes of the future. Even though his sight only extended a couple of seconds, it had made him an effective fighter. And fighting had been a primary tool for his previous lifestyle. It was hard to shake a fighter's mentality.

The flash he had was brief, but the image played for him like a ghostly figure. The man placed his hand on the ground, using the momentum of his weight to turn the heel of his foot into the other fighter's ribs. Too bad for his opponent, he didn't have Amana's gift of short-sight.

Smack!

Reality caught up. The man was hit full force and crumpled to his side. Out cold. Amana raised an eyebrow when the victor didn't pump his fist or pound his chest. Instead, he knelt before his fallen opponent, almost in prayer. A noble gesture, but one only suited for a sparring match like this.

Amana turned back to speak with one of the Ya-Seti when a man covered in blue paint brushed his shoulder. The man was a shaman by the looks of it—ceremonial staff clutched in one hand with a spirit crystal lodged in his right eye. White streaks decorated his head, torso, and legs, all in different shapes, each representing a different spirit that the shaman could call upon by ritual.

With the shaman's arrival, the festival quieted. The fighters put cloth to bloody noses and open wounds, the serving party left their food and drink unattended, and the dance circle was all but broken up.

As everyone settled, Amana caught sight of the broad shoulders of the guard he had escaped from. The warrior's eyes were darting like a hawk, pulling at villager's shoulders, checking if their faces matched the runaway. Amana smiled. *He'll have a hard time finding me if he's going to be so aggressive about it.*

Drummers took positions around the shaman. The Ya-Seti soldiers perched atop their war elephants remained; more alert now with the change of movement.

Amana found a spot between a family of boys and a girl. As he sat, a masked man walked away from the gathering. Everyone else, even the Ya-Seti, were gathering around the circle. Why had this man decided this was the best time to leave? Amana reached out with his short-sight but felt nothing amiss.

The shaman was fantastic, getting the crowd involved in only a few moments. Satisfied with the energy, the shaman began his ritual, using the drummers and the sand beneath his feet to conjure up the spirits of the lands.

"Commune … spirit … union … blessed" were all the words Amana could understand. It was the Old Tongue of the Gods that

once lived before men. Amana was familiar with some of the base words, those that dealt with certain witchcrafts. Those who still practiced the art could even be deadly if needed. The words in this ritual were friendly, however. The shaman called upon one of the nurturing spirits rather than one of war.

Once the spirits manifested from the flames encircling the invocation, the Ya-Seti bride-to-be and the Bajok prince—or second Chief or however the Bajok designated their higher-ups—entered the center of the ritual.

This was apparently new to the young woman. When the first spirit passed through her chest, she almost jumped right off the ground. The Ya-Seti were a noble people, but her response reflected how disconnected they were from their magical roots. She wasn't even familiar with the most basic of rituals.

Amana almost laughed out loud when he caught sight of the guard again. He was rounding closer, still looking from head to head, even pulling some of the men's masks off. With the village dispersed across the festival grounds, it was much more difficult to play keep-away from the guard. Amana crawled back into the shadows of the surrounding huts just as the Bajok guard passed.

When it was clear, Amana stepped forward again, into the thick of the villagers. The village Chief was speaking with the spirits now, and his voice was deep and defensive.

What did I miss? Amana thought.

Amana could not understand the Chief at first; his accent was particularly thick. But a Ya-Seti woman decorated in silver and gold translated to another group of her people nearby.

From what Amana could gather from her translated words, the village was tainted with demons of some sort. Dark spirits were tricky things. Like insects, they were difficult to kill and nearly impossible to exterminate. If the spirit's warning was correct, this village would be in a very dire situation.

"*Something dark remains!*" the spirit shouted through the shaman's mouth. "*This marriage cannot be claimed!*"

Something dark remains. Amana reached out with his sight, but again, he couldn't feel an immediate threat. Instead, he found something perhaps even more chilling: nothing. There was no danger, but there was also no energy to latch on to at all, as if his senses were cut off.

Some of the villagers blamed the Ya-Seti, and the visiting nation shouted back. Amana couldn't decipher any one voice, and the Ya-Seti woman who translated had a hard time keeping up, as well.

Amana wondered if he should have intervened. After all, as a potential monk, he should seek to help others. Or perhaps the solution was more passive than that. Maybe he only needed to lead by example. He wasn't sure how to model his life as a monk quite yet.

But it was the young woman, this bride-to-be, who calmed the situation.

"I trust the people of Bajok will keep us safe during this time." The woman's use of the Bajok language was perfect. Her accent was not as rough as the Chief's, which was easier for Amana to understand. "In my homelands, we often are tested like this. Not by our ancestors, or our spirits, but by the elements and our own enemies. My father, our Kor, has taught us that men should be given the chance to prove themselves before we cry out against them. Are these festivals not held to cleanse the village of such evil spirits?"

This young woman was a well-practiced diplomat, a Kor-in-training. Amana scanned the crowd for the Ya-Seti royal head known as Mosai, the Undying Kor. By most accounts, he was the oldest mystic in the world. He was well over one hundred years old, though some claimed he was nearing his two hundredth birthday. His magic was long-lived and powerful. The scholars said it had to do with his regenerative organs and bones that healed at twice the rate of other mortals.

Did this young Ya-Seti hold the same power? That would be a

powerful ally to have indeed. Her heirs could hold a dynasty—if they were good rulers—for as long as they wanted.

The Undying Kor had ruled for countless decades. Now it was time for his reign to pass on. If this small speech by his daughter was any indication, his legacy was in good hands.

The shaman directed his drummers to play again, and the festival was back on, though with less energy than before. The Bajok gave their visitors sidelong glances, and the Ya-Seti returned their gazes with steeled looks of their own. Amana looked at the archers; they too were on high alert.

With the drum circle and the royal retinue back on their stage, Amana went back to his search for someone who could understand him. Just as a Ya-Seti soldier walked past him, someone tugged at his leg.

It was a boy, no more than twelve years old, a shadow of a mustache above his lip. At first, Amana could not understand what the boy was saying. It sounded as though he asked where Amana's face had come from.

"I'm sorry, it's been a while since I've spoken your tongue, little one." Amana smiled kindly.

"He's asking where you are from," said an older woman. It was the same woman who'd translated for the Ya-Seti earlier. Her clothing had looked expensive before, but up close Amana could not look at it for long. Not because he was averse to wealth, but because the firelight reflecting off her gold crown and silver sash made Amana squint. Each of her ten fingers bore a jeweled ring, and her braids were strapped by golden clasps. Her gown was made of fine silk. With all that jewelry—and the pair of guardswomen at her side—this woman could only be the leading lady of the Ya-Seti: their Kor'de. "He has never seen a face quite like yours."

"Tell him it's a very long story." Amana smiled down at the boy. The Kor'de translated.

"He says he loves stories, especially long ones."

Amana chuckled, brushing the boy's head of locs with his palm. "Tell him I will share it another time. I intend to be here a while."

The Kor'de translated, and the boy gave a hand salute. Amana hoped it was an affirmative gesture and not an expletive. But the boy's smile was a good sign.

"Excuse me, I've not introduced myself." The Kor'de bowed her head. "I am Kor'de Neema of Ya-Seti, but as it seems now, translator for my people. I told them they needed to learn the language but few heeded my word."

"I am honored to meet you. I am Amana." He bowed his head.

"What brings you to this small village?" Neema was just as cordial as her daughter. "Are you also looking for a suitable groom for your child?"

Amana frowned. He'd done well to put away the memories of his dead daughter.

"I'm sorry, I didn't mean to ..."

"No, it's all right," Amana assured her. He thought he was past that. His Junga teachings should have helped him shadow his face from that old wound. All the more reason he needed to find Elder Uzoma. "I'm here on a personal pilgrimage."

"Ah, that's the reason for your beard and hair, is it not?" Neema pointed out. "Correct me if I misspeak, but that is the tradition of the Junga monks, yes? Are you pledged?"

"Not yet," Amana admitted. "But I intend to be. That's what brings me to this village. I am searching for Elder Uzoma."

"Ah yes, he is perhaps the most famous of these villagers. Surprising to not find him here tonight."

"You know Uzoma?"

"Only by reputation," Neema confessed. "He was one of the greatest warriors of my time. He gave some of our allies in the south trouble before he retired to this place."

Neema was well-read and well-informed, even for a Kor'de. Amana stole a glance at her wrists. Sure enough, several beads were wrapped around her arms, a sign she had studied at the Kinali Academies.

Over Neema's shoulder, Amana saw a Bajok warrior speaking with a young woman. Amana flinched for a moment, thinking it was the guard from earlier. The man had a similar build, but his face was different, his eyes uncrossed. Then the warrior was speaking with a masked man. Had it been the same masked man who had left the festival circle before? He had the same walk … a kind of swagger.

"What do you know of these dark spirits?" Amana asked Neema offhandedly.

"Only that they do not help with our relations with these people. In time, I'm sure they'll realize it was not us that brought in this dark entity," Neema said.

A vision flashed through Amana's head. The Bajok warrior was going to give the masked man a good kick. Though Amana was certain that a fight was coming, he waited for his vision to come true. But instead, the warrior turned away with clenched fists, leaving the masked man unharmed.

These false sights happened from time to time. It meant that the man had had the thought of actively doing harm yet didn't follow through. This was sometimes used against those with short-sight as a countermeasure, a mental feint.

The situation was resolved, yet his sight was still flashing an elusive warning. His long-sight was far less developed, only manifested through extensive ritual and meditation. But those sorts of meditations took weeks. Amana couldn't see what his magic was trying to show him, so he used his eyes.

The masked man and the girl were leaving the festival, but they were stopped by another young woman. Amana heard pieces of the argument. The girls had come together. One had found a partner to share her night with; the other had not.

Kor'de Neema was still speaking, though Amana ignored her, letting her voice buzz at the back of his mind. One of the archers never took her eyes off Amana. Could she tell he was not listening? Amana couldn't see her face clearly through her helmet, but she was more beautiful than any guard he'd ever seen before, with large golden eyes and bushy dark hair tinted with red, pulled back in a tight bun.

"Excuse me, Your Highness," Amana cut in as politely as he could. "I left my boat by the river. I tied it down, but the post was lodged in the mud. I want to make sure it has not floated downriver and become crocodile food."

"By all means. We will speak again, Amana. I'm very interested in learning more about your studies." Kor'de Neema stepped aside to let him pass through the festival throng. "I look forward to our continued conversation as well. It was an honor, truly." Amana bowed, dismissing himself. He stole one more glance at the guardswoman. Her eyes were still locked on him before she moved aside to let him pass. Amana could have sworn she was looking at his bare chest.

Amana didn't see the couple. They must have left. He turned to the girl who had been left alone at the party. She was crying now.

"What happened?" Amana placed a hand on her shoulder.

"She left me. I can't believe she left me." Her tears ran freely. "I don't believe it."

"Who was that man she was with?"

"I don't know. You a Ya-Seti, too?" the young woman asked as she wiped her eyes. She looked to Amana with a raised eyebrow; his accent, another dead giveaway. "Who are you anyway?"

"Name's Amana. You?"

"Yejide."

"Yejide, do you know where the two of them went?"

Yejide shook her head. "Down that way; they couldn't have gone past the river. You don't have to go. I'll just tell one of the warriors."

Amana lifted his eyes. The guard was still searching the village for him like a mad man. Now he was talking to Rafiki. His arms were waving up and down as though asking if he could climb the elephant for a better view.

Amana's head rang again; it was like a wasp stinging the inside of his temples. There was danger; there was danger *now*. And not from the Bajok guard.

"That's a good idea, Yejide. Go tell someone from your village—someone who isn't too drunk. I'll go find her," Amana said. Yejide nodded, the last of her tears cried out.

Amana bumped shoulders and tripped over feet to get to the other side of the village's center, but eventually, he made it. Still, his sight was flashing. He clutched at his head, nursing his eyelids.

Amana had been told that his family was a ruling people, generations ago, dictating the future and the outcome of wars and battles well before they started. He wondered what it would have been like to use his abilities to their fullest. It would have helped in situations like these.

The farther he moved from the village, the darker it got. Even the two moons didn't light the ground around the riverbank. It took a moment for Amana to get his bearings, but eventually, he realized where he was. He turned a corner of a hut and found the couple by the boats.

The sight was horrific.

The woman was bloodied—chewed and mangled—yet, somehow, she was still breathing. The man, his mask fallen to the side, was not really a man at all, though not entirely beast. It looked as though he was crawling, though his back was to the ground and his belly faced the night sky. His arms were bent backward, planted on the ground like a lion or—a hyena. Where the back of the man's head should have been was a hyena's face. It ravenously ate away at the girl, oblivious to Amana's presence.

Amana reached for the sword at his hip, but grasped at empty air. An old habit. But he had to save the girl somehow.

Amana shouted—it was all he could think of to get the creature off the girl. The hyena-form turned, snarling. It whipped forward, meeting Amana face-to-face, protecting its meal.

"Leave her be." Amana put as much courage into his voice as he could.

The hyena-man stalked toward Amana, back arched, ready to pounce. Amana set his foot back in a balanced stance. He prepared his sight for what would likely be a one-sided battle in the creature's favor. He hadn't fought in years and had no weapon.

But it didn't matter. The girl needed help. He just had to buy her some time.

Amana let his gaze drift to her. She lay just beside his boat, barely holding on. Amana lifted his fists, and the demon ran—not to the left or right down the river's edge but *across* the river, scampering atop the water as if it were sand.

That was odd. Amana didn't think himself that intimidating, but he didn't give the demon's retreat a second thought. He rushed to the young woman. Was she even breathing? He tried to cover the open wound on her neck, but dark fluid kept pouring out like a roaring red river. She would bleed out; there was no stopping that. Still, Amana lifted her head to reduce the blood flow.

"Who was he?" Amana rushed his words. "Tell me."

The girl could not answer—the gash in her throat was too large. Amana wasn't even sure she was still alive, though her eyes were wide open.

"Stop right there," a woman said behind Amana. He lifted his hands in forfeit. That was why the demon ran off. They had company.

"I did not do this." This looked bad, and Amana knew it. He side-eyed the woman.

"Turn around; keep your eyes on the river." Her words were

sharp and curt. It was the Ya-Seti archer with the golden eyes. Her arrow was aimed straight at the back of Amana's neck.

She was with a small band of Ya-Seti soldiers, with the Bajok warriors coming up at their rear. The villagers shouted in their native tongue, and Amana understood them. Like anyone who knew a second language, curses, slurs, and insults were some of the first and most vital words one learned. Seeing one of their own dead elicited closed fists and furrowed brows. Soon after, the Great-Chief arrived with the rest of his entourage.

"And so," the Chief said in a broken accent of the Mother Tongue, though he stood confident and tall, "we find demon."

CHAPTER 3

MOONSBEAM

THIS HAD NOT BEEN PART OF AMANA'S PLAN. BEFORE HE could utter another word, someone pinned his arms behind his back—the Bajok warrior he had given the slip to earlier. The warrior held Amana tight, locking Amana's hands behind his back. Amana hadn't realized how large the man was—a head taller than Amana and twice as wide. The warrior's skin had spotted scales up and down his arm like the back of a pangolin. Getting away by physical force a second time would not be an option, and Amana would not attempt to do so while the Ya-Seti archers had their arrows trained on him.

They took away his traveling bag, which did not have much apart from his scrolls and a few pieces of dried mango—and other items used during light travel. Amana gave no protest nor claimed his innocence. From the outside looking in, he knew how it seemed, and he knew it would sound twice as ridiculous to say this was the work of an *actual* demon.

And that demon had been unlike any dark spirit he had ever seen before. There weren't many creatures like these where he came from, just huge cities filled with lowlifes and noblemen.

Amana had heard stories of sea creatures that swallowed ships whole, flying monsters that rained terror from above—though Amana had, in fact, seen a northern dragon once before—but none were like this.

If he had to compare the creature to something he knew, it had to be a shape-shifter. There were many among the Ya-Seti, in fact, and Amana suspected a good number of the Bajok were shape-shifters, as well. He turned his head toward his captor. The warrior's eyes were a normal brown, but Amana could not get over his scaly skin.

"Eyes forward, Demon," the warrior hissed.

Amana was sure there were at least a few shape-shifters in the soldiers' ranks, too. Most soldier types had the ability to turn themselves into fierce lions or agile leopards. While traveling through the jungles of Kunda, Amana had heard of the legend of the Gorilla King—a shape-shifter whose human form had never been seen—who led wild gorillas through the forests. More commonly, these shape-shifters were messengers, birds who could travel great distances—at least, in Amana's experience. In warfare, they were used for scouting, but between peacekeeping nations and commoners, they were used to transport the mail.

No, the creature Amana had come face-to-face with was like nothing he had encountered before. It was like a shape-shifter gone wrong. The spirits were right—this was neither man nor demon.

When the Bajok warriors and Ya-Seti soldiers returned Amana to the village square, the people whispered to each other. Amana could not make out any of their faces; they were all silhouetted by the large fire crackling behind them. Women carried their daughters close, and young boys hid behind their fathers. The hushed voices sent a shiver down Amana's spine. What was the justice system like here in Bajok? Judging by the silence, it did not seem good. Not good at all. How would Amana wiggle his way out of this one?

The Bajok warriors made their way through the crowd, pushing Amana toward the blazing fire. There were more whispers exchanged between the villagers. If he knew the language better, he might have been able to pick up what they were saying. Still, he knew that what they were saying was not favorable. He must have looked like a madman with his unkempt hair and beard—and that he was shirtless and covered in a young woman's blood.

The warriors sat him mere meters away from the village center's fire pit. They placed him so close, the edges of his locs started to catch alight. Amana winced at the stench.

The Ya-Seti archers did not follow them into the circle, taking positions around their Kor and Kor'de, along with the young Princess. Another set of Bajok warriors surrounded the Great-Chief, who approached the center of the circle. These warriors carried large weapons, odd poleaxes by the looks of it, with one end thin and sharpened to a tip and the other wide and blunted. Would those be the tools of his execution? Amana would place his own bets on the fire.

Speaking out of turn would do him no good, so he waited for his opportunity. Another set of warriors dropped the young woman's mangled body a yard from Amana. The crowd let out cries and yells as a woman spat at Amana. She missed, but Amana got the message.

"Demon," the Great-Chief said in his accented Mother Tongue, "death comes for you."

The Kor'de stepped forward, her guard matching her every move. She spoke to the Great-Chief in the villagers' tongue. The Chief considered her words but did not answer right away. After a short moment, he nodded his head, waving a hand for her to come forward.

"The Great-Chief Oba," Neema began, as she stepped into the circle, "will allow me to translate for you. I will recite your terms of execution."

Terms of execution?

"Do I get to speak?" Amana asked, figuring this was the best chance for him to get his say—or rather his *only* chance to get his say. "Or do these *dikala* not give fair trial?"

Neema frowned and turned to the Chief to translate. Amana hoped she left out his insult, though. Chief Oba chuckled. *Uh oh.*

"You guilty, Demon," Chief Oba spat into the fire pit. "No trial."

"There must be some way for me to claim innocence," Amana said in the Mother Tongue, but the Chief's eyes glazed over. Amana switched to the local tongue, gesturing to himself. "I. No. Demon. I prove this."

Oba did not respond at first. The shaman, with his staff in hand, stepped forward, speaking in the Mother Tongue.

"We have tests that can reveal this man's true nature," the shaman admitted to Neema. "Though it would take much time and energy on my part."

Neema translated for the Chief, who responded with gritted teeth, shaking his head so hard Amana thought he might burst a vein.

"Chief Oba does not wish to waste the strength of his shaman on a man he knows nothing about," Neema said to Amana. The Bajok warrior holding Amana agreed, shaking his head just as hard as his Chief.

Then Amana caught a familiar eye. Yejide, the young girl from earlier. But the moment he looked at her, she shook her head, rubbing the inside of her elbow nervously.

"This girl." Amana nodded his head. "She know me. Your name is Yejide, no?"

Yejide pushed herself deeper into the crowd. Why didn't she speak up for him?

"Do not speak to her!" the Chief bellowed. "She does not know you."

"She does; she's scared, is all ..." Amana caught himself

speaking in the Mother Tongue again. He whipped his head to Neema, who spoke to the Chief.

"The Chief says he will not coerce an answer from one of his people who does not wish to speak," Neema said with arms folded. Amana turned back to the girl, but she was gone now. He clenched his teeth, exhaling hard through his nose.

"So, instead I die while the true demon runs free?" Amana felt a darkness well up in him. His fear turned to anger, and that anger would have him do something he would regret. These people did not understand what he could do if pressed.

Amana considered his chances of escape. There were three warriors around him with poleaxes trained at both of his cheeks and the back of his head. The large warrior still had Amana's hands pinned tight behind his back, but Amana's feet were free. If he could just kick some of the embers from the fire into the warrior's eyes, then maybe, just maybe...

It did not have to come to that. Amana wasn't favored in this situation, and even if he did get past the warriors who held him hostage, there were at least two dozen others that lined the crowd of villagers. Now was the time for Amana to use the diplomacy of the Junga, not the strength of a warrior. Fortunately for Amana, the young boy from earlier spoke up.

"Foreign man is good," he said with his eyebrows pressed together in confusion.

The boy's father pulled him aside with haste. Amana frowned. The boy might have been his best chance. But his father seemed to not want him getting involved; or rather the father did not want to further provoke his Chief's anger.

That's what Amana thought at first.

As the father moved what Amana assumed was his son, he spoke on his behalf. His voice rang with confidence and grace, though he never looked his Chief in the eye. He seemed no older than forty, just a decade over Amana's own age. Like Amana, his hair was worn long, in a band of locs, but his face was clean-shaven. He was not as attractive as some of the other men in the village, though. His ears were puffy, and his nose looked like it had been reset several times.

He's a fighter. Amana thought he might have recognized him from the fighting ring, but he couldn't be sure. The man did not seem to be a High-Chief or even a low one. Unlike the young men who wore their chests bare, he wore a long, simple *kanzu* robe. He had no silver nor gold, but he had a simple bronze charm tied around his neck, an odd shape of spirals at its end.

"This man, Kojo, says it is the right of the village to weigh in on any execution," Neema translated to Amana. "'Fine,' says the Chief, 'if the village agrees.'"

Amana nodded. Oba raised his hand, closing it down in a fist with his thumb sticking out. Then, he crossed his neck with his thumb. The locals grunted their approval, more warriors than villagers, but the grunts were low.

Chief Oba raised his hand again, stopping the voting process. The Chief then waved his hand toward the shaman, indicating the vote for a trial. The villagers' grunts started low, not very encouraging for Amana's chances of survival. But Kojo, who had vouched for him, grunted the loudest. He locked eyes with Amana, a hawk's gaze. Kojo didn't even look to see who agreed or disagreed with his approval. Somehow, his confidence spread to the other villagers. They joined in his chant. And soon, the votes for the trial outweighed those for a blind execution.

This man had influence. He may not have been a Chieftain, but he must have been a leader for the commoners here. But why had he been so intent on helping Amana? Or had it been his son's approval that had spurred him on? Whatever the case, Amana could relax his shoulders, grateful he could keep his life at least for a few more moments.

"So, a ritual we will have," the shaman said.

"No matter. Demon will die," Chief Oba said in his best

version of the Mother Tongue. Surprisingly, he was smiling. "The ritual will be by moon fire."

The village shaman walked toward the roaring fire where Amana had been. He spoke a few words to the warriors who surrounded Amana. Though reluctant, the warriors released Amana, lifting their sharp poleaxes from Amana's face.

No more poleaxes. Good. That'll make getting away at least possible, Amana thought.

Amana massaged the red rings around his wrists, getting circulation back into his numb limbs. The shaman took Amana away from the fire. He tapped both of Amana's shoulders with his staff. And then with the tip of his staff—which Amana did not realize was sharp—he pricked Amana between the eyes, drawing blood. All the while, the shaman chanted in the Old Tongue, calling to Deh'ala again to open the gates of the spirit lands.

He flung the drop of blood into the fire from the tip of the staff. The flames turned white, shooting straight up into the sky in two radiant beams. The beams shot out to each of the moons. Amana could make out the names "Yem" and "Aya" during the shaman's chant, the twin spirits that guided the tides of the oceans and the flow of the rivers. From what Amana could discern of the chant, his trial would be set under the judgment of these spirits. They would reveal what his true ancestral magic was.

"Now, the accused must step into the fire of the moonsbeam," the shaman said as he turned his staff from hand to hand, keeping the portal between the mortal world and the spirit lands open through his chant and dance. Amana made no movement toward the fire, lifting a questioning eyebrow at the shaman.

"It will not harm you." Neema winked at him. "Unless, of course, you are lying. Otherwise, the shaman will close the portal and burn you alive."

No wonder the Chief was so willing to go through with the ritual, Amana thought.

Amana shook his head, but he did not have much of a choice.

His muscles tensed, determined to prove his innocence before these people. He looked at the young woman's body again. She had been such a beautiful girl. There was nothing she could have done to deserve what happened to her.

Taking a deep breath, Amana stretched out his hand into the roaring white flames. It did not feel hot at all, but instead, it was cool like the rushing water of a waterfall, though without the wetness that came with it. Amana dipped the rest of his body into the flame-portal and saw nothing but white. Just as in darkness one could not see their own hand in front of them, Amana could not see his own body now. All there was was the white and the two beams coming down from the moons, like two eyes looking down on him, like a predator in the bush. Amana never understood the Old Tongue, but now within this beam of light, it made complete sense to him. He could hear the shaman as he spoke to the twin spirits of the moon.

"We bring before you a child of the ocean. We ask that you reveal his true magic," said the shaman.

"*This one is talented,*" the spirit of Yem said.

"*But within him lies a dormant darkness,*" the spirit of Aya added.

"Does a demon rest within his soul?" asked the shaman.

"*No, he is pure in this way,*" Yem decided.

"*But he is not in balance,*" Aya concluded.

"Is this child of the ocean a shape-shifter, one that takes the form of a beast?" the shaman asked.

"*No, this one does not change form,*" Yem said.

"*But he does have the eye,*" Aya concluded.

"*Yes, the eye! He has arrived at last,*" said another voice. It, too, was female, but Amana could not see a third spirit among the others. Yem and Aya seemed to speak from the moons, but this third voice spoke from within Amana's mind. The voice differed from the spirits. It was more … human. "*You must leave this place, Amana.*"

The voice grew louder and louder. Could the shaman hear

this? Could the spirits? They were still passing judgment while this other voice kept shouting over them.

"Go! Go! Go from this place! It will only bring death to those you care for! Go!"

And then Amana was thrown out of the portal. He was flustered but unharmed. Next to him lay the shaman, who looked as though he had run for a day straight, sweat pouring into his eyes. There were already several villagers tending to him, giving him water in wooden cups.

Amana tried to make eye contact with him. "Did you hear that voice? Did you hear her?"

"Yes, they are the twin spirits."

"No, the woman. Just the one voice."

Chief Oba was yelling now.

"The Chief says you've exhausted his shaman," Neema translated. She stood just beside Amana.

"He did not kill the girl," the shaman said through labored breaths, though he gave Amana a questioning look.

So, he didn't hear her voice, Amana thought.

The shaman turned over again to his Chief, translating the same in the local tongue. Oba smacked his lips.

"'It doesn't matter; you heard what Ula said. The dark spirit is not mortal nor immortal. He can still be the demon,'" Neema translated again.

"But I have been seen under the moon spirits. I am no child of shape-shifters or demons." Amana stood up, dusting himself off. He figured now he could argue with Chief Oba more openly. At least, now he had the spirits backing him. But he would need to do it in the local tongue. "Twin spirits say"—he pointed to himself—"I all right. All good."

"Who are you?" the Chief said in simple words, impatient with Amana's accent and his butchering of the language. "A warrior from Guela?"

"I am no warrior," Amana managed to answer.

"Then you are …" Chief Oba could not find the word in the Mother Tongue. He directed his question to Neema.

"He asks if you are a mercenary or a merchant of some sort. He says your face is not common here and wonders if you are traveling for someone's head or for trade." Neema turned to Amana with a relaxed brow. She too must have been relieved he was no demon.

"Neither. I am no one." Amana said.

"He lies," the shaman said. Amana turned to him with a furrowed brow.

How dare he say I'm lying? The dikala …

"This one has the sight."

Oh, that. Right.

"You have sight?" Oba said in the Mother Tongue, his tone much softer now.

"Yes, I do," Amana rolled himself over in the dirt. "But it's not very good."

"You can see the future, no?"

"Only a few seconds, no more. I can't find this dark spirit for you, if that's what you're asking." Amana lifted himself up. His head only reached Oba's chest. Were all the men in this village so large? The Chief nodded his head slowly.

So, now you know how to speak the Mother Tongue? Amana thought.

"What did you see by the river, then?"

"It was neither man nor demon exactly," Amana said. "It was half man, half hyena, from what I could tell. It was like no shape-shifter I have ever seen. His form was not completely changed, neither man nor beast," Amana said this all while looking directly at the Great-Chief, never wavering.

While Neema was translating, Amana observed the villagers. The story of the man he described stirred whispers and small conversation among the people. Was this a familiar fiend among the Bajok? Even the Chief frowned when he heard Amana's story, the color of his face drained. He almost looked scared. Almost.

"Why you here?" Chief Oba finally asked once the chatter around the village died down.

"To meet Elder Uzoma," Amana said.

"Everyone knows Uzoma; he lives out by the Great Rocks." The Bajok warrior who had bound Amana's hands together stepped forward. "I can take him to Elder Uzoma tomorrow."

"I can escort myself; I need only to know the way."

"No. You get taken by Nanga," Chief Oba interjected. "Zoba will be punished for letting you in."

Zoba bit his tongue. Perhaps it was better if he had not spoken up. Amana did not like it, but he really had no choice. He agreed with a nod.

"Get yourself some rest," Nanga, the warrior said. He had been the one holding a poleaxe to Amana's neck. "Uzoma's farm is a good ways away."

"It's not even a half day. The walk will only take the morning," another warrior said. This one had held a poleaxe to Amana's cheek. His hair was shaved on the sides but was long down his back.

"Yemi," Oba started to say to the new warrior. Amana could not understand the rest except for the word "daughter" and the name "Oluchi." It had been a while since Amana had interacted with the words of this land. But he was beginning to understand more already. The more he heard the nuanced vowels and cadence of the language, the more he picked it up. The language was a carry-over from the Golah Empire, with subtle changes to certain words, especially the vowels.

"What did he say?" Amana whispered to Neema.

"He says while you're out there to inform Oluchi about what has happened to his daughter."

"Right, of course," Amana said.

He had almost forgotten the girl might have had family in the village. The Ya-Seti archer who had caught Amana approached. She whispered into her Kor'de's ear.

"I must say." Neema sighed, nodding to her guardswoman. This time, the archer did not look to Amana. "I didn't think our next conversation would be like this. But I must attend to some other business. I will see you around the village, Amana. That is, if you'll stay now."

"And have one of those warriors coming after me?" Amana laughed. "No, I think I'll stay for now. Don't want to look any guiltier than I seem now."

"Smart move." Neema nodded and walked away from the festival circle. Amana's thoughts turned to the young woman's corpse, which still lay next to the flames.

Her eyes were still open, and the blood around her neck had begun to dry. The fire reflected off her eyes like little fireflies. Amana could not help being reminded of his own daughter. Those same flickering fireflies were the last things her eyes had seen, as well.

CHAPTER 4

THE FARMLANDS

THAT NIGHT, AMANA DREAMED OF FIRE. SWEAT BEADED THE top of his forehead, but he did not care. He had to get to Sanaa, had to get to his daughter.

The ship was overtaken, the battle lost. Men died at his side, their cries muffled by the roaring fires. Wood cracked with snaps and pops. But something was odd.

Though Amana knew he was on a ship, wood splintering underfoot, everything was covered in fire. It was as though he had gone straight to the land of demons. Each flame attempted to slap him across his arms and legs.

Then he heard her screams.

Even above the cries of dying men, he could single out her voice. Those screams were for him; Sanaa was calling for *him*. Amana tried to shout back, but nothing came out of his mouth. With the tenacity of an enraged animal, he shoveled through the burning embers, not caring that his hands were blistering from the heat. He needed to save her before those vicious flames swallowed her whole.

Finally, he caught something other than fire. It was flesh and bone. Amana pulled it out, but the sight was grotesque. It was only a head. He turned it over in his hands. The face was not Sanaa's. It was the young woman who had been attacked—Imani. But her eyes were open, her mouth agape as she started to screech. Her scream had sounded like Sanaa. As the shrieks grew louder, the skin cracked, piece by piece. When the screeching grew unbearable, the head shattered, drifting like ashes into the fire that now enveloped Amana.

AMANA WOKE EARLY IN THE MORNING. THE COOL AIR SPURRED goosebumps on his skin. Had he imagined everything from last night? He still saw those bright moon-eyes looking down at him, judging him. Those eyes uncovered memories and actions he had tried to bury away forever.

The dream was unlike any he had before. It was lucid—it was like he was there, as though it were really happening. Was he touched by those twin-spirits somehow? Did it have to do with that woman's voice?

After rubbing the sleep from his eyes, Amana let it go. The dream was already fading as he reoriented himself in the hut in which he found himself.

It was a small space, barely enough room for him to stretch his legs without hitting the other end. He tried to shake out the cramps in his calves, but he couldn't even manage that—his elbows kept bumping into the mud walls.

Though he was not officially a prisoner, the hut was no better than a common cage. There was a large post in the middle with dried blood and nail markings in the base. The mud-work wasn't well maintained. And the walls were dotted with holes and gaps that let in the night winds. It was a blessing it had not rained, or else Amana would've gotten soaked.

His captors—or at least that's what they seemed to Amana—

had given him no bedding or pillow, so he had slept on the flat ground. They had returned his traveling bag to him, his items still inside. He'd thought it would make for a decent pillow, but the ache in his neck suggested otherwise.

Amana poked his head outside the hut to find Nanga and the other Bajok warrior named Yemi—if Amana remembered correctly—outside his door. Nanga was asleep, but Yemi looked Amana dead in the eye. Amana smiled feebly and returned to the hut. He wasn't sure how long it would be before they departed, so he meditated.

But he couldn't manage more than a minute or two. Each time, he felt the heat of the fire, the visions of the twin-spirits, and that woman's voice—intruders in his mind. Amana slapped the dirt beneath him. He would've smashed his fist into the wooden post, but thought better of it. He focused on his breath, turning his thoughts to the words of the Junga monks.

At least for now, his name was clear of murder, but Great-Chief Oba was still wary of him, perhaps as some co-conspirator. Amana could not blame him. A man no one had seen before last night came into the village, and the next moment one of their own was savagely murdered. To top it off, this same man came on the night the Ya-Seti arrived. A man like this must have been working in concert with these people. That's what Amana would think if he had been put in Chief Oba's situation.

Amana hadn't known Imani at all, and he had seen many die before, but something in those eyes stuck with him. She looked almost betrayed before she passed on, as though something failed her. It was a look Amana was far too familiar with. With these images troubling him, meditation was put on hold. Perhaps Elder Uzoma had a solution against such nightmares.

It was not long before Nanga and Yemi came for him. They shoved him out of the hut and into the early morning. The sun had just started peeking over the eastern horizon. Only a few villagers were awake—those cleaning up after the festival. Most of them averted their eyes from Amana.

As they walked, Amana took measure of the village. Down the path they walked and along one edge were two great huts, one of which was guarded by four Ya-Seti archers—probably the guest hut for the visiting Royal Family. Farther down were the festival grounds, right up against the largest hut in all the village. It stood at least twenty paces high, less a hut and more a small building, squared instead of rounded.

Nanga and Yemi had a body sling made for Imani. Her mauled face had been covered, though a small spot of blood dotted the wrappings near her head.

"If you wouldn't mind," Amana said, "I would like to help carry the girl to her father."

The warriors looked at each other. Nanga shrugged.

"Better for me." Nanga handed his end of the sticks to Amana. The weight wasn't bad, but a few moments of walking would change that. Amana pulled back his hair to keep it from falling into his face.

Before leaving, the warriors knelt in prayer, asking for the blessing of the Hunter's eyes and the strength of the Warrior—Amana thought he heard the name "Ugara."

As they prayed, one of the Ya-Seti archers approached them—the woman with the golden eyes and dark red hair. In the morning light, Amana could make out the freckles that dotted the bridge of her nose. She didn't wear a helmet like she had before. Her face was longer than Amana had thought, and her eyebrows were thick.

"The Kor asks if I can join you," she said in their local tongue. Her accent was perfect.

"That depends on a few things," Nanga said, looking the woman up and down. "What do we get in return?"

"A healthy relationship with the Ya-Seti."

Amana didn't understand what Nanga said in response to her,

but the Bajok warrior leaned to one side, wanting a better look at her backside.

"That's enough, Nanga," Yemi said in the Mother Tongue. He gave Amana a sidelong glance and a wink. Unlike the other villagers, this warrior had no accent in his words. "My name's Yemi. You can come with us. It is time we learned more about your people."

The woman nodded. "My name is Nya. I am the head guardswoman to the Kor'de."

"A *woman* guard?" Nanga coughed in disbelief. "The Ya-Seti can make you archers, sure, but the head of a guard? You sure you know how to use those things?"

Nya did not flinch at Nanga's rude remarks. "I'm sure I could teach you a few things about the bow, *Bajok*."

"I'd like to see you try, *Ya-Seti*."

"I think it's time for us to set out," Amana butted in—for Nanga's benefit. There weren't many women warriors in Bajok, if at all, but Amana knew of the Ya-Seti guardswomen. They were not ones to trifle with. Judging from Nya's unbroken expression, she was one of their elite. Her golden eyes were intimidating on their own, but her furrowed brow gave them a fierce malice. "I'm sure you both can continue this conversation when we return."

It did not take long for the group to leave the village. Nanga brought up the rear with Nya in front of him—it took another moment for her to agree to that. Amana was pushed between Nya and Yemi in front, with Imani's body swaying between them in the sling.

The village gates to the north, tall and wide, were almost a mile from the hut where Amana had slept. Of all the villages Amana had visited so far, Bajok was the largest, though still nowhere near as big as some cities of the Great Nations in Esowon. The people here were certainly bringing themselves back into the fold, though. The marriage proposal was already a sign of this. Still, the sheer size of the place was awe-inspiring.

The Golah Empire was once one of the largest in the west, but infighting had broken it apart into the smaller territories that now made up its borders.

From the edge of the village, Amana saw their destination. Just on the crest of the horizon were the tops of large rocks.

"Are those the Black Rocks?" Amana asked Yemi as he shifted the weight of the sling in his hand.

"Hah, are those the Black Rocks, he asks," Nanga said, then chuckled.

"That's the Little Brother," Yemi said. "It's much smaller. We'll need to go around it before we see the big ones."

"So, get comfortable with that sling. I told you it's a decent walk," Nanga said.

Amana shook his head, directing his next question to the friendlier warrior. "Why are they called the Black Rocks?"

"It was once the land of demons. If you go deep enough into them, you will be lost to its maze," Nanga spoke over his comrade again. He used the bottom of his spear as a walking stick.

"What kind of demons?" Nya asked.

"The kind Amana said he saw," Yemi answered before Nanga opened his mouth. "Half man, half hyena. I was a young boy the last time I heard of one; before the Great-Chief Oba eradicated their kind. They've been gone for years now. But they used to hide away in the hills when they took women from the village. Our Chief might not believe you, but I do. That's why everyone was on edge last night. We've not heard of such a creature in some time."

"Do you know where they came from?" Amana asked.

"No one knows for sure. Doesn't matter to me. All I care is that they're gone now."

Amana nodded. At least someone, even if it was only this lone warrior, believed his story.

The quartet—dead girl in tow—walked through the tall grass toward what Yemi had called the Little Brother. The morning sun painted the plains to the east a brilliant orange. But to the west was a vast expanse of green, acre after acre. The farmlands kept stretching farther than Amana could see.

"How many people does this all feed?" Amana asked with his mouth wide open.

"Far more than those that live in Bajok. We have quite a surplus going," Yemi said casually.

"How much are you producing here?" Nya asked, her face betraying nothing, though she took extra time to look over the crops.

"You saw those huts back at the village. The big ones. Go ahead and take a guess," Nanga said.

Nya sighed. "How much?"

"Enough to last us quite some time" was all Yemi said. Amana couldn't help thinking all these questions were more than the stirs of friendly conversation. It felt like everyone was sizing each other up. "So, Nya," Yemi said. "Tell us more about the Ya-Seti. The Chief only said that your First Daughter was special."

"I can speak your language if you want," Nya said, giving Amana a furtive glance.

"Oh please, I need to work more on the common tongue." Yemi waved his hand. Even with one hand, he had no issue carrying the sling. "If Bajok wants to become a player in the larger world, we'll all need to speak the Mother Tongue."

Nya shrugged. "Not much to say. Ya-Seti is the greatest nation Esowon has ever seen or ever will see." Her words sounded like a mantra.

"Not exactly humble," Yemi replied. "I heard you have competition from those … Vaashi? Vaakee? Vaadi?"

"The Vaaji? They're no more than poets and scholars. They are no match for our armies."

"There's more to power than might," Yemi pointed out.

"The day I see a book defeat a bow is the day I marry a tokoloshe," Nya said.

"That can be arranged," Nanga said, though Nya ignored him.

"Are all the women in Ya-Seti as strong and confident as you are?" Yemi asked.

"Not all of them." Nya's lips betrayed a smirk. Yemi was more nuanced than Nanga.

"Amana, what do you think?" Nanga broke into Yemi's conversation. "Have you seen a finer ass? I swear, a woman like this is wasted as a warrior. Put her in a nice *gomesi* dress, or without one … Maybe do something with those eyebrows, and I would ask the Chief if she could stay."

Nya turned swiftly, too fast for Nanga. Before he realized it, he had been struck across the face with the end of her bow. Nanga crashed to the ground with a thud.

"Nice thrust," Amana said. He had seen the Ya-Seti at work, but not for a long while. Her form was perfect. "That was the style of the *desert scorpion*, right?"

"Close," Nya said as she slung her bow back into place. "It was the style of the *seaside crab*, a similar striking technique as the way of the scorpion, but with the Ya-Seti port-side touch."

Nanga lifted himself from the ground, nursing his jaw. "That was a cheap shot!" he shouted after the group, finding purchase on the ground again. Everyone ignored him. "Hey! I said that was a cheap shot! Face me head-on, and see if you can do that little trick again."

Nanga ran after Nya. Amana dropped his side of the sling to face him, legs planted in a fight-ready stance.

"Stop it, Nanga," Yemi said. In an instant, Nanga had stopped, though his breathing was still quick.

"Don't do that, Yemi," he said as his breathing eased.

"You need to calm down," Yemi said. "It was a fair shot for what you said. Why don't you take the lead ahead of me?"

Nanga obeyed. As he stomped past Nya, he shoved into her shoulder. When Nanga took the lead, Yemi pulled up his side of the sling again.

"Were you a warrior before all this?" Yemi asked Amana.

"What makes you say that?" Amana asked.

"The way you talk, the way you walk, the way you move your eyes. You have the spirit of Ugara."

"When traveling alone, you have to be alert," Amana answered, not wanting to join in this game of questions.

"But you're trained, yes?" Yemi added.

"I ... was."

"Are you a deserter?" Yemi pried.

"Nothing like that, no. I just know my way around a spear and sword, is all."

The group passed a woman tending to her harvest, infant slung around her waist. She saluted the warriors. Acknowledgement from other farmers continued until the group reached a bridge that went over a river.

Amana continued to gape at the large expanse of green. The closer they got to the Black Rocks, the richer the soil was. These farmers were producing more and more food. He knew the Bajok were looking to restore their previous Empire, but at this rate, they would have had a surplus that could feed the whole of the Westerlands.

"What is this river?" Amana asked.

"The Nyoka," Yemi said as they passed over the bridge.

"It can't be. The Nyoka is how I came here from the south," Amana said.

"It curves north a little ways down. It ends a bit farther to the east," Nya said.

"You did your research." Yemi smiled.

"I try." Nya bowed her head.

The Black Rocks were closer now; Amana could make out their base. Most were dome-shaped and rose, it seemed, to the bottoms of the clouds. Vegetation grew along the sides.

Amana shifted his grip again on the sling. He might have

known how to fight, but he was out of practice. And being out of practice, he was also out of shape.

"When I was younger, there were more people here," Nanga said as he gazed up at the rocks. Then he took the sling from Amana. "I've got it from here. You can stop struggling."

Amana gave up the weight, shaking his arms back to life.

"We used to pray atop the rocks," Nanga continued. "The shaman and priest said it brought us closer to the Creator and the Source. But with the attacks, we retreated down by the river. We've braved our way back into the rocks recently, though. The soil there is perfect for harvesting. In fact, Elder Uzoma's is perhaps the deepest farm within the rocks—if I recall correctly."

"That's right," Yemi said. "Nothing scares that old man."

"What do you know about him?" Amana asked Yemi. Amana shook his hands, forcing blood to circulate back into his fingers. It had taken the better part of the morning, but Yemi finally showed strain under Imani's weight.

"In his prime, he was one of the greatest warriors known to Bajok. I've never seen a man kill so efficiently before. He was like a piece of art." Yemi's eyes glazed over.

"No one really knows where he came from, though," Nanga added. "He's not a native of Bajok. But he wanted a wife. After helping the Chief with our demon problem, he was given one of the most beautiful women in the village."

"The man has piss-poor luck with women, though," Yemi added. "His first wife died giving birth to their first son."

"The son's name is Ikenna, right?" Nanga asked Yemi.

"Yeah, I think so. You'll get to meet him, too, if he's tending to the farm this morning. You'll know exactly who he is. All the girls love him, well, until they get to talking to him."

"Why's that?" Amana asked.

"He's a bit … strange," Nanga added. "You'll see. But Yemi is being modest; he's the one the women can't get enough of."

"True enough," Yemi admitted. Nanga nodded his head to Nya. She didn't pay the conversation any mind.

"Anyway," Yemi continued, "same thing happened to his second wife."

"He was just too big for them, I say," Nanga said with bouncing, raised eyebrows.

"She died like the first," Yemi said. "Uzoma got himself another son, but the baby died shortly after, too. They say he tried something strange during the pregnancy to keep his wife alive. Some say he's cursed by the—" Yemi caught Nanga's eyes, "the demons at the rocks."

"Piss-poor luck." Nanga shook his head. "It's a shame. A warrior like Uzoma didn't deserve that. I guess no one is perfect," Nanga chuckled. "You can't be blessed with both perfect fighting skill and a wife that can handle you. Isn't that right, Ya-Seti?"

Nanga winked at Nya again. She returned the gesture with a scowl. On the horizon, appeared the silhouette of a man trotting down the road.

"Oh, Ugara's spear! Here comes Oluchi now," Nanga said, dropping his end of the sling.

"He will have to know one way or the other," said Yemi.

"I'd rather it be closer to his home, not here in the middle of nowhere."

"What're you going to do? Hide the body?" Yemi questioned.

"Of course not. I guess we'll just have to give it to him straight. Or maybe we'll have the woman speak to him. She's probably got a kinder tongue for this sort of thing. And you heard her speaking our tongue. Hell, if it wasn't for those dots on her face I would have thought she was a local. She's got the eyes for it, too. Your parents shape-shifters?"

Though it was Nanga's first legitimate question, Nya continued to ignore him. Amana, too, wondered about her parentage. If she were a shape-shifter—and likely a strong one if she was the head of a guard—Nanga wouldn't want to get on her bad side.

"Maybe she should speak to him," Yemi agreed. "Where did you learn our language anyway?"

Nya lifted her chin. "Our Kor'de wanted her entire retinue to learn. She gave us six moons. Most of my comrades didn't take it seriously, but I got the hang of it within a season. Knowing the language was vital, especially if this deal went sour. It's better to know what kind of tactics your enemies are throwing at you without them speaking in code."

She's really one of a kind, Amana thought.

"You're really one of a kind," Yemi said. Amana lifted his eyebrows at that.

"But no, I will not help you talk this man down. He has no idea who I am, and I have no relation to his daughter. This one is on you," Nya concluded.

The silhouette grew larger. Amana could make out the aged lines on the man's face, and his arms were as thin as twigs. The figure must have been Imani's father, Oluchi. The elder looked bewildered and flustered. He must have known by now his daughter was missing. When he finally took notice of the group and the object that lay behind them, he realized why they had come. The man dropped to his knees, tears welling in his eyes, his mouth agape.

"Amana," Yemi said as he dropped his end of the sling. He wasn't even sweating. "Uzoma isn't far down this stretch of land. Just follow this road between the rocks. He's the last settlement on the road. You can't miss him. We'll deal with Oluchi while you attend to your business. This might take a while. Oluchi is an emotional man."

"Can you blame him?" Nanga turned. "The man lost a daughter. And a fine one at that."

"Whatever happens, you and I know this won't be over anytime soon," Yemi said. "Amana should go on ahead."

"Thank you," Amana said before Nanga could reply. He set down the road toward the old man.

"And don't try running off! Those rocks are like a maze, and with these demons about, we can't promise you'll be safe!" Nanga shouted after Amana.

"We'll be waiting for you at the mouth of the rocks! Don't be too long!" Yemi chimed in. Amana waved a hand in acknowledgment. As he passed Oluchi, he wondered if he should say something to console him.

"I understand how you feel" was all he could whisper to the man. Oluchi stared up at him with red eyes—a look of pure defeat that Amana knew far too well. Those grief-ridden eyes could easily turn hot. It was just a matter of when. "Hang in there; these people will take care of you."

CHAPTER 5

ELDER UZOMA

IT TOOK AMANA ANOTHER HALF HOUR TO REACH UZOMA'S farmstead. The rocks were enormous, blocking out the morning sun. Shadow covered the landscape, with only the tops of the adjacent rocks reaping the warmth of the meager sunlight. Amana suspected that when the sun rose high enough, the rock valley would be lit for most of the day.

The clearing stretched one-hundred fifty strides, the soil a deep brown, with worms wiggling throughout. There were all sorts of crops growing: horned melons, figs, nuts, brown rice, and lots and lots of beans. The variety of crops were far more diverse than the other farms Amana had passed.

Like Yemi and Nanga had said, the rocks were slotted, all leading down different natural corridors. Each lane was a new maze for Amana to get lost in.

Uzoma's hut—no, not a hut, a building—was grander than most everything Amana had seen in Bajok. It would never be mistaken for a royal palace by any means, but Uzoma was living comfortably. His home was more a fortress than a homestead.

Unlike the huts of Bajok, Uzoma's was squared instead of round, rising at least fifteen paces.

Just outside the main threshold, a young man tended to a row of crops. He favored his left shoulder as he pulled at weeds, and there were scrapes on his elbows and knees. In Bajok fashion, he wore his hair long, pulled back by twine, wearing nothing but cloth around his middle, with sweat glistening off his back.

"I come with open palms." Amana used the local greeting, stretching out his hands. "Elder Uzoma lives here?"

When the boy lifted his head, Amana knew him instantly as Uzoma's first son. Nanga and Yemi were right: he was a handsome man, his skin almost too perfect, chin cut with sharp angles.

"What's it to you?" he said. The young man rose to his full height and—like the other men in Bajok—he stood a head taller than Amana. But the boy's height came mostly at the neck.

"You're Ikenna, are you not?" Amana asked.

"Like I said, what's it to you?"

"Now, now, play nice, Ikenna," a voice bellowed. Amana turned to who he assumed had to be Elder Uzoma. He was quite a burly man, worthy of mention among the warriors of Bajok. His hair was gray now, long like Amana's, though it grew well down his back, and his beard fell almost to his belly, not unlike the Junga monks. His eyes, by the looks of them, were once brown. Now, they were a more opaque gray. There was no question where Ikenna got his looks from. Though Uzoma was well past his prime, his cheekbones had not yet sunk. They still carried a healthy—and handsome—frame, the perfect face for one who was called a "lady charmer." If Ikenna was tall, Uzoma was a giant. Next to his broad-shouldered father, Ikenna looked almost bony.

"I apologize, Father." Ikenna dropped his head.

"I'm not the one owed an apology."

"Sorry …" Ikenna stopped short, not sure how to address Amana.

"My name is Amana."

"Sorry, Amana," Ikenna finished.

"Don't mind my son." Elder Uzoma switched to the Mother Tongue.

"I understand the Golah Tongue," Amana said.

"Perhaps, but you speak the Mother Tongue much better." Uzoma only smiled. "As I was saying, he's becoming a man. Not sleeping as well as he should. Last night was particularly tough on him."

"Was he part of the festival last night?"

"No, I try to keep the farmhands focused on their work. We just started our harvest, and I didn't want to miss a day. There will be other times for festivals. That right, Son?"

Ikenna nodded with his long neck, keeping his eyes low.

"It was particularly eventful," Amana started. "Though a girl was killed."

Ikenna's eyes went wide.

"Oh no." Uzoma stepped closer to Amana, giving his son a side glance. "Do they know the girl's name?"

"Imani, I believe. Oluchi's daughter, they say."

"Imani?" Ikenna dropped the weeds in his hands. "What do you mean she was killed?"

"There was a demon that passed through the village last night, half man, half hyena. I wasn't entirely sure—" before Amana could continue, Ikenna ran toward the threshold of the rock structure.

"Ikenna, come back here now!" Uzoma shouted, but his son was already several yards away.

"Did he know her?"

"Oluchi's only a farm or two south of ours. Ikenna had a soft spot for his daughter," Uzoma confessed. "Again, I apologize for my son's attitude. As I said, he's been going through a change."

"I don't mind, truly," Amana said. "We were all young once."

"Too true," Uzoma agreed. "So, what brings you to my farm, Amana?"

"The teachings of the True Path," Amana said, withdrawing his scroll from his travel pack and handing it to Uzoma. Uzoma turned the scroll gently over with his hands.

"And what makes you think I can help you with this?" asked Uzoma.

"If the stories from the east are true, you are the Great Elder Uzoma. The Enlightened Warrior."

"So they say," Uzoma said. "Come, we'll talk more inside."

Uzoma led the way into his home. Before crossing the threshold, he said a short prayer to Deh'ala, the Gatekeeper. That was a tradition of the locals, but not of those who followed the True Path. Amana wondered what sort of teachings Uzoma followed. Not wanting to be rude, Amana mirrored Uzoma's actions.

"You don't have to do all that," Uzoma chuckled. "It's something I do for me. Local traditions rubbed off on me and all that. No need to suck up to me. Praying to the Gatekeeper will not bring you the answers you are looking for, at least not yet."

Amana nodded, hoping his ears hadn't gone red in the presence of such an elder.

Uzoma's home was well-lit, a window for every room, all held up by strong clay. Most of the villagers only had one large room with perhaps a corner for a fire pit. But Uzoma had set himself something a step above, a Chief among farmers. The architecture was influenced by the east—there were arches carved above each threshold and high ceilings.

The most noteworthy piece of furniture in the room was a small table. It was bedecked with a simple but elegant cloth. There was clean water in a wooden cup atop it, with a white candle and miniature statues of figures Amana did not recognize. Next to the statues were various objects: farming tools, small weapons, and a long spear that stretched the length of the table. At the center of the table was a dish of fresh meat—beef, if Amana's nose placed it right.

"You can do with a bite to eat, I'm sure," Uzoma said,

responding to Amana's rumbling stomach. "It's a long trek from Bajok. Can I offer you a fig? Some meat? Lucky for you, my wife cooked up some beef yesterday. There's plenty left."

"Yes, please," Amana said as he set down his travel pack.

"Esi!" Uzoma called toward the back of his home. After a moment, a beautiful young woman—though gaunt around the eyes—came from the back. Her eyes were big, her hips were large, and her stomach pregnant.

"Yes, my love," the woman answered. She did not say hello to Amana or even make eye contact with him.

"We have a guest. Could you fix something for him?"

"Of course." She gave Amana a polite smile after Uzoma mentioned him as a guest, though her eyes were still locked to the ground. After a short bow, she disappeared into another room.

"You have a nice place here," Amana complimented.

"Thank you," Uzoma replied as he sat down in one of his rocking chairs. "It took some time, but I've had help over the years."

Even the ground was well-kept, the entire floor covered in various rugs and skins. Amana walked over to the chair next to Uzoma, lifting a hand for permission. Uzoma nodded his approval, allowing his guest to sit.

"So, have you already pledged yourself?" Uzoma asked, taking a sip of his morning tea. "You've been growing your hair for some years now, haven't you?"

"I'm not pledged, no," Amana said. "But I have taken the steps."

"It's not the most glamorous life. Forgive me if this sounds rude, but you don't seem the type for this sort of thing. What did you do before? Mercenary work?"

"Something like that."

"Personal bodyguard? You have the physique for it."

"That came with the job sometimes."

"What is it then, boy?" Uzoma asked, his voice agitated. He

was a peaceful individual by reputation, but he was an old man. And old men had little patience for most things.

"I was a pirate … smuggling mostly," Amana confessed.

"Ah, so that's why you have that look about you." Uzoma sipped his drink.

"What look?" Amana raised an eyebrow.

"Your eyes are darting every which way. Relax. It's just my home."

Amana relaxed his shoulders, sinking back into his seat. Had he really been that obvious?

"You from the east?" Uzoma asked. "I can't quite place it."

"My mother is from the Isles. She says my father was from the east, though," Amana said as Esi brought out his food—a plate of sliced peaches and a reasonable cut of beef. Amana's stomach grumbled again.

"Go ahead." Uzoma nodded. "I don't mind you talking through your food." Amana nodded and took a bite of the meat first.

"Your father is from the Esterlands, you say?" Uzoma started up again.

"Not the Esterlands, even farther," Amana said, taking a bite of the fruit. Uzoma raised his eyebrows.

"I don't recall any recent engagements between the Isles and the Far East."

"There was no war if that's what you mean. It was nothing like that. My parents' relationship was amicable. But my father didn't want any little *kijana*."

"Ah, so you're a love child then?" Uzoma said with a toothy grin.

Amana frowned, leaving a pregnant pause in the conversation. He never liked the term love child, as though it implied he was lesser somehow.

"Don't fret about it. We're all children of passion, are we not?" Uzoma chuckled. Somehow, Amana felt better about hearing his words. There was a friendly quality to Uzoma he could not quite place. He came off more enlightened and amicable than warrior and gruff. It was no wonder the villagers and so many others seemed so fond of him.

"What have you studied so far?"

"Just the tenets of Boism," Amana said.

"Ah, yes that is a good one. Have you found success with its teachings?"

"It's gotten me far enough."

Esi walked back into the main room. She changed the food from the altar and filled the cup on the table with new water. Still, she did not look toward the talking men, keeping to herself. Amana didn't think she liked him much.

"So, you want to be a monk. But why?" Uzoma shifted forward in his seat.

"It's the best way to live out my days. Being a pirate doesn't amount to anything," Amana said casually.

"Don't lie to me. I can always tell," Uzoma said, eyes peering over his cup like a lion looking over tall grass.

"That's no lie."

"You don't have to tell me the exact reason, but you first have to be honest with yourself," Uzoma said. He lifted himself from his rocking chair and walked toward a crate near the front of the hut. It took him some time, but he found the scroll he was looking for.

"It's one of the first tenets of Boism, is it not?" Uzoma said over his shoulder. "One must not speak anything but the truth, or something to that effect, right?"

"But I did not—"

"Your answer was not honest within your spirit."

"How could you know that?"

"You said it yourself. I'm one of the enlightened ones," Uzoma said as he sat back down in his chair. "The Gods' gift to me was elevated once I studied the True Path. I'm sure you've experienced this yourself, even if only to a minor degree."

Amana nodded. It was true that his short-sight had been honed over the years.

"And this is your wish, to make it stronger, right?"

"Yes. That is part of it ... What is your gift?"

"I thought you would have guessed by now." Uzoma grinned. "I've been using it the whole time you've been here."

Amana raised an eyebrow, not quite sure what Elder Uzoma meant. He should have felt uncomfortable and uneasy, yet he still felt oddly contented with the situation he was in. The chair he sat in was soft, the smell of Uzoma's home was sweet, the warmth of the morning sun hitting the back of his neck was comforting. There was nothing that made Amana feel amiss.

Ah, that was it! Amana thought. The questions that had been hurled at him would usually irritate him, even anger him, but the reason those feelings were kept at bay was clear now.

"You're an empath!" Amana concluded. He should have known. With the other empaths he'd encountered, he could feel the artificial moods they created. But Uzoma crept into him without warning. Amana thought his good mood was of his own accord. This elder was truly a master of his craft.

"Very good, Amana." Uzoma clapped his hands. "And you have quite a bit of anger within you that needs to be kept at bay."

Amana clenched his jaw. It was true.

"May I?" Uzoma asked, lifting his index finger and thumb toward Amana. The younger man nodded, though he was not entirely sure what Uzoma was about to do.

It wasn't so bad. Uzoma only touched Amana's forehead, but as he did so, a rush of warmth filled Amana. He could feel Uzoma in his body like he had felt the twin spirits the night before.

"What is this?" Amana said with clenched eyes, his body shaking uncontrollably. "Are you reading my mind?"

"No, my gift does not work that way. I am reading your emotions. It's a similar principle, but there is a subtle difference. There is a lot of pain within you, Amana—pain you have not yet let go. You can't hope to follow the Junga path with this in your heart."

"No," Amana said through gritted teeth. He had not come this whole way just to be rejected again. He tried to shake off the good-natured feeling in the pit of his stomach. It felt fake. But the harder he pushed against it with his ire, the more he was soothed into complacency. His eyes drooped. "I've already mastered the other tenets."

"Have you now? Should I list off the things you've already failed to achieve in our simple conversation?" Amana had no answer for that as his head drooped. "No, Amana. There is much darkness in you. Teaching you would be futile when you have so little control."

Uzoma removed his hand from Amana's forehead. He walked away as though nothing had happened, sat down, and took a sip of his drink casually. By contrast, Amana's brow was beaded with sweat, and his breath was ragged.

"I don't have time like that anymore," Uzoma said. "It would take too much effort, and I barely have any to spare."

Amana looked away from Uzoma, holding his tongue. Without Uzoma's hand on his forehead, he could feel that darkness sneak back up his spine, his slack jaw clenching in apprehension.

Amana glanced at Esi. Her eyes were wide with shock, but she gave no encouragement, only cradled her stomach. Amana looked down to her belly. She would be due within the moon, judging by her size.

"Your wife ..." Amana panted, still recovering from the empathic experience. Uzoma lifted his head, but did not respond. "It's said that your wives have a hard time in childbirth."

"Careful," Uzoma warned.

"I can help you there. I brought my own daughter into this world. I could do the same for yours."

"A daughter? You never mentioned a child—"

"Careful," Amana warned back with piercing eyes. Uzoma looked at Esi and then back at Amana. Esi's lips parted, but she did not make eye contact with either man. What had she wanted to say? She must have known about the rumors of the wives that had come before her. Perhaps that was the reason for her odd mood. Now that Amana felt for it, he could sense how Uzoma soothed her.

"Esi, you should sit down," Uzoma suggested. "Don't stress yourself." Uzoma stroked her back. Color returned to her brown face. After a moment, she nodded and sat.

"My mother was a midwife," Amana said. "Most of my childhood was spent assisting her. I know the practice well enough."

"A smuggler, a pirate, and a midwife's assistant? Are you sure you're not some King, as well?" Uzoma chuckled.

"That's a story for another time," Amana said, smirking.

Uzoma stroked his beard, inspecting Amana from head to toe. After a few moments, he looked to a crate stacked against the wall. It was filled with scrolls. Amana stole another glance at Esi. This time, she looked right at him.

Her gaze was unsettling. She never blinked. Her eyes were a normal brown, but the whites around it were bloodshot. When was the last time she had slept?

Poor chana, *she thinks her pregnancy a death sentence,* Amana thought.

Esi broke the eye contact first when Uzoma brought his attention back to Amana.

"No." Uzoma shook his head. "I will not train you, nor will I help you."

"But I've come all this way—"

"That's my decision. Thank you for visiting me, but it's time for you to go." Uzoma turned to his wife, then back to Amana. "If you'll excuse me, I need to tend to my wife. You can show yourself out."

Amana wanted to say something, but he couldn't decide what might change Uzoma's mind.

"Thank you, Elder Uzoma." He clenched his jaw. Uzoma nodded, waiting for the younger man to depart.

Amana took a few deep breaths through his nose, then got up, dusting off his traveling cloak. As he turned on his heel, the back of his foot hit the table, knocking over his water onto Uzoma. Esi dropped to her knees to clean her husband off.

"I'm sorry, Elder, I didn't mean to—"

"Just go, young man. Go," Uzoma said, his eyes neutral.

Amana turned away, rubbing his beard. He peeked over his shoulder when he reached the hut's door. Esi continued patting the water away.

"Don't worry, it's only water," Uzoma told her.

Amana crouched by Uzoma's crate, filching the scroll closest to him. He peeked over his shoulder again. The couple was still busy cleaning up the mess. Amana smiled as he let himself out.

THE MOMENT AMANA STEPPED OUT OF UZOMA'S HOME, HE felt wholly himself again. The magic of the empath no longer forced him into an artificial good mood. There was, in fact, an anger brewing inside of him though. Uzoma's little interrogation had done its number. Amana was no master of any tenet … not even one it seemed.

Where had he gone wrong in the conversation? What had triggered his ire? Just about everything. The mention of his daughter, the mention of his past life, the accusation that he was not ready to become a monk. And after all that, Uzoma still refused him.

At least Amana had one of Uzoma's scrolls. But he didn't dare open it until he was well away from Uzoma's homestead. After each step, Amana expected to see Uzoma bounding out of his house, chasing him down for his scroll. When Amana reached the end of the fig trees, he knelt beside one, pulling out his prize.

It was a small scroll, though in good condition—much smaller than the Scroll of the Five. It illustrated a man performing several combative sequences. The martial art was called the Spirit's Dance, or the God's Dance—at least that's what he thought—Amana couldn't make out the symbols well enough. Amana took note of how the fighter often used his legs instead of his hands, much different than the brawling style of the pirates Amana had been familiar with. All the moves seemed to flow from one to the other like a choreographed dance, just like the men at the festival.

Of all the scrolls you could have stolen ... How will this help? Amana thought to himself.

Handwritten annotations were etched on the sides of the scroll. Some Amana could read; others he could not. One of these annotations suggested that the flow of this martial art brought one closer to the spirit of the Warrior. Another suggested, more practically, that the movements were used for inertia, putting more kinetic weight behind each flowing kick. There were also annotations juxtaposing the Spirit's Dance with another local style called the Spirit's Claw, though nothing in the scroll illustrated this other fighting discipline.

Even with all the spirit mumbo jumbo, there was no way this scroll was sanctioned by the Junga. All of the annotations were of the mainland, not from the Far East. Frustrated, Amana stuffed the scroll—perhaps too roughly—into his pack. Maybe he'd come back for another scroll. If Uzoma would not teach Amana, one of his journals might.

Catching his anger, Amana centered himself. He closed his eyes and emptied his mind. Elder Uzoma's lesson was vital, and he respected that. It was also the only lesson he would likely receive from the elder.

Never get too high; never get too low. Amana remembered these as the words the monks spoke. He accepted that he was not as prepared as he thought he was, so he let it go. He would learn the lesson but would not let it bring him down. He already was at a disadvantage by thinking he had conquered all of his studies. A true monk knew to sustain their humility at all times. But they also knew they should never beat themselves up over mistakes. No, Amana would not let that happen. He would take what he had learned and apply it sensibly going forward.

He wasn't entirely sure he could help Uzoma's wife, either, even if the elder had accepted his offer. But he had nothing else to bargain with. Uzoma seemed certain he would not train Amana under any circumstance. Besides, Uzoma's wife looked as if she was not all there, and it had been many, many years since Amana had delivered a child. If it did come down to a delivery, Amana would need to brush up. But first, he needed to figure out how to change Uzoma's mind.

CHAPTER 6

INTO THE BUSH

It wasn't long before Amana found his way to the threshold of the great rocks, but none of the members of his escort were there—they likely were with Oluchi in his homestead. So Amana waited.

He started to pull out his stolen scroll again when he caught sight of two figures in the distance. Judging by their shapes and sizes, it was a man and a woman, though Amana couldn't be sure. Tucking his scroll away, he ducked between the rows of bean plants.

Step by silent step, he approached the pair. They spoke the local tongue in raised voices. The female jawed rapidly, her words strung together like an unbroken melody. Amana still couldn't make out their faces, the bean plants obstructing his vision. But as they grew nearer, another figure materialized through the rows of plants.

This new person was crouched near the pair, just at the edge of the couples' blind spots. As Amana approached, the distinct dark red hair betrayed the identity of this single figure: Nya.

Amana slowed his pace, taking extra care to set his foot down from heel to toe.

"You have light feet," Nya whispered without turning her head. "But they are not light enough." Amana stopped cold.

Nya turned with a finger to her mouth, a smirk at the corner of her lips.

"Why aren't you with Oluchi and the others?" Amana asked, keeping his voice low.

"The wife didn't trust a Ya-Seti coming into her home, so I remained here. These two showed up not too long ago."

"What are they saying?" Amana strained his ears to decipher the female's words. Her words voiced an unbroken stream of sound.

"The boy came from the rocks," Nya said, keeping her eyes locked on the pair. "He wanted to see Imani, but this girl here wouldn't have it."

"The boy's probably Ikenna, Uzoma's son," Amana said. "After I told him what happened, he came running. Do you know the name of the girl?"

"Yejide, from what I can tell," Nya replied.

Amana raised his eyebrows, pushing the bean plants away from his face. Ikenna's back obscured the young woman, but now that Amana was listening for a specific voice it did sound a lot like the skinny girl he had spoken to the night before.

Yejide continued to yap with clenched fists, punctuating each sentence she spoke with a stomped foot on the dirt. Ikenna lifted his hands to her shoulders. The girl flinched at Ikenna's touch at first, but her shoulders relaxed.

"Just tell me one thing," she said. Amana could understand her now that she spoke slowly. "How could you kill her?"

"I didn't," Ikenna said gently. "I swear."

Yejide shook her head. But she did not bring herself to shout as she had before. After Amana's stint with Uzoma, he could feel the influence of an empath. Ikenna nullified Yejide's mood, keeping her calm. The young man lacked the refinement his father had—the manipulation was obvious to Amana, or perhaps Amana's guard was up from earlier.

"Like father, like son," Amana said under his breath.

"What's that mean?" Nya turned her head slightly.

"He's soothing that girl," Amana whispered to her. "Listen to his voice; you can feel it."

"He's an empath." Nya's eyes went wide.

"As is his father," Amana said. "I found that out the hard way—"

"If he's an empath, then we'd better withdraw," Nya said, lifting up on her heels. "He'll suss us out if he pushes his power toward us—"

"I already have," Ikenna said through the plants.

"Yejide, step away from him!" Amana said with steel in his voice. Nya stood to her full height, her bow and arrow trained on Ikenna.

"Come to me, Yejide," Nya said softly in the local tongue.

"The pair of you have no idea what you're doing," Ikenna said as he let go of Yejide. The moment she was outside of his grasp, her glazed eyes cleared and she stumbled to Nya's side.

"Then enlighten us. What do we have no idea about?" Amana asked.

"Don't let him talk to you. He can't be trusted," Yejide said in Amana's ear.

"I could say the same about you last night. What was that about?" Amana shot back.

Yejide spoke fast again. Amana couldn't keep up.

"She says she wasn't supposed to be there yesterday. That her father would've killed her," Nya said.

"I'm not the man you're looking for," Ikenna butted in, speaking the Mother Tongue so Amana could understand. But Ikenna's voice was filtered by the influence of his power.

"Your father tried that on me, as well." Amana stood his ground. "It's not going to work here."

"He'll trick you." Yejide tugged at Amana's shoulder. "It's the way of his kind. He's a kishi, like from the songs."

"What's a kishi?" Nya asked.

"It is the demon that plagued our land many years ago," Nanga said from behind the group, his spear in hand. He turned to Amana. "We all suspected it's what you saw last night. But we wanted to believe it was just a shape-shifter."

"What's the difference?" Amana asked, keeping his eyes locked on Ikenna.

"The kishi are much, much worse." Nanga bent his knees, readying himself to attack. "They hide in plain sight. They could be our neighbors, our family, our friends ... or the sons of war heroes. They're charming enough when you get to know them, but hidden behind their heads are those filthy hyena-heads."

Amana measured the back of Ikenna's head with his eyes. Something *could* be hidden underneath it. But many of the men in the village wore their hair that way.

"You've no idea what you're talking about." Ikenna crossed his arms. "Yejide and the other women in the village—"

"Are safe now that we've found the demon." Yemi approached the group with his own spear held at the ready.

"What took you so long?" Nanga shot over his shoulder.

"There are certain courtesies one has to attend to with a burial," Yemi replied.

"If you would have left before all that we could have taken this kishi already," Nanga shot back.

"You're not taking me anywhere," Ikenna said with outstretched hands. Amana wished he had gotten a better look at the demon. It had been too dark for him to be sure it was Ikenna. But there was an easy enough way to find out. They just needed to see the back of Ikenna's head.

"Yejide, I'm sorry," Ikenna said.

"Why are you saying—" Yejide started to say, but she let out a gasp instead. Ikenna spun on his heel, revealing a hideous beast behind his head. It was just as Amana remembered it, a monstrous snout peeking through the part in the matted hair. Nya let her arrow loose, shooting Ikenna square in the back, but her arrow bounced off as if it were a twig. Ikenna's back—now the kishi's chest—was fortified with a layer of thick skin. Inch by inch, fur grew out of Ikenna's back, and he used it as a shield. In an instant, his elbows bent back on themselves, and his neck cracked forward, the hyena-head taking control.

"He's going for the girl!" Nanga shouted, letting his spearhead lead the way toward Ikenna, jabbing at his unprotected skin.

"Amana, don't let him take her!" Yemi hunched low next to Nanga, flanking Ikenna. The warriors used their spears well, keeping out of reach of Ikenna's hyena-head, but the demon was too fast for them.

"At his back, Nanga!" Yemi barked. "You have to get him from the back!"

"What the hell do you think I'm trying to do!"

Ikenna vaulted over Nanga, soaring at least ten paces in the air. When he landed, he drove his head into Nanga's gut. Nanga flew back twenty paces, skidding into the row of bean plants behind him.

Yemi was alone now. His spear was well built—strong Bajok black-wood topped with a sharp tip—but it looked puny next to the kishi's huge maw. Still, Yemi held firm. Where the hyena-head darted and bit, Yemi bobbed and weaved, always using the tip of his spear to maintain distance. But the kishi recovered with preternatural speed. Yemi was an impeccable warrior and a fighter at his peak, but he was only a man against a demon.

Nanga clutched at his ribs, wincing in pain while Nya kept loosing arrows into a demon hide that was too thick to be pierced.

Amana closed his eyes and took a deep breath, submitting to his short-sight. When he opened his eyes, the kishi was a ghostly figure. But unlike the men at the fighting circle from the night before, Amana could not track the beast. Just as he was given a flash—a ghostly image of the kishi biting at Yemi or snapping at his heels—the demon filled the wispy image, setting into reality before Amana could get a proper read on it. Though Amana's magic was compromised, he couldn't stand there waiting for Yemi to fall.

"Yemi, to your left!" he shouted, but the directive was too late. The kishi hit Yemi across the cheek with the back of its paw. Amana felt the impact even in his chest as Yemi flew back into a set of fig plants. Like Nanga, Yemi grimaced, rolling in the dirt.

"Move aside," Ikenna said from the back of the kishi's head. "I must take the girl."

"You mustn't do anything." Nya trained her next arrow between the kishi's eyes.

"Don't let him take me," Yejide whispered in Amana's ear as she clutched at his arm.

"Stand aside, foreigners," Ikenna barked. "You know nothing of Bajok."

"We know enough," Amana said.

"I don't have time for this." The kishi sprang forward. Just as it reached the apex of its jump, a rock the size of a large fist struck it across the snout. Amana and Nya pivoted away as the kishi fell face first into the dirt.

Where had that rock come from? Amana turned to Nya, who was oscillating her hand in a continuous wave. Hovering around her fingers were bits of earth, forming themselves into a mound of mud-rock.

She's an elemental! Amana thought to himself.

"So, you can touch the earth," Ikenna said, getting up on all fours again. "Good trick, but that'll only work once."

Ikenna started to lunge again, but his follow-through was disrupted. The dirt under his feet was suddenly uneven. Again, Ikenna fell forward.

Clever girl. Amana smiled.

"Enough!" Ikenna shouted, his hyena-head snarling.

"Take the girl and run," Nya said to Amana. Sweat beaded on her forehead as she moved her hands over the ground. In an instant, the loose dirt lifted from the ground in a cloud of dust, obscuring the kishi's vision.

"Let's go," Amana grabbed at Yejide's arm, leading her into the rows of tall bean plants. Yejide picked up the pace, running faster than Amana had expected. There was a roar followed by a scream from behind them, but they kept going, the rows of the plants obstructing the blue sky above. To their right, the Black Rocks loomed over the tops of the plants. To their left—when Amana braved a look—he made out the rising dust cloud. It looked almost like fire, though the tint was brown instead of white or deep gray.

"Wait, wait," Amana squeezed down on Yejide's hand. "We can't outrun him, not like this."

"What are you doing?" Yejide turned to him with shock on her face. "We have to try. We can't *stop*."

"No, wait, listen." Amana held a finger to his lips. The sounds of the fight had stopped. Amana crouched, pulling Yejide down with him.

"You think that woman killed him?" Yejide asked in a whisper.

Amana shook his head, listening for … anything. All that brushed his ears was the wind and the occasional song of a bird. But there was nothing else. It was … too quiet.

Then there was a laugh, the guffaw of a hyena.

"Oh no, do you think that woman is okay?" Yejide asked in a whisper. "We have to go now."

"No, no, no. Just let the beast pass." Amana turned his head, listening for footsteps, but then he remembered that these demons made no sound with no imprints on the ground. After all, the kishi from last night had walked atop the water soundlessly.

Amana closed his eyes, searching for anything that his short-sight would give him. There were tiny flashes from time to time. A beetle here, a worm there. But nothing so large as a kishi.

Yejide finally caught her breath, though her head twitched at every little sound through the bush.

"Do you feel that?" Yejide said, her eyes rolling up into the back of her head. "The wind, it feels nice, doesn't it?"

That's an odd thing to say …

Amana grabbed Yejide by the shoulders. "It's a trick. The wind is not real."

Amana reached out—not with his short-sight but with his own intuition. Sure enough, he sensed it. The breeze felt easy on the skin; the dirt under his feet felt softer than it had any business being. Ikenna was trying to lure Yejide out with his soothing abilities. If he could not find her, he could force Yejide to come to him.

"Let's stand up, Amana." Yejide's eyes glazed over. "I can't feel the breeze down here."

"Sapphire Hells!" Amana swore in the Mother Tongue. "I mean, listen, Yejide." Amana shook her harder, but she was loose in his grip, taken by the spell. If force was not going to work, Amana had to try something else. What had the monks said? One had to empty their goblet before they could fill it? But how would that help here? How could he get Yejide to simply stop caring about the breeze?

"No more cup," Amana said, hoping it would translate. It didn't. But Yejide's confusion at his words brought her out of the spell.

"No cup?" she asked. "What are you saying?"

"I don't know how to say it in your words," Amana said. "But you're back now, so stay focused."

But she wasn't. Once the confusion passed, her head lolled from side to side as though she needed to take a nap.

"The dirt is so soft, isn't it?" Yejide stroked the dirt beneath the palms of her hand. "Maybe if I rub it hard enough I can make it move like that woman did."

"Listen to your breath," Amana decided to tell her, grabbing her hands. Was that fur he saw through the plants? "Do no thinking. Just breathe."

Yejide's eyes widened back to their more natural, frantic state.

"Good, good," Amana patted the sides of her shoulders. "Think of your breath only. Stay silent."

Who would have thought the Junga monks would be so effective against demons?

"I know you are close," Ikenna said from within the bean plants. Amana thought he heard him to the right, but he couldn't be sure. Something told him the young man could throw his voice through the kishi. "Yejide, you will come to me. I will keep you safe. I will take away your fears."

"Don't listen to him," Amana whispered to her. "It's a trick. Like you say to me."

But Yejide was failing. Though she shook her head, trying her best to fight Ikenna's influence, she could not help herself against him.

"Okay, listen," Amana whispered to her again. "You have to run. He will find us sooner or later."

"No, I can't. You have to stay with me. He won't stop until he has me." That got her out of her spell.

"I can hold him off," Amana said. "But not for long. You have to go now."

"Okay, okay," Yejide said, her eyes fluttering again. "Don't be a hero. You run when you can."

"Trust me, I'm no hero." Amana shook his head.

"You are to me," she said as she ducked into a new row of plants.

Amana just shook his head again as he turned back to where he thought Ikenna might have been.

All right, let's try not to die.

He bolted through the plants in the opposite direction of Yejide. His hand brushed over every fig, every rice plant, making as much noise as he could. It only took a few seconds before the kishi sprang from a thick bush, blocking out the sun as it bore down on Amana.

Just before the kishi came down, another warning stabbed through Amana's head. He tucked himself into a roll, barely avoiding the kishi's attack. Without the others, Amana had no buffer between himself and the demon.

"You are no enemy of mine," Ikenna said, though Amana could not see his face. The hyena-head bore down on him with eyes of murder. "But you need to get out of the way."

"Amana!" someone shouted in the distance. It sounded like Nya.

"I'm over here!" he returned the shout. "Need a little help!"

Using all the focus he had, Amana predicted Ikenna's next attack. He slipped back on his heel, letting the kishi swipe at nothing but air. But Ikenna expected the dodge, rolling with the strike and pivoting on his back leg with a sweep that caught Amana at the back of the knee. The momentum of the strike sent Amana in a near full-circle spin, and he landed hard on his stomach. The impact blew the wind out of his gut. He would have gotten back up, but his stomach wouldn't let him.

There was nothing left to do but die. Hopefully, Yejide had had enough time to get away. Amana clenched his muscles, waiting to be bitten or ripped in two, but nothing happened. When he looked up, the kishi was dashing away, a spear and an arrow sticking out of its human front. Ikenna's face, bouncing up and down behind the hyena-head, scowled at Amana before disappearing into the endless expanse of farmland.

"Where's the girl?" Nya asked as she knelt down next to Amana.

"I told her to run." Amana lifted himself to his elbows, still catching his breath.

"Where to?" Nanga asked, holding his back in pain. "My spear is stuck in him."

"Just that way, toward the east." Amana pointed at the plants where she had run through.

"She should have an easy trail to follow," Nanga said as he pushed through the fig plants. "We just have to find her before that demon does."

Yemi stepped up behind him, stretching out a hand to Amana. Blue and purple colored the line of Yemi's jaw, but he still wore his signature smirk.

"Welcome to Bajok," he said. "I promise you, it's not always like this."

CHAPTER 7

BAJOK'S SECRET

NANGA DIDN'T FIND YEJIDE. YEMI SAID IT DIDN'T NECESSARILY mean she had been taken by the kishi, but the endless pit in Amana's stomach didn't make him feel any better. When Nanga and Yemi told Elder Uzoma what his son was, the man simply nodded and asked if Ikenna was dead. When Yemi said no, Nanga turned to Amana.

"You see. I was right, wasn't I?" he whispered to Amana. "The man is cursed. The kishi got to his son, too."

The walk back to the village was silent, save for the shuffling of Nya's arrows at her side, and the bottom of Yemi's spear making contact with the ground. Amana was told not to say anything to the others—the villagers or the Ya-Seti.

When they returned, they spoke directly with the Great-Chief, who listened to their story without interruption, stroking his beard in thought.

The Great-Chief allowed Amana to make camp outside the village near the riverbank. Nanga and Yemi both vouched for him, telling Chief Oba about how Amana helped fight the kishi. So, the next day, Amana settled down near the river docks.

Kojo, the man who had come to Amana's aid during the shaman's ritual, helped him build a makeshift hut. His son and daughter assisted them as well, twisting twine for the roof.

"How long you stay?" Kojo asked Amana in heavily accented Mother Tongue.

"'How long *will* you stay,'" Amana corrected. Amana traded lessons in the Mother Tongue for Kojo's help with his hut.

"How long *will* you stay?" Kojo said again.

"You got it." Amana smiled. "I'm not sure. I guess until I'm ready for the Junga monks."

"The Junga?"

"Uh, you might know them as the mountain monks."

"Ah yes, travelers speak of them," Kojo said, smiling to his children. They worked the twine quickly between their tiny fingers.

"Your children are very skilled."

"They are. They'll be great ..." Kojo could not find the word, so he spoke in the tongue of Bajok. "They'll be great workers for the village's future."

"Nu-uh! I'll be a warrior like the Great-Chief!" Kojo's son dropped his twine, flexing his nonexistent muscles, though a strange scale protruded from his skin.

"Oh, *Baba*, can we show him?" Kojo's daughter dropped the twine, jumping and clapping. Before Kojo could answer her, she was already grabbing a stick, smacking it as hard as she could against her brother's stomach. The boy didn't flinch at all; there wasn't even a red welt on his skin.

"Adeola! Stop that!" Kojo shouted though he was smiling. Adeola dropped the stick, her cheeks red.

"Your son has the gift of strong hide?" Amana asked Kojo.

"Most males here have this," Kojo said. "The parents of our parents—"

"Ancestors," Amana corrected.

"Our ancestors have always followed the way of the Warrior. It's necessary for the plains. They are dangerous."

"Oh, Baba! Can I show him my *a'bara*?" Adeola hopped up and down again.

"You will not! You haven't even finished your work yet!" Kojo pointed a finger at his daughter. She got back to work, her fingers flying through the twine. Kojo turned back to Amana with a smile.

"What is *a'bara*?" Amana asked in the local tongue.

"Uh … it is," Kojo pressed his fingers together, looking for the term. "I don't know how to say it in your words. It's a gift from above, from the spirits."

"Ancestral magic?" Amana asked in the Mother Tongue.

"Yes! That's it," Kojo said excitedly, snapping his fingers. He seemed to always wear a smile. "This is why you have your hair like this, yes? To make your spirit strong? To connect strong to your ancestors?"

Kojo pointed to Amana's matted locs. In truth, Amana did not think his hair had any significant meaning.

It was one of the first rituals of the Junga. They had twisted his hair and maintained it, but he figured it was merely a designation between new students and the elders—the shorter the hair, the newer the student.

Amana had stopped maintaining them like the Junga did, his hair more a fluffy poof with strands spreading out than clean, individual knots.

"Yes … for the spirits," he lied.

"We are alike, yes?" Kojo thumbed at his head. His own locs were down his back, not unlike Uzoma.

"Not everyone in the village has hair as long as that, though, right?" Amana looked to Kojo's son, whose locs were only down to his shoulders, his bangs in his eyes.

"Just the … *oni'baro* …" Kojo looked to Amana for help.

"The believers ..." Amana suggested, though he wasn't sure himself.

"Yes, I think this is the word." Kojo nodded. "The hair holds spirits. The oni'baro keep hair like this to make connection strong. Adami, since child, never cuts his hair."

Kojo's son, Adami, lifted his locs out of his face, smiling at the sound of his name.

"So, how was it out there?" Kojo went back to his work. "I never go close to the haunted rocks."

"Not too many haunts," Amana said, passing a stack of sticks to Kojo. "Elder Uzoma is living well, it seems."

"He is hero of this place." Kojo grabbed the sticks, starting on the hut's threshold. As he finished, he said a short prayer to Deh'ala. "You find knowledge from him?"

"I'm not so sure, to be honest," Amana said. "I took—he gave me—material to study, but I've no clue what use a monk would have for it." Amana went to his pack, withdrawing the small scroll.

"Ugara's Spirit Dance!" Kojo perked up, looking the parchment over. "I did not know it was painted to paper."

"You mean you did not know it was *written* on paper," Amana corrected.

"Ah yes, thank you," Kojo said, nodding his head. "Who marked this?"

"Elder Uzoma, I guess."

"Interesting ... everything here in Bajok is by word ... by the mouth. Uzoma is a bit ... different. He is not from here, you know."

"So I've heard," Amana said, looking the scroll over again. "You called it the Spirit Dance. Is that what it says on the scroll?"

"I don't know these lines, but the pictures are the steps of the dance." Kojo pointed to the first set of pictures.

"I saw men fighting like this at the festival; it looked pretty brutal," Amana said.

"It can be," Kojo admitted. "But it's a way for us to keep the spirit connection strong. The Warrior, Ugara, is most important for this dance. Here, I show."

Kojo laid the parchment aside, pulling his kanzu over his head. He tied his long locs into a knot, removing his necklace with the interesting spiral on it.

His children looked up from their work, grins going ear to ear. They would have themselves a show, something far more entertaining than roof building.

"I can't partake in any violent acts," Amana waved a hand dismissively.

"Like I say, the dance is ritual, mostly. Not really fighting." Kojo was already in a fight-ready stance, though his legs were spread wide.

"Your feet are too far apart; someone could just push you over," Amana noted.

"You want to try?" Kojo challenged, an edge to his voice. Amana wasn't so sure he wanted to push him over, especially with his children there. But his son and daughter were beaming, and Kojo looked cheerful enough.

Kojo started moving the same way the young fighters had two nights before. He swayed from left to right, backward and forward; it was hypnotic. Even without a drum circle, Kojo was keeping to a distinct beat.

That was it! Amana thought. All he had to do was match that beat and cut Kojo off from his tempo.

Amana waited for Kojo to shift to the right. Just as Kojo moved his weight to the left, Amana stepped forward, attempting to shove the older man off his feet. Before Amana could extend his arms, Kojo shifted his weight back instead of left, away from the push.

Amana did not see it, even with his short-sight. Kojo didn't even seem to know he would do the move himself. It was all part of the rhythm of the fight. Amana did not have the time to center his balance, so Kojo snatched Amana at the knee with his own legs, almost like a crab. And with that, Amana buckled and fell over.

"Careful, Baba!" Adeola shouted in the local tongue. "If Mom hears you were fighting, she'll be angry!"

Kojo pressed his finger to his lip, winking at his daughter. She jumped and giggled, covering her mouth. Kojo helped Amana up to his feet.

"How did you do that?" Amana asked as he dusted off his traveling cloak.

"You fell for the dance," Kojo chuckled. "Do not worry, all beginners do. Ugara's dance is meant to ..."

"Confuse the opponent?" Amana finished for him.

"Right!" Kojo lifted his finger with a smile.

"Baba says you have to be jumpy like a zebra," Adami added, hopping and skipping like a zebra. His father nodded.

"The first step is to learn *the sway*," Kojo began his dance. He tilted from side-to-side, forward and back, in one continuous motion. "The spirit's dance is all about the side to side, always moving with the Warrior. Good side-to-side, good connection. You try."

Amana tried to match Kojo's movement, mirroring his bounce. It was unlike any other martial art he had ever experienced. He was used to just smashing his fist into a man's face. No need for training, just hard-fought brawling experience—not this dancing business. He could admit that he felt the flow Kojo had mentioned. But Kojo's children were laughing hysterically at his performance.

"Not like that," Kojo said, lifting his hands. "You're too much like tree. You need to be like leaves. Side-to-side. Like dancing."

"I've never been much of a dancer," Amana admitted. He felt himself stiffen, worse than he was before. The more he tried to find the rhythm, the worse he did.

"Too much head," Kojo's son said in his accented Mother

Tongue. The boy lifted himself to his feet and started doing the sway along with his father.

"Adami is right; you can't think about it," Kojo said, matching his son's movement, throwing kicks above Adami's head. Adeola got to her feet as well, wanting to join the fun. She, too, was a natural, even bobbing her head in rhythm with her movement. The young girl had her own style, looking more like an agile leopard than the strong and jumpy variants of her father and brother.

Amana closed his eyes, thinking of nothing. Just as he had told Yejide to empty her cup, he emptied his own, focusing on his breath.

But it was easier said than done. The moment he thought his mind was empty, it wandered to something else: the sound of birds passing by, the laughter of Kojo's children, or the wind brushing through the trees.

So, he listened to the river. It was silent, undisturbed, but Amana could hear it somehow. It was calling to him as though a prayer were being carried over its waters. As he let himself dive deeper into the water's call, he found his own beat. The movement was not as refined as the Bajok villagers, but Amana could feel an energy tingle through his skin.

"There you go; you have it." Kojo smiled.

"Do you all hear that?" Amana asked. The voices on the water were louder, but he could not make out what was being said.

"I don't hear anything." Kojo shook his head.

"From the water." Amana opened his eyes. There was nothing on the riverbank, just the stillness, the longboats bobbing near its bank.

"You might be hearing the Moon Sisters … probably Aya," Kojo decided. "Ugara is working through them. I wish more of the young are like you. Less and less of the people dance; they're more interested in iron weapons than their God-given hands. I never see someone pick up voices like you. You are fast. Keep your practice, Amana. The dance shows you many things."

Amana nodded. He wasn't confident the call from the spirits was his own doing. It was the same voice that had been calling him since that first night; Amana was sure of it. "Thank you, Kojo. And thank you for helping me set up."

"You are guest to our village. It is our way."

"I wish some of the others remembered that when I got here," Amana said.

"They are scared. That's all. You say the soldiers take liking to you, right?"

"Yeah, they seemed to," Amana said. "What do you know of Nanga?"

"Strong man. Good warrior."

"Is he ..." Amana couldn't find the right way to put it. "Polite to the women in the village?"

"As far as I know, yes," Kojo frowned. "Why do you ask?"

"No reason," Amana lied. "What do you know of Yemi?"

"He is good man. Very ... how do you say it ... attractive, but not with love."

"Charming?"

"Yes, charming. He's very charming."

"I'll take more nice people like you and Yemi any day," Amana said. "Speaking of guests, how long are the Ya-Seti staying for?"

"Not sure," Kojo said, still eyeing Amana wearily. "The ancestors no give blessing to the marriage, not until this demon is gone. But I hear the Ya-Seti are patient. This makes sense. Their leader has more than a hundred years, yes?"

"Does he really? I thought he was over two hundred."

Kojo shrugged. "He's older than the Gods."

"Yeah," Amana nodded his head. "Well, let's hope this episode with the dark spirit resolves itself soon."

From the top of the small cliff, a pair of heads peeked over.

They were two young men—also with long hair. They wore the same necklace Kojo had.

"Elder Kojo!" the smaller said in the local tongue. He was breathing hard.

"Please, I am not old enough to be called an elder," Kojo chuckled.

"The demons are back!" the bigger one shouted, ignoring Kojo. "It took her! It took the beautiful one!"

"What do you mean? Took who?" Kojo's friendly eyes turned stern.

"Shanaki," the first one said. "The demon took the First Daughter of the Ya-Seti!"

GREAT-CHIEF OBA ORDERED EVERYONE TO THE "BIG HUT," AS the Bajok called it. The Ya-Seti royalty and their guard were there, just off the main stage. Amana picked out Nya among them. They traded nods before Nya went back to searching for potential threats in the crowd. Amana approached her.

"Was it Ikenna?" he asked.

"Had to be, right?" Nya said, still scanning the crowd of villagers piling into the hut.

On the stage stood the Chief himself, surrounded by a group of elders who supported their frail, bony bodies with walking canes. Nanga stood close to the Chief, nursing his side which was now black and blue. Yemi stood guard near the First Son, Baako, whose fist was clenched against his wooden throne.

After fifty villagers tried to pile into the hut, a lineup of Bajok warriors cut them off with clubs and spears. Those who did manage to squeeze into the hut whispered loudly to one another. Talk of "kishi" and "demons" was rampant.

When everyone settled, Great-Chief Oba stood, turning his

head to Kor'de Neema. "Tell us again what your soldiers have told you."

"My daughter wanted to go down to the river to fish. She loved that back home," Kor'de Neema said, her eyes misty, though she kept a firm face. One of the Ya-Seti advisers translated her words. Next to the adviser stood Kor Mosai, who had a perpetual statue-frown, his eyebrows pushed down over his lids.

"She should have been here with us. She's going to be my bride, I could have protected her!" Baako shouted, his balled fist white-knuckled. His father put up a hand, quieting the young man. Baako sounded a lot like Ikenna to Amana, though more nasally—rebellious teens trying to play at being men.

"Why do your guards not protect your First Daughter?" Oba asked of Neema in the Mother Tongue.

"They will pay with their lives," Neema responded, looking over her shoulder. The two Ya-Seti guardsmen held their heads low. "They know the price for failing to protect their charge. They know that death comes after a thing like that."

Nya grunted beside Amana.

"What is it?" he asked.

"It's my fault," Nya shook her head. "I was off this morning to find out more about these demons. Usually, I shadow the other guards to make sure they're protecting Her Highness properly. And look. The second I'm away, something like this happens."

"You don't seem that shaken up about it," Amana said.

"Shanaki can take care of herself." Nya shrugged. "I've seen her put better women and men to shame."

"Can she fight?"

"No, nothing like that. Her weapon is even better."

Kor Mosai lifted his finger, moving slowly as usual. "Who took Shanaki?" he croaked.

"We are trying to find that out now, my Kor," Kor'de Neema assured him. The age difference between the two was stark.

Neema had to be at least a century-and-a-half younger than the Kor. How many wives had the Kor taken over his lifetime? Three? A dozen? A score? He must have gone through many wives over the course of his unnatural life. Amana wondered how Neema felt about her position, about being with a man so old and wrinkled. She seemed more caretaker than a wife to him most of the time.

"My archers said they saw a figure across the lake," Neema said to Oba. "At first, they only thought it to be a stray hyena. But then that hyena ran across the water without sinking." Several villagers gasped. "My men were taken off guard. They knew this must have been the demon that showed up a couple nights ago. Nothing should break their focus. Our archers know this. Our arrows are only as effective as those that let them loose. And my men missed. They claim it was not entirely their own fault. They said the creature did something to them, made them feel defeated before they could even reach their arrows. And the demon, they said, was faster than any animal they had ever seen. Before they could attack, they were knocked over, and my daughter was taken."

"I can attest to that," Amana spoke up, looking to the Great-Chief. Was he allowed to mention Ikenna now? "The demon I saw—" Yemi was shaking his head. "On the … first night was unnaturally fast."

There was a weighted silence in the room. The Bajok warriors exchanged furtive glances.

"At this time, I would like to put together a search party for my daughter," Neema requested. "We do not know this land well, and we would need your assistance, Great-Chief Oba."

"I'll go with them!" Baako insisted. "I'll take a group of my men, and we'll find that bastard demon!"

"My son speaks out of turn." Chief Oba didn't need to lift his hand this time. His voice was enough. "My lead warriors need time to recover—"

"What happened to them?" one of the villagers cut in from the crowd.

"Nothing to worry any of you," Oba said, eyes sharp as a knife. "They were hunting yesterday and met a pack—"

"But they went with that foreigner. Does he know what happened?"

"You will not speak unless you are asked," one of the elders at the Chief's side said. "If the Great-Chief says his men need to rest, his men need to rest."

"What of your shaman?" Neema asked, ignoring Oba's statement. "Can he not heal your men back to fighting health?"

"Yes, that would usually be the case," Chief Oba admitted. "But the last ritual we used him on, the one we used to uncover the truth of this foreigner here—" the Chief pointed at Amana, "has left him unavailable for quite some time." Amana lowered his head. Too many eyes darted in his direction for his comfort.

"And I do not think I will risk any more of my men to chase after this demon."

"But this is your land. This demon is attacking *your* land. Would you not protect it?" Kor Mosai said.

"Our shaman assures me that our village grounds are protected. As you may have noticed, none of these attacks are happening within the walls."

"What about Elder Uzoma?" one of the Elder-Chiefs next to Oba asked. "He has saved us from this before. He has kept the peace at the Black Rocks. Can he not help us again?"

"I would not ask my old friend to risk life and limb for someone who is not our own. He is old and done with such things." Oba shook his head. "Perhaps this is a sign from our ancestors. This marriage should not go forward. It's more trouble than it's worth."

"How can you say that?" another Elder-Chief gasped.

"Father, at least let me try," Baako got to his feet, chest pushed out. "We know where these demons live!"

"Something is wrong here," Nya whispered to Amana. "I've been looking into these killings and kidnappings. That Imani girl was not the first. Attacks like these have been increasing all over these lands. It's true, none of them have been within the village, but many of the farmers have been plagued."

"What does that mean for us?" Amana asked.

"It was Ikenna!" The voice was loud and rude. At the threshold of the hut was old man Oluchi, Imani's father. The Bajok warriors at the threshold of the hut held him back with their shields. "Ask Uzoma himself! The boy has not been on his farm this entire day!"

Heads shook amongst the Bajok. Some villagers sucked their teeth and waved Oluchi's words away.

"The kishi, they are back! Uzoma's son is one of them, I tell you!" Oluchi clenched his fist in the air.

"Impossible! The kishi have been gone for nearly two decades," one of Chief Oba's advisers exclaimed.

The word "kishi" set a stir amongst the crowd, the same stir that had brewed amongst some of the villagers from the start. Amana didn't think Chief Oba could keep the secret hidden for long. The villagers would have to know they were no longer safe. But Amana did not want to be the one to tell the truth of it.

"It's true," another adviser chimed in. "There hasn't been a kishi in these lands for many years. It was Uzoma and Great-Chief Oba who did away with them, all those years ago."

"Have you all seen my daughter?" Oluchi continued, ignoring the last man's words. "Her throat was ripped to shreds. What sort of thing does that?"

Oluchi looked around the crowd with wild eyes, searching for some sort of support. Eventually, his eyes found Amana's and he pointed his finger straight between Amana's eyes.

"This one, he knows," Oluchi's eyes widened, his eyebrows like crawling caterpillars. "He saw how my daughter was killed. Why do you all deny it? Half-man, half-hyena! It all fits! When's the last time we've checked for these creatures? We know how they hide themselves!"

The room turned to Amana. Again, he recoiled from the dozens of eyes set upon him.

"I'm sorry, but I'm not sure what I saw …" Amana looked to Yemi again. When he finally looked to the crowd, he couldn't resist their eyes. Some leaned forward to listen, others had raised eyebrows, many of them women. "The kishi have returned."

"I knew it!"

"The farmers aren't safe!"

"I have family out there!"

"We have to kill it now! Before it spreads like before!"

Chief Oba's eyes shot daggers at Amana, yet the foreigner did not feel the fear the larger man wanted to instill. Amana knew telling the villagers about the kishi was the right thing to do.

The Ya-Seti guards turned to each other with looks of confusion and shrugged shoulders.

"I do not understand," Kor Mosai said. "What are these kishi?"

"They are demons, dangerous demons. *Charmers*, as they used to be called." Chief Oba shook his head. "They target the women. Years ago, it got really bad. We were nearly outnumbered by them as they multiplied. But once we found out how they hid themselves, it was much easier to eradicate them. Uzoma and I started to examine everyone in the village. Every man and boy had to cut their hair. It was the only way they could hide themselves.

"Knowing they could no longer hide under their hair, most of the kishi ran off to the rocks near the hills. Our people now call them the Black Rocks. That's where they made their last stand, but Uzoma and I did away with them. And as you know, Uzoma has never left that place. He always thought there might be more we never discovered."

The parts Amana did not understand were translated by Kor'de Neema, who spoke rapidly to keep up with Oba's words.

"And now you think some might have come back?" Kor Mosai asked.

"It seems that way now, yes."

"But if Uzoma's son is one of the kishi, wouldn't that mean Uzoma—"

"That's exactly what doesn't make sense to me. Everyone in the village cut their hair off, and Uzoma was clean."

"Where do the kishi come from? How were they created?"

"No one truly knows where they come from," said another adviser. It was the shaman. Amana hadn't recognized him without the blue paint covering his body. He was hunched in a corner, a blanket wrapped tightly around his shoulders.

The ritual really took a lot out of him, didn't it? Amana thought.

"But folklore tells us these Charmers were made by a dark spirit that tried to mix mortal and immortal, but ultimately failed," he said.

"So how do you stop them? What did you do before?" Amana asked.

"We killed them to the last beast," Chief Oba said.

"And we should start with Ikenna!" Oluchi demanded. "I want Uzoma moved far away from my lands."

"As far as I'm concerned, Uzoma is the most innocent of us all," Chief Oba stated plainly. "If you truly want to demand him off your shared land, you may always challenge him to Ugara's Dance."

Oluchi put his hands down at that. He was no match for Uzoma in that way, and he knew it.

"But if Uzoma's son is being accused, we must settle this now. Nnedi." The Chief gestured to one of the women on stage. Her face was more pointed than the others in the village, and she had a perpetual twitch.

"Tell Uzoma he's to come here at once."

Nnedi nodded her head, then pulled off her tattered clothing. Before anyone could get a good look, she transformed into an osprey, mouth turned to beak, arms turned to wings, and legs into talons. The osprey fluttered its wings and flew between the Bajok soldiers guarding the way out. Amana caught a glimpse outside—nearly half the village waited to hear or see what was happening.

"That girl might be safe yet," Nya whispered to Amana as they waited.

"Why's that?" Amana asked.

"These demons seemed to fancy women, right?"

"Right."

"If he never found that girl, maybe he went for Shanaki as a trade."

"But why? What does Shanaki have to do with any of this?"

"Like I told you, Shanaki is special."

IT TOOK AN HOUR FOR THE SHAPE-SHIFTER TO RETURN WITH Uzoma. The villagers in the hut spoke with hushed voices. With the kishi secret out, many discussed what action the Chief would take. Baako was still fuming. Every few moments, he sat up to speak with his father, waving his arms around like a madman. Oluchi kept murmuring to himself about Ikenna being a kishi.

"Elder Uzoma has arrived," one of the advisers greeted the man with a respectful nod. All the Bajok in the hut bowed to Elder Uzoma.

"Uzoma," the Chief said, nodding.

"Oba." Uzoma returned the nod. He was the only one on a first-name basis with the village leader.

"Has Nnedi informed you why you were brought here?" Oba said. The osprey-shifter was already pulling on her rags.

"Yes, but I must say I can't believe it." Uzoma's arms were crossed peacefully.

"Just a formality," Chief Oba said. "But we must ask where your son has been."

What was with the show? Chief Oba knew that Ikenna was off somewhere, maybe even killing Shanaki now.

"I've not seen him since yesterday," Uzoma admitted. "He was to trade some of our harvest in the market."

"You see! Ikenna cannot be accounted for!" Oluchi shouted.

"Silence, Oluchi," the Chief bellowed. "When was Ikenna supposed to return?"

"No later than noon."

"Send the search party out! He can't have gone far!" Oluchi shouted again.

"If I need to quiet you one more time, I will have you removed from this hut," Chief Oba said. Oluchi's head slumped.

"Have *they* returned, then?" Uzoma asked.

"There is too much evidence in favor of their return, I'm afraid. If your son is involved in some way, we must know. I'll give him another day to show himself, but no more," Chief Oba decided. "But you are right, Oluchi," Chief Oba confessed. "We should take extra precaution to this new circumstance. If the kishi have returned, all men in the village will have to shave again for the time being."

"With all due respect," a familiar voice from the crowd said. When the man stood up, Amana leaned forward. It was Kojo, speaking in the Bajok Tongue. "Cutting the hair of an oni'baro cannot happen again. We've only now been able to regain our connection with the ancestors. That festival was the best we've had in years. We will only go backward this way. Would it be possible to examine each man's hair instead of cutting it all off?"

The words Amana could not understand were translated by Kor'de Neema. Other men near Kojo nodded their heads. They, too, wore their hair long.

"We need to know the enemy by sight. This is the best way—the only way," the Chief said.

"But couldn't—"

"My decision is final," the Chief cut in. Kojo made no additional comment. Almost instantly, he bowed his head and sat down. "As your Chief, I will start."

Oba took off his headdress and let loose what looked like several years of growth. One of his advisers walked to his side with a large knife. Loc by loc, he cut his Chief's hair. After a few moments, the Chief turned to his audience. The back of his head was bare. No hyena-demon there. Next were the elder advisers. All of them were clean. Then it was Baako's turn.

"But father, it's finally down to my shoulders," he protested, but he let himself be shaved. Nothing was on the back of his head, save for a birthmark.

"No man in this room is allowed to leave. Every man here will submit to my advisers, Bajok and Ya-Seti alike. Is this agreeable to our guests?"

The Kor and Kor'de both nodded in unison. There were a few protests, but the Royalty's sharp eyes shut them off quickly.

"All right, then, everyone submit yourself to the stage for your shaving," Chief Oba directed.

Suddenly, a thick elbow jabbed into Amana's gut. The air was knocked out of him as he fell to the ground hard. Before he could understand what happened, there was a man running over his body and straight out into the village.

"Stop him!" one of the advisers shouted. "It's one of them! It's one of the kishi!"

CHAPTER 8

THE CHASE

AMANA ENGAGED IN THE CHASE WITHOUT A SECOND THOUGHT, even though a bruise started to swell over his ribs. It fueled his ire, his short-sight already in full focus. The man who had shoved him was fast, but not fast enough. Amana's feet pounded into the dirt. The man looked over his shoulder, measuring the distance between himself and Amana. But this man—no, this kishi—did not realize Amana was already becoming winded.

Amana stretched out his hand toward the man's shoulder. But the back of the man's long hair started to part, and beneath it emerged a hyena's face. Amana drew his hand back quickly, fond of keeping his fingers.

Women and children came out of their huts to see what the pounding feet had been. Amana slowed, and the man quickened. As the kishi took its true form, the man covered more ground. But his transformation was slow going—the protective magics of the village were doing their work. Amana just needed to stop the man before he got away from the village. He looked from left to right.

There! Amana thought as he grabbed a heavy stick from the ground. He briefly glanced over his shoulder. Bajok warriors and

Ya-Seti archers were gaining ground. Amana's short-sight gave him a head-start, but only just. Focusing himself, he cocked his arm back, stick in hand. Amana's short-sight gave him the target he needed. With perfect aim, he flung the stick at the kishi. It rotated in a perfect circle, aimed not where the kishi was, but where the kishi would be. And Amana's aim was true.

With a loud smack, the back of the man's knee buckled and he fell over, face first. But the fall was only momentary. In perfect balance, the man, now more hyena than anything else, sprang up on all fours. He had managed to get outside of the village's protection, just through the northern wall.

Amana had caught up, but now he was facing the fully-formed kishi. The demon sprang at him, but Amana had already seen the flash. With a small pivot, Amana dodged the first attack. The kishi went face-first into the side of the wall, head tearing a gap in the clay formation.

That was close. Even though Amana could predict the kishi's movements well enough, it was difficult for him to actually dodge him. It was one thing to see where his opponent would hit him. It was entirely something else to be able to react accordingly.

One of the Bajok warriors perched atop a watchtower aimed his spear at the kishi. He flung the weapon, a perfect throw. But the kishi was ready for it, facing the spear head on. The tip thunk off the kishi's strong hide, like a needle thrown against steel.

The kishi scaled the wall, snatching the warrior from his perch and throwing him twenty paces down. There was the distinct crack of bone breaking. Though the Bajok warrior was still breathing, Amana knew he would not be getting back up. Amana was alone. He just needed to stall until the rest caught up. But without a weapon, all he could do was evade.

Another flash.

The kishi sprang from the tower, attacking Amana from above. Amana wasn't ready for it. Instead of rolling away, he put his forearms in front of his face, hoping to simply survive the assault. The impact was hard. Amana could feel teeth sinking into one of his arms, and pain shot up his bicep. His arm was useless now, but he still had his legs.

With as much force as he could muster, he kicked the kishi's belly—no, its back—Amana still hadn't gotten used to the notion. The kick wasn't enough. The hyena's mouth was still latched around his arm. It wasn't going to dislodge that easily.

Amana reached around to the back of the hyena's head, the human head, pressing his fingers into the eye sockets, gouging them. That worked. The hyena's jaw dislodged and gave out a howl. Amana rolled away.

Finally, the Ya-Seti archers arrived—Nya in the lead—already letting their arrows fly free. Four of their arrows found their target, punching into the kishi's back, the human front. Still, the kishi did not stop. And instead of attacking the archers, it still came for Amana.

Amana dodged all its attacks as Nya poured more arrows into the kishi. Amana acted as a distraction, doing all he could to keep out of reach. Then the Bajok warriors took their own openings, using their spears to poke holes in the demon. Finally, Amana was free of the kishi's undivided attention. The demon was completely surrounded now, all but defeated.

"We don't have to kill you," Amana said. "Just tell us where the girl is."

"You know nothing, foreigner!" the human side of the kishi said, though in an unnaturally deep tone. "The time for mortals has passed. That girl is better off serving the kishi."

The kishi bit the air near one of the Bajok warriors.

"What do you mean by that?" Amana said. But the kishi was not interested in giving an answer. Instead, it took one great leap at him. Amana had expected the lunge long before it came, and he slipped away once more. He was now fully exhausted, and collapsed to a knee, unable to muster the energy to stand. His short-sight dwindled.

But there was something else. The longer he fought the kishi, the more dejected he felt. It was like the Ya-Seti had said—they had a way of making one feel dead inside. Hopeless. It was more than just Amana's physical stamina that was drained. His will to fight was diminished.

When Amana lifted his head, he had expected to find the kishi's jaw chomping at this face. Instead, there was a spearhead protruding straight through the kishi's hyena eye. Yemi stood at the north wall's edge, nodding at Amana. Amana nodded back.

"Their human side is their weakness," Yemi said as he stepped forward and freed the spear from the dead kishi's head. The Great-Chief had caught up as well. Yemi turned to him. "We'll need to retrain the men how to defeat them. It's useless to attack them from the front. It's a good thing the Ya-Seti flanked him as they did."

One of the Bajok warriors came closer to the kishi, using his spear to poke at its inert body. Another warrior tended to his fallen comrade. The man gave out a yell when his leg was touched.

"You did well, Amana." Elder Uzoma said with a smile. Amana hadn't noticed that the elder had caught up as well. In fact, most of the village seemed to be there. Men watched the scene with wide eyes. Children clutched at their mother's heels, asking what the kishi was. The elder stood taller than all of them, even the largest of the Bajok warriors. Where most of the elders looked frail, Uzoma rose strong and tall.

"Perhaps I underestimated you," Uzoma said. "Did the Junga monks teach you those moves?"

"I never got that far with the monks." Amana shook his head.

"Hmm. Come back to my home tomorrow. Show me more of what you've learned," Uzoma said, pressing his lips together.

All Amana could do was nod, but he winced at the pain in his arm. Uzoma held out his hand. When Amana took the elder's hand, Uzoma lifted him up with what felt like unnatural strength.

"They don't need to see it anymore," Oba whispered to one of his warriors. "Get *it* out of here."

"Should we stake it, Chief?" the warrior asked.

"No, burn the body. Take it far from here." Oba said. The warrior nodded. "Every man in this village is to report to the big hut immediately," Oba bellowed. A pair of Bajok warriors carried the demon's carcass away, following the Chief. The rest of the villagers followed as well, but the Ya-Seti stayed.

"That means you, as well," said Kor'de Neema to her men. "To those who don't have their hair short, report yourself to the main hut. We must hold our alliance with the Bajok. And you." She nodded to Amana. "My husband would like to speak with you."

Amana turned to Uzoma. He nodded. "Go with them, and make sure you get that arm fixed before you see me."

AMANA FOLLOWED KOR'DE NEEMA TO THE GUEST HUT. THERE, Kor Mosai waited with six of his elite guard surrounding him.

"I don't believe you two have been formally introduced," Neema said. "Amana, this is Kor Mosai, the Undying."

"A pleasure to meet you," Amana gave a courteous bow.

"So you have the short-sight," Mosai said with a husky voice. How was the man kept together? His face looked as though it would fall off his skull.

Amana did not answer right away. People with his gift were often used as tools for Royal Families such as Mosai's. "The Wise and Honorable Kor can be trusted," Kor'de Neema assured Amana.

"Your silence is telling, young man," Mosai eyed Amana knowingly. "Where are you from, exactly?"

"The east." Again, Amana was not sure how much he wanted to give up to the Ya-Seti. It was a possibility they were already aware of who he was. He had raided their ships a number of times on the Sapphire Sea.

"We, too, are from the east, my friend," Mosai said, grinning. "My question is how far to the east are you from."

"The isles" was all Amana divulged. He had to be careful here. The Ya-Seti didn't have the best relations with the Sapphire Isles.

"I expected as much. You have the look about you. Who did you fight for? Jultia? The Vaaji?"

"I fight—fought—for no one."

"I've lived several lifetimes boy. Someone with your gift does not stay away from a fighting occupation," Mosai said. "So you fight for no one you say. That means you are a criminal of some sort. What is it then? A mercenary? A smuggler? A pirate? All three?"

Amana bit his tongue.

"Johari, shoot this man in the head please."

The moment Amana heard the order, his sight went berserk. Just to the left, he saw the ghostly glow of an arrow targeted straight at his ear. Almost involuntarily—instinct at its finest—Amana jerked his head back. His sight caught up with reality, and the arrow passed just by his nose, embedding itself in the adjacent dirt wall.

"Johari, hold," said Kor Mosai. The archer stopped herself from loading her next arrow.

That could have killed me! Amana thought. What was Mosai playing at? Amana clenched his jaw, biting his tongue so hard it almost drew blood. It took every bit of self-control not to hit the old man. But Amana knew it would be bad to attack the Kor when he had so many guards surrounding him.

"Not even my best with the sight are so talented. Who was your father?"

"I don't know," said Amana through gritted teeth.

"Pity," Mosai sighed. He didn't seem to care that one of the veins in Amana's forehead was bulging.

"What do you want?" Amana said with squinted eyes. It took all his rudimentary monk lessons to not spit on the man. Did the Kor think he could toy with Amana's life like a game? Royalty—and the power they dangled above his head—never sat well with him.

I will not commit acts of war, Amana read the words of Boism in his mind.

"My guard saw how you fought that kishi. You were always a step ahead," Mosai continued.

"Not quite." Amana lifted his bitten arm, pain throbbing now that his adrenaline had worn off.

"We have healers who can fix that up right away." Mosai shrugged.

"Even if they do fix my arm, I'm not much of a fighter." Amana patted his bulging gut. "I've been out of it for some time."

"That may be so, but Nya told us about what went on with that creature. You were able to guide that Bajok warrior's actions."

"Yemi was overmatched."

"Yes, but you were able to see so far into that demon's movements that you could give him enough warning."

"Yes. What does that have to do with anything?"

"We would like you and Nya to look for our daughter together." Kor'de Neema stepped forward. Her voice had a much sweeter, more delicate tone than her Kor-husband.

"Where is Nya?" Amana looked to the guardsmen and women lining the edges of the hut. Nya was not among them.

"On assignment," Neema said. "We want this to be a covert mission. These kishi seem to run deep in this village. We don't know who to trust, but the shaman already vouched for you. You're no shape-shifter, and you are no demon. But you do have a gift we can use."

"And what do I get out of this?" Amana looked at the guards

surrounding the room. He knew he'd likely not get much, save for his life.

"Something tells me you want to find out who these kishi are just as much as we do," Mosai spoke up again.

There was truth to the words, but not what Mosai thought. Amana wanted to make sure Yejide was okay. A girl like that—alone in the wilderness—wouldn't last long. He could care less for Shanaki or the Ya-Seti's plight. If it hadn't been for Yejide or Uzoma's sudden interest in Amana, he would have left Bajok.

"Let us help each other," Mosai said as he stood up, though gingerly. "As you already have seen for yourself, Nya is a capable warrior."

"You will meet her on the outskirts of the village, close to the first farmlands," Neema added.

"Do you have a lead on where Shanaki may be?" Amana asked.

"We don't," Mosai admitted. "But we are sure Nya already has several thoughts."

WHEN AMANA LEFT THE VILLAGE, NEARLY ALL THE MEN HAD their heads shaved. He wondered if he would need to shave his head as well, even though the shaman had completed his trial. Amana had meant to cut his hair. It was unyielding and always fell over his eyes, but he did not want to compromise his position with the Junga monks.

As Amana expected, Nya found him before he found her. She stationed herself near a large rock close to the first farm of Bajok.

"I knew you would accept," she said, smiling.

"Like I had a choice." Amana shook his head. "So what are you thinking?"

"Before Shanaki was taken, I was casing the village. It's the women that seem the most shook. They were all afraid of just one kishi, now that there are two—were two—they're really on edge."

"Did they tell you anything useful?"

"Not much new from what we already know."

"It's gotta be those rocks everyone is so afraid of."

"That's what I was thinking, too."

"Well, I'm to meet with Uzoma tomorrow. We could check it out if you're not too afraid."

Nya chuckled. "I'll pretend not to be insulted by that. I forgot to ask what you thought of Uzoma. I never got to meet him."

"He's different from what I expected," Amana looked to see if they were alone. "I thought he would have sworn off of violence, but he does not seem averse to it. He denied my training because … well … he didn't think I was ready. But after seeing me face that kishi, he seemed to … I don't know … have a change of heart."

"He's a smart man, then. After seeing what you could do, I'd take an interest, too," Nya said.

"But this stuff about his son is troubling. Has anyone spoken up about him?"

"No one knows where he is. I'm just about certain he has Shanaki. It's just a matter of if he's here or halfway to the Setting Sea by now. The women in the village all had positive things to say about him, though. He seems to be quite the charmer—"

"Charmer … we know what that means now," Amana said. "But Yemi and Nanga said that he isn't so personable when he gets to talking. Remember how Ikenna tried to influence Yejide? He probably leans on his empathic powers more often than not."

"The men weren't so favorable about him though. Yemi has had his issues with him."

"I don't blame them. He had a bit of an attitude with me," Amana said.

"Does anyone know who the kishi that was killed today was?"

"No," Amana said. "I don't think so."

"I wonder if Ikenna is in league with other kishi. How many of these things are we dealing with, do you think?"

"I really don't know. The Chief and his advisers said they were all but extinct, right?"

"True, if they're to be believed," Nya said.

"We need to learn more about who these kishi are for ourselves. Those haunted rocks are our only lead."

"You get your rest, Amana," Nya said with another smile. "Talk to Uzoma, then let's meet at the rocks."

Nya turned back towards the village.

"But you're not allowed ..." Amana started to say, but Nya had vanished like a shadow.

CHAPTER 9

BOISM

AMANA DREAMED OF RAGE. THE FIRES THAT COOKED HIS daughter, cooked his soul. He knew who had done this. He knew what needed to be done.

His ship might have been overtaken, but he was still alive, still breathing. Sweat glistened on his brow, and exhaustion nearly over took him, but his arms worked well enough, his legs could still carry him forth, and his sword was still sharp.

He did not recognize the men at his side, the only ones loyal to him now. All that mattered was that he continued to press forward through the flames.

They could follow if they could keep up.

Amana reached the upper deck of his half-sunken ship. In the distance was the enemy ship, dark and looming, lifting and dropping atop the turbulent waters.

Amana took a rope in his hand and swung toward the invading ship. It was a fool's action, but rage was the father of foolishness.

He was outnumbered and outmanned. But all he could see

were the eyes of his daughter, her blackened skin, the smell of ash.

Turn away; leave this place. It will ruin you.

Amana stopped. What was that voice?

Was it one of his crew? Were the sea's winds speaking to him? It did not matter. He only had one goal: murder Zuberi. Murder the man who had taken his daughter from him.

"I'D LIKE TO INTRODUCE YOU TO MY WIFE, AMANA," A DISTANT voice said. "Amana?"

Amana shook himself from his stupor. He had been daydreaming this time. He was in the middle of Kojo's hut, staring at an older woman who gave him a kindly smile.

"Sorry," Amana said. "I've not been getting very good sleep."

"None of us are getting sleep," she said. "The women in particular."

Her name was Ime. She was still beautiful for her age—if a little portly. The purple gomesi dress she wore brought out the deep brown of her skin.

She was the cook of the home and the village. The festivals food had been made mostly by her hand. Amana had a plate of seasoned beans and okra before him, already half eaten before he dozed off.

"Your Mother Tongue is very good." Amana noted as he fed himself a spoonful of beans. "Why haven't you taught your husband?"

"He don't learn too good." Ime winked.

Amana laughed, but his smile turned to a frown when he got a proper look at Kojo. The man looked much different now with his head shaved, though Kojo seemed undeterred, still beaming like always.

"I told you not to fret," Kojo said, noticing Amana's dour eyes. "It's dry season anyway. No need for all that hair, right?"

"How does the village feel about all this?" Amana asked, less as a friendly gesture and more as an investigation. He still hadn't made a contribution for Nya.

"Scared mostly," Kojo said. "No one really cared about cutting their hair if it meant we'd all be safe. But everyone is keeping a closer watch on everyone else."

"The man that died, do you know him?" Amana asked.

"You mean *did* I know him?" Kojo corrected. Amana was still having trouble with the past tense translation of the local tongue. "And Akua? He was one of the merchants from somewhere west. I didn't know him much, but he seemed friendly. Never would have thought he was one of the kishi though..."

"Always knew they'd come back," Ime interjected in the Bajok Tongue. "We really should think about taking the kids to Guela. My brother still has that farm over there."

"There's nothing to worry about. The kishi are weakened in the village ... you saw that yesterday," Kojo reassured her.

"Any wall built by men can be torn down, whether by nature or by our a'bara," Ime said, offering Amana a bowl of plantains. When he lifted the bowl his arm felt like daggers were cutting into his muscle. The Ya-Seti healers had done their job well, but the wound had still scarred. "But if *this* man could stick around, maybe we have a shot." Ime beamed, speaking in the Mother Tongue.

Amana smiled, but he did not understand why he was so praised. He did not defeat the kishi, and he had nearly died himself.

"I could help find the girl if you would just let—," Kojo started.

"No! You have a wife and children to protect here." But Amana did not catch the rest of what she said. Her local tongue was too fast in her tirade against Kojo.

"The men trust me," Kojo said much more slowly, to the benefit of Amana's comprehension. "The *fighting* men trust me."

"The answer is no." And that was it; Kojo did not protest further. "It's the Chief's job to be rid of them, though Moons know he has little chance."

"What do you mean?" Amana said through a mouthful of food.

"All that nonsense about defeating the kishi all those years ago," Ime started, stirring a pot of beans. "I was young when that all happened, but I remember it well enough. It was Uzoma who did all the work. The Chief was lucky to have him. Oh sure, the Chief puts on a good face, and he's a good talker, but when it comes right down to it, those muscles he has don't amount to much. Hell, Uzoma could have been Chief if he wasn't a foreigner. He can at least keep his word. A man who can't keep his word isn't worth a damn."

"Uzoma never wanted the title," Kojo added. "He was a warrior first, he said. He wouldn't know the first thing about leading a village."

"Well he should," Ime said, stirring the pot with more force. "What has the Chief done? Given a few haircuts? The good that will do!"

Kojo frowned as he rubbed the back of his bald head.

"So Amana, I hear you're training with Uzoma," Ime said, perking up again. "What do you think of him?"

"Ime fancies him," Kojo said, thumbing toward his wife.

"Oh who wouldn't?" she waved him off.

"He's different from what I expected," Amana admitted. "But he's a kind enough man."

"Oh I bet." Ime smiled. "He hardly ever comes around here. It was nice seeing him in the village again. Too bad about his son though. There has to be a mistake."

"My wife fancies Ikenna as well." Kojo chuckled.

"Oh who wouldn't? He's an angel of a boy. He's always so

nice when he trades harvest with me. Saves me the best of his crops."

"Amana saw him. The boy runs around with those demons. There's no way around it," Kojo made sure to point out. "Sometimes it's the nice ones you have to watch out for."

"He's only been gone a day," Ime said, waving her hand dismissively. "I'm sure he has a good explanation—"

"He would have killed me if he had the chance," Amana said.

"Is that so?" Ime turned to Amana, who had finished his small breakfast.

"I'm heading to Uzoma's home a little later this morning. I intend to ask about his son," Amana said.

"Oh don't press him too hard, you hear?" Ime said. "He's an old man now. I remember him back in the good old days. Tough as a lion, that one. Oh! If you could..." Ime jumped up, looking almost like a younger girl. She went to her pot and emptied the rest of her plantains into banana leaves. "Could you give this to Uzoma. Tell him it's from Ime. Ime from the market, the one with his favorite dish."

Kojo rolled his eyes.

"Amana, before you go." Kojo stepped up, speaking very rapidly in the local tongue. Amana turned to Ime.

"Yeah he speaks a little fast when he's excited," she said. "He says he wants to give you pointers on that silly dancing, doesn't want you embarrassing yourself in front of Uzoma. I'll tell you, I never saw much purpose in Ugara."

"So what do you say, Amana?" Kojo asked.

"I like practice." Amana sat up. "Let's go."

"It was very nice meeting you, Amana," Ime bowed. "Let Deh'ala bless all your passings."

"Thank you, Ime. It was nice meeting you as well."

AMANA AND KOJO WENT DOWN TO THE RIVER TO PRACTICE *THE sway* once more. After a brief meditation, Amana cleared his mind of yesterday's events. He focused only on the task of the moment. With the small scroll perched up on a rock, Amana read and moved at the same time. Each step was illustrated on the scroll, demonstrating how each move should flow from one to the other. But it was very different when applying it in reality.

Amana got the steps down well enough, but he was not sure he could feel the spirits guiding him. There was something missing, some element to the technique that was not clicking for him.

In truth, Amana did not really know what spirits he was calling to. Before his studies with the Five, he never took much interest in any spiritual group.

It was not as though he did not believe in what they believed. Ancestral magic and demons were a very real thing, but Amana always felt that the practical overrode the mystical.

"That won't do." Kojo shook his head. "And here I thought you would do better, not worse." Kojo removed his kanzu and started his own sway. Somehow, watching Kojo helped Amana clear his own head.

"That kishi, Akua. He always live here?"

"No, he was from a neighboring village further down the river, almost to the Setting Sea. He and a few other merchants came for better trade."

"Does he—*did* he—have a wife?" Amana asked.

"No, he didn't. He was always alone, though he was with many women in the village. Recreationally, if you know what I mean."

"What was it like this morning?" Amana asked. "Are there many men with hair cut?"

"Just a few stragglers like me." Kojo started to practice his kicks.

"Are there more kishi?"

"None that I know. Most of them—like Akua—were merchants from other villages. Carry-overs from the festival."

Amana nodded, continuing his back and forth motion. Many of these merchants seemed to be associated with the kishi in some way. Nya would want to know about that—if she didn't already know.

Amana started to feel something well up in his chest as he spun around. Was this the spirit guide that was supposed to direct his moves?

"There you go, you're getting it again," Kojo congratulated.

"I'm not sure how. I don't know what it is I'm taping into."

"It's Ugara. The elders say its unrelenting passion that moves the Warrior. But to be honest with you, I find better results when I call to the river." Kojo kept his movement going as he drifted down by the riverbed's edge. "You see, if you're doing *the sway* correctly, it should not disturb the water. It should flow with the water seamlessly. It's really a matter of balance. A warrior's passion is necessary, but using passion alone will lead to frustration if not handled correctly."

That was it. That's what he needed to unlock. It wasn't the moves themselves that needed to be mastered, but what inspired them.

Uzoma had already uncovered that Amana had difficulty bottling up his anger. But here, with this spirit dance, perhaps he could achieve some sort of peace or clarity.

"I think that's when you mess up," Kojo said, as the water lapped around his legs softly. "When you got here, it seemed like your mind was everywhere, when really it should be nowhere."

Amana joined him in the water. He continued his steps and he could feel it now. The ebb and flow of the water helped him realize how connected the Dance was. His body moved freely now.

"Do you fight in those festivals?"

"I used to, but I'm too old now." Kojo didn't look a day over forty.

"Are the fights that tiring?"

"No, but I got married. And Ime wanted me to take no part in them anymore. I train up some of the villagers, but that's about as far as it goes."

Amana had the basic steps down, that he knew. For the first time, he was actually having fun with it.

Kojo got fancy with his own sway. He started to kick up water, leaning in close, then swung his leg over Amana's head.

"You're not ready to start applying styles yet," Kojo said. "But this is the way of the zebra. It's good for keeping your balance and setting up back kicks. With a partner, you'll want to get your shoulder in close, brush against their side, then turn around for the strike. Next time you go out to the wilderness, look at the animals and how they fight. They'll teach you a lot."

Amana tried to imitate Kojo but he was sloppy.

"No, no, no. Don't try now." Kojo laughed. "If you try to apply a style, it will mess you all up. You gotta get the fundamentals down first."

"Thank you for today, Kojo." Amana nodded his head, wiping sweat from his brow.

"Of course."

"If you hear anything new about the kishi, tell me please."

"I'll keep my eyes open like everyone else." Kojo put his kanzu back on. "And your Bajok Tongue is getting better already."

IT TOOK ALL MORNING TO WALK TO UZOMA'S HOUSE. THE elder was already working on his farm when Amana arrived. Amana hadn't recognized him at first.

The sun reflected atop Uzoma's newly shaved head. But unlike Kojo, the look suited the elder, made him look younger.

"Do you have no one to help you?"

"It keeps me alive." Uzoma shrugged. "So, how are you liking Ugara's Dance?"

"What?" Amana's heart dropped.

"Oh come now, I know you stole the scroll."

"I have no idea what you're talking about." Amana tried to keep a straight face.

"Your eyebrows give you away when you lie." Uzoma wiped sweat from his brow. "Don't worry about it. I wanted to see what you would do with it. Show me what you've learned."

At first, Amana stared at Uzoma. Was this a trick? Uzoma waved a hand to the open dirt ground, inviting Amana to begin.

Amana set down his traveling pack, never letting his eyes drift from the elder. After a moment he began his sway. But this time, he thought of water, how it pushed and pulled at his legs, how he could feel the spirits within him—whatever they were.

Uzoma nodded his head, stroking his beard pensively. Amana could feel the energy within him well up. His flow was even stronger than it was by the river.

Had Uzoma's presence elevated his performance? He hoped the elder was not using his empathetic abilities on him now. Amana waved the thought away. Uzoma would have wanted him to learn properly, without any aid.

"You have the basics down," Uzoma admitted. "I did not expect you to do as well are you are now. Did you have help?"

"One of the men in the village. I didn't realize right away that these scrolls were the same movements from the festival fighting."

"It's true," Uzoma confessed. "Why did you not use this against the kishi you faced."

"I was too busy thinking about staying alive." Amana chuckled.

"Smart. Remember, anything you learn from a mentor—or any scroll—can only go so far. When it comes down to it, use your instincts above all else. Just remember to keep at it. Then, your instincts will become what you practice naturally."

Amana nodded.

"Oh, I almost forgot." Amana pulled out the plantains wrapped in banana leaves. "Kojo's wife wanted me to give these to you."

"Oh yes. Ime, I believe?" Uzoma asked. Amana nodded confirmation. "Sweet woman, that one."

"Indeed, she is very kind."

"Have you touched the spirits today?" Uzoma asked.

"Yes, but I'm not sure who or what it is I'm getting in touch with."

"Follow me inside," Uzoma waved a hand. Before he entered his home he prayed to the Gatekeeper. Amana internalized his own prayer, seeing if he too could feel the presences of this Deh'ala. There was a whisper, a female voice, but nothing more. Was Deh'ala associated with a man or woman? Amana could not recall. Uzoma watched as Amana's forehead creased in thought.

"The Gatekeeper is the first step to all the others," Uzoma said. "It's likely the reason you're only getting flashes instead of full callings. One must consult the doorman before they can enter the dwelling of the spirit world."

"Will you be teaching me about the spirits of Bajok?"

"Not exactly, or rather, the spirits of Bajok reside in the teachings of the Five."

Uzoma's wife was there again, tending to the family altar again.

"What is this exactly?" Amana asked Esi.

"An altar to the ancestors," she said, her eyes hovering at the edges of eye contact.

"How is she doing?" Amana asked Uzoma, looking down to Esi's belly.

"Well enough."

"What has she been drinking?"

"Besides water? Nothing else."

"There is a special brew I can make for her. To ease her pregnancy."

"What would that be?"

"Did your harvest produce any kinkeliba?"

"Yes it has," Uzoma answered, nodding to his wife. Esi went to one of the pots in the hut to retrieve the tea leaves. "What will this plant do?"

"It helps soothe the birth passage. I used it with my own wife almost exclusively. She drank it all through her pregnancy, but it should work fine even so late into your wife's own."

Esi came back with the leaves. There was a pot already brewing near the hearth.

"Is your water already purified?"

"Yes," Esi answer meekly, her head down. "It's already been boiling for the better part of an hour."

"Good," Amana said. "Pour yourself a cup full of the water, then add the kinkeliba for no more than a few minutes. The taste will be strong and a bit bitter, but you'll feel better."

"Thank you." Esi bowed her head again. She walked over to the pot and prepared herself the tea.

"Was that also part of your mother's duties?" Uzoma asked.

"No, it's something I learned from the western merchants that came to the Isles. I brought this back to my mother and it helped the women she assisted a great deal. I never let the merchants know that, though. They didn't sell at a very high price."

"You were a smart boy, then." Uzoma smiled.

"I'd like to think I'm a smart man now." Amana smirked.

"Those monks advise humility do they not?" Uzoma asked. Somehow Amana felt he was being chided, but he could never tell with Uzoma.

"I've not read anything of it within the Five," Amana answered.

"The Five is only one facet of their studies," Uzoma turned to the wooden chest in the room, searching through it with deft hands. "I've been wondering about this 'self-pilgrimage' of yours. Why is it that you are not studying with the Junga monks now?"

"I wanted to be sure I was prepared before I pledged myself."

"I told you, lying to me will not work."

Amana clenched his jaw, biting back his anger. "The monks did not accept me."

"I figured as much." Uzoma finally found what he was looking for. It was an odd instrument, a flat wooden circle with five ribbons attached to it. "Did they say you had to embark on this little mission to join them?"

"No, but they did not say anything against it."

"You'll have to remind me, I'm so old," Uzoma said. "Why is it you wish to join these people?"

"For a purpose, for meaning in life. To be one with the Supreme One."

"Do those people really have a purpose?" Uzoma asked. "They sit atop their mountain and meditate, but do little else."

"I mean … For my own reasons, my own purposes. To find a power—enlightenment I cannot achieve on my own."

"Fair enough," Uzoma said, lifting his hands in front of Amana. In one hand was the odd instrument, in the other—which Uzoma had gloved—was a marble ball, black and opaque, with a white sliver going up and down the middle. "Have you seen this before?"

"It looks familiar," Amana said. "Wait, that can't be—."

"It's the second part of Boism. You see, with those mountain monks, there is more than one part of their discipline. There is the mental and the physical, both are intertwined, both nurture the other. There are the teachings they have, like your scroll, but there is always a physical manifestation. Here, take this. These ribbons wraps around each of your fingers."

Amana examined the ball in his hand. It was much heavier

than he expected, more the weight of a sack of rice than a light marble.

"It's a ball from the Great Tunnel of Akeem," Amana said. "They call it the Glass of the Gods."

The ball was very valuable, though this one was almost used up. The glass orbs were almost the size of a man fully grown at their largest, but each time it was used it shrunk down to the stone at its center.

How could Uzoma trust anyone with this—or the information that he had one, maybe even more if he was so willing to share this one? It could fetch a hefty price. Uzoma could rule his own city with this God Stone.

"That's right," Uzoma nodded his head. "Do you know why it's so valued?"

"It has magical properties," Amana said.

"Go ahead." Uzoma nodded his head. "Use your a'bara. You will feel its power."

Amana stretched out his focus to his sight. The stone's energy coursed through him. Amana's sight extended out of Uzoma's hut and into the farmlands. He could even sense the insects that ate away at the crops.

"You have pests eating away at your southeast fig trees," Amana said. His eyes were hazed. Uzoma took the ball from his hand. The protective glove over his hand separated his skin from the Gods' Glass.

"Yes, the ball has powerful properties," Uzoma said. "But men have gone insane holding onto it for too long. But I have used it as a tool for focus. And the mountain monks use it as well in their training. The ball is easy enough to hold in hand, but balancing it on this wooden plank is difficult. And herein lies the exercise. Go ahead and sit along the ground here." Uzoma pointed to the space just in front of the hearth. "You see, Amana, what you lack is balance. You have compassion, and you have zeal, but you fail to hold them up as twin pillars. You are either one or the other but hardly ever both."

"Does this mean you're training me now?" Amana beamed.

"Let's say you're on a trial period," Uzoma corrected.

Amana nodded seriously, but inside he was elated. Was Uzoma really that impressed with how he dealt with the kishi?

Amana finished tightening the ribbons around his fingers. Uzoma placed the ball on the plank and it fell off immediately.

"Once you balance this ball, you will have mastered yourself," Uzoma said.

"Have you?" Amana asked, then realized the question might have come off defiant.

"No one can hold a balance indefinitely. But the teaching is to strive for it, rather than fall to chaos."

"How long have you been able to hold it?" Amana asked as he gave it another go. This time he kept the ball on the plank for a brilliant two seconds.

"Long enough" was all Uzoma answered.

"Why is the glass so heavy?" Amana asked.

"It's a God Stone," Uzoma explained. "They're different kinds of these stone that align with different properties, different forms of ancestral magic—elementalism, telepathy, short-sight, and so on.

"This one is special because it works with every type of magic. Most of these stones have been surrounded by this glass, which are composed of the Gods' energy. Each time one uses the glass a layer of the magic is removed.

"The center of this particular glass—it's stone—is unbalanced. It holds too many magical abilities that are at odds with one another. The Junga use these specific stones to practice mediation between these properties.

"The trick is to find that magic's center, then one can properly balance it on the wooden plank. Keep at it. That's my next task for you. I don't expect you to have it down as quickly as Ugara's

Dance, but next time I see you, I expect progress. If the kishi come back for you, it will do well to defend you."

"The villagers seemed eager to have you fight the kishi again," Amana said, placing the ball and the instrument into his pack.

"I'm too old for all that now." Uzoma sat down in his chair, bones creaking as though to confirm his words. Esi stood up to rub her husband's back. "I'll leave that to you and the others. I can protect this land well enough—I have my own securities here. But I can't go out looking for fights anymore."

"Can a compromise be made with the kishi?" Amana asked.

"With a demon like that? Unlikely. What compromise would you propose?"

Amana shrugged. He didn't know enough about the kishi—their origins or their motivations.

"That's not their way. Not everyone can be compromised with in that way. You'll come to understand that with age. Sometimes—most times—they have to be stopped indefinitely. That's the best way. These kishi want this Ya-Seti girl; there is no fair trade there."

"Is that what you had to do with the original kishi you and the Chief destroyed?"

"There really was no other way. It was kill or be killed."

Amana pressed his thumb and forefinger to his chin. Uzoma was truly different from any other monk Amana had met. Amana wasn't even sure he would call Uzoma a monk, or if the elder would even refer to himself in that way.

"I don't mean to be rude, but I did not see Ikenna. He only has few hours before he needs to show himself to the Chief." Amana had to ask, though he knew Uzoma would see it as an interrogation.

"Like I told those other Bajok warriors and the Chief," Uzoma said. "I do not deny that my son may be involved with that riff-raff." Uzoma's shoulders tensed. Esi pressed her hands deeper into her massage.

"What do you know of these kishi?" Amana asked.

"Only that we defeated them many years ago, drove them back into the rocks."

"Could your son be there now? Have you gone looking for him?"

"I did," Uzoma said, his tone betraying insult. "But the rocks are as quiet as ever."

"I wonder why he would take Shanaki after what happened with Imani. He really did seem to love the girl," Amana said.

"Who's to say he took that Princess anyway?" Uzoma said quickly, his tone rising. Amana had found a touchy subject with the man.

"All the evidence is pointing to your son right now."

"That might be so, but none of us know for sure. This isn't the first time he's gone missing. He always comes back. Trouble might find him most of the time, and he might be away with those girls, but that doesn't mean he's one of those demons. As you might have noticed, he's quiet the charmer."

"That seems to be the common trait among these kishi."

"True enough," Uzoma conceded.

"And I saw him, Uzoma," Amana said, not meeting the elder's eyes. "I fought him. He's one of them." Uzoma was silent. Amana looked up, but Uzoma did not meet his gaze. "How many were there when you pushed them back?" Amana finally asked.

"Nearly a village full of them. There had to have been at least fifty back then."

"Is it possible any of them slipped by you and the Chief?"

"Impossible. I made sure I took out all of them. And we know how to find them now. They hide their demon head behind their hair. And my son was checked years ago!"

"Sorry, I did not mean to disturb you with this." Amana bowed his head, but he was not finished. "The kishi I fought and the other men who have gone missing were merchants from other villages. It's a possibility these kishi might be more far-reaching than the small village of Bajok."

Uzoma sighed, dropping his shoulders. Esi stopped rubbing him, not daring to look up.

"There might have been a few who could have slipped past us." It seemed hard for Uzoma to admit. His fingers dug into the sides of his chair. "And yes, I have suspected some may have returned to the village."

"Where do they come from? Could Ikenna —"

"No, Ikenna wouldn't know—he couldn't." Uzoma was still in denial. "But keep an eye out in the village Amana. For me."

Amana nodded. This was the first directive he had received from his mentor, a man who now seemed well past his prime in his flustered anger, a man who now wore his age on his sleeve.

Amana would have to pick up the pieces for him. If there were other kishi in the village still hiding—and Amana was the one to uncover them—Uzoma would surely teach him all he knew.

"For the Great and Mighty Elder Uzoma," Amana said with a respectful nod, "anything."

Amana smiled, but a sharp pain shot through his head. Amana clutched the sides of his temples. Images of his wife and daughter flashed before his eyes.

The voice returned to him.

The danger is too great. Leave this place.

"Are you all right Amana?" Uzoma rose from his chair, placing a hand on Amana's shoulder. Amana relaxed. Uzoma's touch was euphoric, like an instant cleanse. The visions left his mind, and the voices were silenced.

"Sorry, it's these visions I keep having." Amana blinked his eyes thrice.

"This land will reveal many things to you. But you must control yourself and these visions. Only you should be able to call to them. Don't let them force their way into your mind. Not all voices are beneficial guides."

"I'll be off now. I'll see you again soon." Amana turned to Esi, who was quietly drinking her tea. "Be sure to keep up with the kinkeliba leaves. I assure you it will help ease what you're going through."

Esi nodded with a smile, though she looked tired.

"Come Esi, it's time for a nap," Uzoma said, lifting his wife up with gentle care.

A nap wasn't such a bad idea, but Amana had a date with a Ya-Seti archer.

CHAPTER 10

THE BLACK ROCKS

NYA WAS ALREADY WAITING FOR AMANA BEHIND UZOMA'S homestead. She wore light armor plating—signature Ya-Seti style of blue with gold trim—armed with a dagger at her side and her bow slung over her shoulder. Nya's quiver was loaded with arrows, which hung just in reach of her fingers.

"Somehow, I feel underdressed," Amana said with a chuckle.

"Do you know these rocks and what's within?"

"No."

"Then perhaps you would do better to wear something more protective." Nya looked him up and down. All Amana had worn for the past few moons was a light traveling cloak and strapped rawhide sandals, occasionally donning a straw hat or head wrap for inclement weather.

"What is on my back is all I'll ever need for the True Path," Amana answered.

"Didn't seem that way when that demon was snapping at your neck," Nya shot back. "I would feel more comfortable if you at least carried a dagger."

"One must abstain from taking the life of living creatures," Amana recited from the Scroll of the Five.

"No one said anything about killing, but you need to defend yourself."

"I won't need a dagger, I assure you," Amana said, waving his hand.

"Suit yourself. Just keep your eyes open. You're no use to me dead."

"I do not intend to die today."

"Well, that's good to hear," Nya said, stuffing her dagger back in its sheath. "All right, let's head out, then, shall we?"

Before setting out, Amana took one look over his shoulder. Amana hoped Esi would be okay. She looked well enough, healthy—healthier than the women his mother often tended to. But he would have to take a closer look at her next time he visited Uzoma, check the vitals of the baby, at least.

"Well, come on then," Nya said. "I'd like to get this done before the sun sets."

Amana nodded and followed her into the first threshold of the rocks. Once he passed from sunshine to shadow a chill passed over his bare skin. Nya's skin pricked, but she made no motion or sound to suggest it disturbed her.

Amana thought her an interesting woman. After watching her fight, he knew she was quite formidable. Yet he attributed that more to her gifts than her physical prowess. Still, she was scrappy, and often that's what counted when it came right down to it.

"So you're an elemental?" Amana asked idly as they approached their first fork.

"Not a very good one," she said, eyeing both paths.

"Why's that?"

"You're the well-read sort. I'm sure you know why."

Her family's magic had probably all but died out. A true elemental could cause the clouds to storm, or the oceans to manifest tsunamis. But those were few and far between now. Those of such talent were usually guarded and used sparingly in wartime. Even if the Ya-Seti had any, they wouldn't bring them across the continent for a simple marriage proposal.

"Which way should we go?" she asked Amana, nodding to the fork.

"My gift isn't all that strong either. Your guess is as bad as mine."

"The Kor says you're the best he's seen with the sight," Nya said.

"My sight doesn't work like that. I can't predict which path we should take."

Nya frowned, taking the path to the right.

"Well, that was a quick decision. Why that way?" Amana asked.

"I always follow my gut," Nya said.

"Then why ask for my input?" Amana followed her through the narrow path.

"Wanted to see if my gut and your sight were aligned."

"Something tells me if I had said the left, you would have still gone to the right."

"And you would be correct." Nya gave him a brief smile.

The path here was well-traveled. It was likely the reason for Nya coming this way. It was probably the path Uzoma walked when he patrolled the area. Or better yet, it could have been a new path carved by someone—or something—who wanted to remain hidden.

"Did you find out anything new in the village?" Amana asked as he trotted over the uneven earth.

"Nothing," Nya admitted. "Though a few other men have gone missing."

"More merchants?"

"Locals."

"What do you think of that?"

"I think this village has a kishi infestation."

"Why did the Ya-Seti choose this place? Why this Chieftain? And why his son?"

"I'm not privy to any of their reasoning, I just follow orders."

Like a good soldier, Amana thought.

"Just be careful when going into the village," Amana said. "If the Chief knows you're spying on the goings-on ..."

"I'm well aware of the consequences. And I would not be the head of the Kor'de's guard if I could be easily caught." Nya took the next fork to the left.

The rocks here seemed to rise higher than the ones in Uzoma's canyon. Flowers and plants grew out of the rocks, overgrown near the bottom. One of the rocks was carved with what looked like writing. It was faint, but Amana could make out the words, which were written in the Mother Tongue.

"*Beware the path that lies ahead,*" Nya read. "Looks like we're going in the right direction."

"Wait," Amana said as he received a flash. It was distant. There was no immediate threat. But Amana focused his attention on what had warned him. There was a fight somewhere deep in the rocks, but he could not tell between who or what. "Something, no, someone is fighting in there."

"Let's pick up the pace, then," Nya said. She jogged off between the rocks. Amana set off behind her. They jogged for a few moments before Amana lost his connection, sweat beading his forehead. He was already exhausted. Nya's breath was barely heavy.

"It's lost, I feel nothing," he said with his hands on his knees.

"You're a bit of a mystery, aren't you?"

"What's that mean?"

"I don't get you. You look like you were once a fighter, but now you've got ..." She waved her hand up and down at Amana. "I don't know, the whole monk thing ... it doesn't suit you."

"I suppose it doesn't really suit anyone, does it?" Amana said through strained breaths. Nya rolled her eyes and continued down the tight corridor of rocks.

For what seemed like hours, they twisted and turned between different rock structures. It all looked the same, save for some animal bones they came across here and there. Nya was antsy, eyes darting side-to-side at anything that wasn't a rock.

"I'm sure it'll take us more than a day to navigate these rocks." Amana had been drawing a map of the path they were taking, marking each turn on parchment.

"I can see why none of the Bajok come here," Nya said. "They aren't afraid of dying to some beasts. They are afraid of dying from boredom. Here, let's stop for a moment."

Amana welcomed the break. Nya was doing fine, but he was well past his exhaustion point. From his pack, he pulled a sack of water and drank. When he finished, he gave it over to Nya who only took a sip.

"You can have more than that if you like." Amana nodded.

"I'm trained to only take as much as I need in the moment. You never know when you need to ration."

"Can't argue with that logic, I suppose." Amana stuffed his water sack away. He pulled out the Scroll of the Five and the new instrument Uzoma had given him. He read the scroll as he tied the ribbons to his fingers. He recited the words softly to himself as he set the Gods' Glass on the flat wood—making sure to touch the orbed glass with his robe instead of his hand.

Nya watched him. He tried to balance the ball as best he could. Two seconds. The ball fell. Three seconds. The ball fell. Four seconds. The ball fell. But each time, Amana got better, each time, he centered himself in the shadow of the rocks. After a few moments he was able to balance the ball for seven heartbeats, eight heartbeats, nine heartbeats!

"What the hell is that anyway?" Nya blurted out.

Damn, only nine heartbeats. Amana took a deep breath, trying to control his frustration. He read from the scroll in his mind before responding to Nya's interruption. *Abstain from words of war.*

"This is an instrument of Boism," Amana explained. "It's supposed to help me find balance in my life."

"It just looks like a silly game for children," Nya said. Amana ignored her.

"It's a sacred ritual that has been handed down through many generations of monks."

"Whatever floats your boat, friend. We're going to head out in a few, so get yourself and your toy ready for another trek."

Amana sighed and balanced the ball again. This time, he stopped reciting the words from the scroll. Instead, he thought of the water back in Bajok. He thought about how it felt as it passed by his ankles, the motion of the spirit dance.

When the Gods' Glass rolled left, he did not fight it, moving with it, catching it under its center again. When the glass spun right, he followed it again, drifting with its rhythm. He did that for what seemed like another second before dropping it.

"Not bad," Nya said, clapping.

"Not funny, that wasn't even three heartbeats."

"Three beats? You were balancing that thing for at least five minutes," Nya said, slinging her bow over her shoulder. "Come on, time to go, monk."

"Did you say five minutes? That's impossible, it only felt … wait." Amana stopped her before she walked off. "Do you see that?"

Nya followed the path of his eyes. "See what?"

"Just there, up the rock. That language, it's …" Amana pointed just past Nya's head. The words were only somewhat familiar.

"There's nothing there but rocks," Nya said with raised eyebrows.

"It's the Gods' words, the Old Tongue," Amana said. "But I

never understood it before. It's just there. How can you not see it? It's glowing."

"You sure there isn't something special in that water you gave me?"

"A hand cannot be kept in a scorpion's burrow. The soup does not move around in an elder's belly. Little by little is how the pig's nose enters the yard."

"Okay, there is no way you made that gibberish up," Nya said, following Amana's gaze more intently now. "What the hell does any of that mean?"

"I don't know exactly. I'm not familiar with the local proverbs." Amana was already writing the passages down in the Mother Tongue. The glowing texts were written all over, repeating all the way down the rock's side. But there was one larger than the others.

"It is not everyone with a quiet disposition who is kind-natured." Amana read another.

"You do realize when you read that stuff you're speaking in the Gods' Tongue, right?" Nya said.

"Oh, you couldn't understand me? I didn't even realize."

"Yeah, what the hell are you saying?"

"Well, they all seem to be warnings. The first essentially says that it's risky business to play with a scorpion. The second says something about an elder and his food, I'm not sure about that one. The third says a pig can get into anything as long as it tries bit by bit. But the last one, the big one, it says that a peaceful and kind face is not to be trusted."

"We know the truth of the last one, at least," Nya said. "The face of a man hiding a beast behind his head."

The kishi did put on a good act. They all seemed to charm their victims into complacency before they pounced.

"You sure you're not one of these demons?" Nya asked with a smile. The response took him by surprise. Was she calling Amana handsome? Amana was reminded of the first night he saw her.

Her eyes looked the same then, too. "Oh, lighten up, it was a joke, Mana. You monk types are never any fun."

"Sorry." Amana shook off the shock on his face—he also ignored Nya's shortened version of his name. "The spirits already vouched for me."

"I know that," Nya said. "If you were really a kishi, you would have made a pass on me, or I on you, right?"

"Right," Amana got red around the ears, but his eyes locked with Nya's. "I've been meaning to ask you. I mean, I know you can touch the elements, but are you—"

"A shape-shifter, as well?" Nya smiled. "No. Just an elemental."

"Your eyes." Amana nodded to her. "They look like the women's in Bajok. I suspect many of them are shape-shifters, too. But with you ... your hair ... usually, only lion-shifters have that look about them. And your face, it's very ..." Amana caught himself before he likened her face to a big cat.

"Many thought that would be the case when I was a girl," Nya said. "My father was a lion-shifter. His hair was an even deeper red than mine, great big beard and everything, just like a mane. But yes, my face does have that shape about it, doesn't it?"

"There's nothing wrong with that," Amana said, betraying a smile. "I like it."

"Well, I think that's enough for today," Nya said, turning her face away from Amana. Were her cheeks getting red? Or was that the reflection of the setting sun? "You have all that gibberish written down?"

"Yes."

"Let's head out, then," Nya said. Amana nodded, but there was a loud laugh just on the other side of the rocks, the kind of laugh that could only belong to a hyena.

"The kishi?" Amana asked Nya.

"I guess we won't be leaving just yet." Nya set off in a dead run toward the high-pitched laughter. Amana went after her, keeping up as best he could. There was no mistaking the laugh of a kishi.

As they ran toward the disturbance, they found something … unexpected. Baako was lying on the ground with a bite on his neck. He was flanked by two Bajok warriors—Nanga, who had his guard up, and Yemi, who tended to Baako's wound. There was a small clearing, a quarter the size of Uzoma's little valley. But the sun peeked straight down into the small canyon.

"What happened?" Nya already had her arrow at the ready, aiming at every hole in the valley. She seemed prepared for any kind of surprise.

"We found that damned beast!" Baako said, blood spilling from his mouth. "He's here! Hiding where his friends hid!"

"Was it Ikenna?" Amana asked.

"Yes! It was that damned—" Baako started.

"We don't know that for sure, sir," Yemi said.

"You know damn well it was him, Yemi. You're the one who convinced me to come search this place."

"I remember saying we should have sent out a party to look, not come ourselves." Yemi wiped blood from Baako's neck.

"He took my bride away from me because he couldn't have that farmer's daughter!"

"You need to calm him down," Amana said to the warriors.

"He's right," Yemi said, holding the back of Baako's head. "You need to settle down or you'll bleed out."

"Do you know which way the demon went?" Nya asked, ready to pounce.

"We didn't get a good look at him. He came at Baako so fast, it was all we could do to protect the First Son," Nanga said.

"Did you wound it at least?"

"It was too fast for any of that, Ya-Seti," Nanga spat. Nya ran off to examine every crevice in the rocks, observing the ground for any disturbed dirt or rock.

"They don't leave any marks like that," Nanga said.

"It's true," Amana said. "The one I saw didn't even disturb the water it walked over."

"There has to be something!" Nya shouted. "They have our Princess. She is close."

"We have to get the First Son back to the village," Yemi said. "Our shaman has to tend to this wound quickly, and we'll need your help getting us back."

"My priority isn't your damned First Son," Nya shouted, desperately looking for any kind of clue.

"They're right, Nya," Amana said. "We're not going to find this kishi today, but we are getting close. The First Son is intended to be part of your Royal Family someday. In a way, he is your charge to protect."

"There has been no marriage," Nya corrected Amana with sharp eyes. "He's no responsibility of mine. I've known Shanaki my whole life. I've known these Bajok a couple days!"

"Trust me," Amana said, stepping close to her. "We will find Shanaki ... I want to find Yejide just as bad."

"Use your damn sight!" Nya said. "They have to be close!"

In truth, Amana had already tried that when they first arrived. But he had only sensed the danger Baako was in, not where the kishi had run off to. He considered using the Gods' Glass, but he remembered what Uzoma said about the stone driving men mad when used frivolously.

"The sight is gone," Amana said, placing his hands on Nya's shoulders. "But at least we know the beast is here. He won't get past Uzoma's homestead without us knowing, the elder has protected these lands for years. If you'd feel better, you can stay outside of Uzoma's farms for the time being."

"We don't need that Ya-Seti's help!" Nanga said. "This is still Bajok land and our right."

He was right. If the Chief got wind of this, he would not be too kind to Nya—or Amana. But they would need her help if they were going to get Baako safely back to the main village.

"We will need the Ya-Seti's help," Yemi chimed in, placing a hand on his comrade's shoulder.

"Are you sure you can't see them?" Nya said to Amana, ignoring the Bajok men.

"I'm sorry, Nya, I can't. There's nothing we can do for the girls right now. But Ikenna isn't going anywhere. He's stuck in these rocks."

Nya sighed. "Fine, but let's make it quick."

"All right, let's get the First Son back to the village." Amana slung one of Baako's arms over his shoulders. The First Son cried out in pain.

CHAPTER 11

THE PLAINS OF PREDATORS

FIRE AND BLOOD. FOR THE NEXT MOON-CYCLE, THOSE WERE Amana's dreams. Each time he felt the heat of the inferno, he turned it away. Each time he felt that blood-curdling anger, he smashed it out. Over time, the voices subsided to whispers, and then, they were silent. The dreams went away, and he could rest easy.

A MOON-CYCLE PASSED WITH NO SIGN OF THE KISHI OR THE girls. Some of the Ya-Seti were starting to think Shanaki could never be found. The Bajok had given up on Yejide the day she had vanished. They said she would be lost forever, like the others.

"It's just like it was before," one woman had said when Amana was trading in the market. "Girls gone missing. Never to return again. I don't let my daughter out to the river anymore."

The Kor and the Kor'de never came out of their guest hut anymore, either.

There was one Ya-Seti whose resolve was unhindered, however. Nya had yet to leave the haunted rocks ever since Baako was returned home to get proper care. She was certain that the kishi would come out one way or the other, with Shanaki alive or otherwise.

Nya and Amana had gone deep into the rocks several times together—when Amana wasn't training with Kojo or getting acclimated to Bajok—but they found nothing. Amana could no longer find the markings he had found on their first day there. He did speak to some of the villagers about the passages. All of them were familiar with the words, but none knew how they could relate to the kishi. They couldn't even agree if they were left by the kishi or their ancestors. So Amana turned to Uzoma, who said that the words were indeed left there by the last of the kishi, who were, of course, former clansmen in the tribe. But he waved it off as nothing more than desperate men finding solace in their last days.

Amana's training had come a long way in the past few weeks. Now he could hold the Gods' Glass for five minutes without it toppling over. He could also feel his short-sight strengthening, sometimes extending his gift past the threshold of a few milliseconds to full seconds. This also helped his parallel training with the spirit dance.

"It might not be obvious to you, as you are self-trained," Uzoma had said. "You treat the teachings of the Junga as though they do nothing but meditate on mountainsides. They are probably one of the fittest peoples in the world. They understand that one can only conquer their metaphysical self if they can control and maintain their physical body."

So Amana had gone back to regular exercise, running each morning and night, training with Kojo and the other villagers before and after. He had to admit that it was beneficial. His pudgy mid-section was going away, but weight loss was easy. He knew he'd need to work harder to get back to the shape he was in before taking up the True Path. The ease of his breath, due to his workouts, helped the ease of his meditation. And the ease of his meditation enhanced his sight, and his enhanced sight made him nearly unstoppable as a fighter.

This is the power I will need, Amana had thought.

"I swear, I've never seen anyone catch onto Ugara's Dance as quickly as you have, Amana," Kojo said one morning.

"It's not all me, I swear," Amana said as he checked Kojo with a kick to his mid-section. After a moon-cycle in Bajok, the strange vowels of their language returned to Amana. He still needed correcting with his tenses, but the language rolled off the tongue more easily. "You see, that kick was sloppy. But I could see you turning into it long before you even knew you would."

"I've heard of those with short-sight before," Kojo said. "One of our older warriors has it, too, but nowhere near this good. He's an elder now, so he rests a lot. Sometimes, he can predict the weather for a week if he concentrates enough."

"I'll admit," Amana said, sweeping Kojo off his feet. "This is the best I've felt with it my entire life. I should have taken up this … soul … um …"

"Spirituality?" Kojo suggested in the Bajok Tongue.

"Yes. I should have taken up this spirituality stuff years ago."

"Don't get too ahead of yourself, eh? *One must abstain from words of war and violence* and all that, right?" Kojo recited some of the Junga scrolls in the Mother Tongue. Amana had been teaching him and some of the other villagers as best he could. "Let's all be glad you're a man of peace."

Amana smiled as Kojo tagged him with a kick. "You see, I'm not perfect." Amana stumbled back. In truth, he was exhausted. And with exhaustion, his sight was less accurate, even with his heightened abilities.

"But I've heard there are ways to even the odds with your

kind," Kojo said as he helped Amana back to his feet. "Some of you are too reliant on your sight. You live and die by it. But I know that those of us without the sight can give you bad reads."

This was true. Amana did not like confessing this to anyone who did not know, even his closest confidants. Anyone he fought, if their mind and willpower were strong enough, could mentally feint an attack to throw someone with short-sight off. Kojo started *the sway,* but he started giving off false reads.

Flash.

Kojo's ghostly image went for a low sweep, but it also collided with another image that went for a high punch. Amana could not read which one was his true intent, so he had to trust reality.

It wasn't enough.

Kojo went neither high nor low, instead, kicking straight out at Amana's mid-section. Amana lost his breath. He'd have to figure out how to subvert something like that.

"That's enough for today, eh?" Kojo said, smiling and grabbing his kanzu.

"Shall we pray to the Warrior?" Amana had grown accustomed to the spirits of the land. He was told of the main four that the village followed: The Warrior—sometimes known as The Hunter—Ugara, The Farmer, Eke, and The Twin-Moon Sisters, Yem and Aya.

"We're rubbing off on you that much?" Kojo smiled, kneeling down for prayer.

"I admit, it helps me. As you say, they all flow through us, do they not?"

"Has it helped with the dreams?" Kojo asked.

"Yes, it has. In truth, I've stopped having them, all together."

"It's not wise to shut them out entirely. Spirits do not like to be ignored."

"They were hindering me," Amana said as he took a drink of water. "Uzoma said I should stop letting them in so easily, that *I* should only initiate it through the spirit dance or through prayer."

"Fair enough. Just be careful about the one-way relationship. What do your monks feel about you praying to other spirits?"

"I'm not sure, to be honest." Amana shook his head.

"Those religious types can sometimes be pretty territorial with their followers."

"Elder Uzoma says the Junga monks believe in all types of religions. They're not as dogmatic as Jultia, for example."

"Jultia?"

"Another land far from here. They're probably the most religious of any of us. Some of the greatest palaces a man has ever seen, all in the name of their Supreme One. 'The One True God.'"

"You mean Ogó'ala?" Kojo asked.

"Is that the Supreme One here?"

"There is only the One, isn't there?" Kojo chuckled. "You're telling me these people believe only one entity can do all the things that need to be done in the world?"

"You'll have to ask one of the Jultians," Amana said.

"Maybe one day I'll be able to visit this place."

"Nothing is stopping you, friend."

"I can think of one person who would stop me."

Kojo looked over his shoulder to his hut.

They laughed and started their worship. After their prayer was done, they headed back to the village for lunch. Bajok warriors stood in front of each hut. Ever since the kishi had tried to escape, the village had been on high-alert. Baako wanted to go back out immediately, but the healers said he would be out of commission for at least another week. The bite on his throat had already begun to scar. Battle scars was a sacred thing in this village, apparently. Most of the warriors gave him respectful nods when they saw his wound. It was a show of experience and survival. Amana had received similar nods when his cloak exposed his bitten arm.

The Chief wanted to station more warriors near Uzoma and his homestead as well, but Uzoma denied them. He said he'd done well enough to keep the kishi away these many years, there was nothing different now. But some of the warriors in Bajok felt the old man was slipping. The attack on Baako was right in his backyard.

The scent of seasoned beans wafted from inside Kojo's home when they approached. Amana's stomach grumbled, ready to replenish the energy that was depleted from his morning workout. But he caught sight of Elder Oluchi trading meat in the market. He, too, was surrounded by a pair of warriors overseeing each transaction.

"I'll catch up. Tell your wife I'm sorry for not coming," Amana told Kojo. "I want to see what's going on with Oluchi."

"All right, brother," Kojo said. "More beans for me."

"Make sure to pinch those cheeks, eh?" Amana winked.

"Is that Amana?" Ime shouted from within the hut. "Ask him if he's gone to see Uzoma recently!"

"Ignore her," Kojo said. "If she knows you're here, she'll talk your ear off. Go ahead, I'll catch up with you later, yes?"

Amana smiled and waved, trotting off towards the market. The Bajok warriors watched him all the way, though they were far more trusting of him after he had brought the First Son back.

"Oluchi!" Amana waved. Oluchi returned the wave, though halfheartedly. As much as Amana was happy with his current circumstance, that did not stop him from his investigation. He might not have been as passionate as Nya, but he was still looking for ways to find the girls alive and well. "How's the farm? Any more troubles out there?"

"It's quiet. A bit too quiet I'd say. I'm helping tend to some cattle now. One of my neighbors has had an increase in his losses."

"How many has he lost?"

"A dozen of his n'dama. And that was just his farm."

"Is that normal within a few weeks?"

"Not at all," Oluchi said as he gave his next customer a pound of meat. "He only loses one a moon-cycle usually."

"Do you all know who's taking them?"

"He thinks it's the lions in the east, maybe even a leopard or two."

"But you think it's something else."

"You and me both know what else would be so ravenous." Oluchi locked knowing eyes with Amana. Oluchi was old, but the shadows under his eyes were deeper than Amana had remembered them. "Did you hear that Kofi's son went missing? And that boy Okoro hasn't been heard from either."

"What do you think about that?" Amana already knew the answer.

"Those demons are coming back," Oluchi said, slamming another slab of meat into another's hands. "They're like rodents, they are. The Chief is slipping, I tell you. Uzoma, too."

"There haven't been any sightings since Baako's return. Nya—I mean—Uzoma has made sure of that."

"That may be true enough," Oluchi said—paying no mind to Amana's slip. "But follow the trail. Those beasts are just waiting for the right time."

"I'll look into it."

"At least someone is," Oluchi spat. "All *Great-Chief* Oba wants to do is hunker down and hope for the best. All these warriors, yet all they're doing is watching an old man trade some meat."

"Watch it," one of the warriors said, gripping his poleaxe tightly.

"And what are you going to do about it, youngster?" Oluchi pushed his chest up against the warrior. He only reached the young man's belly. Amana put a friendly hand on Oluchi's shoulder.

"That's enough. Let the kijana off with a warning this once. I assure you, I'll take a look at these animal attacks myself."

Oluchi scowled at the warrior but nodded at Amana's request.

Amana turned away from the farmer and out toward the wilderness. This was the best lead he'd had in weeks. He had half a mind to tell Nya, but he knew she wouldn't leave the Black Rocks. Plus, they hadn't been on the best speaking terms the last few days. She was frustrated that they left when the kishi were supposedly so close.

It might be better if I go at it alone this once, Amana thought.

AMANA SET OFF TO WHERE OLUCHI HAD SAID THE ATTACKS originated. The land in the east was far more desolate—the plains of the predators—as some of the Bajok called it. Even during the height of the Great Empire of Golah, many had not ventured there. But Amana was confident he could suss out anything that might do him harm, confident in his short-sight.

Nothing about the day suggested there was danger. The sun rose high in a cloudless sky. Elephants roamed peacefully in the distance, antelope grazed, and wildebeest fed their young. No predator was in sight. Amana knew this was not a true peace. The usual predators in the land knew there was a new alpha, and that alpha was the kishi.

Though the general atmosphere was serene and calm, Amana did feel a presence stalking him. At first, he expected it was a lioness or a leopard ready to pounce on a lone human, but this presence felt all too familiar.

"If you wish to follow me, you'll have to do better than that," Amana said.

"Damn, your sight really is one of the best, isn't it?" Nya said. She was crouched behind a long bush.

"So I'm told. Why are you following me?"

"Why didn't you tell me where you were going?"

Amana did not want to answer. The truth would have been

too hard for Nya to hear—Amana had come realize he needed to be sensitive with her or else she lost her temper.

"I didn't realize I had to report to you."

"My Kor'de said we were to do this together."

"I don't recall those exact words."

"She definitely specified 'together.' Anyway, I keep tabs on all my suspects."

"Suspects? But my name was cleared almost a moon-cycle ago," Amana said, taken aback.

"You might not have done the deed, but you could be in league with these demons. How else could you read those words?"

"You know very well how I was able to do that."

Nya bit her tongue. Amana was caught in a half-truth.

"Fine, so my other leads dried up."

Amana wondered if she really meant that all of her other leads had been beaten to a pulp. Amana heard rumors of some of the Bajok warriors encountering something in the night. Most assumed it was the kishi, but their black eyes—rather than bitten necks—said otherwise.

"Or you were too bored waiting for a kishi to pop out from those rocks. You don't settle down in one place too often do you?"

"That's why I came along on this expedition." Nya smiled. She nocked her arrow into her bow, then let it fly free. The arrow found its target—straight through the head of a savannah hare. "I'm also quite handy with a bow. You hungry?" Amana shook his head. Nya took the little rabbit and stuffed it in her traveling pack.

"So, what lead are you following that didn't need my assistance?" Nya asked, walking ahead of Amana down the path.

"Oluchi's friend lost a lot of cattle to animal attacks."

"And you think it's the kishi?"

"It's the best lead we've had since those rocks."

"*We,* I like that." Nya smiled. "So what was your plan, just walk around until you find something?"

"I didn't have a plan exactly," Amana admitted. "Worst case scenario, it would be a nice walk through the savannah."

Nya and Amana walked together for a few moments. The day grew hotter as they walked deeper and deeper into the long grass, the sun peaking in the sky. The trees were spaced out, only providing shade every hundred yards or so. Before long they settled under one of the larger trees. Animal bones were stacked against the root of the tree, but the creature was long dead, the last of its fur decomposing.

Nya removed her light armor plating, fanning herself with her hand. Her dark skin glistened, sweat drifted down the line between her breasts. Amana found himself staring—and so did Nya. He looked away furtively but knew he was caught. She laughed.

"One must abstain from sexual misconduct." She chided, imitating the monotone voice Amana had while reciting from his scroll. "It's okay, I won't tell your mountain monks. You're only a man."

Amana went red around the ears. He had admitted to himself privately that Nya was a beautiful woman, a strong individual, not unlike Asha, his wife. But he never saw her like this before, so … exposed. To take his mind off the thoughts he had—like ripping the rest of her clothes off—Amana set himself to the spirit dance. After a short prayer to The Warrior, Amana began the sway, shadow-boxing away from Nya as she removed the rest of her clothing.

"Where did you learn to fight like that?" she asked.

"Elder Uzoma and Kojo are teaching me."

"I noticed the Bajok all fight like that. It's a bit strange, isn't it?"

"It's quite relaxing once you get the hang of it."

"Have you tried it out in a real fight yet?"

"No, it's not used for combat ... not for me," Amana said, stopping his dance. Though in truth, he did not use it in a fight because, one, he was not looking for a fight and, two, he was still uncomfortable with the unfamiliar martial art. He turned to Nya, who had discarded her bow and arrow against the tree, her armor resting against her weapons. All she wore now was enough to cover her womanhood, not unlike most of the women in Bajok. "It's used to balance the—"

Look up, Amana.

"... the body with the mind."

"That doesn't seem to be all that useful then. Here, show me." Nya stepped into a fight-ready stance. It was the opening style of the Ya-Seti sea crab, as Nya had told him before.

"I'm done fighting women."

"What's the matter? Afraid I might defeat you? I promise not to touch elements so long as you leave your short-sight out of this."

"No, really—"

"Come on, I'm sure this fits within one of your tests. See how well your self-discipline works when I've rung your head like a bell."

"I doubt that—" Amana started, but was pushed by Nya. Before he realized it, he was flat on his back.

"Yeah, that's what I thought." Nya dusted her hands off. "That style is only good for dancing."

Amana had bitten the inside of his lip. Though he swallowed his own blood, he smiled. Kipping up, he was ready for her now. Nya circled him like an animal, measuring the offbeat sway Amana was using.

"You see it, don't you?" Amana smirked, locking eyes with Nya. "That dance; that sway. You know it's a distraction, you think you know my timing. But it's a farce. I'm hypnotizing you. Just when you think you know my rhythm—"

Amana swept his foot behind Nya's ankle. She buckled but

did not fall. Instead, she went with the blow, cartwheeling back and catching her foot under Amana's jaw. Amana fell back hard.

"Fancy words, fancy dance," Nya said, strutting from left to right. "It doesn't matter. I'll still beat you."

That one really hurt. Amana shook his head. He was in far better condition than he had been last moon, but he didn't realize how much more he had to go to get back in proper fighting shape. Amana removed his own robe to free up his movement.

"Oh, getting serious now," Nya chided, though Amana noticed her eyes drifted across his chest a second too long. Without a second thought, Amana dipped and sprang up with a front kick, slamming his foot into Nya's abdomen. Her stomach was strong, but he still managed to knock her off her feet, finally.

"Good one, old man," Nya said, springing straight back to her feet as Amana had done before.

"Old?" Amana raised his eyebrows. "I can't be more than seven years your elder."

"Like I said—old."

They sparred for another few minutes as a pair of passing antelopes watched. It had been a long while since Amana fought without his sight. Though he would never admit it to Nya, he could not help but use it. Some of the flashes were involuntary, instinct. He tried to ignore them, but with Nya landing so many shots, he started to lean on those flashes, anticipating her moves. Eventually, he was able to get his legs around one of hers, the same move Kojo had used to take him down. But it didn't work. Nya always found a way to slip past him.

Amana changed tactic. His spirit dance was a bit too soft for Nya's more brutish assaults. Amana needed to revert back to what he knew. Bouncing from left to right, trying to lull Nya back into his rhythm, he suddenly stopped. Nya flinched for a second. That was all Amana needed. Instead of shifting his weight within the sway, going for a kick or a leg-lock, Amana ran straight at her. He wrapped his arms around her, placing his foot behind her ankle; then he shoved. She fell back, and he was right on top of her in a grapple. But Nya was not deterred.

She used her body weight perfectly, countering Amana's own strength by redirecting him. Nya was as good a fighter as Amana had ever seen. Amana had started the tackle and grapple, but Nya had already turned him around. Now *she* was on top.

"That last move wasn't part of that Bajok dance," Nya said, on top of Amana. Their wet bodies slid against each other.

"Nah, I learned that one from somewhere else, *chana*," Amana said. Nya's eyes widened slightly.

"Chana? I know that word—and that move. Those Islanders use it. The low-life. Is that where you come from?" With that, Amana pushed Nya off of him, his jaw clenched. "Sorry I didn't mean to—"

"Don't worry about it." It was the first time Nya had apologized for anything. Why did she care to say sorry? Amana changed the subject. "How long have you been fighting?"

"That good, huh?" Nya patted herself on the back. "I've been fighting all my life, and I was formally trained up by the Ya-Seti when I turned twelve."

"You'll have to teach me some of those moves."

"Only if you ask nicely."

On the distant plain, there was a pair of dust clouds, the signs of a chase. Amana and Nya were close enough to see it—a dark figure chasing two little cheetah cubs.

"Where is its mother?" Amana asked.

"You don't think that's ..." Nya looked to Amana. Amana looked to Nya. They both bolted. Nya picked up her bow and arrow along the way but left her armor behind. Amana ran behind her shirtless.

When they approached the scuffle, they saw what they were looking for. It was another kishi, running impossibly fast; the cubs had no chance. In what looked like two fluid motions, the kishi snapped both their necks, one after the other. Nya shot an arrow into the kishi, but it bounced off its strong hide. The kishi remained unfazed, with the pair of cubs between its jaws.

"Remember, hit their backside," Amana said.

"Noted," Nya replied, grabbing for another arrow.

The human head of the kishi resembled one of the merchants that had left a moon-cycle ago. Before Amana could approach the kishi, he received a flash—the cheetahs' mother was making a dead run for Nya's back.

"Nya, get down!" Amana shouted. Without a second thought, Nya dipped. The cheetah mother leaped over her and lashed out at the kishi, who dropped one of the cubs. The two beasts tussled briefly, but the kishi retreated into the thick of the plains, a meal already between its jaws. Still, the mother growled at Nya and Amana. Nya started to oscillate her hand, rocks and sand swirling around her fingers.

"No, don't," Amana said with an outstretched hand. "She's just protecting her cub." Amana turned back to the growling cheetah, her back arched, ready to pounce. Slowly, Amana took a step back with an outstretched hand, making sure not to look the cheetah directly in the eye. Amana cooed softly, continuing to tread back lightly.

Nya mimicked Amana, stepping back slowly. When they were fifty strides away, the cheetah mother started nuzzling the dead cub that was left behind, trying to bring it back to life.

"Those demons are getting desperate now," Nya concluded later as she pulled on her armor. "Bajok has been on lockdown ever since Baako was attacked. That's why there are all these attacks on animals. They need to feed. If they can't have the Bajok women, well, they'd need to eat somehow."

"It still doesn't make sense." Amana stroked his beard. "Like you said before. If they really do have Shanaki, shouldn't they be long gone from here? Why are they sticking around and why this far out? The Black Rocks are completely on the other side of this land. Is their reach really that far?"

"I don't know," Nya admitted. "But that's good news for us. It means Shanaki might still have a chance out there—"

"And Yejide."

"And Yejide, wherever they are, and whatever those beasts are doing to them. We just need to trap one of these things. It can't be that hard."

"Not hard. Just impossible."

"I can do impossible," Nya said, smiling.

CHAPTER 12

GUESTS UNWELCOME

AMANA RETURNED TO ELDER UZOMA. HE HAD NOT SEEN THE man in nearly a week, too busy with the goings-on in the village and the nights he stole with Nya, planning their next move. But the progress he had made on his own was significant—or so he thought. When he arrived at Uzoma's home late in the afternoon, he showed that he could balance the Gods' Glass for a full five minutes.

"Impressive." Elder Uzoma nodded his head. "But by now you should be able to balance it for at least ten minutes."

Amana dropped his head. He'd really thought he had made a lot of progress.

"I'll admit, you are doing better than most," Uzoma said. "But your method is too lenient. You have to control the stone, don't just sway with it. You have only carved out the cusp of what can be gleaned from this meditation technique."

"But the Junga say—"

"Do I look like a mountain monk to you?" Uzoma took the instrument and demonstrated. He walked about his large hut, cleaning off his chair as he balanced the ball on the flat wood. Amana's lips drifted apart, a dazed look on his face. Each time Amana tried to balance the thing, he needed to sit, unmoving. And here was Uzoma, walking around and tending to his chores as though there was no heavy ball he needed to balance. The ball did not even seem to move. When Amana balanced it, it swayed to and fro, and he flowed with it. But Uzoma seemed to will the ball to his command, rather than the other way around. The ball followed Uzoma, rather than Uzoma following it.

"You're distracted. You've not been here for quite some time," Uzoma finally said after he finished dusting his altar. "It's that Ya-Seti woman you go off with, isn't it?" Amana opened his mouth. "You think I didn't know you two were lurking off into the rocks. And how has that turned out for you? Have you come any closer to finding my son or those girls?"

Amana shook his head.

"I'm not telling you to abstain from sexual misconduct as your scroll would say." Uzoma stuffed the instrument back into Amana's hand. "But don't you dare grow attached. That's the true reason for that tenet. You'll need to maintain focus if you are to be a match for these kishi."

Amana hardly thought Nya was distracting him. There was their brief time on the plains, but that was innocent enough. And nothing came of it. But had Amana wanted more to happen? Regardless, he never felt such clarity in his abilities. Nya was not clouding or hindering him at all.

"I've already conquered that tenet." Amana lifted his shoulders with confidence. "Surely, you've heard of the Sapphire women, some of the most beautiful in the world."

"Conquering your ability to turn away from attractive women is the least of it." Uzoma laughed. "It's true attachment that's the worst. That's what you should be wary of. Romance comes in more than one form."

"Does this mean you'll no longer train me?"

"I already told you, I'm not one of those mountain monks. I won't benefit your goal if you wish to become a pacifist."

"But the Balanced Five says pacifism is the way to salvation. It's how the Junga achieve their great power, right?"

"Why are you so insistent on having me as a mentor?" Uzoma ignored Amana's question.

"You were one of the best warriors known to this land. Now, somehow, you have become a farmer with no real anger. You seem genuinely happy. I can feel it within you; it makes you stronger."

"I made my peace long ago."

"But how? How did you let go of that hate? All those years of war, all those fights with the kishi. They do terrible things. I've seen it."

"I had to. If I left myself in that state, if I did not step away, that anger would have eaten itself through me. That kind of hate is empty emotion." Uzoma turned to a boiling pot near his hearth.

"How is your wife?"

"She is due very soon. She rests most of the day now. If my prayers are answered, it will be in the next fortnight."

"What happened to your other wives, if you don't mind me asking?"

"None of the shamans understood what went wrong," Uzoma said. "They were all healthy. I just happen to be unlucky. But I'm confident Esi will pull through. I will not lose her like the rest." Uzoma's eyes were sharp.

"Has she been drinking the tea I recommended?"

"Yes, I made sure of it. Only time will tell if your recommendation will help."

"How's her color? May I see her?" Amana stood up and made for the back. Uzoma lifted a hand.

"No, she's sleeping now. But her color is troubling, I'll admit. She's a bit purple."

"That's a good thing. It means the tea leaves are working.

There's a second step to the process, though. Just before her water is released, you'll need to change the dose. She'll need to drink every half hour until she's ready to birth. I should be here when that happens, to make sure everything is okay. I'll be sure to make my sessions more frequent. I won't miss my days anymore."

"I thank you for that," Uzoma said as he added the hot water to the cup. "But I want to deliver this baby on my own."

"It would be no trouble," Amana said.

"It will be done by the father, as I've done before," Uzoma said sternly. Amana didn't understand it. Uzoma didn't have the best track record with his wives, why risk doing it himself?

"If you change your mind, I'll be here each morning, I swear it," Amana said.

"Give me a moment," Uzoma said, lifting the cup of hot tea and starting for the back room. "My wife has been waiting for her tea."

Uzoma left Amana alone in the room. A few scrolls were strewn across the table. For a few minutes, Amana gave them sidelong glances. Uzoma was more receptive, but something told him he'd need to steal another scroll. But the old man would know. He had probably left them out on the table so openly as a test. Just as Amana was about to examine one of the scrolls, there was a knock at the door. Who would be visiting at this time?

"Could you get that for me," Uzoma said from the back room.

"Of course," Amana answered. He stood up and walked to the door. When he opened it, two men stood before him. Both had handsome faces and very long hair.

"Where is he?" asked the one on the left.

"I don't know who you're talking about," Amana said.

"You know who we're looking for, *foreigner*," said the man on the right. Amana recognized this man; he was another merchant. Amana had a strong feeling about what hid behind their thick hairs. Slowly, he shifted his weight to his back foot.

"Amana, who's there?" Uzoma called from the back.

With that, the two men rushed the door. Amana tried to hold them back, but the strength of the pair was too much. Amana looked over his shoulder. Uzoma had come out from the back room. His face was placid, but his fists were clenched. Before Amana fell under the weight of the two men, Uzoma came barreling down on them at full force, jumping into the air when he was a pace away. He led his forward momentum with the bottoms of his heels, connecting against both men's chests. The pair flew out the doorway and into Uzoma's farm. Their falls were cushioned by the bean plants.

Amana's raised his eyebrows. Elder Uzoma moved much faster than he should have been able to. Amana thought he was well past his prime, retired from anything so physical. But that flying kick was smoother than of any man even half his age.

"We just want to know where he is, Uzoma," the larger of the two men dusted beans out of his locs.

"And what makes you think I would tell you youngsters?" Uzoma crossed his arms.

Are they talking about Ikenna? Amana thought.

"You're slipping, old man. It's past time we took these rocks and these lands back."

"You will try," Uzoma said, uncrossing his arms. He grabbed one of his farming tools, a long stick with a hooked metal edge. "But you will fail."

The two men didn't miss a beat. Their joints started to pop; their hair parted. Within a moment, their kishi form was manifested.

"Amana, now will be the time to get up. Arm yourself."

Amana looked for something useful. He found a sickle near Uzoma's porch.

"Take the small one on the right," Uzoma said. "I got the big one." Uzoma was already in a fighting stance. His rhythm was different than Amana expected. It was neither the local spirit dance nor anything Amana had experienced in the east. But something about Uzoma's style was familiar. His footwork was grounded, but his sway definitely belonged to Ugara—brutal punches strengthened by the turn of his hips, and his whirlwind kicks given speed by his the pivots of his heels. He used elbows and knees along with his farming tool, knocking the larger man off his feet.

Amana was wrong. Uzoma wasn't fast. His timing was just perfect. Years of fighting experience allowed him to work the larger man the way he wanted. He might not have been as athletic, but he was far smarter.

Amana almost forgot he had to deal with his own adversary, who was already barreling down on him. This kishi was slower than the three he had faced before, but he was still incredibly fast. Amana had never fought with the weapon he had, but it was long and sharp, and it would keep the kishi at bay. The demon bounded from left to right. Amana could sense its incoming attack and used the long farming tool to block its path. The kishi fell right onto its hooked edge, but the blade did not pierce its skin.

Come on, Amana, you knew that wouldn't work.

Each time Nya's arrows had tried to sink into a kishi's skin, they always bounced off. Yemi had said their human sides were weak. Amana needed to target the kishi's back somehow. But how would he pivot around such a fast foe?

Amana kept one eye on Uzoma. What was he doing to bring the kishi down? Uzoma kept setting the kishi up to overextend itself. Then when he had it where he wanted, he slashed its back open with the back-side of his improvised weapon.

Amana replicated the tactic. It should have been easier for him to do with his short-sight. But his insides went cold. The kishi was altering his spirit. Amana fought the crippling sense of dread, centering his thoughts around the spirits of the water. It helped. Though the kishi was still prying into his fighting spirit, Amana could function.

He saw where the demon would attack from just before it did.

Amana settled into the rhythm of Ugara's dance, everything one fluid motion. He swayed right, leading the kishi, then step back and left, bringing his weapon-hand over in an arc.

Smash!

The back of the kishi—its human side—split open. Blood spewed freely from its wound. The kishi and the human head yelled in unison.

The kishi that Uzoma fought now had several wounds on its chest, belly, and leg, and it had slowed significantly. Uzoma still looked fresh, the bounce in his step sharp, ready to make his kill. But before he could slice at the kishi's neck, it retreated.

"Gazini, let's go," the human head said as it trotted away from Uzoma. But Gazini had far less pain tolerance than his friend. Amana had only cut him once, and he could barely stand now. Gazini's friend did not seem to care for him much, running halfway down the canyon without looking back.

Amana used the blunt end of his farming tool to take out the back of Gazini's knees—the blow was strong enough to break the back of the leg. Blood still spilled from Gazini's cut.

"Kill him," Uzoma ordered.

"He's defenseless." Amana didn't see the point in killing the kishi or the man.

"There's no reasoning with these types. They are tricksters."

It was true—where the kishi had put dread in Amana's heart before, now it tried to nudge Amana's heart toward sympathy

"Don't kill me, please." Gazini turned his hyena face away, using his human face instead. Amana could have sworn the inside of Gazini's eyes were moving into themselves—almost hypnotic. "It's not my fault. It's the hyena; it takes over."

"Amana, kill the beast." Uzoma had an edge to his voice. "It tried to kill you, it will do so again."

"Please, all we want is the girl! Don't listen to Uzoma." Amana wasn't sure what he should do. There was no immediate threat from the kishi, but could he deny Uzoma's orders? The act of fighting was a bit of a gray area within the Junga discipline, but killing was definitive. Would all of Amana's training go to waste if he murdered an innocent foe? Were the kishi innocent at all?

Gazini wasn't going to wait for Amana to make a decision and changed his tactic. "We know about the Ya-Seti you go around with. If you do not help me, he will kill her."

Amana smacked Gazini across the face.

"He? Who's he?" Amana asked.

"We weren't sure before, but you do fancy the woman, don't you?"

Amana smacked Gazini across the face again. This time Gazini's eye swelled.

"She hides out near the rocks. Bathes near the springs. We've never seen a body like that before. The Warrior's-Way has done her well. Some of us were thinking she'd be a nice one to take as well."

Amana went to strike Gazini again, but the human side moved away, revealing its hyena head which bit at Amana's hand. Amana did not see it coming, distracted by Gazini's words. He could feel it now, so subtle. The demon had pushed against Amana's fear, enraging his consciousness.

Lucky for Amana, Uzoma did see it coming.

Before the kishi could bite down on Amana's wrist, Uzoma slammed his sharp tool into the kishi's neck, separating head from neck at its human side.

"When I tell you to kill, you kill." Uzoma lifted his blade, blood flying into the air, a few drops landing in Amana's beard. Uzoma stomped back into his home, leaving the body.

Amana sat alone with his thoughts. No matter what he did, it was wrong. He looked at his arms. He hadn't noticed the wounds he'd acquired—the benefits of adrenaline.

The kishi were desperate if they thought they could simply take Uzoma as they pleased. Was it a power play? Did Ikenna want Shanaki for himself? Did he take her when the others advised against it?

"Thought I might find you here!" said Nya as she approached from behind. The golden trim of her Ya-Seti battle armor reflected the setting sun. "Is the old man here?"

"He's in the back tending to his wife."

"Good. We need to go," Nya said. "I have a new lead—what happened to your face?"

"The kishi just showed up."

"Here?" Nya's eyes lifted.

"Yes, here. And they know where you're hiding. They are watching you. They might be watching us now."

"What do you mean they are watching me?"

Amana pushed the bean plants aside to show her the dead kishi. "This one said he's seen you by the springs. That they were thinking of taking you as well."

"Dikala ... I thought I had been careful."

"Careful enough against the Bajok, maybe. The kishi are another thing," Amana reminded her. Nya scowled. "We have to find these kishi, fast. And the girls. What's this lead you have?"

Nya perked up. "I've figured out a trap."

"Good to see you, Ya-Seti," Uzoma said from his porch. Amana turned. Uzoma was looking the woman up and down, then his eyes drifted to Amana. He was smiling. "What brings you to my home?"

"Just need to borrow Amana for the night."

"Yes, he's quite the special one, isn't he?" Uzoma grinned, showing all his teeth. He was never this friendly with Amana. It was strange he was being friendly at all, with a dead man on his farm. Nya glanced at the corpse furtively. "Please, excuse my mess. I've had some rude visitors today. Could I interest you in some tea? I apologize for its taste. It's for my wife."

"Yes," Nya started to say. Had Amana seen her eyes go dewy? "I mean, no, I have to be off. Pressing business for the Kor'de."

"Oh, yes, I've not been able to speak with your leaders. Do give them my well wishes."

"I will," Nya said.

"All right, then. We'll be going now." Amana stepped in, grabbing his travel bag, stuffing his scrolls and his balancing instrument into it. Should he have done something about the body? He figured he should at least move it.

"Leave it to me," Uzoma said. "You did well today, Amana. Come back soon." Uzoma turned to Nya.

"It was nice meeting a Ya-Seti as lovely as you." Uzoma waved. "I can see why Amana speaks so highly of you."

Amana went red, his jaw clenched.

"FOR AN OLD MAN, UZOMA DOESN'T LOOK HALF BAD," NYA said as they walked back onto the plains of the predators. Night had fallen, but Nya walked with a confident pace. "If he was fifteen years younger ..."

"He's a married man," Amana cut in. Nya shrugged, her smile betraying that she was only teasing.

"You're not jealous, are you?"

"No. It's just not appropriate, is all."

"Ah, come off it, you're from the Islands. Your lot are supposed to be promiscuous. Not even your monk training could drive that from you fully. Just a few days ago you couldn't keep your eyes off—"

"Okay, that's enough," Amana said, a little curt. "We're here now. What is it that you've done?"

"I set up a trap for our demons," Nya said. "You see that wildebeest over there?"

Amana followed the path of her finger. A hundred yards from them was a wounded wildebeest, limping by a tree-side.

"The kishi are getting desperate and hungry," Amana said. "But they wouldn't be that stupid. That's clearly a bait."

"I wouldn't be so sure about that," Nya said. "If they really are that hungry, they'll take what they can, even if they suspect bait. They attacked Uzoma. They wouldn't have done that unless they were desperate."

Amana shook his head. "How long has the beast been out there like that?"

"No more than two hours."

"Why hasn't he walked away from that tree?"

"I have him tied off to it. He tried to break it at first, but he settled down quick enough."

"Fine, we'll wait here," Amana said.

So they waited.

"What did the kishi want with Uzoma?" Nya asked.

"They said they wanted to know where *he* was."

"Ikenna?"

"That's what I think."

"Do you think there's an internal competition for Shanaki?"

"I'm not sure." Amana stroked his hair. "But the kishi thought Uzoma knew where Ikenna was."

"Do you think he knows?"

"I don't think so. He's a proud man. If Uzoma knew where his son was, he would have brought the boy in already. You should have seen him fight."

"He can still fight, too?" Nya lifted an eyebrow.

"I wouldn't have believed it either if I hadn't seen it with my own eyes. He fought like a man no older than myself."

"Did that kishi say anything before you had to kill him?"

Amana gulped. How was he going to explain that one?

"He didn't say much" was all Amana said.

"You're a terrible liar, you know that? You always do this thing with your eyebrows." Nya smirked through her helmet.

"A thing with my eyebrows?" Amana touched them.

"Yeah, they sort of scrunch up like caterpillars." Nya chuckled. It was a lovely laugh, light and easy on the ears, a laugh he often heard when she teased him.

The thought of the kishi's words were in his head again. His feelings for Nya were something he meant to suppress. Uzoma saw it, even the kishi. It troubled Amana that they were being watched, especially Nya. Could the kishi be stalking them even now? No, they couldn't have. They had caught that other kishi by surprise when they were on the plains. Still, Amana shifted in their hiding spot with unease. He was about to suggest they move camp or leave the trap—which he didn't believe would work anyway—when a hyena came sniffing about.

"Not exactly what we were looking for," Amana said.

"It's exactly what *I* was looking for," Nya said, her eyes intent on the hyena. "See there, it's caught the scent of blood."

Sure enough, the hyena stopped in its tracks, ears pushed forward, listening for where its next meal could be. It didn't take long for it to find its mark. And the wildebeest saw its predator. With a second wind, the wildebeest tried to escape from its rope. The hyena made a full sprint for the beast, snipping at its legs. But the wildebeest put up a good fight, bucking its head.

Hyena had powerful jaws, but alone they were manageable. Another predator or even a weakened wildebeest could handle just one. After a few minutes of back and forth, the hyena laughed, calling its brothers and sisters.

"Perfect," Nya said.

"Perfect?" Amana questioned. "It's calling hyena, not the kishi."

"Just wait." Nya shushed Amana.

In just a few minutes, the rest of the hyenas came. A dozen, maybe more. But Amana realized straight away what Nya was looking for. There was a gray-backed hyena that wasn't quite right—it was the way it walked, or the way it sniffed, Amana couldn't quite tell. It did not move like the rest of them.

"Is that one a runt?" Amana thought out loud.

"You can't tell?"

"The way it's walking so strangely, like it's a—" it clicked in Amana's head. "Like it's a human!"

"You got it!"

"A shape-shifter?" Amana watched as the group of hyenas surrounded the poor wildebeest.

"I think so. Yemi said there was one always sniffing around the watering hole."

"You saw Yemi? You know that's dangerous! He can't keep lying for you—"

"Relax, relax, I was eavesdropping, of course."

Amana let his shoulders drop.

"You can't be so cavalier about all this. The Bajok don't make idle threats. The Chief doesn't want anyone interfering with their affairs. He nearly took my head the first day I met him."

"Hell, I almost took your head myself." Nya laughed. "Anyway, I wasn't sure at first. I thought the hyena could just have been wounded or something, but it favors its back legs. You can tell it wants to stand up half the time."

Amana turned back to the strange hyena. His mind clicked again. "I think I may know this shape-shifter."

Nya's eyebrows lifted at that. "What do you mean you know it?"

"Well, not personally. The villagers at the market talk about him often. They say he spends most of his time as a hyena, now that he's banished."

"Banished?"

"Yeah, the Bajok have bad blood with the hyena. And after all this business with the kishi ... They just didn't trust his sort. I don't blame them." The hyenas were now ripping into the wildebeest, eating through its flesh while it still grunted against the dirt. "This must be his pack. Even with them, he seems like an outsider."

"I noticed that, too. You'd think he would have taken the alpha position with his human intellect."

"That's usually the case," Amana said as he crouched in their hiding spot in the brush. "Well, let's go get him, shall we?"

"Shouldn't we wait for some of them to clear out? He's likely to stay around for the scraps."

"Where's your sense of adventure, Ya-Seti?" Amana said, smiling. "We have a man with the sight and a woman who can touch the elements. They're really no match. I'll show you a few more moves from the Isles."

Nya smiled and got to her feet.

"We'll need to go in smart, though," Amana said. "We'll need to break them up first and get the shape-shifter isolated. What I want you to do is shift that tree if you can."

Nya nodded, ready for some action. She shifted the leaves atop the tree. All it did was startle the hyenas, but they kept eating.

"I have another idea," Nya said. She shifted her hands, and a small dust cloud surrounded the hyena pack and the half-eaten wildebeest. Again, the hyenas were startled, but they did not see anything that they should fear.

Amana rolled himself in a mud puddle to mask his scent. Then he crawled closer to the pack. The dust cloud gave him additional cover. He found himself next to one of the hyenas. He could not see it through the cloud, but he could predict its movements, its ghostly image shining through the dust. Amana encircled the cloud until he found the hyena that was not quite right. Then, he sprang into the dust cloud with a yell.

The hyenas flinched at first, but when they noticed it was only one human, they grouped together and started growling. But the shape-shifter seemed to know better, running out of the dust cloud. Amana gave chase, losing ground quickly, but the hyena-shifter was headed straight for Nya in her own hiding place. She popped out and shot an arrow through his leg, pinning him to the ground.

The rest of the pack was still after Amana, but their movements were easy to adjust to. The fight was short. Amana always found it easier to fight animals; their movements were always more direct. Most of the hyenas ended up crashing into one another, some even biting their comrades by mistake. Amana continued dodging them until they realized he was no ordinary human. Eventually, they gave up the chase.

Amana turned to the shape-shifter, who was trying to dislodge the arrow from his leg.

"What's your name?" Amana asked wrapping his hands around the hyena-form's jaw. He knew if he let go for a moment, he'd never see his hands again. "Go ahead, show your birth-form. We only have questions." It was strange when the protruded jawline shrunk back into the hyena's head, replaced by a human mouth. Now, there was only a naked man for all to see. He had the face of an animal, pointed and long.

"Name's Ayo!"

"Good to meet you, Ayo. I think we have a mutual friend in Ikenna," Amana said, nodding to Nya. She went for Ayo's back, pinning his arms.

"Don't try anything funny," she said. "Or I'll put a dagger in your neck."

"You don't have to go doing that." Ayo jumped. He was a frantic sort of man, his head twitching from left to right like the beast he was. He smelled like he hadn't bathed in years and emitted a pungent odor that could not be washed away with a simple bath.

"Answer my friend's questions," Nya said, "and you won't have to worry about that."

"Have you seen Ikenna around recently?" Amana asked, kneeling down next to Ayo's slumped body.

"I don't know nothing about no Ikenna."

"Something tells me you're not telling the truth. These are your hunting lands are they not? There have been increased attacks on your turf. Surely you have some new rivals who've relocated here."

"I told you already, I don't know nothing about that."

"Or maybe it was you who took the girl. I'm sure the village would love to hear I found her captor, and it was Ayo all along. The banished shape-shifter who wanted to get back at the people of Bajok. They'll have a stake ready just for your head."

"That's a lie!" Ayo shouted, shifting his weight. But Nya had him locked down good. "I didn't take that girl! It was Ikenna."

"Ah, but I thought we did not know where Ikenna was?" Amana smiled. He almost felt at home interrogating this man. It was like putting on an old glove. But Amana didn't take too much satisfaction in breaking him. He was as dim as they came.

"I'm not telling you anything else."

"The other kishi don't like what Ikenna is doing, am I right? They are fighting over the Ya-Seti princess?" Ayo kept his lips shut now.

"All right, then, my turn," Nya said. She took the butt of her knife and hit the side of Ayo's head.

"Nya!" Amana shouted.

"Back up, Amana," she held the knife out at him. "He's not going to answer us. Your way is too slow and too unreliable. But this ..." she held up the knife, "always gives answers. I'm not losing another lead on Shanaki."

Amana could not think up a good enough response, so he stepped aside and let Nya take over. Nya grabbed Ayo by the nape of his neck. Ayo winced, and Nya answered him with a punch to the face.

"Where is she?" Nya shouted.

"I already told the other guy! I don't know nothing about that girl." Ayo started pulling at the arrow in his leg. "Take it out, please!" he shouted.

"Oh no, you don't want me to do that. My people are masters of the bow and arrow," Nya pulled out one of her arrows from her quiver. "You see this spiked tip here? It's made specifically for idiots like you. The moment you pull it out, you'll cut up even more vital veins than when it went in. And I assure you, my shot was not meant to kill you. You will lose some blood—that can't be helped—but you will not pass out before telling me what I want to know. I have the tool to remove it properly, but I'll need answers first."

Ayo gritted his teeth. The color underneath his dirty face was leaving him. Still, he persisted. Still, he did not speak.

Nya used her palm to smack Ayo right on his throat. He coughed. But no words came out. Nya raised her hand again.

"Okay, okay! All I know is that the girl was taken. She was taken by Ikenna."

"Where does he have her?"

"I don't know," Ayo flinched at Nya's raised fist, but a punch never came. "Honest, I don't know."

"What does he want her for. Why her?"

"He wants revenge. No, he wants to protect her. No, that's not right. He needs her for his plans. It was the only way."

"What are you talking about? One thing at a time. What revenge?"

"I don't know." Ayo clutched his head, shaking it back and forth. "The kishi, they're back. They want revenge."

"Who's trying to protect Shanaki?"

"I don't know, I don't know," Ayo repeated.

"How about Yejide, Ayo. Did you hear anything about her?" Amana leaned forward.

"I don't know!"

"We're pressing him too hard, he's confused." Amana stepped in. Nya batted his hand away.

"Dikala, tell me where they are. You must have some idea!"

"The rocks! The rocks! They have to be there."

"We already tried that. Where else can they be?"

"I can't ... I can't ... they'll kill me." Ayo was crying now. "I don't bother nobody. Why you have to come around here and ask me all these questions?"

"Tell us what we want to know, and it'll be over," Amana said over Nya's shoulder. She smacked Ayo across the head again.

"He was out here with her, he was out here, he needed food, he needed his revenge on that man. The Chief doesn't like me, never has, never trusted me. I was his best servant. I tended to everything he needed, then he threw me out. Serves him right what's happening now." Ayo was on a tangent of his own now.

"You're not going to get anything useful out of him. You have to calm him down, Nya." Amana stepped in again with more force.

"Amana, this is the last time I'm going to ask you to step back." She lifted the ground below Amana, and he fell over its uneven lumps. "He's almost there. He's almost broken. I'll get him to 'fess up."

Nya turned to Ayo again. She pressed her thumb into his collarbone and applied pressure until it was at the edge of breaking.

"Stop it, please!" Ayo's eyes went wide. "I don't know. I won't tell! They'll kill me. They'll kill you all!"

"It's one or the other, Ayo. You know, and you will tell me."

Ayo started to shape-shift back into a hyena, but Nya was ready. She rubbed her hands together, and a small flame appeared. With her scalding hands, she grabbed Ayo's wrist, burning him. The man hollered, a strange mix between a human scream and a hyena laugh. Just like that, he stopped his shift, remaining in his human form. The pain from the flames was too much, though, and he passed out. Nya slapped him a few times, but he didn't wake.

"You will compromise the truth by getting answers through

pain. The Scroll of the Five says to abstain from such dark words and actions …"

"Enough with your damned scroll," Nya shouted, giving Ayo one more slap to make sure he couldn't be brought back for questioning. "Do you even have a mind of your own? Will that scroll get Shanaki back?"

Amana shook his head. "Whether it gets Shanaki back or not, I don't want to see you going down this path. It's one I know all too well, and it amounts to nothing useful."

"I got more out of him than you ever could trying to be his friend. And I don't need you saving my spirit or whatever it is you're trying to do. My mission is simple. I serve my Kor'de, and I will return her daughter to her. What would you have me do?"

"Exercise some patience," Amana advised. "What you're doing is foolish."

"So, I'm a fool now?" Nya stood up to her full height, her nose almost touching Amana's.

"You know that's not what I meant."

"What did you mean, then, Amana? What?"

"You're being hard-nosed."

"That's what gets the job done, and you know that. What's wrong with you? Why are you so weak? You have the body of a warrior and the skill to back it up, and you're wasting it on what? To live a life at the feet of other mountain monks?"

"Don't disrespect the clan. They have something I need." Amana threw his finger into Nya's face, and she batted it away with the palm of her hand.

"Forget that clan," Nya said. "You're so much better than this, Amana."

"No, Nya." Amana pointed down to the bloodied Ayo. "You're much better than this."

Nya shook her head, her brow pinched tight in frustration. "You're not helping me on this mission anymore. Ayo is mine. The trap was my idea, my claim. Go back to your elder and your villager. I'll get answers out of this shape-shifter one way or the other."

"Uzoma was right about you. You're just a distraction." Amana said.

"The feeling is mutual then."

They stood there in silence for some time, only Ayo's labored breathing pierced the dead air. Everything was said that could have been said, and there wasn't much either of them could have done to change things. Nya turned back to Ayo, lifting him atop her shoulder. Amana did not want to get involved or provoke her rage further, so he turned and walked away.

"Both of you step away from the shape-shifter."

A group of a dozen Bajok warriors surrounded them, hidden in the bush. Amana couldn't make out their faces in the night, but he could see the outline of their figures. They must have approached Amana and Nya as they argued. Nanga led the group with Yemi at his side.

"Over my dead body." Nya stepped in front of Ayo's unconscious body.

"That can be arranged," Nanga said with a smile, clutching his spear. They were all on their guard, knowing what Nya was capable of now.

"Now, now, calm down," Yemi said with a friendly smile. "Nya knows Ayo falls under our right. This is our land. Otherwise, she can be taken to our Chief for execution. It's your choice, Nya."

"Execution?" Nya tilted her head. "After everything I've done?"

"To hell with negotiations." Nanga gritted his teeth. "We know she's the one going around giving us hell. We should take her in."

"You will not." Amana stepped in. "Nya's done more for this investigation than any of you."

"We're not going to listen to a foreigner," Nanga spat. "She's overstepped her bounds. She doesn't get any more chances."

"How about this," Amana proposed. "You take Ayo and—"

"No, they're not taking the shape-shifter." Nya's voice was sharp.

"You really have no say in this. You should listen to your friend here," Yemi said peacefully.

Nya sucked her teeth at the use of the word *friend.*

"She's too wild." Nanga stepped forward. "I'm taking her in. That's what the *Chief* wants."

"Nya is not the enemy here." Amana moved between Nanga and Nya. "You both want Shanaki and Yejide back—"

"The foreigner could give a damn about the Bajok. All she cares about is that princess and breaking our noses in," one of the warriors said in the local tongue. Amana recognized the man as Zoba, the guard he had slipped past on the first night.

"The kishi attacked Uzoma and me," Amana said.

"When did this happen?" Yemi stepped forward, the rest of the warriors leaned in as well.

"Late this afternoon. They came looking for Ikenna, I think. Uzoma didn't have a good answer for them, so they attacked."

"They never attack Uzoma. Not since the war ..." another of the warriors said, his eyes downcast.

"Did you get a good look at them?" Yemi said, his eyes squinted.

"Not really, but one of their names was Gazini? Uzoma killed him," Amana said.

Yemi frowned. The other warriors whispered to one another.

"So the old man has still got it!" one of them said enthusiastically.

"They are getting desperate," Nya spoke up. "Ayo knows something about that."

"Maybe we can work together then," Yemi decided. "If these kishi truly are attacking Uzoma, this could get out of hand very quickly. We'll have another war."

"Work together?" Nanga butted in again. "Do you hear yourself, brother?"

"Amana is right. Nya is working towards the same goal. Everything rests on that Ya-Seti girl." Yemi turned to Nanga.

"What about *our* girl? Yejide is still out there, too, or did you forget that?"

"Of course, I didn't."

"Do you remember what that foreigner did to me? What she's done to the others?"

"Of course, I do."

"Then you'll know why I won't just let her have her way with the shape-shifter," Nanga said, pushing Amana aside.

When he grabbed Nya's arm, she flung a rock at his nose—the following *crack* indicated she had broken it. Without looking at the damage done, she adjusted Ayo on her shoulder and ran. It was a futile attempt. She was outnumbered, and it didn't help that she had the weight of Ayo to deal with. It only took two of the warriors to stop her.

"I really wish you hadn't done that." Yemi looked down to Nanga, who was clutching at his nose. "And I really wish you hadn't done that, Nya." He looked at Nya, pointing to Nanga's bloodied nose. The man was livid. "I'm sorry, Nya, but we'll have to take you back to the village … as our prisoner."

CHAPTER 13

EXECUTION

AMANA RETURNED TO UZOMA THE FOLLOWING MORNING AS HE had promised. They started with the ball balance training. Amana was doing even worse now. Both Ayo and Nya were being held captive in Bajok. Yemi had been able to talk the Chief down from executing Nya on sight—but only after the Chief found out about how she had helped capture Ayo. Though she was safe for now, there was still a pit in Amana's stomach.

Kor'de Neema had tried to negotiate for Nya's immediate release, straight back to Ya-Seti. But the Chief had denied the request.

"She's had chance," the Chief had said in his broken accent.

Nya, surprisingly, had accepted her fate—no choice words for the Chief or the captors who tugged at her arms. Amana could not bring himself to say anything to her. She was still angry with him about what had been said. Ayo, on the other hand, looked as though he might soil his pants at any moment. Even when they brought him food, he thought they were coming for his head. It was going to be difficult getting concrete answers out of him. But Nanga had already thought up a few ways to get Ayo to talk.

Nanga's methods were about the only thing he and Nya could agree on, though Nanga also campaigned for her immediate execution.

When the Chief heard about the attack on Uzoma, he stationed two Bajok warriors at the elder's home. Amana had waved at them when he had arrived, but neither acknowledged the gesture, intent on watching the farmlands.

With everything on Amana's mind, he could not balance the ball for more than a few seconds.

"What happened?" Uzoma asked.

"You're right, women are distractions."

"It's not all women that can be distractions. Just the ones we care for."

"I don't ..."

"You don't know it yet, but you do," Uzoma said. He walked to Amana and took the Gods' Glass. "No balancing today. I have something else for you." Uzoma searched inside his chest. "You promised you'd bring my wife into good health. I think it's only right I do right by you."

"The baby? It's okay? Did she give birth?"

Uzoma shook his head. "No, nothing like that yet. But I've been through this twice before. And Esi looks better than the others. I have a good feeling she'll pull through."

Amana smiled, but after the kishi attack, he had been thinking of something.

"Yemi said the kishi put a curse on you," Amana said this slowly, seeing if this was a subject he was allowed to comment on. "Is that why your wives have been dying?" He was glad to hear she was doing all right—and that he was the one to help—but he could not help wondering if his efforts would ultimately be futile. He was no alchemist after all. There was no special tea he could brew to lift any kind of curse placed on Esi by the kishi.

"Yes, those are the rumors that have sprouted around the

village," Uzoma said. "But no, I am only cursed with an aging body."

"You took on those kishi well enough," Amana pointed out.

"I haven't been completely honest about why I came to these lands," Uzoma said as he pulled out a dusty old scroll. "You see, I used to fight for the Golah Empire before its fall. We had reached the jungles of Kunda when I came across one of the Junga monks. He was imparting wisdom to our enemies and refused to share that wisdom and knowledge with us because our conquest was unfounded. I was the only one who stood at the mountain monk's defense, and I saved him from execution.

"The Empire never could get past the jungles. Our leader fell, and the state was broken. After the war, I was invited to join the monks on Junga mountain because of my talents as an empath. I think they were more interested in studying me than anything else. I stayed with them for a time, and I learned a lot. And what they taught me ... that helped me find balance.

"But I still did not achieve what I was looking for. You see, like you, I have been trying to step away from the darkness. A life of war, a life of combat, that's all I could think about. It was all I knew. I needed to *control* it. But I could never manage it.

"So I thought about returning to the former Empire, bringing it back to its heyday—through conquest, of course. I could go back to what I knew; perhaps then I could find a purpose."

"And did you?" Amana asked, reading over the new scrolls Uzoma had brought out. It was a twelve-scroll series about the Junga monk's balance. Boism was just one of the chapters in the large volume.

"I did. But it did not come from the teachings of the Junga at all. It was the teachings of this land. I know you've become familiar with some of their spirit-Gods, yes?"

"I have," Amana said. "It's all Kojo talks about whenever we spar."

"Do you know what their core value is?"

Amana shook his head.

"You see, the mountain monks saw good and bad as two separate entities, when really, one cannot exist without the other. To the Bajok, and the greater nation of Golah, it's not a matter of either-or, but a matter of both-and. Consider a storm. We do not see it as evil, but mother nature's natural state. A storm does not wipe out a village because that village has wronged them. It's simply living out its nature. But what happens after that storm? It wipes away the weak, and the strong remains."

Uzoma went to his altar. He lifted one of the statuettes. "So I fought the kishi all those years without malice, but with control. Finally, I found out what I was missing. I needed both the Bajok and the Junga to teach me the truth of our world. Well, that and many other things. You see this figure? It's the Great Warrior that they pray to. You've come to know him as Ugara. They believe prayer to him will give them good fortune in battle."

"Yes, I've felt him in the sway."

"Indeed, as have I. But power comes from within and without. One's power doesn't just come from the Gods." He lifted the statuette. "It also comes from humans." Uzoma pointed to his heart. "Remember that. Never focus yourself on one piece of information or one lesson. Ever since you started your training, you've felt your power increase, yes?"

"Yes," Amana said. "I admit I use both teachings to help me in this way. I use the spirits, but I also use my natural talents."

"As you should. Never lose sight of that, Amana. As you can see from my small library here," Uzoma pointed to a pile of books in the corner, "knowledge is indeed power. And control is its manifestation. That will defeat these kishi. Stay vigilant. Use your tools to your benefit, including your darkness. But control it, as I have controlled mine."

"Thank you, Elder Uzoma." Amana bowed. "I'll heed your words."

"Keep that scroll there. I've committed it to memory already,"

Uzoma said. "And continue speaking to the Bajok. The farmers, the villagers, the elders, the children, everyone. The True Path will become clearer the more vessels you study."

Amana nodded.

"What happened between you and that woman?" Uzoma asked after a short pause.

"We just had a disagreement."

"If you don't mind me asking, what about?"

"Nothing substantial, just about this mystery with the kishi. We were questioning a shape-shifter out in the predator's land. She had him beat down pretty good, even knocked him out. It didn't seem the best way to get answers out of him."

"A shape-shifter, you say?"

"Yes, a man named Ayo," Amana said. Uzoma lifted his eyebrow. "The villagers spoke of him in passing."

"Yes, everyone knows about Ayo," Uzoma said. "What happened to him? He always gets away from most of the hunters that try to capture him."

"He wasn't so hard to trap when you—"

"Have the short-sight," Uzoma said, eyeing Amana. "So, this Ya-Seti still has him?"

"No. Some of the Bajok came, took Nya and the shape-shifter. He's in their custody now. I believe Nanga is interrogating him now, or soon. I'm not sure."

"Did he say anything about where my son might be … or those girls?"

"Not too much. At least, not before Nya knocked him out."

Uzoma nodded, stroking his beard in thought—the only hair he had left.

"Well, thank you for this, Elder Uzoma." Amana stood up, his pack weighted down with even more material to study. "I'll see you tomorrow at the same time?"

"Yes." Uzoma smiled. "I look forward to it."

WHEN AMANA RETURNED TO THE VILLAGE, HE WENT STRAIGHT to see Nya. She was being kept in the same hut he had been put into on his first night. Her hands were bound to the scratched and bloodied post that stood in the hut's center.

"Yemi?" she asked. She turned and frowned when she saw it was Amana.

"Am I really such a disappointment to see?" he asked. She did not answer. "Why were you asking for Yemi?"

"He's the only reason I'm still alive. The warriors want me dead, and the Great-Chief isn't averse to the idea. No thanks to you."

"You know I didn't want this."

"Honestly, I don't know what you want, Mana."

"I want ..." Amana started, but he wasn't sure himself. He stepped closer to Nya, though he was still talking to her back. "Well, first, I want to get you out of here."

"Don't be silly." Nya shook her head. "They've got a twenty-four-hour guard outside my hut. There's no way."

"What about Yemi? Is he truly a friend?"

"I suppose so. As good as any that I have in Bajok. He trusts me, at least. But it doesn't matter. The only way I'm getting out of here is if we find the kishi that took Shanaki. Then maybe, I could make a case for why what I did was necessary."

"So you *were* breaking the warrior's noses, then?" Amana said. He couldn't help smiling.

"How else would I get them to talk?" Nya said, without a grin. "My case will be even better if Ayo is the one who leads us to the demon."

"Where are they keeping him?" Amana asked.

"I'm not sure. But I heard the warriors talking about his interrogation happening in the big hut."

"Have they started questioning him?"

"I haven't heard any screams yet."

Amana sat down next to Nya, watching her in silence. She gave him a furtive side-eye.

"What?"

"I'm sorry, Nya," Amana finally said. "You're right. I've been too passive, too weak. I've been trying to bottle up my emotions, but I have good reason to ..." Amana stopped himself before he told her too much. Nya grunted. "What?" Amana said, finally seeing her face for the first time. She had a black eye and a busted lip.

"I thought you would have at least told me what that reason was," she said. "I suppose Uzoma was right, then." Nya turned her head away from Amana. "I'm just a distraction."

"You might be." Amana's words were met with a scowl. Amana smirked. "But I like distractions."

Though Nya's brow was furrowed, she let the hint of a smile curl across her lips. She stopped that quickly.

"Listen." Amana got closer to Nya, close enough to smell her. "How about I speak to Yemi? We don't have to cut our way out of the village, but we can certainly talk our way out of it."

"Talk to Ayo," Nya demanded. "He's the best chance of me getting out of here."

"If they'll let me. But first, I'll need to speak with the man who's keeping you alive."

Nya frowned, but she nodded.

"Don't go dying on me just yet." Amana stood up, dusting himself off.

"You still have to teach me that silly little dance of yours," Nya smirked.

"CAN I TRUST YOU?" AMANA SAID WHEN HE FOUND YEMI playing a game of wood and marbles with another warrior.

"Good morning to you, too," Yemi chuckled. "Can I finish my game first?"

"Ah, don't matter none," the older warrior said, old muscles hanging from his arms. "You is two moves from beatin' me anyway."

"Well then, looks like I'm free." Yemi stretched his arms out. "Can you trust me with what?"

"Nya's life," Amana said plainly.

Yemi raised his eyebrows, but he lifted himself up. "Walk and talk?"

"That's fine by me." Amana led the way down the village path. "Why are you keeping her alive?" Amana asked when they passed the market.

"I couldn't waste such a beauty."

"What's the real reason?" Amana frowned.

"Nya doesn't seem like a liar to me. Does she to you?"

"No, she doesn't. She's quite blunt."

"Isn't that the great thing about people like her? Never any surprises." Yemi waved at a woman passing by with her day's harvest stacked on her head. The woman smiled back.

"You were promoted recently were you not?"

"I am a War-Chief now, yes," Yemi nodded. "Part of the First Son's guard and the Chief's adviser. I was the one who found you two out in the plains."

"I thought Nanga outranked you."

"I have a more … delicate touch than he."

They stopped near the festival grounds.

"Nya doesn't have much time to live," Amana said. "You can't keep her alive forever. Your comrades want her dead, and the Chief doesn't care about her life either way."

"I can be quite persuasive," Yemi said, smiling with all his teeth. "I can keep the girl alive. What's it to you anyway?"

Amana did not answer. He didn't think it was right to let out that he had developed feelings for Nya.

"I made a promise to the Ya-Seti," Amana said. "And I still think Yejide is out there … somewhere."

"That girl may be lost, like the others." Yemi shook his head.

"So, there have been other attacks?"

"Of course, there have been. All out in the farmlands. We've been told to keep it quiet, of course."

"And you don't have any idea who is behind all this?"

"Ayo's our best bet," Yemi admitted. "That was one of the main arguments that kept Nya alive. I convinced the Great-Chief that she was the only one to capture Ayo when none of the others in our village could. She really is quite the woman."

Amana did not think it was prudent to correct Yemi. Nya had captured Ayo only with his help—they were a team. But the way Yemi spoke of Nya made him feel uneasy. Did Yemi share similar feelings for the woman? Had Nya shared those feelings for this man? After all, it was Yemi she asked for in the hut, not him.

"Why haven't you questioned Ayo yet? It's nearly midday," Amana said.

"As you know, Ayo is a bit mad. It will take a more delicate measure to get the answers we need from him. Nanga wanted to start this morning, but I convinced him we should give Ayo more time to recover. He's emotionally unstable, after all."

"Would it be possible for me to speak with him?" Amana asked.

"That would be up to the Great-Chief. But like I said, he's in no condition to speak with anyone right now." Yemi turned. "Look, it's been nice speaking with you, Amana. But that's all I can do right now. Trust me, Nya is safe."

"War-Chief Yemi!" A Bajok warrior jogged toward the pair. "War-Chief Yemi, he's been killed!"

"Damnit, I told Nanga to wait until he questioned—"

"It wasn't Nanga, Chief. It was one of *them.*"

"Them?" Amana stepped forward.

"One of the kishi!"

AMANA, YEMI, AND THE BAJOK WARRIOR SPRINTED TO AYO'S hut. There were already several villagers surrounding it, including Great-Chief Oba and the First Son Baako. The straw door was lifted up for all to see inside. Ayo was dead, his throat ripped open like Imani's had been.

"Who was on guard duty?" Chief Oba asked of one of the men.

"Nanga!" said someone in the crowd. "Nanga was guarding."

Everyone looked left and right for the warrior, but he was nowhere to be found.

"You and you," Oba pointed to the men nearest him. "Find him and bring him to me."

The men nodded their heads and jogged off. More onlookers came out of their huts or from the markets. Women screamed. Children asked their parents what had happened.

"This wouldn't have happened if we took the fight to them," Baako spoke up. "Ayo knew where Ikenna was. Now he's been silenced. It's time we took on new leadership, Father."

"What are you doing, boy?" Yemi said under his breath. "This is not the time, and you are not ready."

"What is it?" Amana asked.

"Looks like Baako is fixing to challenge Oba's claim to the title of Great-Chief."

"How does that work out?"

"It's a fight to the death."

"Oh." Amana raised his eyebrows.

Just as Baako was about to speak, one of his guards placed a hand on his shoulder. The man whispered something to the First Son. Whatever was said, it made Baako pause.

"Where is the Ya-Seti woman? Do we know what Ayo told her?" Baako said.

"Nya!" Amana had almost forgotten. "We have to get her now."

"I think that's for the best," Yemi agreed. While Baako spoke to the crowd, the pair jogged off to Nya's hut. When they arrived, the guards stationed outside the hut smiled.

"Nanga is already working on her," one of them said. They could hear whimpers inside the hut.

"Did you not hear about Ayo?" Yemi asked them. They both shook their heads, dumbfounded. "Report to the big hut. The kishi have returned."

"What do you mean?" one of them said. "They can't get into the village. The shaman said—"

"That was an order, warrior," Yemi said with an edge to his voice. The two warriors trotted off. When they were far enough away, Amana opened the hut to find Nanga hitting Nya across the face.

"What did he tell you, Ya-Seti?" Nanga's eyes were blood-shot and wide.

"Nothing important, or I would not have wanted him so bad," Nya said through a bloodied nose.

"Stop it, Nanga," Amana said, his voice booming.

"Oh look, your lover's here to save you." Nanga turned. "Yemi? What are you doing here?"

"Stopping you," Yemi said as though it were obvious.

"I never thought I'd see the day where a Bajok would help a foreigner." Nanga spat.

"What happened at Ayo's hut, Nanga?" Amana spoke quickly, knowing he had little time to trade insults.

"We're doomed" was all Nanga could say. "Those things. They're too fast. Too strong. It came out of nowhere. I couldn't believe it."

"A kishi?" Amana asked. "Did you get a good look at the back of its head?"

"I was too busy trying to stay alive. I wasn't just gonna stare at it!"

"The kishi are here?" Nya words were slurred through her busted lip. "They said that was impossible."

"Well, it was possible," Nanga said. "The thing was in the village, and it killed Ayo."

"Ayo must have known too much," Amana concluded. "The kishi didn't need him spilling their secrets. But how did they know Ayo was here? Most of the kishi have left. Do you think we were followed from the plains?"

"It's possible," Yemi said. "The kishi are silent. They could have seen Ayo return with us. None of you spoke to anyone else about Ayo, right?"

"No," Amana said straight away. But he remembered that he had told Uzoma about the shape-shifter.

Warriors were trotting outside, but they didn't check the hut, passing instead.

"We need to move this little party," Amana said.

"You aren't going anywhere." Nanga grabbed Amana by the arm.

"The Great-Chief is looking for you," Yemi added. "Seems like he'll have your head for this."

"My head?" Nanga scowled. "I nearly died for that shape-shifter."

"Right now, it looks like you deserted your post." Amana pulled at Nya's bindings.

"You can come with us, or you can try to leave," Yemi said. "The choice is yours."

Amana checked Nya's wrists. They were raw and torn. "Did he hurt you?"

"He wishes." She smiled. "Hits like a girl."

"I've been hit by a girl or two." Amana winked. "They can hit pretty hard."

"I have to let my Kor'de know what has happened," Nya said to Yemi.

Yemi nodded. "Right, I'll take Nanga away from here until things die down. No one should be disturbing the guest hut. Just keep away from the market and the festival grounds. There is bound to be a handful of villagers there."

"I know how to keep to the shadows," Nya said.

"That you do," Yemi agreed.

"Thank you, Yemi," Nya bowed her head.

"Of course."

"All right, let's go," Amana said.

Amana and Nya made it to the Ya-Seti hut without incident. The village was bustling. Rumor of a kishi on village grounds spread like wildfire. It was unprecedented.

"The shaman is no good anymore," a man they sneaked behind had said.

"It's the Great-Chief. He needs to step down. Baako should take his place!" someone else had said.

"It's not the shaman's fault really. It takes time for him to reinforce the ancestral wall," a woman replied.

"Ritual or no, if the kishi can come into the village as they please, it might be time to move to Guela."

"Guela? I'd say it's better to move to Kunda. No kishi has ever gone there."

"Kunda? Hah. I'd take the kishi over the Gorilla King."

Many of the conversations went on like that as Amana and Nya sneaked from one hut to the next.

"I knew Ayo had something good." Nya crouched down, not looking as though she had just been beaten down several minutes prior. "I've no clue how I'll find Shanaki now."

Two Ya-Seti archers were posted outside the royal hut.

"I heard they captured you," one of them said when they saw Nya.

"You know I don't stay captured for very long," Nya smirked. "Is the Kor'de here?"

"They both are," the archer said. "Do you have news?"

"We might know where Shanaki is," Amana spoke up.

"That's good to hear," the other archer said. "I'm getting tired of this little village."

The soldiers stepped away from the door and let them pass.

Inside, advisers to the Kor and Kor'de were huddled around the hut. When they saw Amana and Nya, their words turned to hushed whispers. Had they been discussing what had been happening in the village?

"You should not be here." Kor'de Neema eyed Nya. "If you escaped, you should be far from here."

"I intend to leave, but you must know ..." Nya turned to Amana, realizing she was not sure what the Kor'de needed to know.

"I don't believe it myself." Amana shook his head. "The shape-shifter that was brought in was murdered."

"A shape-shifter?" one of the advisers said with narrowed eyes. "We were not told of this."

"I know what happened, Amana," Kor'de Neema said. The adviser shut his mouth with wide, shocked eyes.

"But how—" Amana started.

"It would be unwise for me not to know what goes on in this village."

"Then you know that it was a kishi that took Ayo's life."

"That is the rumor right now, yes. But it's supposed to be impossible for them to reveal themselves within the confines of the village. So the rumor seems unfounded."

"I think I know what kishi that might be."

"You and Nya have already given us that Ikenna boy's name, with little result." Neema's lips went tight.

"Not Ikenna, Your Highness."

Amana thought it over again. The only ones who had known about Ayo were Yemi, Nanga, and their men—and apparently the Royal Families in the village. But none of them would have been motivated to kill Ayo. Amana trusted Yemi. He wasn't on the best terms with Nanga, but Nanga would not have killed Ayo before finding out where Yejide was. The Great-Chief and his son were just as shocked to find the dead body.

What still did not make sense to Amana was how the kishi got inside the village grounds. He had chased one out of the village, and that one had been hard-pressed to transform before it broke the shaman's boundary. Even on that first night, the kishi he saw near the river had transformed just outside the village. If there was a kishi who could transform within the village, that kishi must have had a power that surpassed that of the village shaman. There was only one man Amana knew who wielded such power. And it was the only other person who knew about Ayo.

"What?" Nya turned to Amana. His eyes were darting left and right as he worked it out in his head. "What is it?"

"There is someone else who knew about Ayo."

"Who?"

"Elder Uzoma."

Amana could not believe the words even as he said them.

"The old man? But ..."

"I can't believe I didn't see it before," Amana said. "It was obvious, wasn't it? His own son was the one to take Shanaki—"

"But the Bajok think him cursed," Neema said. "And he shaved his head like the others."

"How did you come to that conclusion?" Kor Mosai finally spoke up, his voice hoarse as usual.

"When I spoke about Ayo—I didn't notice it then—but Elder Uzoma was keen to know more about what he had said and what the warriors might have gotten out of him. And just a few hours after, we find him dead."

"Do you think he's a kishi?" Mosai sat forward slowly.

"It should be impossible. Like Her Highness said, Uzoma shaved his head like the rest, and he's free from the demon. But I've seen him do the impossible. He took on a kishi by himself, even in his old age. I know he's legendary for fighting them, to begin with, but still … He controls Gods' Glass easily, and he … knows how to manipulate emotion. But it just doesn't make sense that the kishi would attack him that night if he were one of them," Amana said.

"Do you have anything more solid than your gut?"

"No, Your Highness." Amana frowned.

"Sometimes, one's gut is the best thing we can follow. And it might save our daughter." Neema pressed her hand to her chin. "At the very least, Uzoma could be in league with the kishi, if not one of them."

"It's possible," Amana said. "He could be protecting his son. Ayo must have known exactly where the boy is."

"Well, it's time for us to get some answers from Uzoma, then." Nya stepped forward.

"I agree," Amana said with a clenched jaw. "I'm supposed to meet with him tomorrow morning, so it won't be out of the ordinary."

"I'll come with you," she said.

"You can't come inside with me. I'll have to go in alone. But you can back me up if anything goes wrong. Just watch the door until I give you a sign."

Nya nodded her head.

"Uzoma has a guard stationed outside his home. To protect him from the kishi," Neema reminded him. "And they know Nya should still be captured or—if they are not yet informed—nowhere near the Black Rocks. You'll need to be very careful around them."

"You know I will, Your Highness." Nya bowed.

Neema turned to Kor Mosai, waiting for his final word. He

did not take long to nod in affirmation.

"Go to Uzoma," he croaked. "See what he knows. But do not engage with him. Bring back whatever information you can, and await further orders."

Amana and Nya nodded in unison as one of the Ya-Seti guards entered the hut.

"Kor'de Neema." The guard gave Nya a side eye. "The First Son is here. They're asking about Nya."

"Right," Neema said. "You two, hide yourselves here."

Neema pointed to the fur on the ground—lion skin by the look of it.

"There's no way we would fit under there without being—" Amana was saying as the guard pulled the skins. There was a wooden slat under it. Beneath it, a hole had been dug in the ground—enough room for three or four grown men.

"You can never be too safe." Neema smiled.

"When did you have time to do this?" Amana's mouth was agape.

"No time to explain. Get in."

Amana and Nya hopped into the hole. The guards quickly dropped the wooden slat, leaving them in complete darkness. All Amana could do was listen. First came the footsteps. The First Son seemed to have at least two guards with him.

"Good morning. What brings the First Son to our hut today?"

"Your Ya-Seti archer. She's gone missing. Has she been through here?" This voice seemed to belong to Baako.

"I've not seen her since she went to those dreaded rocks. Funny, I did not know she had returned to the village. Why was I not informed?"

"We didn't want anyone interfering with our questions."

"She's one of my soldiers. I am a guest here. This should have been brought to my attention."

"With all due respect, *Ya-Seti,*" Baako said this with no respect at all, "this woman has been more than a nuisance for my soldiers. The best that can be done for her is a swift execution."

"I'd like to see you try," Nya whispered in the dark. Amana placed a hand over her mouth. Nya, of course, did not like that, slapping him away.

"What was that?" one of Baako's guards said.

"Must be your imagination." It was Yemi.

"No, I think I heard it too," Baako agreed with the first guard. "What was that noise, Ya-Seti?"

There was movement above their heads. It sounded like Baako was getting closer to the Kor'de. There was more shuffling, and the sounds of arrows being notched onto bowstrings.

"That's close enough," one of the Ya-Seti guards said.

"I'll tell *you* what's close enough, Ya-Seti." It sounded like Baako had turned on the guard, probably nose-to-nose.

"First Son Baako," Yemi said, "please. There is no need for this."

The room changed, Amana could feel it.

"Don't do that, Yemi!" Baako shouted. "I can control myself."

The sensation went away, but Baako did seem to bring himself under control.

"My apologies, First Son," Yemi said. "I just feel as though we're all a little on edge because of the kishi."

Another set of footsteps entered the hut.

"First Son," said a Bajok warrior. "You have to come. It's shaman Emeka."

"What is it now?" Baako said, annoyed.

"It's better if you follow us, sir," the warrior said. Amana could picture Baako eyeing the Ya-Seti. He probably did not want to divulge the information in front of their guests.

"I suppose you're right." Baako's weight was pressed at the edge of the wooden slat that covered Amana and Nya. "Excuse my outburst, Ya-Seti."

"We have all been on edge these past few days, young one,

especially the leaders of our people," Neema said diplomatically. "If we do hear anything from our soldier, *your father* will be the first to know."

"Yes, my father." Baako's words were harsh. "We'll be watching you. Even your daughter isn't worth this much trouble."

"Is that all, First Son Baako?" Neema said politely. Amana could hear the smile in her voice.

"That's all," Baako returned. The sounds of his feet made it known that he had gone. But it took several minutes before the guards lifted Amana and Nya out of the hole.

"What the hell was that?" Nya said.

"You were about to get yourself killed!" Amana returned.

"He was insulting me!"

"Amana is right, Nya," Kor'de Neema said. "Your talents are great, but you need to learn self-restraint. And both of you will need to trust one another. Uzoma will challenge you in ways you will not expect. I remember Uzoma during the Kunda sieges. He's not just great because he knows how to swing a sword decently. He knows the minds of men … And women. I wish you good fortune," Neema said. "Now leave. Before you get us all killed."

CHAPTER 14

WORDS OF CAUTION

THE DREAMS RETURNED SHARPLY THAT NIGHT. AMANA HAD done well to repress them, but the prospect of questioning the man he looked up to left him deeply distressed. So the anger and the flames returned. Amana felt himself screaming. His words were unintelligible, muffled, as though he were hearing them from underwater.

A figure engulfed in flames stood between him and his wife, Asha. But it wasn't the face Amana expected. It was the face of a hyena.

"You cannot save her," the figure said. "You have failed her."

Amana refused to believe that. He failed Sanaa, but he still had Asha. Without thought, he sprang for the figure in flames, his own mortality be damned. But at the apex of his jump, he was stopped. Was it the figure that stood before him who impeded his vault? It did not seem so. Amana felt nothing from the figure. In fact, everything had stopped. The flames were static, the hyena no longer spoke, and his wife no longer sobbed. There was no sound. Everything was void.

What is this? Amana thought.

"You should not be here. You are headed in the wrong direction." It was the female voice Amana had heard before. The one he meant to shut out. *"You should have left."*

But how can I? I need training, I need to stop these demons. I need to avenge them.

"It is too late for that, Amana," the voice said. *"This is your last warning."*

And then Amana was released from the stillness. He descended from his jump, his right fist ready to make contact with the hyena's jaw. But the hyena turned around, revealing the face of Uzoma, who was ready with a spear in hand. The sound of the flames grew louder, and Uzoma guffawed like the hyena that he was. Uzoma's spear pierced through Amana's heart. Pain shot through Amana's body as he watched his wife drift away like ash. He had failed her, too.

AMANA WOKE WITH A JERK. THE FIRST THING HE SAW WAS Nya's big, golden-brown eyes. She had been hugging him. And for the first time, Amana saw true worry on her face, her eyes delicate and soft like a lover's.

"How long have you had them?" Nya spoke first.

"For a while. But they've gotten worse since I arrived here."

Nya broke away from Amana, but part of him didn't want her to let go.

"I made them stop for a time," Amana said as he pulled a piece of cloth to cover himself. He and Nya had camped outside the farmlands leading into Uzoma's canyon. The cold air rippling through the makeshift tent felt like morning.

"You're nervous, then?" Nya asked without being cruel or judgmental.

"I suppose so, yes," Amana said. "Half of me is hoping I'm wrong."

"All of me is hoping you're right."

"If he is in league with the kishi—or is a kishi himself—I don't know who will train me." Amana dropped his head.

"I don't think you need it." Nya pulled on her light armor. "I've seen you. You're more talented than you let on. I meant it when I said you're better than that." Nya pointed to the scrolls that laid next to Amana's traveling bag. "You just have to believe it, Mana."

The tension in Amana's shoulders eased. It was nice having someone who believed in him for a change. He couldn't say the same for the Junga monks. But he was not any more confident about the task at hand. How would he even begin to navigate what would be a very awkward conversation with Uzoma?

Elder Uzoma, would you happen to be hiding a demon spirit in your body somewhere? It sounded silly even within his own thoughts. But he set off with Nya anyway, keeping a confident stride that did not betray the butterflies that fluttered in the pit of his stomach. It had been a long while since Amana had been this nervous.

When they arrived, Nya hid alongside Uzoma's hut's wall, pressing her back against it so as not to be seen through the windows—or by the guards. Would she be safe there? Amana shook the thought away, focusing on what he would say first. He knew if it came to it, Nya would be able to fend for herself.

The first Bajok warrior nodded to him.

"Why are you sweating so much? The sun hasn't even peaked."

"Morning run," Amana said, wiping the sweat from his forehead. The Bajok exchanged looks of raised eyebrows. Amana took his time to knock on Uzoma's door, going over what he would say, how he would say it, trying to anticipate how Uzoma would react. Maybe Amana was wrong after all.

"Well, are you just going to stand there?" the other warrior said to Amana, irritation cutting through his tone. Before the warrior could knock for Amana, the door opened. Uzoma stood there with a bright expression.

"You're here early." Uzoma smiled. "I could hear you coming up."

Amana paused, wondering whether or not he knew Nya was there too. "I was just wondering if it was too early to knock."

"Not at all. Come right in." Uzoma waved him inside. Amana prayed to Deh'ala before he passed the threshold. Uzoma was in a better mood than he usually was—his movements had a bit more pep to them.

"So, I've decided," Uzoma said.

"Decided on what?" Amana asked as he took his usual seat across from Uzoma. He let his eyes drift only briefly on the window that sat behind the elder, where Nya watched.

"Your training. I think it's time we go to the Junga monks and have you initiated."

Amana raised his eyebrows, eyes wide.

"What did I do to deserve this?" he asked with genuine surprise.

"My wife," Uzoma said, offering Amana a cup of water. Amana accepted it warily. "I've never had a wife who looked so well. She will definitely make it."

"I'm glad to hear it." Amana sipped, eyeing the window again.

"Did you heed what I said yesterday? About the spirits of this land and how these people worship?"

"I did, Elder, I did." In truth, he had forgotten all about the task, but he wanted to keep Uzoma in an agreeable mood. Amana's eyes drifted to the window again; he cursed himself privately. He knew he was looking over there too often. Nya ducked out of sight before Uzoma turned to follow Amana's gaze. She'd be angry at Amana for that later.

"It's nothing," Amana assured. "There's a bird that keeps flying by. Sorry, it's distracting me."

"Well, pay it no mind," Uzoma said.

"I've been meaning to ask you something, if it isn't too personal." Amana decided to start with direct questions. In his previous line of work that was always the best method. But he would have to tread lightly with this. There was a wit yet uncovered that Amana had not seen from this man. Kor'de Neema was right to warn Amana and Nya.

"I'll let you know when you've touched on something off limits," Uzoma said through his beard, sipping more of his drink.

"The reason I came to you, as you know, was because of what people said about your warrior spirit," Amana began. Uzoma nodded his head, letting Amana continue. The rapid pounding in Amana's heart would not stop, but he made sure to keep his feelings stoic or else Uzoma's empathic abilities would uncover something off. "And as I've discovered, you truly are a man of peace. Whatever you have done, whether it was the teaching of the mountain monks or the people of this land ... it worked. I've only known you a short time, I admit. But you have never once shown any darkness about you, no 'words of war,' as the monks would say. But I'm still not sure how you did this. So I wanted to ask about your fight with the kishi all those years ago. What actually happened? I've seen these demons for myself. They are cruel and unrelenting. How did you defeat such an enemy without succumbing yourself?"

This was the first test. Amana needed a story from Uzoma—some sort of foundation—that he could test. Then he needed to catch him in a lie.

"I think I can give an abridged account. It was many years ago."

Amana had hoped for a longer story but did not want to push harder. Most elders loved to tell never-ending tales, especially if it included heroics on their part. Had this been any other elder, Amana may not have been able to stop the man from talking. Why wouldn't he want to go into every detail about what made him a legend in this village, and many villages and cities abroad? What did he have to hide?

"Whichever tells the story best. So I can better understand how you've gained the control you have." Amana made sure to add that bit at the end. He had to make sure Uzoma thought this conversation was for his benefit; let him boast a little.

"I came here, where the kishi were most concentrated. There was something about these rocks that they were tied to. There were so few of us then, no more than a score of men, maybe a few more. None of them were all that good, mostly farmers who could barely hold a spear properly. Oba was as fierce a warrior as I had ever seen, but he needed help. He was War-Chief back then. He did not get the Great-Chief title until after we destroyed the kishi. There isn't too much I can say about the fight. The enemy was unrelenting, so we had to be as well. We never took prisoners. Never asked questions. Just war."

"After the kishi were defeated, was it difficult for you to come back to this?" Amana gestured around the hut. "A life as a farmer?"

"It was difficult at first, of course," Uzoma admitted. "A lot of men went on fighting each other in those spirit dances; others, abroad in the fighting arenas. But I had had my fill. I was old—even then. My bones weren't working the same."

"But the other night you defended yourself pretty well," Amana reminded him.

"True enough. But you start figuring out shortcuts when you're my age. Good enough against a wild youngster, but not for warfare. No, those days were—are—gone for me. And I never thought much of it again."

"Why did those kishi attack you?"

"You were there, boy, you heard them," Uzoma said through pressed lips. "They wanted to know where Ikenna was. I don't know where he is. If I did, I would tan his hide."

"Too bad about Ayo," Amana said.

"Yeah, he was a young fellow. Didn't deserve what happened to him."

How could Uzoma have known that? It hadn't even been a full day yet. His land was several leagues from the main village, and the guards outside switched out every few days. No word could have come to Uzoma yet. Amana's heart started pounding against his chest, the hairs on his back sticking up. Amana gripped the side of his chair to calm his nerves. It would do him no good to let his intentions be known before probing Uzoma further.

"Did they tell you?" Amana thumbed toward the door.

"Yes," Uzoma said over the cup of his drink. It had taken him a split-second too long to answer the question. "Just before you came in. I didn't think the kishi could get into the village like that."

"Yeah, neither did I. Had to be someone very powerful to penetrate the shaman's ancestral magic."

"Well ... it might not have been a kishi necessarily." Uzoma stuck out his bottom lip in a frown. "The villages are bordered by the plains. The hyena don't get along with them very well. Ayo ran with them, didn't he?"

"He did," Amana nodded. "But Nanga said he saw the kishi. Said he nearly was killed himself."

"That right?" Uzoma raised an eyebrow. Amana could have sworn he saw a faint smile across the edges of Uzoma's lips. But it could have been his imagination.

"Lucky for me," Amana said. "Sometimes I don't make it back to the village before nightfall."

"Ah, you held yourself well against our attackers the other night. I'm sure you could fend for yourself." Uzoma sat up. He moved to his pot to refill his drink.

"What did you do after I left yesterday?" Amana asked. There was a brief pause. A casual observer might not have noticed it, but Amana was waiting for it.

"Excuse me?" Uzoma asked plainly over his shoulder.

"Yesterday morning, after I left," Amana said it as though it should have been clear the first time he posed the question. This time the pause from Uzoma was more deliberate. The room went cold, Amana's blood chilled.

Uzoma's back was still turned to Amana as the silent moment passed. When Uzoma finally did turn, he wore a smile on his lips.

"Can I offer you some palm wine?" Uzoma started for one of his curved standing pots.

"It's a little early for that, don't you think? Besides, *one must abstain from that which can alter the mind* and all that, right?"

"Right, so silly of me," Uzoma said, sitting back down, his eyebrows slightly furrowed. That was it, the change of expression Amana was looking for. "Esi, can you get Amana another drink?"

Esi came from the back room. She did look a lot better. Her skin was clear, and she walked as though she wasn't pregnant at all.

"Of course," Esi said meekly. She knelt down near Amana's cup. Her skin brush against his. Amana felt a sharp sensation. It was not pain exactly, more like a shock. It felt familiar, but he could not place it. As soon as Esi took the cup away—and her hand with it—the feeling was gone.

"Oh no, allow me," Amana sat up and poured another drink for himself. Amana knew better than to let someone serve him when he was questioning them. "Ayo seemed a bit mad to me, out of his wits. I don't think he would have given up anything significant. Even if he did, I'm not sure the Bajok would be able to discern what was mad-ranting and what was not."

"Ayo, you said." Uzoma's eyes never left Amana's.

"Yes, Ayo." Amana feigned remembrance. "He was a vital person for the investigation. An investigation that could lead to the discovery of your son and the young girls."

"I'm fully aware of this." There was an edge to Uzoma's voice now. Then, it turned ice cold. "What is the meaning of this conversation, Amana?"

Amana whistled. After a short moment, Nya kicked in the door with her bow drawn. The Bajok warriors were already laid out unconscious. Uzoma did not even look up to her—though he smiled—as Esi covered her stomach instinctively.

"Do you have any idea what you're doing, boy?" Uzoma said with an even voice.

"Not quite, but I feel as though I'm getting close." Amana lifted himself from his chair, taking another victorious sip of his drink. "You still haven't answered my question."

"Yes."

"Yes?" Amana pushed out his lips. "Yes to what?"

"What you'll ask. 'Do you know what happened to Ayo?' The answer is yes, I know."

"And what happened to Ayo, then?" Amana asked. He felt his heartbeat in his fingertips. Nya had complete focus on Uzoma, her eyes narrowed.

"I killed him," Uzoma said.

Nya drew her arrow back further. Esi gasped, her eyes darting from Amana to her husband. Amana stood, placing a hand on Nya's arrowhead.

"Why?" was all Amana asked.

"Because he knew too much."

"About the kishi?"

"Yes, about the damned kishi."

"Do you know where they are now? Are you hiding them in the Rocks?" Amana asked.

Uzoma laughed. It took Amana aback. He had never heard Uzoma laugh before—at least not like this. It was just like his dream. It was almost ... inhuman.

"For a moment there, I thought you knew." Uzoma still chuckled. "The kishi are not hiding in the rocks. Not for many years now."

"Tell us where Shanaki is!" Nya blurted out.

"Oh, she is a feisty one, isn't she?" Uzoma beamed. "In another lifetime, young one, you could have been the one.

"As you know, I'm an empath, Amana. I can not only sense others' emotions; I can control them too. Did you think I could not tell you were hiding something from me? I'll admit, you did a good job of cloaking yourself, but you were trying too hard to do so. You gave me no read at all, which is more jarring than if you had been nervous." Amana gulped. Esi rocked in her chair as though she were about to have a seizure. "And right now, I'm controlling my wife from blurting out something very stupid."

Amana looked at Esi more closely. It did seem as though his wife was being controlled. That could have been the reason she seemed so unnaturally docile. "But I'll say it for her so she can rest easy. There is something about the kishi I did not tell you earlier. You see, all kishi are empaths. Some better than others."

Amana shook his head. "So what you're saying is ..."

"*Dikala!*" Nya cut in.

"I'm a man of peace, Amana. And that peace comes by way of control—*utter* control." Uzoma took his time with his last words. "This village, it is mine. These people, they are mine. Yes, Amana. I am a kishi. And not just any kishi. I am *the* kishi."

Nya didn't need to hear any more. In an instant, she let her arrow loose.

But Uzoma anticipated this. He dropped straight into the sway of Ugara, in a balance more perfect than even Kojo.

This did not dissuade Nya, who already had another arrow ready to go. But this time, Uzoma showed his true form. With a bone-crunching sound, he morphed almost instantly.

Uzoma didn't need a full head of hair because he was able to hide the hyena's snout under his skin. He was powerful enough to control the demon spirit, to hide it when it was not needed. And he had been strong enough to subvert the shaman's magic around the village. What other strengths did he possess? Amana didn't think Nya could do anything to overcome him.

Before Uzoma could pounce at Nya, Amana slammed his shoulder into the elder, shoving him back into his altar. The statues, water, and food that sat atop it fell over in a crash.

Unfortunately, Amana didn't realize he had pushed Uzoma next to his collection of spears. The elder stood back up without missing a beat, lifting the shaft of one of the spears, using it as half-man and half-hyena interchangeably, flipping his body from back to front. It was bizarre. In one moment, he was attacking Nya on all fours with the hyena-side, and then in the next moment, he was bipedal, attacking her more conventionally as a human-form with his spear.

Amana had seen this type of fighting before but only between shape-shifters. Fights between them were often split between human and animal form depending on the situation—and the benefit of each transformation. But Uzoma was fluid in his hybrid form, using both human and hyena as one unit. It was not a battle of two to one, with him and Nya facing Uzoma. It was a fight between two and two—and as it was, Amana and Nya were outmatched.

Nya did not seem to be deterred by this at all, shooting arrows faster than Amana had ever seen her shoot them before. Her aim was true, but Uzoma never allowed her to hit his softer human form, letting the arrows bounce off his demon back and turning around to attack her with his spear.

Amana tried his best to simply not get himself killed. He didn't have a weapon, but he had been able to stop Uzoma from landing a blow on Nya. Uzoma was going too fast for Amana's short-sight so he could not direct Nya's action. He could barely evade Uzoma on his own. Amana suspected this wasn't even Uzoma at his best, as he continued to suppress his wife's mood, keeping her away from the fight.

"Get back, Esi!" Uzoma shouted, his voice more guttural now.

Esi tucked herself away deeper into the hut, away from the fight. Nya took that split-second to land an arrow in Uzoma's human side. The arrow sank deep into his rib. With an unnatural movement, Uzoma cracked his arm back into his human form, taking the arrow out.

But that was a mistake.

Nya had warned Ayo before, but Uzoma had not been around to hear about Ya-Seti arrows. One needed a very specific tool to take the arrows out without injury. Now Amana saw why that was the case.

When Uzoma pulled out the arrow, he did far more damage than when it went in. Along with the arrowhead, Uzoma pulled out what looked like muscle. His side was pooling with blood and oozing part of his intestines.

Nya smiled, letting another arrow loose. Uzoma blocked it with his kishi hand. Then he turned towards Esi, snatching her between his teeth by the back of her gomesi dress. With his wife in his jaw like a lion cub, Uzoma swung his arm at the chair and table where his tea still sat. The furniture flew towards Nya, who was forced to duck out of the way. Amana was the last thing between the door and Uzoma. Bravely—or stupidly—he stood his ground.

Uzoma ran straight at Amana on all fours. Amana scooped up the pot of boiling water, using his sight to time it just right. Just as Uzoma swiped at Amana's neck, Amana pivoted, letting the beast pass, but not before he poured the hot water straight into Uzoma's wound.

Both Uzoma's hyena and human head screamed in unison. In a blind rage, the old man spun around, still with his wife under his jaw, to smack Amana right across the face. Amana flew back into the wall, his entire body aching and the wind completely knocked out of him.

Uzoma started to launch himself at Amana again when Nya sunk another arrow into the wound. That was enough for Uzoma, so he turned around and burst through his front door, running away into the morning light.

Amana's breath was harsh as he choked on his own breath, unable to catch it.

"No, no, no, Mana, breathe." Nya came to him. "You're not done yet. Take deep breaths. Focus on your stomach. Yes, like that. There you go."

Amana stopped panting, letting his stomach expand.

"Did you break anything?"

Amana tried to lift himself up. He was bruised—that was for sure—but nothing felt broken, miraculously.

"I don't think so," he said through his gasps.

"Good." Nya nodded with a hand on his cheek. "It's time to run."

"What?" Amana exclaimed. Nya was already out of the door, continuing the chase for Uzoma. Amana jogged behind her with a limp.

CHAPTER 15

INTO THE CAVERNS

Nya led the way while Amana hobbled behind. Nya followed the blood trail Uzoma was leaving behind. Amana was still recovering from his disbelief—and his bumps and bruises.

It still did not make sense. The image played in his mind on repeat. The dislocated bones set in unnatural ways, the way Uzoma bounded away with his wife between his mouth. It was all so wrong. But none of it affected Nya.

"Hurry up, Amana," Nya said. "He'll get away if you keep that pace."

Amana set himself into a hurried jog, though Nya was nearly in a full dash. She would have gone into a full sprint if it weren't for the twisted rock path of the Black Rocks. The image of Uzoma distracted Amana as he tried to keep up with the twists and turns.

"With this kind of blood trail, he's sure to pass out before too long," Nya said over her shoulder.

"If these kishi bleed as we do," Amana noted.

"Let's hope for both our sakes they do. He was incredibly fast.

I'm not sure how we would be able to fight him at full strength, even with your sight."

Amana agreed. Uzoma was even faster than the other kishi he had faced before. He was a master at work. If he hadn't pulled Nya's arrow out the way he did—and wounded himself in the process—there was little Amana or Nya could have done. Now Amana knew why he was the noteworthy warrior that he was. They were lucky to be alive.

"We should go back to the village for support," Amana said.

"And lose this trail? That's not happening. Why aren't you angrier? You trusted the dikala," Nya said as she ducked a low hanging branch.

"I want to see him brought to justice, but we have to be smart about this."

"He wouldn't have run off if he thought he could take us."

"Only because his wife was there," Amana noted.

"Well, good thing he's carrying her through these rocks then."

She had a point there. The insight gave Amana a new resolve. Nya reminded him of Asha again. Nya mirrored flashes of his late wife's spirit from time to time, radiating a vibe that said no one could mess with her or her squad. And Amana knew there was more to their relationship than two partners that needed to stop an enemy.

"No!" Nya said as she stopped running. Amana almost ran straight into her back. "No. No. No. Where is the trail?"

Amana looked around; it was gone. Just a few paces behind were the blood paw prints. But a few paces ahead they turned into the rocks and then ... simply vanished.

"Did he climb the rock side?" Amana asked, looking up. But he knew the answer was no.

"Do these kishi fly as well?"

"I doubt it." Or at least Amana hoped they couldn't. No, something else was amiss.

"Wait, we've been here before, this clearing." Amana pointed to each of the rocks' top-side edges.

"You're right." Nya followed his finger. "This is where we found the First Son and his guard."

"There has to be something about this place." Amana stroked his beard between forefinger and thumb. He pulled out his Boism instrument, sitting down for meditation.

"No, Mana, this is not the time for your monk practice."

"Shhh, this isn't practice." Amana closed his eyes, focusing all his attention towards the Gods' Glass and the stone within it. It did not take long for Amana to find the balance. Now, it felt as though the ball did not move at all. Like Uzoma had shown him, he did not just move with its energy, he imposed his will on it, locking it in place with an energy he could not name—something between determination and passion.

The power drew his mind to the spirits who whispered to him, their archaic language now intelligible. Amana opened his eyes, and the answer was clear to him, written in plain text across one rock wall:

I have two bodies that are joined in one. The more I stand, the quicker I run.

"What the hell did you just say?" Nya said.

"Was I speaking the Gods' Tongue again?"

"I think so."

"Good."

The glowing words seemed like some sort of riddle. The answer, Amana suspected, would open whatever hidden passage was within.

"A lot of these crags and crevices seem to have entrances. What we saw before were other proverbs, but we never gave the right answers to pass through. I thought they were just words that the kishi used for religious purposes."

"Like the Tablets of Truth from Ya-Seti?" Nya asked.

"Something like that. But these aren't just passages extracted for moral reasoning or reminder. It's a security system."

"You mean all these rock structures ..."

"I think so," Amana said, gazing behind them to all the other rocks they passed. "This isn't just a place kishi came to hide. This was their home. Some of them might still be here."

"Like Uzoma. So what's the password?" Nya lifted her bow. What if all the rocks held even more kishi? They were completely boxed in if other kishi were hiding in the rocks.

"I don't know," Amana confessed. "It says 'I have two bodies that are joined as one.'"

"Easy, a kishi," Nya blurred out.

"I thought that at first, too, but there is no way it's that simple."

"Did you even try?" Nya said with a tilted head. "Open kishi! Kishi open! Kishi! Kishi! Kishi!"

Nya turned to Amana, who was smirking. "Fine, read the rest of that thing."

"The rest of it says 'the more I stand, the quicker I run.'" Amana recited.

"That's almost as confusing as when you were talking in the Old Tongue."

Amana pondered the riddle. What ran quicker when it stood?

"What about a river?" Amana offered.

"Rivers don't run," Nya said with a raised eyebrow.

"They do if you think about it as a metaphor. Remember, we have to think about it figuratively."

"Ugh, I hated these riddles in school. Scholars can keep their riddles, I'll stick to my bow."

"Right now, a learned person is kicking our ass." Amana started to pace. "No really, think on it. Rivers run. They can have two bodies that meet as one at a fork. And if they 'stand' on the side of a mountain, they run down. The taller the hill or mountain, the faster they 'run.' And it even has the look of a standing person. A long neck with two legs at the bottom."

"Sounds good to me."

Amana turned to the words glowing on the rock side and said the word. But there was no response.

"Oh, come on, that was as good of a guess as any." Nya scoffed.

"But it was not the right answer. Maybe I should go a more literal route."

"Let me try," Nya stepped in. "The captains in Ya-Seti have always said that a warrior and their weapon are two entities that work as one. And the longer we stand on logs during exercises, the stronger we become. We run faster."

"I'm not following. What's your guess?"

"A fighter and their weapon."

"But what about the standing and running?"

"Well, our weapons, they ..." Nya stuttered over her answer. "Our spears stand and—and ... damnit, I don't know!"

Nya kicked the dirt. Amana was frustrated as well, but he knew being flustered would not help the situation. In truth, he thought his first attempt would have revealed something. And he couldn't think of anything else that would match up. What would the Junga monks have done?

"He's going to get away." Nya punched her palm. "We don't have enough time for this."

"That's it!"

"What is it? What did I say?"

"Time, that's the clue!" Amana beamed. "You're a genius Nya! What has two bodies that relate to time?"

"A clock."

"What kind of clock?"

"I don't know."

"The kind that runs faster when it stands."

"Stop it with the riddles! We have to catch that old man!"

"Sorry—sorry, it seemed obvious to me." Amana turned to the wall and involuntarily spoke the Gods' Tongue: "*Hourglass.*"

The rock began to split in two. Amana would have never known the crease was there. It was almost seamless, a perfect cut between the rock.

"So, what was the password?" Nya asked as the passage opened.

"An hourglass."

"Those timepieces with the sand?"

"That's the one."

"Good thing you're here. I would have never guessed that."

"I'm surprised I guessed it myself." Amana went back to put his Boism instrument away, but his pack was darkened in a thick shadow. When had the sun gone down? When Amana looked up, he saw what had blocked out the sun.

"Could this door open any slower?" Nya said with a huff.

"Uh, Nya, I think I'll take your dagger now," Amana said. Nya turned around, following Amana's gaze. At the top of the opposite end of the rock structure was a score of skeletal demons.

"What the hell are those?" Nya asked.

"Demon animations."

One of the skeletons led the rest. It wore a feathered crown, brandishing a large and pointed spear. With a demonic scream, the rest of the skeletons poured over the rock cliff into the canyon. They climbed over each other, bounding towards Nya and Amana. Nya let arrow after arrow loose into the skeletons, but they kept coming—even without their heads.

"This I can do. I'll take the undead over riddles any day."

Amana unsheathed Nya's dagger from her belt and went to work, cutting through any skeleton that was reckless enough to come at him. But every time he smashed them apart, they came back to life.

"They won't die!" said Amana. "These undead are meant as a nuisance. They'll just tire us out. They won't stop," Amana shouted over his shoulder as he dodged one of the skeletons. "What do your academies say about the Cursed?"

Nya ducked under an attack from the skeleton wearing the feathered crown. "I don't remember much about the Cursed. There was a saying—how did it go?"

"Meeting with the Cursed can turn out dire," Amana said, smashing through the knee of a skeleton. Despite it losing a leg the demon dragged itself closer to him.

"But they cannot resist heat of fire," Nya finished the saying, still evading the skeleton with the feathered crowned. It never stopped coming.

"Is your elemental magic with fire as good as it is with earth?"

"We'll see," Nya shouted back, putting her bow on her back. She brushed her hands together and streams of flame streaked between her fingers. She caught the skeleton with the feathered crowned. The fire blacked the bone, making it brittle with hints of ash, but the demon kept coming, undeterred.

"They're too strong for my magic!" Nya shouted.

"It's time to leave this party. Retreat to the door, it's already closing." Amana made his way back toward the cavern's threshold, but the skeleton with the feathered crown—now only arms and torso—clutched at his ankle. Amana fell back-first. Pain sheared through his spine, aggravating his already aching back. Despite the pain, Amana kicked at the skeleton as more surrounded him.

"Amana!" Nya shouted from the threshold.

"Go on! Get Uzoma. I can't get out." He swung his dagger at an oncoming skeleton. It shattered at the ankle but kept coming with its arms.

"Damnit, Amana!" Nya started to brush her hands together vigorously until there was a ball of fire between her hands. When she lifted her hands, Amana lost sight of her. Skeleton arms and legs start pounding on his exposed flesh. Amana blocked many of the skeletons that wielded their own sabers and daggers, but some of their strikes and slashes were finding their targets, splitting skin.

Just as one knife looked as though it would pierce Amana's heart, a roaring blaze soared over Amana. The top layer of the skeleton pile turned to ash. The lower half was burnt enough that they stopped clawing at him. At his side, Amana saw Nya at the cavern's threshold, looking as though she had run several leagues.

"Get … over … here …" she managed to say.

Amana kicked off the nearest skeletal arm before getting up. The rock doors were only a few paces apart now. Amana limped his way to the cave, desperately trying to reach it in time. He barely managed to squeeze himself through the slit before it closed, though one of the skeleton's hands—still connected to its spine and pelvic bone—held onto his leg.

The magic that held it together seemed to disappear within the cave. It no longer clawed at Amana's ankle. But now it was pitch black. Nya snapped her fingers, and a flame appeared between them.

"That was brilliant," Amana said, grabbing a torch from the cave's wall. "I haven't seen a fireball that large since the Jultia sieges."

"I couldn't let them get you. If anyone gets to kill you, it's me." Nya smiled as she lit the end of Amana's torch. When he lifted the light to her face, Amana saw the sweat dripping into her eyes.

"Are you going to be okay?" he said, placing a hand on her shoulder.

"I'll be all right," she said. "Just need to take a breather—" Nya's eyes were distracted by the skeleton torso—which seemed to twitch.

"These bones," Amana stepped on the pelvic bone to stop its residual movement, "these bones are of a woman."

"How can you tell?"

"It's the pelvic bone. Females have a wider bone and smoother structure." Amana pointed the differences out with his finger.

"Who were they?"

"I'm not sure," Amana said. "But let's find out. We know Uzoma went through here."

Amana pointed to the empty torch holder and the blood trail that led deeper into the cave.

AMANA AND NYA WALKED THROUGH THE ROCK STRUCTURE which looked less and less like a natural cavern and more like a deliberate infrastructure. There was a stream running down one of its sides, possibly an off-shoot from the Nyoka river to the south. The air was cool, but not freezing. The cavern was not entirely man-made. Some of the corridors simply led from one unconnected cavern to another. This cave was not unlike the ones pirates hid themselves away in throughout the Sapphire Isles.

Eventually, they happened upon cave paintings. They were crude and primitive, nothing out of the ordinary from what Amana had seen before. The typical depictions of hunters chasing large game, the occasional painting of prehistoric people fighting the large monsters that once roamed the lands.

"How did you know about that bone stuff with the women?" Nya asked.

"Just a hunch." Amana shrugged. "The bone structures of a man and woman are quite different when you look close enough."

Nya's raised an eyebrow. "But how do you *know* what to look for with just bones?"

"Could you help light this area here?" Amana asked, ignoring her question.

Nya walked over to Amana and held her manifested flame above his head. The light showed a new kind of art—less primitive, though the tools used were just as crude. Amana suspected it was blood.

"It's telling a story, I think." Amana pointed at the first image, which depicted two large hands crafting animals and humans one by one, a hybrid being.

"The Supreme One?" Nya questioned.

"I don't think so. The Supreme is usually denoted by his ring of power. These hands are bare. It has to be one of the lesser Gods, I'm just not sure which. My guess would be the shape-shifting God. What was his name?"

"Beats me. I don't spend much time in the temples," Nya said. "What's he doing?"

"It looks like he's trying to create his first subject." Amana traced his finger across the next set of drawings.

"Wait, no." Nya lowered her light to show more of the drawing. "This can't be the shape-shifting God; they had special rings, too, right?"

"Right." Amana agreed. "This had to be the work of some other entity. But whatever it is, it seemed to have failed many times. Look at the art here." Amana pointed to the portion of the drawing showing dead humans and animals in bloody and grotesque poses.

"Wait, this could be the beginning of the God's war, look there." Amana pointed at another portion of the painting, where the many Gods battled each other in the skies. But the hands still went to work beneath them in secret.

"Why doesn't the artist ever show the God's face?" Nya asked.

"Maybe no one knew what the God looked like," Amana said. "Look there, this is definitely the war. That's the Massacre of the Meteor."

"And there's our little guy fleeing and … oh, he does have a figure, but he's more a shadow now." Nya pointed. The hands were now a shadow with human hands. The shadow inserted itself into a hyena.

"The first kishi," Amana gasped.

The picture went on to show the figure take human form, with a hyena head still protruding from the back of its head. Over time, hair grew to hide the hyena and the human form began to interact with other humans—particularly women.

"This is how it all started, then." Nya waved her torch farther down the cave.

The next set of images depicted this first kishi charming a woman, marrying her and eventually having a child with her. But the next set of images set Amana and Nya on edge. It was the most gruesome childbirth either of them had ever seen. A hyena cub chewed through the woman's stomach and then proceeded to eat its mother whole. Then it trotted straight into the hands of the beastly father. And the art showed this happening again and again and again until there was an army of them, and they ruled over all.

"Esi is in more danger than I thought." Amana realized, standing in front of the bloody mess that depicted the kishi birthing cycle. "We have to get to her now."

"She's as good as dead," Nya said. "The best thing to do is to kill that beast inside her and give her a quick death."

"Let's worry about the details when we catch up. The blood trail isn't lost."

"No, no, no, not that way, he'll kill you," a voice squeaked behind them. Nya turned around with fire, ready to throw the flame at the interloper. Amana held his dagger out in front of him.

"Who's there?" Amana shouted into the darkness of the cave.

"Kwachi means you no harm!" the voice squeaked again. "Kwachi has been in these caverns many years, I know why you are here. But no one ever gets out."

"Show yourself," Nya said.

"Only if you promise not to burn Kwachi, sweet woman."

"That depends on a few things."

"What do you mean no one gets out?" Amana asked.

"Kwachi knows what happened to Ayo. It will happen to all of us. There is no stopping them. No, no. No stopping them," the voice continued squeaking, the sound reverberating off the cave walls.

"How do you know Ayo?" Amana asked again.

The figure showed itself. It was a hyena, a fully-formed hyena, a shape-shifter, not a kishi. But it seemed like this hyena had not seen the sun for many, many years. Its fur was almost colorless, a shade of ash-gray, with patches of skin showing through thinning hair.

"Ayo was Kwachi's brother," the hyena spoke, its squeaking voice matching its look. "He and Kwachi are servants of the Great and Mighty Elder Uzoma."

Amana and Nya looked cautiously to one another.

"Kwachi calls himself Kwachi," the hyena form said to them. Like his brother Ayo, he was very twitchy, never looking either Amana or Nya in the eye for too long. "Kwachi can show you the way to the Great and Mighty Elder."

Amana did not trust the shape-shifter, but he did not have much of a choice.

"You can tell us the way, and we'll take it from there," Amana said.

Nya nodded in agreement, she seemed ready to throw her flame at Kwachi—no matter how exhausted she was.

"These chambers are ever-changing to ward off the bad people. But you two are not the bad people, are you? Kwachi can see this. Kwachi could tell you the way to go now, but 'now' is not always in this place. The rocks like to change."

"What do you mean?" asked Nya.

"The Great and Mighty Elder has many nasty friends who've helped him enchant this cavern. He's had help from some of his wives, too, but some of them weren't easy to convince."

"What do you mean *wives?*" Amana asked. "You make it sound like he had more than two before Esi."

"Oh, the master has taken many, many wives over the years.

There was Bosede, Onyeka, Yewande, Folami—the other Folami—Ebele, Chioma—"

"Does he have Esi?" Amana asked, cutting Kwachi off.

"Yes, he's taken her into the main chamber. She will have another of his sons soon, within the week. Quite a shame. The Great and Mighty loved this one truly. She was an oh so special mystic. A perfect part of his grand plan."

"A mystic? What is her magic?" Amana never sensed anything in her.

"She can speak to minds." Kwachi grinned.

"Those are rare," Nya said.

"She also has the sight."

"She's Twice Blessed?" Amana asked.

"Those are *really* rare," Nya added with a raised brow.

"Extremely," Kwachi agreed.

"Shanaki is Twice Blessed as well," Nya said to Amana. "But she needs a lot of work with both her magical abilities."

"Esi's abilities are quite special," Kwachi said through his slack jaw. "She knew you would come to us." Kwachi nodded to Amana. "She has the long sight, the longest the Great and Mighty has ever seen."

"Why endanger her with a pregnancy, then?" Amana asked.

"You, sir."

Uzoma had known Amana was coming all along? Why had Uzoma made Amana go through training to prove his worth when his future-telling wife knew Amana would pass all his tests?

"Why help us?" Nya asked.

"The Great and Mighty Uzoma has gone mad," Kwachi answered. "He's never been kind to Kwachi, never kind to poor Ayo. He's grown more evil in his old age. He knows he only has so much time before his days are gone. Ayo was the last straw. He did not have to kill him; he wouldn't've talked."

"Oh, he would have talked," Nya said, cracking her knuckles.

"What of Yejide? Do you know if Ikenna took her?" Amana asked.

"No, not even the master knows. But he thinks his son took the Ya-Seti princess. Ikenna means to challenge him with his own powerful bride."

"But Uzoma has a wife with the long-sight, he should see where his son went," Amana noted.

"Remember, I told you Shanaki is special," Nya said. "She's a dampener."

"Magical suppression?" Amana asked. "That's why she was to be married to this village?"

"Right." Nya nodded. "And it's why there's a good chance she's all right. The kishi wouldn't be able to transform around her—if she wills it."

"Yes, that was most troubling for the master," said Kwachi. "He was so frustrated when he could not find the girl." Kwachi turned to Nya. "Master thought Ikenna was hiding that Ya-Seti Princess. But it must be the girl who is hiding them. Ikenna is probably forcing her to do this. Master was very displeased with that. That's when Kwachi got this." He tilted his head down to show a gash across his eye.

"Why punish you? It wasn't your fault." Amana tilted his head to see the shape-shifter's scar better.

"Kwachi never questions the Great and Mighty. He does as he wishes, and Kwachi serves. But this servant will serve no longer, not when his brother is dead. Some things cannot be forgiven."

"Revenge is one of the strongest human—er—animal emotions," Nya said.

"All right, then, Kwachi, lead the way." Amana gestured.

The hyena-shifter turned and walked down the rest of the cavern path.

"You can change back to human form whenever you like," Nya suggested.

"Oh no, Kwachi has not walked on his human legs for years now. And human eyes are no good in the dark."

He had a point. His steps were not like his brother's. He did not have that distinctive tread that bipedal humans had when trying to imitate quadrupedal animals. His hyena walk was as natural as the real thing.

Kwachi walked with confidence even in the dark. Amana suspected Nya was afraid of losing him by the way she tailed his back legs. Amana kept his short-sight active, though he sensed nothing that suggested Kwachi wanted to make a run for it. His words seemed to be as honest as his actions.

There were several passages Amana would have never seen had it not been for Kwachi, and the cave did move around, folding itself into a labyrinth. Kwachi navigated the caverns with no trouble at all, proving the integrity of his words.

"It was the third wife that really helped build this place. You met her outside. She was the skeleton queen with the feathered crown. She was one of the few who actually went along with the master. She was willing to sacrifice herself. Not very powerful, she was not a mystic, but she had a lot of loyalty. The master loves that. She was a genius architect, as you can see. Earned herself all those mathematic beads from that academy up north."

They turned down another set of carved corridors. The cave must have been at least a league underground. There were more carvings on the walls. Some depicted humans with hyena heads, probably the intention of the original Creator—shape-shifting done right.

Finally, they arrived at an open chamber. The dome was about one-hundred paces high with a hole at the top. It was still daylight outside, and the sun was peeking through. The chamber was spotted with open crevices, radiant with a spotlight at its center that was cast from the ceiling's hole above. There was one huge stone structure—thirty yards wide—in the middle, surrounded by a gap all around, almost like a moat, except instead of water, there was nothing but an empty abyss. There were only two entrances, the drawbridge that led onto the stone slab, and the bridge on the other side, which led out of it.

"The master is just past this chamber," Kwachi said, walking across the unbalanced bridge.

"I don't know about this. Doesn't feel right," Amana said.

"We'd be trapped on that platform," Nya agreed.

"You would have been trapped anywhere else in this place, in much tighter confines. If Kwachi wanted to trap you, he would trap you," the hyena-shifter noted.

That was fair enough. It was true that they had passed narrow passages that would have been perfect for a trap. Just cave in the top rock, and they'd be goners. The blood trail had dried up once they followed Kwachi, so Uzoma was likely healed, wherever he was.

"You go ahead," Nya said to Amana. "I can cover you from here if anything happens."

Amana nodded and followed Kwachi across, maintaining his focus. Nothing seemed amiss. But there was something far off, a sort of fluttering. It sounded like wings echoing off the cavern walls. Then came the screams.

"Oh no," Kwachi said.

"What does 'oh no' mean? What is that sound?" Amana asked.

"Kongamatos."

"Bullshit! Those things have been gone for centuries!" Nya shouted from her position.

"The Great and Mighty has been breeding them for decades. They are to be the vanguard of his kishi army. He knows we're close. He must be desperate. Most of them are no more than infants—far from being battle-ready."

The screams grew louder, echoing off the cave's walls. The first one to appear was a great big thing, the size of four large men, with a multicolored beak of red, yellow, and orange. Its beak was spiked with large teeth as it yelled its animal call. Its body was furred like a bat, and each of its talons was the size and shape of a sickle sword. But it was shackled by a long chain, thankfully.

"These things were supposed to have died off with the last ancient beasts in the Kunda War," Amana said.

"Most of them were, but the master nurtured a few still hiding in the depths, such as these."

"How have they survived? They are supposed to be creatures that feast on rivers and swamps." Amana ducked behind a loose rock.

"He keeps them well-fed. But they seem rather hungry."

At least a dozen smaller kongamatos followed what Amana assumed was the mother. It was hard to tell how many there actually were with their fluttering wings. Amana felt very under-equipped with just his dagger.

"Only the big one is chained," Amana noticed.

"They all follow the mother. No need to chain up the children. Kwachi suggests you take better cover."

The mother came straight down for Amana, beak spread wide for her next meal. Before she could snap her beak over Amana's head, a flaming arrow skidded across her face. Nya sat atop her perch, enchanting her arrowheads with magical flame. As the mother-beast careened to the side, her children followed.

"Focus on that big one," Nya shouted down to Amana. "The little ones keep following it. They'll follow exactly what she does."

"What do you expect me to do with a dagger?" Amana shouted back. Nya shrugged.

Amana was sure she was thinking how silly it was that he never brought proper weapons with him. He was starting to agree. Despite his monk training, perhaps it would have made sense to carry at least a sword at his side—if he kept crossing paths with demons and ancient beasts.

The mother kongamato doubled back. This time, she aimed for Nya, who continued to shoot fire-arrow after fire-arrow. But like the kishi, the kongamato's hide was too thick.

"Quick, move to your left!" Amana warned Nya as he saw the flash of the mother beast's attack. Nya rolled just in time; the kongamato only snapped at air. As it turned to swipe at Nya again, it hit a loose rock that crashed down on the drawbridge, cutting off their exit.

"Any help here would be nice!" Amana shouted to Kwachi. "How do we defeat these things?"

Kwachi was too busy keeping himself alive, dodging the attacks of the flying beasts as they followed behind their mother. Kwachi doubled-back when one of the smaller creatures came too close. In Kwachi's retreat, he hit Amana hard across the legs. Amana fell to the stone floor, reminded of the pain in his back once again.

Moons! Can I not fall on my back anymore, he thought through his aching movements.

With Amana vulnerable, the mother came barreling straight down at him, screaming that terrible call. Amana could see the flash of her attack, but he had no means of actually evading her in time. Flaming arrows still shot at the kongamatos, but they were undeterred. One arrow, however, found its mark in the mother's eye. The mother screamed a horrifying cry, still falling straight at Amana.

"Amana get out of there!" Nya shouted. But he couldn't. His muscles ached in protest. Just as the great beast was about to smash into the ground, Kwachi pushed Amana out of the way. Amana rolled and rolled, nearly to the edge of the rock structure's edge, looking down into the endless pit. Kwachi cleared out of the way too, avoiding a crushing blow from the kongamato.

The mother lay dead—Nya's arrow had found a weak point through the beast's eye. The other flying beasts immediately flew back into the crevices. Without a mother, they would need to find a new leader.

"He's leading us to a trap," Nya said as she ran to Amana's side, pulling him away from the edge.

"Kwachi would never! Kwachi wants the master dead! He treats us like dirt, and he should be returned to it!"

"You knocked Amana down. He wouldn't have been in that situation if you hadn't rammed into him like that." Nya held Kwachi at arrow point.

"Kwachi saved the good man! He saved him!"

"He did, Nya." Amana finally got to his feet. "He knocked me down, that's true, but that beast was about to crush me under its weight. I'm only alive *because* Kwachi pushed me out of its path."

Nya frowned, shaking her head. "I don't trust him. Something is off about him."

"You can trust Kwachi," the shape-shifter said again.

"Prove it. You should know a way out of here." Nya pointed to where Kwachi said Uzoma had been, across the cavern where the bridge had fallen.

"The bridge is gone! There is nothing Kwachi can do." Kwachi turned to Amana for support. "Please, you know I saved you."

"I don't know what he's playing at, Mana." Nya glared at Kwachi. "But you didn't see his eyes when he pushed you. It did not look like he was trying to save you."

Amana turned back to Kwachi. "Get us out of here, Kwachi." Amana's voice was cold. The shape-shifter did not meet his eye.

"Kwachi can jump across it but—but—"

"I don't want to hear it," Amana said. "Jump."

Kwachi was reluctant to move, but he obeyed, his head held down. He sniffed at the rock's edge, judging the distance between the gap. After a few moments, he decided it was manageable. The shape-shifter stepped back a few strides, ready for a running start. Then he was off, galloping as fast as he could. When he reached the edge, he pushed off with all four legs.

He's not going to make it, Amana thought.

Kwachi's front legs reached the other side of the gap, but his back legs hung below the edge. Without human hands, it was hard for him to grip.

"Use your hands, Kwachi!" Amana shouted. "Your hands!"

Kwachi almost forgot he was half human, whimpering a hyena's cry. But then he transformed his paws into fingers, lifting himself over the edge. At first, it sounded like he was screaming for joy—happy to be alive. But the scream was more like laughter. The laughter of a hyena.

"The master will get you good for this." He chuckled that horrible hyena sound. His hand transformed back into a paw, pressing into one of the stones near the open crevice—a collapsing point. The cavern began to fall all around, their exit blocked, the way they came cut off. They were trapped on all sides with no way out.

"You know what, fuck these kishi," said Nya.

CHAPTER 16

NO WAY OUT

It did not take long for Nya to start looking for ways out. Amana knew it was futile; they were outsmarted. Uzoma may not have wanted them to follow, but he had the advantage—this was his turf, and he had set them up in a perfect trap.

"We did not have another choice," Amana said. "We would have lost the trail like you said."

Nya was testing the strength of the rocks that fell into the gap, using her elemental magic to break them apart, but she only managed to puncture small fissures. Her magic was all but expended. The fire blast she used against the demons—and as an augmentation for her arrows—had exhausted her energy.

"Can you climb this?" Nya asked.

"I don't think so. It's too jagged and too tall." Amana looked up at the cavern wall. Even if he had the strength to climb, the slope at the top would have been impossible to scale.

"Damnit!" Nya's voice echoed off the cavern wall. "Why aren't you helping?"

"It would be wasted energy," Amana sighed. "He means to wait us out, to have us weak."

"I just don't have anything that could help us here." Nya's shoulders slumped.

"What elements do you have control over?"

"Mostly rock, some fire, lightning—on an overcast day. I told you I'm not very impressive."

Amana looked at the rocks that had fallen from the cave-in trap.

They just might be big enough, he thought to himself.

"How confident are you with rock?" he said.

"It's the best magic I got."

"If we used one of these rocks as a platform, could you lift it a hundred paces to that opening?" Amana pointed to the cavern's top side.

"It would take some effort," Nya bit her lip, "but I could do it."

"Could you do it with one of us on it?"

Nya thought it over, pressing her hand to her temple. As Amana suspected, she couldn't.

"I wouldn't want to tire you further."

"I can do it!" she shot back. "Just … give me some time to rest."

"Would it be easier for me to get on or for you?"

"I'd say you. I'm lighter, but if I lift myself, I'll have to balance my body and the rock together. You're heavier, but if it's just you, you can balance yourself, and I can focus on the rock."

"All right, it's worth a try."

"But if I fail, you could hurt yourself pretty bad."

"Do you think you can do it?" Amana placed a hand on her shoulder, searching for an honest answer. It was his life on the line, after all.

"I think so," she answered after a pause.

"You know so. I believe in you," Amana said. Nya smiled at that. "But test some of the rocks out first. I'd rather not break my legs today." Nya's smile turned flat, and her eyes narrowed. She hit Amana across the chest, and Amana laughed. Joking aside, she did test out a few rocks she felt she could potentially lift. After a few minutes, she decided on one she liked.

"This one," she said. It was the smallest rock she could find that could still hold Amana comfortably. "This would have been much easier if one of us was a bird-shifter. If you have any other tricks up your sleeve, this would be the time."

"No, I've just got the sight. And like you, I'm not a master."

Nya frowned but sat herself down with her elbows on her knees. Her arms were tilted up, her thumb and forefinger pressed together.

"What are you doing?" Amana asked.

"I'm trying to meditate," Nya said, trying her best not to crack a smile. Amana was the first to snicker.

"You?" He tilted his head down. "Meditate?"

"Shut up and let me be," she said with her eyes closed. Amana gave her space, trying his best not to criticize how tense her shoulders were—or how uneven her breathing had been. After a few moments, she opened her eyes again. "Let's get started, then."

Amana stood on the rock and waited. Nya concentrated.

"I should have taught you some of my meditation techniques properly."

"Too late," Nya said.

"We have to do this now. If we make it out, we'll want to be gone before nightfall."

"Agreed."

Nya lifted the rock under Amana slowly. Amana nearly slipped off but quickly found Nya's elemental hold on the rock. It reminded him of the balance he held with the Gods' Glass. Then it occurred to him that the meditation technique could benefit the situation.

"What are you doing?" Nya said, her hands oscillating control over the rock. "Don't move, it's hard enough moving you when you're still."

"I have an idea." Amana pulled the Gods' Glass from his pack, using his robe to hold it. What had Uzoma said about it? That it would make a man go mad if used improperly? "Do you have something to wrap your hand with?"

"Yes … why?" Nya said, her hands stretched out to the rock.

"I still have this." Amana lifted the stone, the light above glinting off the sliver in its center.

"I don't know how to use that monk-balance-thing you use," she said.

"You don't have to. The Gods' Glass should still elevate your abilities if you touch it. But you have to be careful …"

"What happens if I touch it?"

"I don't know exactly, but nothing good," said Amana. Nya bit her lip, straining under the weight of Amana and the rock. A moment passed before she ripped the tunic under her armor. She wrapped it around her hand.

"All right, throw it down." she lifted her hand. Amana dropped the stone. When it landed into Nya's hand, it snapped into her palm like a fish to bait. And then the rock platform that Amana stood on shot up twenty paces in the air. He nearly fell off the rock, caught off balance by the change in speed.

"Woah!" he shouted as he regained purchase with the platform. "Slow down!"

"Sorry, I didn't mean to!" Nya said with flushed cheeks. She held the stone with the ripped piece of her tunic. "I can feel everything in the rock, all the way to its center. I've never had this much control."

"Don't press too hard into its influence. It's very easy to lose control. You just as easily could have thrown me against the wall." Amana sat back down on the rock platform, concentrating on his balance.

"Less talking, more monk stuff." Where Nya had strained under the weight before, lines creasing in her forehead, now there was an ease to her elemental hold. She lifted Amana with little difficulty, and the rock gained more and more height.

As Amana rose higher, he heard voices. Was there someone at the top? When Amana strained his ears, he could not hear anything. Then he realized the voice came from within. The spirits must have been speaking to him again—that same female voice that he heard in his dreams. Who was speaking to him? Was it the Moon Sisters like Kojo said? Amana could not understand what the voice was telling him—the sound only a whisper. But when he neared the top of the cavern, unscathed and perfectly balanced, the voice grew louder and clearer.

Turn back, they are there! They are waiting for you, the voice shouted in his head.

Amana was elated to reach the top. Nya was beaming too. But Amana realized why he had been warned away.

Five kishi were waiting to meet him, their mouths ready to bite.

"Get me back down!"

"Why? You're almost there."

"Kishi! Five of them!"

"Damnit!"

Nya tried to adjust the rock's direction, but panic took her. The platform shot off to one side, crashing into the cavern's wall. And Amana fell.

One-hundred paces was a long fall, one that Amana knew would be lethal. He grabbed for the edges of the cave wall, but he was too far. All he could grasp was air. Nya went into overdrive, flinging small rocks in his path for him to grab onto. Amana managed to hold onto a couple but his grip kept slipping, and he continued to fall.

Amana flung his arms out, arching his back to slow his fall. The ground was still coming at him much too fast. One of Nya's rocks caught under his cloak, hanging in mid-air. But Amana's momentum was too great. Instead of hanging along with his cloak, he slipped out of it. He desperately snatched for the fabric, looking for any kind of hold. Just at the end of the cloth, right at the tip, he managed a tight grip. But his hold on the cloak did not end his descent. It only slowed it. The fabric eventually slipped through his fingers, but the fall was only fifteen paces instead of one-hundred. Still, Amana landed awkwardly on his shoulder, pain tearing through him.

"That was a bad idea," Amana sighed through pinched eyelids. The color in Nya's face was gone, but the lines in her forehead softened. She dropped the Gods' Glass to her side, and her shoulders relaxed.

"Damn these kishi," Nya said as Amana lay next to her on his back. He was bruised, but nothing seemed to be broken. That was one blessing. "Didn't think I would die like this."

"We're not dead yet," Amana said with his eyes closed. "He needs me to save his wife. He needs me to deliver his child. We still have value."

"I don't think he cares about that anymore."

"Those kishi could have killed me. They were playing with me."

"Uzoma can just get another wife."

"You heard Kwachi. She's special. He's waited a long while to impregnate her. He knew I would come. She's even more powerful than me, it seems."

"More powerful? I thought the difference between those with short and long-sight were different abilities." Nya lay next to Amana with her hand holding up her head.

"It's true. I liken it to someone who can sprint very fast—that's me and my short-sight—to someone who can carry on for leagues at a time—that's someone with long-sight. Those with short-sight are coveted for our abilities in combat—"

"Yes, I know about all that," Nya said. "Most of our mainland guard have the ability."

"Those with long-sight are a bit rarer. But for some, they are more valuable. Having a score of short-sighters in an army is well and good, but take that army and set them against even one gifted with long-sight, the long-seer will always win."

"Not always," Nya said. "Those with long-sight have to know what to look for, right? Their visions aren't omniscient."

"True. But Esi knows who to look for."

"Like I said, we're dead." Nya looked around the cavern, eyeing the silhouettes of the kishi that poked their head over the open gap above. She scowled at them.

"Uzoma's doing this to weaken us." Amana turned to her. "He's injured and needs to heal. He must be gathering reinforcements, probably forcing Esi to communicate with the other kishi. But I think he's locked himself in as well. We must have him cornered."

"So what's the plan?" Nya asked.

"We wait him out as best we can. You should rest first. We'll be here a while."

FOR THE FIRST FEW HOURS, IT WAS EASY ENOUGH FOR AMANA and Nya to sleep—both were completely exhausted from the day's efforts. Then night fell. It was cold beyond cold. It was the kind of cold that hurt, each brush of the wind like a dagger to the exposed forearm or calf. The rocks held no form of warmth, absorbing the freezing temperatures into themselves. But the cold wasn't so bad compared to the nasty laughter of the kishi, who were likely ordered to keep Amana and Nya awake.

On the second night, Nya finally accepted Amana's cloak—after he had offered it several times. Though his cloak was thick, Nya still shivered. And with the laughter of the hyena heads echoing throughout the chamber, it was impossible for her to sleep.

She drifted every so often. Amana knew it because her

breathing changed. When she was awake, her chest barely moved up and down, as though her heart stopped, as though she were prey sniffing for a predator, hyper-alert. But when she allowed herself to rest, she breathed easily—softly even. It was a new aspect of Nya Amana had never seen. She *almost* looked vulnerable, petite.

The moons' light was hitting her face just right, crafting highlights across her smooth cheekbones. Amana had never seen her face like this before. So peaceful, without a scowl or a furrowed brow or a joking smile, just stoic. Her nose was a nice shape, if a bit small, with freckled dots spotted under her eyes. The thickness of her lips favored the bottom. She truly did look like a lioness in human form, dark-red hair and all. When she did open her eyes—the hyena's laughter was too much—Amana was reminded of her golden-brown eyes as they twinkled in the moons' light. Nya was a beautiful woman, that much he was certain of. She was a fierce woman as well. A woman Amana once longed for, but had turned away from since ...

He could not stand seeing her so cold, shivering and waking every five minutes. She had held him the night before, nullifying his nightmares. It would only be courteous to do the same. He shifted his body next to hers, pressing himself close to her, arm wrapped around her middle. Amana squeezed firmly, just enough to lock in the heat around Nya, but not enough to disturb her sleep.

He did not remember when he fell asleep as well.

"WHY DID YOU FALL ASLEEP?" NYA'S VOICE WAS THE FIRST thing Amana heard. Morning had broke. Nya shoved Amana off of her, deep lines cut through her forehead.

"I—" Amana started. "Sorry, I shouldn't have."

"Uzoma could have come at any point in the night and done

whatever he pleased with us. Don't go soft on me now, Mana. We have to be alert." Nya turned away from him, taking the next watch.

THE WORST OF THE DAY WASN'T THE LACK OF FOOD OR WATER, but the boredom, Nya's weakness. She tried to start a conversation with Amana several times, but he spent most of the day meditating. Still, she persisted.

"Would you rather have no one show up for your wedding or your funeral?"

Amana rolled his eyes. It was another silly game Nya wanted to play, but he did not feel like playing along.

"Come on, Mana, we might die here. It wouldn't hurt to get to know one another, would it?"

"Funeral."

"Agreed." Nya smiled. Amana surprised himself. For hours he had only made rote responses from the Scroll of the Five. Perhaps boredom had caught up with him as well. "Why?" Nya asked.

"Doesn't really matter who shows up to my funeral. I won't be there to know."

"Hmm, I took you as the type to believe in the afterlife."

"I don't." Amana frowned.

"How does that work for the mountain monks? Are you allowed to be a non-believer?"

Amana shrugged.

"What kind of monk are you?" she asked.

"A bad one. My turn."

Nya sat up beaming, ready for a question from Amana.

"Would you rather find true love or have all the riches in the world?"

"All the riches," Nya said straight away.

"You don't believe in the power of true love?"

"Hardly. True love is a farce."

"You've never felt it, not once? There's been no man to capture your heart?" Amana asked. Nya rolled her eyes.

"I've been with many men, but none of them I would say I loved," Nya shrugged. "I suppose *you* have."

"I have," Amana said straight.

"And how was that for you?"

"It was the best thing to happen to me." Amana lowered his eyes.

"And the worst ..." Nya added. "Did she break your heart or something?"

"I wish that were so."

"What then?"

"It's your turn."

Amana knew this was not what Nya had in mind, of course. The game was meant to get answers out of him, not cryptic responses.

"Would you rather have an easy job working for someone else?" Nya asked. "Or have a very difficult job working for yourself?"

Amana frowned at this. "Another question."

"Nope." Nya denied him the out. "My question stands."

Amana was slow to respond. "I'd rather have an ... easy job working for someone else."

"That's a lie," Nya shot back.

"Maybe my life would have been better that way."

"What were you doing before all this anyway?" Nya cocked her head, her hair falling over one eye. She had finally let it down after the first night.

"Whatever earned me coin" was all Amana gave up.

"A criminal then?" Nya surmised. "Don't give me that look, I couldn't care less what you've done. I figured you were up to something like that before this whole monk thing. You have to do what you have to do in this world."

"Would you rather …" Amana thought his next question over. "Would you rather be deaf or blind?"

"Hmm, that's a hard one," Nya admitted. "That's a good one, Amana. See, we can have fun with this. It's just a game. No need to get all serious all the time. But let's see. Deaf or blind. I suppose deaf is the best answer, right? Who wants to go through life without being able to see anything? If I were deaf, I could at least still be useful to the Royal Guard, if they would still have me."

"Have you been in their service all your life?"

"Just about."

"How did you come into their service?"

Now Nya was the one to go cold.

"Come on, I thought this was just a game." Amana chuckled.

"I was a little girl." Nya swallowed. "At the time the Ya-Seti were in conflict with the Aktah just north. They raided the riverways where my family lived."

"You were fishermen?" Amana asked.

"Yes, on my mother's side. My father was from the south." Nya sat cross-legged. "When the Aktah came, there was no warning. They didn't come to attack us directly, but we were caught in the middle. You see, the Kor'de and her first daughter were traveling through the Ipe river that day. It was a leisure trip. Everyone knew about it. I sat on my father's shoulders to see them going by, just to catch a glimpse of what it was like to live the good life.

"When they came, it was fantastic. Their riverboat was beautiful, better than any of the boats we built. Perfectly crafted, painted blue and gold. And they were both so beautiful, Kor'de Neema and Shanaki. Shanaki was waving right at me when it happened …"

"What?" Amana asked.

"When they killed my father," she continued. "They shot him right in the back—an arrow through his heart. The dikala that got him was a terrible shot, wasn't even aiming at him. They were trying to shoot Shanaki."

"Any higher and they could have got you," Amana added.

"I would have rather it been that way," Nya said. "My father was a good man, a strong man. If he'd had the chance, he could have fought that archer, would have torn him to pieces. If I died, it wouldn't matter much. I was a bad kid. Always getting into all sorts of trouble."

Not much has changed, Amana thought. "I'm sure your parents would disagree," Amana said.

"Of course, they would. They were good people." Nya sat up, turning away from Amana.

"They got to your mother, too ..." Amana finished for her.

"After I fell off my father's shoulders, I dropped into the river. When I came back up, I saw my mother had been shot through, too. I still don't know who got to her.

"It was a stupid attack. The Kor'de had her best archers with her, and the Aktah were disorganized. As soon as it all started, the Kor'de's guard protected her. It didn't even look like the Aktah sent a full force. Some say it was a rogue unit that didn't agree with the peace treaty being signed. That attack alone almost caused the war to go on for another few years.

"They found most of the archers who were responsible. Captured them and everything. When I saw the big guy who killed my father, I went straight for him. The Ya-Seti guard stopped me, easily of course, but Shanaki stepped forward, told them to let me through. I said how that man was the one who killed my father, possibly my mother, too. Kor'de Neema deferred to Shanaki. She was already learning how to rule even back then.

"Shanaki asked what I wanted. I said I wanted to kill the man myself. I was surprised she wasn't shocked to see a young girl ask something like that. I was no more than seven or eight then. Shanaki was twelve. But she let me have my wish. Didn't even bat an eye. The Kor'de objected at first. Shanaki told her it was her personal decision and it was final. And with that, the Kor'de let her decision go through."

"How did you kill the man?" Amana asked. "You were only a little girl."

"With my gift, of course." Nya turned back to Amana. "The guard thought the same as you. How can such a little girl do anything? That's probably why the Kor'de agreed initially. She thought I'd just hit the man a few times and that'd be the end of it. But I called to the water, I let it circle around me, then I filled every hole of the man with water. His nose, his mouth, his … other parts."

"You drowned him?" Amana gasped.

"Yes." Nya nodded.

"How did that feel?" Amana sat forward.

"It felt good at the time. I felt like I got the revenge I deserved, and I made the man suffer for it," Nya said. "But over time it felt hollow. My father and mother were still gone. As you can probably guess, the Ya-Seti were all impressed with me. Shanaki took me in as her own, wanted me to train up in their military academy. She groomed me to be in her guard. All because my mother and father were murdered."

There was silence in the caverns as Nya sat back down. Even the kishi up above had stopped laughing.

"I lost my family, too," Amana finally admitted.

Nya did not lift her brow in shock. Amana suspected she knew as much already.

"Before all this," Amana lifted his scroll and his meditation instrument, "I was part-time smuggler, part-time pirate, part-time con artist, full-time criminal. And I was the best."

"Moons! The pirate who ruled the Sapphire Seas. The one who suddenly vanished …" Nya said with her mouth half open, revelation dawning on her face. "You're Captain Lekkun."

"That's what they called me, yes."

"I thought you looked familiar that first night," she said with a wagging finger.

"And here I thought you were looking at *me*." Amana laughed.

"You were quite the headache for the Kor. You had trade in the Sapphire Seas locked up for years. We didn't have much of a navy then, so we turned to land trade, but you affected just about every coastal nation for the better part of a decade. No one's ever banded so many pirate companies together. It's said you're one of the five richest men in the world." Nya said all of this very fast, listing off everything she remembered about "Captain Lekkun" before she forgot.

"All in the past," Amana said. "I lost more than my riches."

"What happened to you? Most figured you were killed. The Golden Lords took most of the power, though now it's mostly just disorganized companies feuding for their treasures."

"I was betrayed by one of my own. Don't look so shocked; it's the way of our people. But we still have a code. And that code was broken with my family."

"She didn't break your heart," Nya realized. "They killed her."

Amana nodded slowly.

"Did you find out who did it?"

"Oh yes, it wasn't much of a secret. The *Great* Captain Zuberi made it clearly known he was the one to kill Captain Lekkun's lover."

"I'm sure he didn't live long."

"I brought my whole company down on him. But I didn't realize how deep the betrayal went. It was a trap, only the crew most loyal to me stood their ground, but most of the rest sided with Zuberi. It was a massacre. I barely made it away with my life. I nearly drowned trying to escape, but I did.

"My next attempt on Zuberi's life was more covert. But even then, I was not smart enough to defeat him. I just didn't have enough power, not enough influence anymore. But I did have a talent—my short-sight. I knew if I could train it, maybe I could grow stronger, figure out his next steps before he made them. But short-sight and long-sight are different. It seems simple in practice but … it's a rare crossover. It didn't seem like my sight could be helped with training, at least, none I could find in the scrolls I stole from the coastal academies.

"One day, I came across a trader from the east, a Junga monk, who spoke about enlightenment and heightened senses and all that. So I disguised myself as a devotee, spent the better part of a year apprenticed to him until the day I was kicked out. One of the monks told me that my intentions were not genuine—which was true. I followed the code, said all the words, but there was a darkness in me they could sense, an eagerness. I only sought enlightenment for my own betterment, not to get closer to the Supreme One.

"But the monks often spoke of a man named Uzoma, especially as they were deciding if they should kick me out or not. They said I reminded them of him. So I did my research, found out who he was, and how he was connected to the Junga. I stole one of their scrolls from their library and continued my studies self-taught.

"You have to understand, they don't teach you anything as an apprentice. You're just a glorified servant with the promise of something more. Finally, I found the Great and Mighty Elder Uzoma here in Bajok, living out his retired days in a fallen Empire that was nothing more than sprawling farmlands. Looks like I got my wish. Looks like I got what I deserved."

Amana ran his fingers through his hair, letting the silence have its moment. The kishi were still quiet.

"You'll get your revenge," Nya decided. "I'll make sure of it. You're not the only one to have hurts, Mana."

Nya lifted herself from the ground and started pummeling the rock with her magic. She was barely making a dent. Amana stood up as well and did as best he could. Using the blunt end of the tiny dagger to pound what looked like weak spots of the cave-in.

For several minutes, Amana and Nya poured their frustrations into the rock. Neither intended to die like this. After a half-hour of continual pounding, there was only a small impression left in the rock. Amana had the sinking realization that there was nothing that could be done. But he still had so much pent up anger, so much passion that needed an outlet.

Amana looked at Nya. Sweat dripped down both their chests and brows. Without conscious thought, they joined in a vicious kiss—their swelling ire finding an outlet, inhibitions be damned. Amana didn't care about the kishi that laughed above.

It had been years since Amana had known a woman's body like this. He had forgotten how soft their lips were, how supple their breasts felt against his skin. More than that, this woman seemed to understand him. The pain, the angst she felt was all communicated through the parting of her lips, the way she bit his lower lip. Amana finally shared his true self with her. A true self that was hidden by the teachings of the monks. Without these things to hold them back, he finally could know Nya the way he truly wanted to.

Nya was the first to strip Amana of his clothing, nearly ripping his shirt from his body in one tug. Amana took her tunic and threw it down to the rocks, then lifted her up onto his hips. With a small trot, never letting his lips part from hers, he pushed her against the rock wall. He started for her neck, using his tongue in spirals that made her moan.

Amana had forgotten the language of lovemaking, the most honest kind of communication. Their moans and hurried breaths said more than any conversation they'd had before. Pure, fundamental, bare communication. And Amana and Nya knew each other completely in that moment.

AMANA AND NYA MADE LOVE UNTIL THEY WERE EXHAUSTED.

The emotion triggered by their intimacy nulled the fact that they had not had water for nearly two days. But once that exhaustion set in, their bodies reminded them how vital water was.

Nya fainted at least twice at the end of the second day. Amana had to shake her back to consciousness, each time reminding her of Shanaki, and how the Princess was waiting for her.

Nya wasn't the only one to drift. By the end of the second day, Amana had fainted thrice.

"Wake up, Mana," Nya had said, stroking his hair. "Zuberi is still out there. You still need to make him pay."

And for the next few hours, it went like that. Faint, encouragement, faint, encouragement, until neither could resuscitate the other, until their bodies forced them to rest. Nya was the first to black out for good, speaking Shanaki's name and apologizing to her Kor'de.

"Death is the rightful punishment for failure of duty," she said softly before drifting off, reciting what seemed to be a Ya-Seti proverb.

Amana was too tired to keep her awake. After only a few minutes, he blacked out, too. No words on his lips, only the image of Uzoma on his mind.

CHAPTER 17

THE DELIVERY

SPLASH!

Amana awoke with a start. Drops of water fell between his eyes.

"Drink," the figure said. Amana could not make out the figure through the red spots in his vision. But the voice was familiar.

"Uzoma," Amana said with a raspy, parched voice.

"Just because I'm a kishi does not mean you can be disrespectful," Uzoma said. Amana could not tell what Uzoma was doing on the other side of the room—or was it another cavern? "You will still address me as *Elder*."

Amana scowled.

"Drink, son," Uzoma ordered again. This time, Uzoma pressed a cup to Amana's lips, forcing cold water down his throat. The act was more violent than Amana expected, but the water was refreshing. Amana tried to grab the cup but realized his wrists were bound by twine.

"Sorry about all this," Uzoma started. "I didn't mean for you to find out so soon. But you seemed like you'd be able to handle the truth. That Ya-Seti woman, I told you she would be a bad influence."

"Nya …" Amana said. "Where is she?"

"She's only a woman, Amana, nothing but a tool," Uzoma said with the condescending tone of an instructor. "You shouldn't care about what happens to her."

"Tell me," Amana said, his throat was already feeling better with the wetness moistening it.

"She is safe. Kwachi is watching over her." Uzoma frowned.

"Is she being cared for?"

"Yes, Amana."

But then Amana knew why she was still alive and not left for dead in the chamber where they blacked out. There was only one reason. Uzoma said it himself. She was a tool. But how would Uzoma use Nya against Amana?

"I thought you would understand. I felt the darkness in you; I still feel it now. You only need to control it, just like I have." Uzoma touched Amana's head. "Good. Your fever has broken."

"I understand that you've killed many women," Amana said. "How many? Three? Four?" Uzoma laughed.

"Quite a few more than that." Uzoma chuckled some more, in that eerie high pitch. Amana could hear the hints of the hyena in him now. For the first time, he got a good look at Uzoma. The wound from Nya's arrow had healed … but it was only a few days —or was it more? How long had Amana been out? Did the kishi have regenerative strength as well?

"I still don't believe it," Amana said. "You can't be a kishi. Your head is shaved. I don't see the hyena even now. How did you do it?"

"I thought you would have realized it by this point." Uzoma forced more water down his throat. "My studies over the years have helped me a great deal. I couldn't spend my life relying on my hair or a hat to hide what I really was. I needed to suppress it when I could. So I used what I learned from the mountain monks and the elders of Bajok to control it. And you can learn this control, too. You, like Esi, will learn. You've only scraped the surface of your abilities."

"Esi …" Amana had forgotten about her too. "The baby …"

"Both are fine," Uzoma said. "The baby will be here very soon, she has seen it. And you will help deliver my child and keep her alive."

"You're getting soft, Uzoma."

Uzoma smacked Amana across the face. He had far more strength than Amana expected.

"Respect, Amana."

"Sorry, *Elder*," Amana said defiantly. "Why do you care what happens to your wife? She's just a tool, after all."

"This is true," Uzoma said, turning back to his workstation. Amana could see him better now. He was boiling something in a small pot. "But Esi is a particularly useful tool. One I've been waiting for, for quite some time."

"She's Twice Blessed, one with the sight and the voice. Aren't you lucky …" Amana said.

"It was rare enough to find such a good seer, but with the talent of the voice as well … You can understand why I've gone through all this trouble. And with you, we can bring order to this world."

"With demon magic and murder. Not interested," Amana said.

"Oh, but I think you are. You're not unlike me, Amana. We both were denied by the mountain monks for the same reason. You wanted the power to avenge those you could not protect."

"How did you—"

"Esi told me all about you. Or rather, I forced her to. She's still so stubborn after all these years. Join me, Amana. With you and Esi using your abilities to their fullest, you'll be able to do whatever it is you want. It's already what you had planned. Esi told me about your dreams. Whatever you tried to do, that rival of yours always seemed to be a step ahead. What is it? Does he have the sight as well, or someone working for him has it? Am I getting close? You need to be more powerful than they are so that you can get to him. You know what you must do to get there."

Uzoma's smile widened as Amana's brows pinched together in thought. That was truly Amana's goal, after all, the power to finally defeat Zuberi, the power to avenge his family. Uzoma was very sharp, that much was true. Amana had suspected something was at play with Zuberi, something he could not surpass.

"I understand with all these hostilities you may be feeling a bit raw," Uzoma said, still smiling. "But I was wounded, and you and that Ya-Seti woman were not letting up. I had to set my wives on you and the kongamatos. I knew neither could kill the pair of you. You're too strong for that, too talented."

"I suppose those kishi at the top of the cavern were yours too, then?" Amana asked.

"What kishi?" Uzoma's eyes narrowed.

There was a cough to one side of Amana. Amana turned his head—which hurt a great deal. Esi had been sitting there the whole time. But her eyes were wide, and she still looked like she had before.

"Esi, please stop straining yourself." Uzoma went to the boiling pot and scooped some liquid into a cup. Amana caught a whiff. It was the kinkeliba tea he had suggested. Uzoma fed it to her gingerly. Yes, he was particularly fond of this tool of his, indeed. After the tea went down Esi's throat, she calmed down immensely. "Now please, tell Amana what you've told me."

"You will bring forth the child of Uzoma," she started in a trance-like state. "And you will become more powerful with the help of the kishi."

That voice! That ghostly yet ethereal voice. It was the one Amana had heard in his dreams. Amana locked eyes with Esi, but there was no recognition there—no human emotion. Amana did not want to let on that he had been communicating with Esi for weeks now.

"You see, Amana," Uzoma said, clenching his fist, "we are meant to be partners in this, it has been foreseen. I can show the Junga monks true power, and you can show Zuberi what it means to cross you. I know it's a lot to think over. And you need your rest. But Esi will deliver in the next few days. I know you'll make the right decision when the time comes."

After a few moments, Uzoma left with Esi. Amana was alone with his thoughts. He had never known someone with the long-sight before. Esi spoke about the future with such ease, even through the strain of Uzoma's control. Amana had no intention of delivering the child, but he knew it would happen ... It was foretold. Esi said it was so. And what had she said about Amana being more powerful? It was because of the kishi? Maybe it wasn't so wrong to continue his training with Uzoma. After all, Uzoma wanted to do him no harm. Amana got into this mess only because the Ya-Seti wanted to use him. Would it be so bad to join the old man?

Of course, it would! This man was a murderer, a cold-blooded killer. His victims were well in the dozens, perhaps even in the hundreds. What had he said about setting his wives on Amana? Were all those skeletons once Bajok women lost to the rocks? Amana had known some wicked men in his lifetime, and none of them had been suitable allies either, let alone mentors.

But Amana had no idea where he was. He had no idea where Nya could be. For the time, he was at Uzoma's mercy—and the mercy of Esi's vision.

Many men, much wiser than Amana, had said it was futile to avoid the foretelling of a seer. No matter what one did, the truth of their words always manifested.

Forget her words, Amana thought to himself feebly. Part of him knew what Esi said would come true. He would deliver the demon child, and the kishi would make him more powerful. He just needed to figure out how that could benefit him.

Uzoma was right. He did have a lot to think over.

After only two days, Amana had to make his decision. Uzoma ran into Amana's cavern with a naked Esi under his arm. He laid her down on a soft blanket.

"It's coming," Esi said. It was the first time Amana had truly heard her voice. It sounded younger than he expected. "The wretched thing is coming."

Her belly was convulsing. The demon head was already trying to find the strength to chew its way to freedom.

"I'm sorry, Esi, but I can't let him use you anymore," Amana said.

"Good, let me die," Esi said freely. Amana was surprised Uzoma was not silencing her. "Kill the beast if you can."

After that comment, Uzoma came out of his stupor. Had the elder been too focused on his new son? It dawned on Amana that the beast would likely be very powerful. Not only a powerful beast but possibly a telepath and a seer like its mother. Uzoma set his empathic abilities on Esi again, nullifying her temper.

"Amana, you have to do this. How can you let my wife die?" Uzoma challenged. Amana could feel Uzoma's influence sneaking into him.

"Don't pretend like you care for her now." Amana tried to push the influence away, keeping his mind his own. "Sympathy will not work here. She and I both know she's better off dead. And if it is up to me, the child will die as well."

"Then we'll have to do it the hard way. Kwachi!" Uzoma called out. From the corridor came the grunts of what could only be Nya. She was dragged in by the mouth of Kwachi, bound at her hands and feet, thrashing as best she could. But the grip of a hyena-shifter was too much to struggle against.

She wore rags, her hair was matted, and her knees were bleeding. Bruises colored her legs and arms. It looked as though she had tried to escape several times and had been punished for it.

"This will not break me," Amana said, never letting his eyes betray him.

"I'll give you another chance to start," Uzoma said. Amana didn't change his expression. "All right, have it your way." Uzoma shrugged, nodding to Kwachi. The hyena-shifter bit Nya's thumb straight off. Nya was gagged, but her scream was still blood-curdling. Amana bit down on his cheek, forcing himself to watch, expressionless. He couldn't let Uzoma get to him.

"Will you really let your lover be so disfigured?" Uzoma said with a toothy smile.

"Stop it," Amana said calmly. Uzoma ignored him. He walked to Nya's side as she sobbed. Her thumb was gushing blood. Uzoma took a hot iron from a fire near the cave's clearing and cauterized the wound.

"So sorry, was that your shooting hand?" Uzoma said. "Tell Amana. Tell him to make it stop. Tell him to help me, help you. Truly, I do not want to be doing this. It would be much easier if everyone just gave me what I wanted." Uzoma removed her gag.

"Go to hell, *ðikala*!" She spat blood into Uzoma's face. "Don't you dare help this cunt, Amana. Don't do a damned thing."

Uzoma wiped Nya's saliva and blood from his brow. He nodded to Kwachi again. Amana expected him to take another finger, but instead, the hyena removed her entire hand. Without a gag, Nya's scream was too much. Amana visibly shook, holding in his breath.

"I can ease her pain, Amana," Uzoma said. Amana's mouth was agape. He was not shocked by the evil. He had seen worse done to people. But this was Nya, the woman he had come to care for. She wasn't just Nya, the indestructible Ya-Seti soldier, she was the woman he saw shivering in the night. And she needed his help, even if she didn't ask for it—or want it.

"I'll do it," Amana said softly. He was barely audible under Nya's screams.

"What's that?" Uzoma said with his hand cupped around his ear.

"I'll do it." *You dikala,* Amana thought.

"Very good." Uzoma set another heated rod to Nya's hand, but this time she did not scream. At first, Amana thought she might have blacked out, but he realized that Uzoma was keeping his word. He was easing her pain through his empathic abilities.

"You see, Amana, I can be reasonable. Truly, I do not wish to kill or harm Nya, nor you. I will keep her soothed so long as you deliver my child and keep Esi alive."

"I'll need my hands if I'm going to do this right." Amana stuck out the twine binding him.

"Oh yes, of course. Kwachi would you?"

"Of course, master," Kwachi went over to Amana and freed him of his rope with two good bites. They both eyed each other as Amana rubbed life back into his hands.

"I would have to cut her through the stomach," Amana said. "But I cannot promise she will survive. I didn't know she was carrying a demon, or that she would have to deliver through her stomach. No woman I've done it on has lived through that. I only ever did the procedure on those who passed. It was the safest way to get the baby out."

"Something tells me you are properly motivated to make it work." Uzoma stretched his hand out to Nya, who twitched on the cold ground. She, like Esi, was at Uzoma's mercy.

"Just make sure you keep the pain away," Amana said. "Most of the women died due to the pain. And I need something clean to cut with. This cave isn't the most elegant place for a delivery."

IT TOOK HALF AN HOUR TO GET EVERYTHING SET UP THE WAY Amana wanted it. But Uzoma followed his directions exactly.

Amana had some sort of control—at least within the parameters of the operation.

"Has she eaten anything in the last day?" Amana asked.

"No," Uzoma said. "I'm aware of the risks that come with it."

"Good." Amana nodded. He didn't want to have to go through the procedure of extracting anything unpleasant from Esi. It was more than likely that Esi would die and her son would survive. If it came to that, Uzoma might not be angry—so long as his son shared his mother's ability. But mystic mothers did not always pass down their magic to their children. It was possible Uzoma would have to try time and time again before he found a child with the exact talents he wanted.

"You'll need to go deep," Amana said. "Don't let her feel anything if you want her to live."

Uzoma nodded, pushing his eyebrows together. Amana could feel the influence he held over Esi, like a cage strong enough to contain an elephant.

It was time. Amana ripped a piece of cloth from his cloak and tied it around his mouth like a mask. With the smallest and thinnest knife Uzoma could provide, he started the procedure.

First, he cut a small horizontal line across the top of the pubic hairline. Then he made another small incision halfway to the belly. It was important that Amana did not cut too deeply. When he first learned to do the procedure, his hands had shaken uncontrollably, but after years of practice, his hands had stilled.

"Why are you cutting her there?" Uzoma asked. "The baby is supposed to come out the other way."

"This is no ordinary baby. There's no way for me to get it out that way while it's trying to chew its way out. We have to get it out this way," Amana answered. "I need you to stay quiet if I'm to do this correctly."

Uzoma silenced himself, though he kept moving his mouth as though he wanted to speak. Amana smirked under his makeshift mask. It was nice being able to tell Uzoma off. But he knew that would only last so long.

The first cut was a success, but Amana would have to cut into the second layer of skin, which he found was always the more difficult of the two. It would be all the more difficult now with a demon underneath. Amana could see the second layer of flesh bulging with the impression of a small snout. How powerful would the tiny kishi be? Would Amana be able to settle it down before it chewed away at its mother?

"Wait." Amana stopped before he made his next cut. "This isn't going to work. I don't have anything to patch her up with after the baby is out."

"What do you mean?" Uzoma lips pressed together hard.

"I told you, I've only done this on dead women," Amana reminded him. "I never had to close them up before because they were already gone. But if Esi survives this, I'll need to mend the cut."

"Would a healer do?" Uzoma asked.

"You just have one of those lying around?" Amana raised an eyebrow.

"Kwachi, bring me Emeka."

After a few minutes, Kwachi returned with another man. Amana did not recognize him at first. Not until the man looked up.

"Didn't think I'd be seeing you again, foreigner," the man said. It took a moment for Amana, but he remembered those eyes.

"The shaman from Bajok," Amana gasped.

"One and the same," he nodded.

"That's how you got into the village." Amana turned to Uzoma. "You got rid of his protection first."

"There will be plenty of time to sing praises of what I've done." Uzoma smiled. "Right now, tend to my wife. Tell Emeka what needs to be done."

"I'm trying to deliver the baby through a cut in her stomach.

It's the best way to stop it from chewing through. That way I'll be able to control it better. I think I can get it out with Uzoma keeping Esi calm, but I'll need to heal her afterward."

"And you need me to mend the wounds," Emeka said with a nod. "I can do this. The cut will be small enough. Only a small ritual is required. I'll just need my …"

Kwachi threw the shaman's jeweled staff to the ground.

"Thanks." Emeka clutched the wooden staff. "I must say, your creature here has been most … hospitable."

The sarcasm in Emeka's voice was not lost on Amana. Turning back to Esi, Amana continued with the second cut, terrified of what monstrosity he would find. The head looked more like a bat than a hyena. The teeth were already growing. The underside of Esi's skin was bleeding where the kishi had been gnawing. Esi must have been in pain for weeks! The skin was almost chewed through.

How would Amana get the hyena cub out without it chewing at the rest of its mother? He caught a glimpse of the human side, which started to cry as it took its first real breaths. By contrast, its hyena brother was just snapping its jaws. Amana took the bottom of its snout in his hand, forcing the thing to close its mouth.

"Emeka could you help me here?" Amana asked, gesturing to the rest of the baby and cub's body. Emeka's face was just as shocked as any mortal man's would be. He had never seen anything quite so grotesque. "Please, Emeka, I need your help now."

"Right, right." Emeka shook himself from his stupor, helping to free the legs. "I never knew an operation like this existed. I've delivered my fair share, but never this way. Where did you learn to do this?"

Amana ignored his question. "Please, concern yourself only with what you're doing."

"Right, right," Emeka said, grabbing at a foot.

The rest of the pull was only a matter of procedure.

Don't let the shaman heal me. Use me against Uzoma. Don't let him win. Amana heard the voice in his head like a shout. Now he knew it was Esi. Her eyes were closed, but he knew it was her. Amana stole a glance at Uzoma, who was fixated on the birth of his son. Amana tried to reply, but he wasn't sure how to do it.

Just think it, I will know, was Esi's answer.

Amana asked how he would go about it. How would he convince Uzoma that she was in danger?

Cut me. Say something went wrong.

Amana mentally told her she might die.

Then so be it.

Amana stole another glance at Esi. Her eyes were still closed. Then Amana asked her about Kwachi and what should be done about him.

Your girl seems to have that handled.

It took all he had not to look over his shoulder. It might've given Nya away, whatever she was doing. So he trusted in Esi. He did not see a better way to go about it. He cut her just before cleaning the baby and the cub off.

"Congratulations, Elder Uzoma, it's a wonderful demon boy." Amana handed the bloodied mess of a baby to Uzoma. Uzoma was as happy as Amana had ever seen him, wearing a smile that went from ear to ear. And the boy seemed to be happy to see his father. It was a strange scene. Even Uzoma's hyena head was showing itself, trying to look upon its newborn child.

But Esi started to shake.

"What's happening?" Uzoma frowned.

"She's ..." Amana could not recall the term. "Her blood is running too freely. I don't remember the word for it."

"What's that mean?" Uzoma's eyes darted from Amana to Esi.

"It means she's losing more blood than she can handle to lose. But I can fix her."

"Well, do it then!" Uzoma said with his baby between his

arms. It started to cry as both human and hyena at the same time, the mood of its father less nurturing now.

"I will not, at least, not yet. You have to tell me the way out of here. And let Nya go, as well." Amana held out the largest knife he was allowed to have straight at Uzoma. He wasn't sure he was ready for a fight, still light-headed from dehydration, but he would make a good effort of it if he had to.

"I'll just have Kwachi kill Nya," Uzoma said, turning. But Nya already had herself free, with her own knife in her remaining hand. The point was stuck to Kwachi's throat. "How did you—" was all Uzoma could say.

Nya only smiled, though she looked as though she might pass out.

"I don't wish to harm your wife any more than you do, so give me what I want," Amana said, matching the tone Uzoma used with him earlier.

Uzoma sighed. "I have something better."

"Forget his tricks, Mana," Nya said. "Just kill him and be done with it."

"I have information on the girls, including Shanaki," Uzoma said.

"Where? Where is she?" Nya's dark expression changed.

"It's likely Ikenna is ensnaring her in our ritual. The same one I've done to keep Esi under my thumb all these years. It takes near a moon to complete, but knowing my son, he's already done the job."

"Where the hell are they?" Nya shouted.

"He doesn't know. His son is likely a rival. He took Shanaki for himself, to fight against you, didn't he?" Amana asked, though privately he wondered if Uzoma knew about Yejide as well.

But Uzoma's silence spoke volumes.

"Ayo had mentioned something about it, though it didn't make sense then. Is that why you wanted him silenced?" Amana stepped to his feet. He would need to work fast if he was to save

Esi. The blood from her cut was pouring out freely. "You have nothing to bargain with, and you are as ignorant as we of Shanaki's location."

"I know the way," Esi said through tired breaths. If she was awake now, she'd likely be feeling the pain soon. "The riddle that got you in here … You need only say the words, and it will lead you out. You do not need me."

"Shut your mouth, woman!" Uzoma said. Instantly, Esi was back in a stupor, back under Uzoma's spell. At least, she would not feel the pain now.

"I do not wish to kill you, *Uzoma*," Amana made sure not to use the "elder" title, "but you are giving me very few choices right now. If I let you live, then I'll have to keep looking over my shoulder. But if I kill you, I would go against the teachings."

"You still try to aspire to that broken doctrine?" Uzoma smiled.

"It's gotten me this far." Amana shrugged. "Keep your child. I want nothing to do with it."

"What the hell are you doing, Amana?" Nya said. "You can't let him get away with that beast."

"Leave me, Amana, truly. Leave this place as soon as you can," Esi said. She was fighting Uzoma's powers hard now, her brow beaded with sweat. Had Uzoma not tried to divert his empathic influence into Amana, Esi would have been silenced.

Amana turned to leave, but Uzoma had one last thing to say.

"You will stop," Uzoma said. Amana could feel the influence of Uzoma's power sneaking into him. But he batted it away.

"Yes, you see how strong you are. Even *my* abilities cannot influence you. Use that rage, Amana. I can help you make your gifts even greater. You just need to learn how to control it, use it to *your* will … like with the Gods' Glass."

"There is no rage," Amana said. "I *am* in control here. And we are leaving."

"You never did tell me how you knew so much about childbearing," Uzoma said quickly. "My guess is you never told Nya either. Esi and I know, of course. Oh yes, she told me all about your mother, and the father who never wanted you."

"Stop it," Amana said, his back still to Uzoma. Amana felt his face getting red.

"Why are you so ashamed of where you come from, Amana? You should be proud of how you climbed up from the gutters of Ajowan. So few have."

"Shut up." Amana gritted his teeth.

"I wasn't sure at first. I worked most of it out on my own. You are a bastard child, a child of passion, that much I could discern. But Esi helped fill in the blanks." Uzoma cradled his baby as he spoke. Emeka looked from Amana to Uzoma. "There is a reason you know how to deliver children ... Because your mother put you to it. Because there were so many children that needed to be delivered where you were brought up, isn't that right, Amana? Tell Nya, tell her what your mother was."

"I will kill you where you stand if you do not shut your mouth, old man."

"Be careful with your anger," Uzoma said. "We both know what happened the last time you truly lost control. Does Nya know about your wife, as well? I'm sure she would like to know."

"What's he talking about, Amana?" Nya asked.

"His mother was a whore, Nya. His mother was a whore, and his father was just another client. He lived his entire life in a whore house, surrounded by it. That had to mess up a kid his age. He grew up with quite the temper. Zuberi knew that was his weakness. He even used that against him. Tell her, Amana. Tell her how you killed your wife!"

CHAPTER 18

ACT OF WAR

THAT WAS ENOUGH FOR AMANA. WITHOUT REALIZING IT, HE was slashing at Uzoma with all his might. Uzoma dodged the first blows easily. Amana was wild with rage, and his slashes were wide and predictable.

"Good, good, Amana. Keep pushing that energy." Uzoma set his child down. It stood itself on all fours at that unnatural kishi angle, looking like it was already ready for its first hunt. "Stay back, son. This one is mine."

Uzoma morphed into his kishi form, on all fours in an instant. His son squeaked a tiny hyena laugh.

"Any last words?" Nya said to Kwachi.

"Kwachi didn't ..." Nya smacked the back of Kwachi's head before he could finish. She gave the shape-shifter a good kick before joining the fight.

"Emeka," Nya said as Amana continued to attack Uzoma. Amana's eyes were bloodshot, his visage that of a crazed man. "Now would be a good time to tend to Esi."

"Right, right," Emeka said, shuffling over to the new mother.

Amana's sight was in overdrive. There were ghostly images

everywhere, movements that were being made several moments in the future. Yet Amana could not capitalize on his advantage. His singular focus dampened his ability. There was just too much information. It all muddled together. So all he could do was attack at them all. All he wanted was for Uzoma to shut his mouth, to see the old man's throat cut open.

Uzoma tagged Amana just under his eye, smacking him with his hyena paw. It wasn't meant to be a lethal blow, the paw no better than a padded, blunt weapon. Even in Amana's rage, Uzoma wanted him alive.

"Now, that's enough," Uzoma chided. "Settle yourself down. This is getting out of hand."

Uzoma's words were laced with his metaphysical grip. He was desperate to use it, trying to stop Amana by empathic force.

Still, Amana kept coming, undeterred in his rage. Nya tried to assist him, using her knife to keep Uzoma backed into the corner from which he fought.

But Amana just got in the way, trying to trap Uzoma on his own. His sight gave him ample warning of where Uzoma would move to next, but he was chasing ghostly images too early.

Amana stepped to the right, but Uzoma didn't even make the motion to the right, shifting his weight to the left. Amana tried to re-adjust, chasing Uzoma to the left. He was exhausting himself, hunting specters that did not matter.

Uzoma's movements were flustered, less of that smooth sway he had had against the kishi he faced before. Though he evaded each of Amana's knife strikes, he kept pushing himself into the cave wall. With his back legs, Uzoma climbed the side of the cavern wall, using his leverage to propel himself over Amana and Nya.

That was a mistake.

With Uzoma in the air, Amana was finally able to use his ability effectively. There was only one way Uzoma could go, and that was down. Amana brought his knife arm back, slashing it across the human side of Uzoma's belly—near the healed wound where Nya had hit him before. The skin split and blood spewed from Uzoma's body. The hyena head whimpered. Uzoma's new son whined near the cavern's edge.

Uzoma recovered as best he could, landing on all fours with a vicious growl. Nya was closer to him now.

She sprang forward to slash him with a strike of her own, but Amana stepped in front of her, and he took the hit to his back, blood dripping down his skin.

"Get out of the way!" Nya shouted. "I could have had him."

Neither Nya's voice nor the wound that stung at Amana's back seemed to register. He was seething. Uzoma dropped into his rhythmic fighting bounce.

"I know how to fight someone like you Amana," the human side of Uzoma's head said. The hyena head simply growled. Uzoma started to give Amana false reads, projecting his ghostly image into opposing directions.

Amana, the mess that he was, went for one of Uzoma's feints, overstepping his stroke and into the range of the hyena's bite. Just as the hyena was about to close its jaw, Amana withdrew his arm, and the hyena's teeth bit nothing but air.

False reads or not, Amana was too fast for the kishi now. For once, Amana could contend with a kishi as though it were like any other man. Perhaps Uzoma was right, he just needed to tap deeper, let the depths of his anger direct his action.

Amana refocused his efforts, with only one thought in mind: his knife in Uzoma's heart. Nya tried her best to keep up. The movements of the kishi and the reflexes of Amana were too much for her to keep pace with. Both men were working at their best.

Nya rubbed her thumb against her fingers, conjuring a fireball, letting it get as big as it could with a single hand.

Amana locked in on Uzoma, his eyes focused like a predator's. And those eyes said one thing: *I will end you.*

Amana could see it play out in his mind's eye. Uzoma tried to slink his way out of the corner again, but Amana gave him no quarter this time, mastering his focus. Uzoma's eyes went wide. Amana could tell the elder's confidence was waning. The ghostly images that were Uzoma's movements were blurred now, a string of motion that Amana simply had to follow. Amana let himself become a slave to the movement, saw nothing but its careening pivots. But those streaks of images collided with one another in a collage of light. Amana paid it no mind, he could see Uzoma's death, and nothing would stop it.

The first stab came without warning. The knife lodged into the back-side of the kishi, right under the human side of Uzoma's collarbone.

It wasn't enough for Amana.

He kept stabbing, finding new pieces of skin that were untouched by the knife's tip. Three holes. Six holes. Ten. Blood drenched Amana's arms. Uzoma tried to resist, clawing at Amana, but each strike took his energy away, his resistance nothing more than small pats against Amana's forearms.

"Stop this!" Uzoma pleaded. "I know …" Nineteen stabs, twenty stabs. "… where the girl is."

Images of Zuberi sprang to Amana's mind. Images of his traitorous crew. This was the power he needed! This was the whirlwind he needed to become. Not even a demon could stop him like this, not even the Gods!

"If you … kill me," Uzoma said through mouthfuls of blood. "My sons … will come."

Amana didn't hear his former mentor; he was drowning in bloodlust.

There aren't enough holes, not enough holes, he kept telling himself.

His arms were flinging wildly, tearing holes through Uzoma's clothes as though it were rock being chiseled from a mountainside. Skin flung from his knife with each swipe. After the thirtieth strike, the fortieth, fatigue started to set in. Uzoma's body had stopped moving a dozen strikes before, but Amana struck a dozen more, just to be sure.

Amana looked like a demon himself. His body was covered in blood. His beard and matted hair stunk of it. His breathing was powerful, deep and strong. Muffled sounds echoed off the cavern wall, like Amana was underwater. He did not turn to listen to them.

Finally, his vision cleared. He got his first good look at Uzoma's dead body. Blood pooled around the old man, the hyena head's eyes were wide but unmoving. Stabs wounds riddled his torso, designed by rage. There was no pattern, no forethought to the cuts, just sheer volume.

The muffled voices grew louder.

What was most surprising to Amana was that most of the hyena side was burnt. The fur that grew out of Uzoma's back was singed off, leaving only a pinkish, brown skin. Had he been able to defeat the kishi because it somehow burnt itself? It hadn't made sense.

Amana, wake up! It was Esi's voice. *Turn around! Look at what you've done!*

The muffled voices became clear now. It was the shaman asking for help. Amana turned around. One side of the room still smelled of burnt hair, the rocks blackened by an inferno. The supplies for the birth were all strewn about, ointments and knives tipped over in the dark clearing. Kwachi was no longer there, and neither was Uzoma's new son. Esi was up now, squatting next to Emeka. They both sat over a body—Nya's body.

"Amana!" Emeka shouted at him.

Oh, they were shouting at me, Amana thought idly.

"We need you to stop the bleeding. Please help. I can't do anything for her if my hands are full," Emeka was saying.

Amana rushed to Emeka's side, taking his place. Nya had a gash that cut from the bottom of her ear, through her chin and to her collarbone.

"You cut her when you were going for Uzoma," Emeka said as he pulled up his staff, speaking in the Old Tongue.

"She was hitting Uzoma with a fireball before it happened," Esi confirmed. "That's why he's burnt like that on one side."

"I did this?" Amana gasped. He looked to Esi for confirmation. Her sad eyes said it all. "But how? I was fighting—"

"It doesn't matter now," Esi said, still naked. Her incisions were healed now. Emeka had done the job.

"Keep applying pressure," Emeka said, saying his spell as fast as he could. "The cut is very deep. I'm not sure I can heal it completely."

Blood poured freely through Nya's face and neck. Amana pressed as hard as he could, but blood kept coming out of her chin and near her ear. Nya looked up at him and he to her. She opened her mouth to speak, but the cut was too deep.

"Don't talk," Amana said, fighting back tears. Nya had none. She was so strong. "You can't die like this. The shaman will make you better. The shaman will make you better."

It was happening all over again. First with Zuberi and his wife, now with Uzoma and Nya.

One must abstain from acts of war, Amana kept telling himself. These were the fruits of war, of violence. These were the casualties. Amana hadn't been able to control himself, and he hadn't cared. He had accepted his rage willingly, and now he watched as another lover died by his hand, because he could not control what he had spent all that time trying to control. And for what? Because Uzoma goaded him? How silly was such pride?

No, Nya is not gone yet. Emeka will save her, Amana thought.

He could feel the wound sealing beneath his grip. The blood stopped flowing down Nya's neck. But it was still wrong. Nya's breathing slowed. Her eyes stopped moving.

"What's happening?" Amana spun toward Emeka.

"The wound is sealed, but she has lost too much blood, it seems."

"Then fix that!" Amana shouted.

"There is no magic that can give blood. At least not in these caverns."

"Give her my blood, or Uzoma's." Amana pointed to his corpse.

"That could kill her." Emeka dropped his head. "We shaman are not sure why, but not everyone's blood is adaptable to another body. If the body rejects the blood, her heart will stop, indefinitely."

"She's dying anyway …" Amana stopped himself from standing up in a fit of rage.

"She's speaking to you," Esi said. Amana turned to Esi. "Look upon her, I will speak for her."

Amana looked back to Nya, whose eyes were half closed.

"She says, 'Mana … it's okay. I'm glad to have known you,'" Esi spoke for her.

Amana caressed her cheek. Her brown skin was paling.

"'So this is what it feels like, then?'" Esi spoke for her again. Nya's eyes drifted. Open and then shut. Open and then shut. Then, they were only shut. Amana's heart stopped. The pit of his stomach dropped.

"No" was all he could whisper. He rubbed the side of her brow, her cheek, her lips.

"I'm sorry." This time it was Esi who spoke in her own voice, placing a hand on Amana's shoulder.

"It's my fault," Amana said in a hushed voice. "It's always my fault."

"You did what you had to." Emeka knelt beside him, moving a piece of Nya's curly hair from her face. "Uzoma was dangerous. He needed to be stopped."

"I could have stopped him some other way." Amana never took his eyes off Nya. He tried to convince himself she was only sleeping. She had looked so beautiful when she slept. "I should have had control."

A full minute passed before anyone said anything.

Then, Nya vomited on the cavern floor.

"Nya!" Amana turned her over so she could relieve the rest of her stomach.

"She was only in shock!" Emeka smiled, clapping his hands.

"I thought I lost you," Amana said as she turned back around. She looked terrible, with bits of vomit on her lips. But Amana thought she never looked better. Nya couldn't speak. All she could do was return Amana's words with a weak smile.

ESI GUIDED THEM OUT OF THE CAVERNS. THE SHAMAN'S MAGIC got her to her feet, but her breath was still labored, and she waddled rather than walked. Still, her feet were motivated, looking for the exit as fast as they could. Emeka had her arm slung over his shoulder, balancing her weight against his.

Amana lifted Nya, who could not walk on her own, still dazed from the significant loss of blood. Amana held her tight, not wanting to let her go.

"How are you holding up?" he asked, frowning. The nub that was now her right hand made him grieve. Her whole life had revolved around the Ya-Seti and being one of their best archers. Without a shooting hand, there would be no place for her.

"I'll have no purpose now," she said, her voice dead. "I'm decent enough with my left, but there's no way I can carry a bow now."

"I'm sure your Kor will have some use for you."

"Maybe cleaning the walls of the palace—or the temples. But there is no real honor in that work."

Amana frowned.

"It doesn't matter really." Nya tilted her head down. "You heard the old man; Shanaki is as good as gone. It's been over a moon-cycle. There's been no sign of her. Nothing."

Amana could not empathize. There was no way he could know what it was like living one's life through one's hands and then having them taken away. There had been men on his crew who had lost hands and legs on raids, but there was always other work for them on the ship. But Amana had to admit, their lost limbs changed them. There was always a certain confidence lost. Men who were the best lovers took fewer women to bed. Men who were the best fighters had no motivation to learn with their other hand—never speaking up for fear of a fight. He hoped the same would not happen to Nya.

The responsibility was Amana's. Nya would not have lost her limb if it were not for him. She would not have that ugly scar on her face and neck if it were not for him. All because Amana broke his vows. He knew that he should have dismissed Uzoma's words. They were nothing more than that, words. Uzoma was in no position to harm him, no position to stop him even; yet Amana took it upon himself to shut his mouth. He had succeeded, but at what expense? He would never be a monk now, never truly achieve the power he sought. Would his power forever rule him, instead of the other way around? But how did it all happen?

Amana turned to look at Nya. He knew it was because of his connection to her. That's when his focus fell apart. He broke rule after rule, thinking he was above it. He gave into Uzoma's teachings. There was no real balance, just those who could control and those who could not.

"Is that what happened to your wife?" Nya asked as they turned near the cave paintings.

Amana nodded. "I thought I had Zuberi cornered. I was still reeling from my daughter's death."

"You had a daughter?" Nya asked, her voice hoarse.

"I did," Amana confessed. "She was the first casualty. She was taken with my ship. When I had Zuberi cornered, I went into a similar rage. My power was strengthened, but I can't make sense of it. I don't use it to control my opponent, I simply follow it with no real guidance. In the end, I never got Zuberi. He escaped, but my wife, she—"

Nya placed a hand on Amana's chest.

"It's okay. I know." She leaned her head closer to Amana.

When they finally found the exit, there were two figures silhouetted at the mouth of the cave. Emeka sat Esi down near the cave's edge.

"Stay here," Amana whispered. "I'll see who that is."

Nya agreed, sitting down without protest. Had this been only a day before, she would have been right at Amana's side.

"Who goes there?" Amana's voice echoed down the mouth of the cave. He tried to put a sense of confidence in his voice.

"Is it true? Is he dead?" the voice called, the vibrations of its timbre echoing off the walls. Amana held his knife close. Uzoma was right—his sons had known that he would die. Already he would have to face two.

"Who's asking?" was all Amana could think to say.

The taller figure turned to his companion, then back to Amana.

"It's Ikenna, son of Uzoma," said the voice. "I'm here with Shanaki, daughter of the Ya-Seti Royal Family."

CHAPTER 19

RUNAWAY

"NAKI!" SHOUTED NYA FROM BEHIND AMANA. IT SEEMED Shanaki had her own nickname as well. Nya's voice was still ragged, but her spirit was changed, uplifted by the sight of Shanaki.

"Nya?" Shanaki asked, placing her hand over her forehead to get a better look into the cave. "Is that really you?"

If she could, Nya would have run to Shanaki, but she was still too weak. She did manage, however, something between a limping walk and a hobbled jog. Shanaki beamed, running to Nya, closing the gap to her. Shanaki's smile quickly turned to a frown when she saw what was left of Nya's hand. The hug still came, but it was more an embrace of consolation than of reunion. "What happened, Nya?"

Nya shook her head. "The kishi."

"They need to be stopped." Ikenna approached the pair.

"Where have you been with Naki this whole time?" Nya's tone turned dark, even through her pain. A little of the old Nya was back. Amana smirked at that, eyeing Ikenna for his response.

"Protecting her," Ikenna said matter-of-factly, as though it was the most obvious thing.

"That's what I'm here for," Nya said defiantly. Amana's smirk turned into a full smile.

"And look how that turned out for you." Ikenna nodded to the stub on her hand. Just on cue, Nya lunged for him, but Shanaki held her back. It was a half-hearted effort. Nya's energy was spent.

"No, he's right." Shanaki tried to lift Nya back to her feet properly. "Without him, I would have been taken by the kishi. That Baako, the First Son, he's one of them."

"So the Chief is a ..." Amana trailed off.

"No, he's not. It's a bit complicated," Ikenna said. "I'll tell you all about it. But we must return to the village now. They're likely congregating."

"Who's they?" Amana asked.

"The other kishi," Ikenna said plainly. Amana was reminded of the kishi that had attacked them at the roof of the cave.

"The kishi! There were four or five guarding us in the cave."

"I took care of them. They were just scouts."

"What did you do with Yejide?" Amana stepped forward.

"I never found her that day..." Ikenna trailed off.

"You never found her, or you killed her?" Amana clenched his jaw. He wasn't going to fail the young girl, too.

"I never found her then, but I did ..." Ikenna said. "I tried to protect her, too ..."

"What happened?"

"One of them got to her first at the Black Rocks."

Amana's heart dropped. "You mean—"

"She didn't make it." Ikenna frowned.

"You did it, didn't you?" Amana felt himself drifting into a fight-ready stance, but he thought better of it. What was the point of it? What would it change? What he wanted to do was get away from this place.

"Naki, listen to me. Step away from that beast!" Nya placed herself between Ikenna and Shanaki. It was a moot gesture—Ikenna made no move to attack.

"So, it was you I saw that first night." Amana pushed himself in front of Nya. He made no effort to hide the bloody knife in his hand.

"No, it wasn't," Ikenna said. "It was another. I'll explain everything if you give me the chance. I saved Shanaki because I knew she was their next target. I can recover Yejide's body if you wish to see it."

Amana stepped back, dropping the knife. For weeks he had clung to the thought of Yejide alive and well. He had sent her to her death, made her run right into the maw of a kishi. Amana's body quivered with anger again. He didn't need to be here at all. If he had known the girl was lost, he could have been away from this place and all it brought with it.

"You were the one that killed my father?" Ikenna said. Amana felt Ikenna's empathetic influence in his chest.

"Does that bother you?"

"Only that it wasn't me," Ikenna said. "Just wondering how you managed it. You're only a man."

"Men can do a lot when they put the right effort into it" was all Amana could say. A fight was the last thing he needed right now. Though his muscles tensed at the thought of Yejide's dead body lying somewhere in the Black Rocks. He knew too well that his power led to more destruction. He needed to reevaluate what it meant to wield his power. But he also had no intention of backing down from a kishi when he had others to protect. "So who killed Imani then?"

"Baako, I believe. When you told me what happened to Imani, I knew it was him straight away." Ikenna was undeterred by Amana's attempt at intimidation, conversing casually. Did he not realize he was speaking to a man who killed a kishi? "That's why I ran off like I did. He and I are rivals of sorts. That's to be expected of brothers, I suppose."

Nya gasped. Emeka's mouth fell open.

"What?" Esi said, holding her stomach.

"That's impossible," Emeka added.

Amana was the only one not to break face. He needed to match this potential enemy, whatever he was playing at. Why was he asking about how Amana killed his father? Did Ikenna want to see how well he'd match against him?

"So, Baako is Uzoma's? How?" Amana asked. "The Great-Chief should have known his son was half demon."

"Like I said, there is a bit of a story to be told," Ikenna said. "But I'd rather not do it here at my father's lair. The other kishi would have felt his death; we are all connected to him."

"You mean you all can sense each other?"

"Just our father. Just a few moments ago, that connection was severed. And we've all been told what must be done when that happens."

"And what's that?"

"Take over Bajok … well, the women of Bajok. Then kill the men."

There was cackling laughter echoing off the edges of the rocks.

"Yeah, let's get out of here," Amana agreed.

IT WAS NOT LONG BEFORE THEY ARRIVED AT IKENNA'S OWN cavern. It was still within the confines of the great rocks, not very far from Uzoma's homestead. Somehow, it was less severe than Uzoma's cave, the walls of which had looked like sharp, hanging fingers. Ikenna's cavern curved with no fissures or impressions at all.

"How did you manage to be so close yet undetected?" Amana asked.

"I can't take credit for that," Ikenna said. "My father would have found me in hours if it were not for the Royal Daughter." Ikenna nodded to Shanaki, who brought up the rear with Nya. The pair of them had been speaking in hushed whispers. On occasion, Shanaki would look up at Amana and smile. The women were closer than Amana had suspected, almost like sisters.

"So, you're a dampener." Amana nodded to Shanaki. "I was told you weren't very good." He turned to Nya. Nya gave him a sluggish wink.

"That's what we tell everyone." Shanaki shrugged.

"She was perfect for me," Ikenna cut in. "I've been trying for years to stop my hunger for, well, you know … being a kishi has its benefits, but sometimes, you can't control yourself. You saw it that first night with Imani, the kishi just takes over.

"Shanaki was able to stop my abilities completely, though I would have liked to transform every now and then. Still, I was cut off from my father and the other kishi. Most kishi would have felt weak from this, but it was liberating for me. Getting to know the Royal Daughter was a pleasure."

There was more whispering between Shanaki and Nya. This time it was Shanaki who looked to Ikenna. Amana stared at the back of Ikenna's long hair.

"So, what's all this?" Amana asked. "How many children does Uzoma have?"

"Last time I counted, I would say there are about forty left in Bajok alone."

"Bajok alone?" Nya said with shock. "You're saying there are more out there?"

"My father traded a lot with the other villages of the former Empire. During his travels, he would take several wives. He wanted all of Golah for himself, bring it back to the days of the Empire—but with kishi as the leading force."

"He was creating an army," Shanaki said to Nya. "Ikenna says, counting all the villages in Golah, the army is in the hundreds."

"We've seen how just one of them fights. They're enough for five or ten men ..." Emeka said in a hushed toned.

"But Amana was able to kill Uzoma," Nya said. Amana lowered his head, not wanting to look at the deep gash across her face.

"That's right. You still haven't answered me, Amana." Ikenna turned. "How did you manage that? Uzoma was the best of us." Amana did not answer.

"He has the sight. Better than anyone I've seen," Nya said for him.

"If you fought a kishi single-handedly, I assume she means a short-sight?" Ikenna asked.

"I can't control it," Amana said. "Not when I'm fighting at that speed. Nya knows that better than anyone here."

Nya did not look away from Amana. She showed her scar proudly. "It was my fault. You could have handled it yourself. A good warrior knows when she is needed and when she is not. I should not have interfered."

"Don't try to pass it off, Nya." Amana winced at the excuses she made for him, even if the injury wasn't intentional. "It's not the first time I've done something like this."

"That's why you wanted to train with my father, right?" Ikenna said.

"It was," Amana replied. "But like I said, either I'm over-matched by a kishi or I'm overkill. And if I'm overkill, I hurt others."

"If my father's training served you enough to face him, I would not shy away from it, especially now. We have to return to the village and get those people out." Ikenna turned to Shanaki. "Your mother and father should be making their way here with the other Ya-Seti, but the villagers, we can't leave them under the influence of the other kishi."

"Your father's training did more harm than benefit," Amana said. "I thought I knew control. I was mistaken … gravely. This is not my fight. It never was. I came here for one reason, but now I realize I'll never really learn to control myself. I thought I could do it … play as a monk, gain their power, and use it for my own purposes. It just didn't work that way."

"Then you waste yourself," Ikenna said. "Look at me. How do you think I've managed?"

Amana had to admit, Ikenna was different than he remembered. The boy was more … relaxed now. But if it was true that his powers were dampened in Shanaki's presence, and for so long, his temperament may have cooled.

"Why are you helping the villagers? Why aren't you running around with the others?" Nya asked Ikenna.

"How much do you really know about the battle with the old kishi?" Ikenna asked. "The ones my father and the Great-Chief fought."

"Only what the Elder-Chiefs told us," Nya confessed.

"It's only a half-truth," Ikenna said. "It's true the fight was with the kishi. And it's true my father and the Great-Chief rid the land of them, but not because my father was fighting away evil demons—he was killing off his competition. Kishi are like lions in that way. They kill all the sons that aren't their own, and my father made a clean sweep. But he never turned into his kishi form when he did it, so none were the wiser."

"Had he already perfected his ability to suppress the demon head?" Emeka stepped forward, curiosity lacing his tone.

"He had. After his time with the mountain monks, that was one of the first things he realized he could do. The battle with the kishi was long-fought. They retreated to these rocks for their last stand, but they were all killed. There were more in the other villages, though, and they killed those, too."

Ikenna stepped over to a table. It was much like the one his father had in the main room. There were fewer objects atop the table, but there was a cup of water and statues that stood on it. Ikenna changed the water in the cup before he spoke again. "The Chief's first wife was pregnant then. They had been trying for years, and many wondered if she was barren."

"But thanks to Uzoma, she could have a baby," Shanaki added.

"Let me guess," Amana cut in. "The Chief had no idea Uzoma was going behind his back with his wife?"

"The bastard probably forced her under his spell," Nya said.

"Not with this wife. This one actually fancied my father." Ikenna sat near the cavern's edge. "My father denied her advances at first. He knew that taking a woman would reveal who he was, especially the Chief's wife. He actually respected Oba, who was only the War-Chief then. Oba had a great mind for strategy. My father wanted him to be the face of his first campaign. He just needed to work out how to tell him most of the army would be filled with demons. But the Chief was ambitious—if he had an army that could bring the return of the Empire, he likely would have gone for it. He still might.

"In the end, my father took her anyway. During one of the away-campaigns, my father made sure the Chief was injured, unfit to travel back to Bajok. That's when this first wife was due to deliver the first child. And when she did, that's when Baako was born. My father had the shaman killed for letting the wife die as punishment. Really, he was just covering his tracks. The shaman would have seen everything, including Baako's true form." Ikenna turned to Emeka who sat forward to listen. "I believe that's when you were employed as this village's shaman, no?"

Emeka counted on his hand. "Seems about right. We all wondered about that. Shaman Udo was always efficient. Didn't seem right that he should be punished for death in childbirth. Those were common enough."

"Believe it or not," Ikenna continued, "the Chief thanked my father when he returned. And he raised Baako as his own without knowing what he really was."

"But how was Baako's head covered? He wouldn't have had control enough to suppress his hyena head."

"My father requested to be Baako's guard until he was older," Ikenna said. "For the first few years, my father kept Baako's head hidden until he got used to it. My father did that for all of us, then it became like second nature."

So, Ikenna didn't need his lump of hair to cover his hyena head, Amana thought to himself.

"But not all kishi could do it," Amana said. "I chased one of them—Akua."

"I don't know that name ... but if he couldn't hide his head, he must have been weak. My father might not have finished his training. Was he a native?"

"No, Kojo said he was a merchant from someplace west."

"Interesting." Ikenna frowned. "My father never mentioned an Akua."

"Were you Uzoma's second child, then?" Amana asked.

"I was. And I've seen over and over how so many women were killed for our—his—conquest. I vowed never to do that to any woman. I never took a woman as my own, never laid with one."

Nya gave Shanaki a furtive glance. Amana was sure she hoped Shanaki did not lay with Ikenna, no matter how attractive he was. When Shanaki shook her head, Nya's shoulders relaxed.

"You have to be at least twenty-years-old," Nya said with a raised eyebrow. "And you've never been inside a woman?" She didn't seem to believe him—or Shanaki.

"And I never will," Ikenna said.

"What about Imani though? You clearly were taken by her."

"I fancied her, sure. I didn't do more than look at her ... But I only meant to protect her, hoped she found someone better than me. Certainly, better than Baako."

"Did you both know who your father was?" Amana asked.

"We did. Baako was the favorite, of course. He was going to be Chief. It would have been a legitimate and covert ascension to power if anything happened to Oba. No need for a massacre."

"Why didn't they just kill the Chief?" Nya asked.

Shanaki was the one to answer this time. "Uzoma's army wasn't ready yet. It's not exactly ready now. He wanted to wait a bit longer before he executed his plan."

"Remember, my father liked the Chief. He thought he was a strong leader, a good speaker. My father never had a taste for leadership like that, he preferred working in the background. But you've seen it, the Chief just has that presence about him. My father wanted that to rub off on Baako—for him to be an effective leader for his kishi army."

Just then, there was a bird call outside the cave's threshold. It sounded like a hawk.

"A message from Bajok." Ikenna got up and walked out into the daylight. With his hands cupped around his mouth, he whistled a short three-beat trill. There seemed to be some sort of code to it.

Amana looked up at the bird—it was an osprey, the river hawk. Under closer examination, Amana could tell the messenger bird was not entirely an animal. The nuances of this hawk were human, fluttering its wings too often—as though it were unsure it would stay aloft. This was a shape-shifter.

After another pass, the osprey flew down headfirst as though it were hunting. But just as it was about to hit the ground, it tilted up. In the next instant, there was a grown man that landed on the ground, completely naked. Amana could not see his face; it was covered by Ikenna's back.

"It's so good to see you," Ikenna said. "Have they already started?"

"There will be a village meeting tonight. The Chief is dead. Baako saw to it, challenged him to Ugara's Dance. I assume Uzoma is gone, then?"

"Yes, only a few moments ago."

"The Ya-Seti should be here by sunset. I saw them retreating this way." Amana knew that voice.

"Kojo?" Amana said. Kojo looked over Ikenna's shoulder.

"Amana here has been busy," Ikenna said with a smile. "He was the one who killed my father."

CHAPTER 20

NOWHERE TO HIDE

"YOU SAID THAT WAS IMPOSSIBLE." KOJO TURNED TO IKENNA.

"I believe, I said it was *improbable*—not impossible," Ikenna corrected.

"I knew this man was special." Kojo eyed Amana. "But to kill the Great and Mighty One. How did you do it, Amana?"

Everyone looked to Amana, everyone except Emeka and Esi, who had witnessed the maelstrom. If Amana was being honest, he wasn't quite sure how he had done it. All he'd seen was red when it happened. When he came back to reality, all that was left was the bloody torso of a demon, and Nya spread across the floor with blood streaming out of her neck.

"Thank the moons, Emeka was there" was all Amana could manage.

"Amana was brilliant, truly. But he was an animal, untamed, unhinged. He was no longer himself," Emeka said.

"But he killed a kishi, and possibly the best one there ever was," Kojo said, looking to Amana, who could not speak for himself. Kojo turned back to Ikenna, his hands on the young man's shoulders. "That's the type of warrior we need if we'll ever stand a chance."

"You knew about Uzoma?" Amana asked Kojo.

"I had my suspicions." Kojo nodded. "I didn't know for sure until Ikenna came to me. It was my idea that he take Shanaki away from the village."

"Who are you?" Amana asked. "Who are you *really*?"

"You know me, Amana," Kojo said. "I wasn't sure if you could be trusted, at first. Perhaps, I should have let you in on everything sooner. But my character has been honest."

"Has it been? Your Mother Tongue is much better than you let on ..."

"Like I said. I wasn't sure how much I should expose to you."

"Kojo is the leader of the Guardians," Ikenna explained.

"The Guardians?" Amana asked.

"The Guardians of Aya, yes." Kojo lifted the necklace with the spiral charm he always wore. "*Protectors of Her will. She flows eternal.*"

"Does your wife know about this?"

"Of course, she doesn't. Not many do." Kojo put the necklace back around his neck. "Ever since the first kishi attack, my father and the other oni'baro put together the Guardians. Uzoma and Oba were a great help, but the community wanted to make sure we could defend ourselves as well. With you here—by way of Aya's river no less—it truly is written in Ula's stars. You must join us and help fight these Kishi."

"My mother has seen this too," Shanaki chimed in. "That first night, after she helped translate for you. She saw something in your future—oh no, she isn't a seer, exactly, but she has very good intuition. That's why she chose Nya to go with you, to keep an eye on you, figure out if you were truly a good man. Nya hasn't told me much, but I see the way she looks at you. I've known her nearly my whole life, and she's never looked at a man as she does at you. And Nya has always been a good judge of character."

"Well, she's wrong here. I'm not a good man. By rights, I shouldn't be here. I should be dead on one of the Sapphire Isles, lost and forgotten." Amana turned away from them all. He didn't deserve the admiration or the praise. He was a killing machine, at best, nothing more. He certainly wouldn't call himself a good man. Turning back to Shanaki, Amana shook his head. "Your family knows who I am."

"Amana, you don't have to—" Nya cut in.

"You all want to know why I'm here? I came to learn how to kill another man. A man who wronged not only me, but my family, too. I didn't come here to be a 'nice person' or live a life free of earthly tethers."

"You *really* don't have to do this," Nya butted in again, placing her remaining hand on Amana's chest.

"You four might not be familiar with me," Amana nodded to the others, "but Her Highness knows me as Captain Lekkun. I was a pirate who raided her people indiscriminately. Among others."

The Bajoks' expressions didn't change. For them, the name meant nothing. Amana had expected that. His attention, however, was on Shanaki. She did not gasp nor did she even raise an eyebrow. Her face was devoid of emotion, taking Amana's words in plainly. Had she been that way when she told a young Nya she could execute a man?

"Never tell this to my mother—or my father—for that matter," Shanaki finally said. "But for me, it doesn't matter. I've seen Ikenna in action before. The first few days we were tailed by the others. You almost found us when you came to the rocks. These kishi are more than a match for any of my archers. If you can do what Nya and the others say you can, you have to help us. With just a few words, I could pardon your name."

"This isn't my fight. Never has been." Amana shook his head. "I've used the teachings of the Junga to further my own agenda, and I paid the price. Maybe becoming a monk was never for me. Perhaps I should—"

"Frankly," Kojo cut in, "I don't give a damn who you are. I've shared my table with you. I've trained with you along with my children. You're as good a man as I've ever known."

"You don't know me truly." Amana shook his head. "Uzoma saw it. Even your shaman here saw it. There is a darkness in me that cannot be controlled. I thought I could. I was getting better, but the moment I was unhinged, there was nothing I could do. What if it's your wife that's in the cross-fire—or your children? There isn't anything I could do, at least, not now."

"What happened in my father's cave that has broken you like this?" Ikenna said. His arms were crossed, eyebrows pushed together, examining Amana as though he were a puzzle.

"Nya was caught up ..."

"No, that's not it. Something else is wrong with you."

"He's right, your spirit is broken," Kojo agreed.

"I broke the tenets of the Junga monks, one by one," Amana said. "And each time I did, something worse happened. I killed, I spoke words of war, I lusted," Nya dropped her head at that, "and I lost control. I paid for it."

"Those monks only speak words," Ikenna said. "They dictate your life as much as the grass that grows from the ground."

"This isn't my fight," Amana repeated.

"This is true, it's not," Kojo said.

"It's not our fight either," Shanaki added. "But we will only defeat these beasts if we are together. As far as I'm concerned, you are a part of us."

"You're important to us, Amana." Nya lifted her head again. Amana forced his eyes away from the scar across her neck.

"I'm sorry, everyone." Amana looked at each of them. "I should have never been here to begin with. I'll get you back to the village, but after that, I'll set back down the Nyoka."

There was another whistle outside the cave. This one was

different, not the call of the hawk. This one was human, a short trill that sounded like the wind. Amana had heard this call before, near the port cities of the mainland. The Ya-Seti were here.

Ikenna and Kojo stepped outside the cave to meet the company. Kojo whistled back.

Amana squinted his eyes. He made out the shapes of heads and the tips of spears. It wasn't just the Ya-Seti who had arrived. They had at least two scores of Bajok with them as well—most of them women and children.

Amana stepped forward to get a better look. The first figures to materialize were a pair of guards stationed in a forward flank around their Kor'de. Behind her were their two large elephants, on which the Kor sat beneath a mounted canopy atop one of their backs. Bringing up the rear were young men Amana recognized from the spirit dances. They, too, were guarding their own. Between them were a set of women Amana did not recognize, save one.

"Ime!" Kojo wrapped his arms around his wife. "Did you take the river like I said?"

"We couldn't," one of the Bajok men said. "They had all the boats. We had to go on foot."

Kojo raised his head over the villagers, mouthing a count. "Where's Dayo? Enu?"

The Bajok man only shook his head.

"They know we have come here," Kor'de Neema spoke up.

"Did they pursue?" Kojo asked.

"No," Ikenna said for her. "They would be too afraid to with my father gone. They wouldn't want to meet who killed him." Ikenna turned to Amana.

"Not Baako!" another man spoke up. "He wanted to chase us down until we were all dead. He would have gotten us too if Yemi hadn't stopped him."

"You mean if we hadn't covered you with our arrows," one of the Ya-Seti archers said.

"Yes, yes, your arrows helped too." The young man waved the notion away.

"Mother!" Shanaki rushed out of the cave. She embraced her mother in a tight hug. Amana had never seen the Kor'de smile so wide. Kor Mosai only gave Shanaki a slight nod, no loving greeting from him.

"Is she whole?" was all he croaked.

"I knew you'd be safe, my child." Neema ignored her husband, patting her daughter's back. Shanaki was at least two heads taller than her mother.

"I would have sent word, but Ikenna said it would be too dangerous. He wasn't sure who he could trust in the village," Shanaki said.

"Where have you been?" her mother asked.

"Out here, among the rocks, mostly. We tried to get out a few times. That was when we ran into Baako."

"I'm so sorry we wished to pair you off with that boy."

"It's okay. There was no way of knowing, really." Shanaki shook her head. "Ikenna kept me safe, and I him."

"Are you the boy?" Neema turned her nose to Ikenna, examining him up and down. She nodded her head approvingly. "You're certainly a looker. You're one of *them,* aren't you?"

"I am," Ikenna confessed without hesitation.

"Why is it you have not yet killed my daughter?" Neema took a small step in front of Shanaki. "I spoke with your Elder-Chiefs. Your kind aren't supposed to be able to handle themselves around pretty girls."

"I'm quite unlike most of my kind." Ikenna caught Shanaki's raised eyebrow. "But your daughter had a lot to do with that."

Neema smiled. "Maybe it was you I should have married my daughter to."

"I wouldn't be so sure about that," Amana finally spoke up.

"Ah, Amana," Neema raised her eyebrows. "We thought you dead. And Nya?"

From the cave, Nya limped her way to her Kor'de. She had been hiding in the cave, tucking her handless arm behind her back.

"I am here, Your Highness," she said.

Neema looked her up and down. First, her eyes scanned Nya's face. Neema stretched out her hand, stroking the scar.

"Your wound looks strange. Was it healed?" she asked.

"Emeka saw to that," Nya gestured to the shaman. Emeka gave a feeble wave and smile.

"I could have healed it better," he said proudly. "But I had to tend to Esi first."

Neema held Nya by the shoulders. Nya flinched.

"Show me," Neema said immediately.

Nya turned her face away when she showed her Kor'de the handless arm. Like her daughter, Neema frowned at Nya's stub.

"What happened?" Neema demanded. "I've never seen anyone get the better of you."

The Kor'de's guard all whispered to each other with curiosity. If the best of them could not fight the kishi, how could any of them expect to do any better?

"The kishi happened, Your Highness," Nya sunk her head down low. Perhaps she was expecting to be chided for her failure.

"I'm sorry, I could not save Naki—" Nya caught herself mid-sentence, "Princess Shanaki. I will submit to your judgment."

"Oh, we'll have none of that." Neema shook her head as she sucked her teeth. "You are alive. That's what matters most here. And you." Neema turned her attention to Amana. "I'm told you defeated Uzoma in single-combat?"

How did she get her information so quickly? Amana thought.

The Ya-Seti archers shifted in their gear, their attention locked on Amana. There were audible gasps from the Bajok villagers.

"By Ugara's spear!" one of them said.

"That's impossible," said another.

"I did," Amana said. "But at a cost."

Amana made an effort not to look at Nya. Neema caught the look.

"Nya, how did you come across your wounds?" Neema said directly.

"I …" Nya trailed off. "I'm not sure I could …"

"Every one of Nya's injuries was because of me." Amana stepped forward. "Her hand was because I did not give in to Uzoma's demands. Her neck was by my hand because I could not control myself while fighting Uzoma."

"But you killed him all the same?" Kor Mosai spoke from the top of his elephant.

"Yes, Your Highness," Amana looked up into the man's wizened face, "I killed him."

"We should attack!"

"Use the foreigner!"

"If he can defeat a kishi, he could defeat them all!"

The Bajok were stirred up now. Where they had no hope, Amana filled the gap. He was a perfect weapon for killing kishi. But Amana wasn't sure killing kishi was the right thing for him to do.

"So, what are we to do now?" one of the young men asked of Kojo.

"It's obvious, isn't it?" Kojo stepped out of the circle to take in the whole group. "We attack."

"No, we won't," Ime stepped forward, lifting a defensive hand against her husband. "It was difficult enough getting out of the village. We can't go back."

"Not everyone." Kojo took Ime into his arms. "I only need a few good men. Enough to get Amana close. This ends with Baako's death. The kishi will fall without their leader."

Amana didn't remember agreeing to any of this.

"Won't another leader take his place?" Neema said.

"Eventually, yes," Ikenna added. "But that will take time. If we can retake Bajok, we can refortify its defenses with the shaman's help."

Shaman Emeka stepped from the cave where he hid. "I'm not so sure I'll survive a battle." He turned to the Bajok men that remained. "How many kishi are holding the village?"

"At least two dozen, maybe more," a small man said.

"They were already calling for reinforcements when we left. The ones hiding out in the plains," a taller man said.

"It doesn't matter. We'll have a kishi-killer with us now!" the smaller man shot back.

"I'm not joining you," Amana said.

Both, the Ya-Seti and the Bajok, turned their heads toward him.

"I've already told Kojo and the others. I shouldn't be here."

"What? What's he saying?" Kor Mosai peered over his saddle.

"My goal was to find Elder Uzoma," Amana spoke a little louder for Mosai. "I found him. I learned from him. He has shown me that I am not ready to carry this magic that I have. I can't put any of you in danger."

"What danger?" Neema asked.

"If you want me to be decently effective against a kishi—if you want me to have that kind of power, I can't tell friend from foe. I can match their speed, but I can't promise ..." Amana caught Nya's gaze. "... I can't promise your safety."

"Well, son," Kor Mosai said over his perch, shrugging, "that's war."

"*One must abstain from acts of war.*" Amana was surprised to hear it was Nya who spoke the words for him.

"Then what?" one of the Ya-Seti archers stepped forward. "We just let the kishi take control of Bajok? That's just as bad!"

"That's not up to me," Amana said. "It's up to the Supreme One."

"What's he going on about?" the small Bajok man spoke up again. "I don't understand. Why will he not fight?" Chatter from the Bajok stirred. Each man and woman had their own choice words for Amana.

"Excuse me, everyone." Kojo raised his hands to the crowd. "Amana has been through a lot. I'm sure he isn't thinking too clearly now."

"I know exactly what I'm doing." Amana's nostrils flared. "None of you can tell me what I can and cannot do. None of you know what I've been through, what it feels like when …" Amana turned away from Nya's eyes again. "… When I have this … curse within me. I have no business here. There is no reason for me to stay—what are you doing?" Ikenna was tugging at his arm.

"I'm saving you from a mob," Ikenna whispered into Amana's ear. The young man pulled Amana away from the angry crowd.

IKENNA WHISKED AMANA BACK INTO HIS CAVERN. KOJO WAS still trying to control the Bajok, who didn't understand the concept of backing down from a fight. The Ya-Seti archers surrounded Nya. They, too, seemed to have the same questions as they pointed at Amana's back.

"I'm sure my father told you how he achieved the power he did, how he was able to hide his demon," Ikenna said once they were far enough into the cave not to be seen.

"It was a combination of the Junga teaching and what he learned from this village," Amana answered.

"It was mostly what he learned from this village," Ikenna corrected. "They know balance so well here. They don't see good and evil as most in this world do. Though, of course, they cannot deny demons such as myself or my brothers. They don't see us as bad, just a part of the struggle of life. The natural order of things. What the mountain monks teach is abstaining from everything in this world. Denying yourself its pleasures, its horrors, as though that will make everything go away. That is a fantasy. It's true for the few of them that have achieved greater insight by internalizing and focusing their energy, but some of their members limit themselves."

"How so?" Amana asked.

"Because not every piece of teaching works for everyone. No man or woman in this world is exactly alike. No one piece of knowledge will help everyone.

"You came here because you could not internalize your energy the way you wanted to. You tried the way of the monks, but that did not work for you. Their teachings may give you the power you desire, but you'll have to break their code if you actually want revenge.

"You came here to find a new way. Whatever it is my father did to you, whatever he taught you, it worked. You matched him. You tapped into something that allowed you to defeat him, no matter who got hurt in the process."

"But I'm still no better than an animal," Amana said. Ikenna held up a hand, and Amana's insides went cold.

"Sorry," Ikenna pulled his hand back, and Amana felt a release around his chest. "It's a habit. Let me finish. My father had a similar story to yours. He was denied by the monks after they discovered what he really was—and what he really wanted. But when he came here, he found balance and control. The Bajok embrace the reality of this world. They do not deny it. They understand this."

"Uzoma tried to feed me that story as well." Amana turned away from Ikenna. "And he was a demon."

"But did he not speak a truth to you?" Ikenna said. Amana stopped in his tracks. "Look at me. I'm just as much of a kishi as he was, yet it is not my desire to see kishi rule over all others. I understand we are a parasite, a curse that must be mitigated. I have to restrain my desire for women everywhere I go. My time with Shanaki was especially difficult. It's the longest I've spent with a woman alone. But I know it was a test, a test I needed to go through to know I was ready. You, in your life, have been tested, I'm sure. When you have been tested did you turn tail or did you meet it head-on?"

"I try to take it head-on," Amana was slow to say. He could work out where this was going.

"Then that's what should be done. The mountain monks have their merits, but for you, I suspect their teachings are not an adequate answer."

"Maybe you're right, and the monk life isn't for me. Then who should I listen to? Your demon father or the Junga in their mountains?" Amana asked.

"Neither and both." Ikenna smiled slowly, the kind of smile Amana was sure earned him favor with many women. "It's the beauty of this place. Remember, it's a 'both-and' mentality here. It's not 'either-or.' Amana must do what is right for Amana."

"But I can't fight in this battle. I've already said as much."

"It's because of Nya, isn't it?" Ikenna said.

"I thought you said you'd stop using your empathetic abilities?"

"I'm not," Ikenna said plainly.

"Yes," Amana admitted. "It's your father, too. Love and war have always been a poor mix for me. Both were my failing. I grew too attached to Nya, and I wanted your father dead more than anything else. I did not separate myself from them as I should have. If I fight in my current state, I may never come back. Each time I go to that place, each time the magic takes over, it's like I'm a monster."

"You're getting in touch with the Old Spirits," Ikenna said. "The true magic of our ancestors. Well ... yours at least, not mine."

"I don't feel human anymore when it happens. Killing and murder. The Junga tenets tell us these should never be the answers to our conflicts."

"Oh, but they are," Ikenna said. "There will always be

violence and conflict. Utopia is mere fantasy peddled by those monks. As good as things can get, there will always be two opposing forces. We see it in nature, we see it even more with humankind. There is no avoiding that. And becoming a pacifist does nothing to prevent that. You just make victory easier for your opponent."

"And what if that opponent is bloodlust?" Amana asked.

"There is a victory that can be made there as well."

"But conflict begets more conflict. If we do fight the kishi, it will just create more fights with more kishi, and we will leave this world in perpetual war."

"Perhaps, if you are unbalanced. The reason I have been able to deal with my condition is that I've given up needless hate. Fight your enemy, for that, is the way of things sometimes. Despite all the diplomacy, all the words of good faith—conflict will still arise. And we must push down those who oppose us. But we must not forget that though we fight our enemy, we do not hate them. That's when the bloodlust creeps in, that's when the corruption festers. Don't make it personal. If you do that, it'll rule you forever, guide your every action and decision. It'll dictate the rest of your life, just as my father is conquering you now."

As Zuberi has conquered me all these years, Amana thought.

"I'm not asking you to make a decision in the next few minutes, but I suspect that you will need to make a decision before the night is done. Choose well, Amana."

CHAPTER 21

PREEMPTIVE STRIKE

THE GROUP MADE CAMP—THE BAJOK IN THEIR CORNER OF THE rock canyon and the Ya-Seti in the other. Amana sat with his own thoughts in his own corner.

Occasionally, some of the Bajok men stole glances at him. Some acted as though they needed something near Amana. They checked the rock structures, making a note of their stability. They kicked at the earth, deciding the soil was good for harvest. A pair of Bajok even did an entire spirit dance mere yards away from Amana. All of it was a farce. They just wanted a better look at the man who had killed the Great and Mighty Uzoma.

The Ya-Seti were no different, though they kept their distance. Many of the archers were huddled around Shanaki and Nya. Every so often, they would look over, measuring Amana from head to foot.

Kor Mosai had finally come down from his elephant where he inspected Shanaki for any injury. Amana could have sworn he heard the Kor question his daughter about any deflowering. Shanaki had gasped and stomped away, taking Nya with her.

Nya was the only one who didn't try to steal glances his way.

Deep down, Amana hoped she would.

Amana tried to ignore it all as he sat cross-legged on the soft soil. The Gods' Glass was lost in the cave. He hadn't noticed until everything had settled. It was probably for the best. All the glass brought was more power that he knew he couldn't retain. Though he wasn't sure what path he should follow, he meditated under the discipline of the Junga monks. He took heavy breaths into his nose, and then light breaths out of his mouth.

And then he felt her in his head.

Decisions, decisions, said the ethereal voice of Esi.

"I would like it if you stopped that." Amana opened his eyes. He scanned for Esi among the Bajok, but she was not there. He turned his head to the Ya-Seti but could not find her there either.

I am unwanted at both camps. I don't know the Ya-Seti; the Ya-Seti don't know me. That's understandable. For the Bajok, I am tainted by the kishi. Also understandable.

"So where are you now?" Amana asked to no one. He must have looked crazy to any of the villagers or the Ya-Seti stealing glances.

Oh, in one of these caves. I think this one was used for my husband's mistresses. You know, I never did thank you for saving me. The moment I realized what was in my belly, I never thought I'd live to see a day past my delivery.

"You're welcome," Amana said. "I didn't think it would work myself. I've delivered many children, but by way of the stomach … It was only my first time. Well, my first time where the woman survived."

You could sell the procedure to the Imtubo Academies … if you wished. Where do you plan to go?

"I'm not sure, right now. Maybe I'll go back to the Isles. Maybe I'll travel south." Amana closed his eyes again, let the villagers think what they wanted. "What about you? Where do you plan to go? Do you not have family in the village?"

My family is long gone. I was a slave of the Golah Empire before it fell.

When the nation broke up, I tried to make my own way. I guess I need to figure out where I should go, too.

"I can show you a few places east. The Sapphire Isles have some of the clearest waters you've ever seen." Amana chuckled. "Or we could both wander the southern fogs together."

Didn't you have enough interaction with demons? Esi's laugh rang out in his head. Amana clutched at his temples. It was like her voice echoed off the walls of his skull. *Sorry, I try to speak softly when I'm inside a person like this.*

"It's all right," Amana said, rubbing his head.

Besides, I think Nya would take issue with me running off with you.

"I hadn't thought about that," Amana said.

You should never lie to a telepath … Your mind is always with Nya.

Amana took a deep breath. It was all a bit frustrating speaking to empaths and telepaths. There weren't nearly as many in the east. "Yes, I think of her often. My relationship with her is … complicated."

It's only as complicated as you make it.

"I don't think she'd want to talk to me right now, anyway."

I can find out for you.

"No!" Amana raised his hand to the air in front of him. A trio of startled Bajok women looked up at him. Amana gave them a coy smile and a wave. "Don't mind me, I'm just crazy." That seemed to be enough for them. They turned back to their conversation with rolling eyes.

"I would rather you didn't look inside her head."

Oh, I already have. She thinks of you, too, you know. She loves you, I suspect.

"No." Amana shook his head. "Nya doesn't love."

Well, I guess you'll find out.

"What do you mean?"

Open your eyes.

Amana opened his eyes again. Nya was walking towards him with food in hand, a feeble smile on her lips.

Good luck, Amana. The sensation of Esi left his body. Part of Amana was relieved at that. He didn't want her listening in on their conversation.

"I thought the Ya-Seti would be three leagues away from this place." Amana tried to start the conversation light.

"You underestimate a Ya-Seti woman scorned. And there are two." Nya gestured back to Neema and Shanaki. Shanaki had no shame; she looked directly at the pair. "Shanaki won't leave until she sees Baako's head on a stake. Dried fish?"

Nya stuck out a handful of fish pieces on a stick. Amana grabbed one and chewed into it. It was salty, but it sated his appetite.

"You know," she sat next to Amana, "we haven't talked about it."

"About what?" Amana asked.

"You know what." Nya's voice went stern. "Don't make me say it, I'm not good at this stuff."

"That's right, you're one of those one-and-done types, huh?" Amana said.

"Stop it, Amana," Nya laughed, grabbing at her missing hand. Amana frowned. Members of his crew would often move as though their limbs were still there. "I'm being serious."

"What's there to talk about?" said Amana.

"I've never been in a situation like that before," Nya said.

"You mean, you've never been with a man?"

"No, not that. I just … never felt that way before, it was strange …" Nya trailed off.

"We were both going to die. Anyone could have felt that way," Amana said when she couldn't continue.

"I thought that at first, too." Nya hugged her knees. "But when we were dying in that cave, I wasn't worried about what was on the other side, not really. I've faced death before plenty of times. I was scared I wasn't going to …"

Nya bit her lip. Whatever it was she wanted to say, it wasn't coming out. She dug her head into her knees, her dark, reddish hair poking out. Amana still wasn't used to seeing her like this.

"Sorry, I never had to do this before. I don't even know why I'm doing it," Nya spoke into her legs. Amana moved his hand to her back, caressing it.

"I was scared I would lose you," Nya said. "For the last few hours, when we kept each other up, telling each other it would be okay … I wanted you to believe that. I wanted you to be better. I really did want you to survive so you could get that man who betrayed you. Because at that point, I understood it."

"Understood what?" Amana bent his head into her shoulder.

"What it must feel like to lose someone you truly cared for." Nya finally showed her face again. Her eyes were watery. "Don't look at me."

Amana looked away as Nya wiped her eyes clean.

"Okay, you can look at me again." Amana turned around to face Nya. He hadn't seen her properly like this since that night. Her golden-brown eyes gleamed in the mid-day light. "I don't want you to hold yourself back because of me. But these people need you. I don't believe in all that destiny stuff, but there has to be a reason you are here."

"I'm just a tool to them. A weapon to be used against the kishi," Amana said.

"That might be so for some of them." Nya put her hand on Amana's leg. "But think of the ones who can't fight for themselves, think of all the ones the kishi will terrorize if they are left unchecked. They need someone like you right now, Mana."

"But I can't even make my abilities work well enough half the time, and when I do …" Amana traced the scar on Nya's face.

"Don't doubt yourself." Nya held his hand in her own. "I know you're better than that. I've seen what you can do."

"Okay."

"Okay?" Nya tilted her head, looking deep into Amana's eyes.

"I mean, okay. I'll help."

"Good. Because if you didn't agree, Shanaki was going to blackmail you." Nya sat up.

"Blackmail me how?" Amana lifted himself up as well.

"Oh, you know, she was going to tell the Kor you were Captain Lekkun and all that."

"She's a shifty one, isn't she?" Amana shook his head.

"She is." Nya nodded her head. "But she's the best future the Ya-Seti have."

"So, what?" Amana said. "All that stuff you said."

"Was all true." Nya stood tall. "You should know me better by now. I'm no good at lying. Come on, Mana, let's go get us another kishi."

AMANA FOUND OUT QUICKLY THAT NO ONE ACTUALLY HAD A plan. Kojo wanted to go in with his own men—along with Amana "The Kishi Killer." Kor Mosai thought they should return with the Ya'Seti's full force, using the elephants as a vanguard. Ikenna wanted to smuggle Emeka in himself, protecting him while he reinforced a mystical barrier that would not allow the kishi to transform. The one thing everyone agreed with was that they should attack that night.

"Well, what are they doing now?" Amana asked.

"They're likely gathering the farmers and villagers that didn't get out," Kojo said.

"Are most of them aware of who is ruling them now?" Amana said.

"No," Kojo shook his head.

"Why are they alive then? Why not have them killed in their homes if that is the goal?"

"My father told the kishi not to go killing anyone right away," Ikenna said. "First, each man would be asked to pledge themselves to kishi-rule."

"That doesn't seem so bad," one of the Ya-Seti archers said.

"Pledging themselves means they have to give up their wife to the kishi," Ikenna added.

"Ah, not so great." The Ya-Seti archer shook his head.

"Many of the men will fight the kishi before they give up their wives," Ikenna went on, circling the map that lay on the soil between them. "If they try to fight back, they'll be slaughtered."

"So, we'll have to make our move before any of that starts." Amana rubbed his beard, turning to Kojo. "Before, someone mentioned something about Yemi. Is he one of ours?"

"He's not a Guardian," Kojo said. "But he's helped us up until now."

"Whatever the case, he seems like an asset," Amana concluded. "Would we be able to get a message to him before we arrived? I would need Baako in a specific location for my plan."

"I can work that out," Kojo said.

"No, send someone else." Ime came forward. "You have a family here. Send one of your dancing boys."

"None of them are shifters. They wouldn't get there in time. Don't worry, I'll be in and out before they know I'm there."

Ime crossed her arms but stayed silent. She must have known Kojo was their best chance for reconnaissance.

"Don't worry about him, Ime," Amana said. "If it's like what the men say, the attention would be on me and no one else. I'll make sure to keep Kojo safe. I promise you that."

"We don't make idle promises in Bajok," Ime said with a stern voice.

"That's a promise I intend to keep," Amana said.

"What's this plan of yours anyway?" she asked Amana.

"I'll need Baako to be on the festival grounds. We'll need to get him to do the pledge ceremony out in the open. That'll be our best chance. If Yemi suggests it, he should listen. I saw how he kept the First Son under control." Amana turned to Ikenna. "How much control does Baako have over himself?"

"You saw what he did to Imani," Ikenna said.

"We still don't know if that was Baako," Kojo cut in again.

"Who else could it have been?" Ikenna shot back. Kojo had no answer. "My father was molding him. He was the first child he claimed, but Baako was jealous of me. Always was. He might have taken me a few times, but girls … I was always better at that."

"Have you fought him before?" Amana questioned.

"I have," Ikenna said.

"Can I assume you've never beaten him?"

"Just use me," Shanaki said. "I was the one to save you that day. I can stop the kishi from transforming."

"I'm glad you volunteered," Amana said. "That's why I want the kishi contained. How many can you control at once?"

"Uh, well, you see …" Shanaki started.

"She still hasn't completed her training at our academy," Kor'de Neema said, stepping into the circle. "As I'm sure you know, magic in the east has weakened. We don't have many good mentors for her."

"I can stop at least two of them!" Shanaki spoke for herself.

"That might not be enough," Amana said.

That would not be nearly enough. Amana thought to himself.

"No, I think we'll hold you back, for now, Shanaki," Amana said. "As much as I know you want Baako's head, your parents would want you protected." Amana turned back to the map. "I'll go in with Kojo and Ikenna's group. We'll split up once we reach the village. I'll go with Ikenna to ambush Baako. Kojo will go with the shaman to make sure his ritual isn't interrupted."

"No offense to Kojo, but I would like to have the kishi or the kishi-killer with me while I'm doing my work," Emeka said hunched over, doing his best not to look Kojo in the eye.

"Do you not have shape-shifters of your own, Kojo? The women … I could have sworn—" Amana started to say.

"We don't have any lion-shifters, if that's what you mean,"

Kojo cut in. "There were a few hyena-shifters like Ayo, but they all ended up being banished. Most of us are osprey or quail."

"I can take the shape of a warthog," one of the older women said. She, like many of the women in the village, had golden eyes, though hers were milky and opaque. It took her at least a full minute to step forward. It took her even longer to transform into a sluggish warthog.

"That's all right," Amana said. To be fair, her tusks did still look like they could tear through a man ... but a kishi ... "I'm sure we'll figure something out."

"I'll go with you," Nya said.

"There's nothing you can do without your hand." Shanaki stepped forward.

"You forget, I can touch the elements."

"We both know that's not as good as your bow."

"I have to agree with Shanaki," Amana said. He didn't need Nya's bravery now. There was no need for her to be in harm's way in this fight. "You should stay back with Shanaki and the Ya-Seti."

"What would you have us do?" one of the archers spoke from the crowd.

"You will be our rear-guard. Once Baako is killed or captured, the kishi will likely make a run for it. We'll need you to contain them within the village. If this is all timed right, Emeka's ritual should be complete, and they should be powerless. Easy picking."

"Like fish in a barrel." One of the Ya-Seti pounded their comrades on the chest. They laughed.

"You're very thorough with your plans," Kor'de Neema noted.

"I've had a lot of experience," Amana said proudly, but realized he should have shut his mouth. Nya was shaking her head vigorously.

"I thought you might have looked familiar. The hair and beard hide your face well." Neema gave him a wink.

"But what about us?" said the small Bajok man from earlier.

"If they find us out before the ritual is complete. How do you expect us to fight those demons?"

"That's a fair point. I'll stay behind with you. But I'm not the only useful one against the kishi. We'll have Ikenna for support, and they can be killed if a small group coordinates their attack. They're weak on their human side. The issue is, they tend not to show it when they are in their kishi form. You'll have to use flanking maneuvers to get at them properly. Just keep your distance using those spears," Amana whispered to Kojo. "They do know how to use those spears, right?"

"I think so." Kojo shrugged.

"What?" Amana said in a hushed voice.

"I mean ... sure ... definitely!" Kojo perked up. "They're my students. They know the way of Ugara. As long as they're guided by the ancestors, they'll be fine."

Amana didn't believe Kojo as far as he could throw him.

"Don't worry," Emeka whispered into Amana's ear. "I should have the ritual done by then."

Amana didn't like it, but he didn't have much of a choice. "All right, everyone! Get your things in order and prepare yourself. We head out in an hour." Amana pulled at Emeka's shoulder.

"I've been meaning to ask you," Amana said. "How will we know when the kishi are powerless?"

"That's where I'll come in," Esi walked through the drifting crowd. "I'll stay with Kojo's group. I'll communicate with you and the Ya-Seti, in case anything goes wrong."

Amana figured he didn't have to explain the battle plan to Esi. She had likely heard it all.

"I'm sure something will go wrong," Amana said. "Always plan for it. Your help would be welcome, but I don't want to put you through anything. You've just gone through a traumatic birth and all."

"Oh, I should be fine," Esi said, smiling. "All I'll be doing is sitting and watching Emeka do his dance."

CHAPTER 22

INTO THE FIRE

AMANA HADN'T PROPERLY HELD A SWORD IN NEARLY TWO years. Kor'de Neema made sure to arm him with one for the coming battle. It was a Ya-Seti curved sword, one he had handled a few times but not often. The sword was well-balanced, forged with the kind of craftsmanship one would expect from the Ya-Seti.

Though Amana pledged himself to the fight, he still did not think he'd have much use for the sword. Ikenna had already taken out two Bajok warriors guarding the river port where they planned to mount their battle plans. Best case scenario, Amana could direct Ikenna without worry of getting his own hands dirty —or putting anyone else in danger.

The Ya-Seti and the elephant vanguard were already stationed north of the village walls. They used the cover of night, hiding away in the tall grasses until further notice. Amana and his group waited for Kojo to return at the southern river bend. The Kor'de had given them six Ya-Seti archers. They had no fear, complete concentration, the same face Nya often wore in battle.

When Amana said good-bye to Nya, leaving her with the Ya-

Seti north of the village wall, he had a suspicion she would not stay put in this fight. He hoped he was wrong.

The song of a hawk sounded across the night wind, marking Kojo's return. They all looked to the dark sky for an osprey. Silhouetted against the moons was Kojo, but his flight path was uneven as he careened downward. When he dropped to the ground, transforming back into his human-form, they all saw a gash across his arm.

"What happened?" Amana asked as he wrapped Kojo's tunic around him.

"Oh, nothing." Kojo pulled his clothes around him. "Just met an unfriendly arrow, is all."

"Do they know we're coming?" Ikenna was on guard.

"No," Esi said from the back of the group. "The one who shot at Kojo suspected it was a scout, but nothing more. They don't know of any attack as far as I can see, but there are so many minds I can't decipher them all."

"That's good to hear," Amana said. "No need for our plan to go to shit just yet. It hasn't even started. Did you get the message to Yemi?"

Kojo stood himself up, fully clothed now. "Yes. He knows everything. Says he'll be able to get the First Son—sorry—the Great-Chief to hold the meeting on the festival grounds instead of the great hut."

"That's the best we could have hoped for," Amana said.

"So what's next?" Kojo asked.

"Ikenna's group will push into the village, warn as many of the villagers as they can, and send them back this way." Amana turned to Emeka, who was already painted and dressed in his ceremonial outfit. "Will this area work for you?"

"The closer I can get, the faster my ritual will take effect." Emeka looked to the dead kishi by the river. "But I'll feel much better starting the ritual here, away from the kishi. Just keep them away from here, would you?"

"I'll try my best." Amana nodded. "How much time will you need?"

"At this distance and if I work fast," Emeka started counting on his fingers, "about an hour should do it."

"You can make that work, right?" Amana turned to Ikenna.

"I don't know." Ikenna shook his head, turning to Kojo. "You did tell Yemi to stall as much as he could, yes?"

"I did." Kojo nodded.

"If something goes wrong and there is a fight, I can take out most of the other kishi. But if it comes down to me and Baako ..." Ikenna trailed off.

"Just go with them, Amana," Kojo decided.

"No, I have to protect you lot." Amana shook his head. "And I made Ime a promise. I can't keep it if I can't keep an eye on you."

"You won't have to," Esi said, tapping the side of her head. "I'll let you know if you need to double back."

Amana clenched his jaw. There wasn't a lot of time, and hasty decisions were usually the worst kind.

"Are you sure you'll be okay here? Your wife will give me an earful even with that wound you have." Amana pointed to the blood seeping through Kojo's tunic.

"It's okay," Kojo said. "She'll forgive you for something like this. Hurry up. The villagers will need you. Once Baako makes the announcement, the men won't stand around to be servants to the kishi. They'll need you and Ikenna protecting them. And don't forget to use them; not all of them are helpless."

"All right, then," Amana sighed. He looked over the rest of the small group. Kojo had brought six of his best men—or so he claimed. One of the boys looked no older than fourteen. Amana would have to work fast, not only for the villagers' sake but also for the sake of this small group. "All right, everyone, this is it. Communication will be through Esi. She'll give us an idea of when the shaman is done. Keep them protected at all costs. If anything goes wrong ..." Amana directed this at Esi, "... you let us know straight away. We'll come right back. If we have to retreat, at least we'll bring a few of the villagers with us. Is that clear for everyone?"

They all nodded their heads. The Bajok men pounded their chests with spears in hand. The Ya-Seti saluted with their national gesture—two fingers shaped like a V.

"Guardians," Kojo said to his men in the Bajok Tongue. "*We are the arrow's tip, the sharpened blade, the shield of Aya and her anointed hands. She is our body and we, the stream. Wash away the filth in service to the Divine. Protectors of Her will. She flows eternal.*"

"She flows eternal," the Bajok men said in unison. Amana noticed that they all wore the same necklace with the spiral charm.

"Do you have anything to say?" Amana asked the Ya-Seti. They shook their heads.

"All right, then, keep low," Amana said to Ikenna at his side. "You're our best chance against these things."

"And here I thought you were our savior." Ikenna smiled. "I'm still interested to see how it is you fight."

"Let's hope for both of us that we won't need me pulling off any heroics."

As Amana and Ikenna pushed forward with their Ya-Seti force, they cleared out each hut with efficiency. The Ya-Seti moved more like assassins than an army, their feet as light as panthers. After the first set of huts, Amana deferred to their clear-out tactics, following the gold trim of their blue armor.

Most of the huts were empty. Many of the villagers were already at the festival grounds, but they picked up as many stragglers as they could, sending them back down to the river where it was safe. Some of them didn't believe they were in any danger, but when Ikenna showed them the hyena on the back of his head, they left without protest.

You all work fast. What should we do with all these people? Esi said in Amana's head.

"Send them downriver. They can stay with the Ya-Seti and their elephants in the farmlands," Amana replied. Ikenna looked at him with raised eyebrows but then realized Amana was talking to Esi.

"No wonder my father wanted Esi so badly," Ikenna said as they cleared another hut.

"They're dead-useful in the Esterlands. It's almost a requirement for any fighting force if you wish to actually win wars," Amana replied.

Ikenna stopped Amana with his hand. "Wait."

Amana hid behind a hut, watching as a pair of Bajok warriors walked down the path ahead of him. Their hair was long.

"Those are kishi," Amana said.

"They are," Ikenna confirmed. "Not very good ones if they needed their hair."

"I think those are some of the ones who escaped when Chief Oba had everyone cut their hair. What do you think? Should we take them out?"

The kishi looked into hut after hut.

"Where are they all at?" one of them asked.

"There were already a lot at the festival grounds," the other answered.

"I don't know," the first said. "Something feels off. The Chief said to have our guards up."

Amana saw two Ya-Seti archers ducked behind a hut adjacent to the warriors, their arrows were trained on the men. Four more Bajok warriors were approaching behind the archers, but the Ya-Seti hadn't seen them.

"Ikenna, cloak them now," Amana ordered.

"Already on it."

Amana could feel Ikenna's influence running through the air. Though the Ya-Seti kept their emotions in check, nothing could stop the thrill of a potential kill.

"Esi, tell them to stand down. Get them out of there," Amana whispered.

Got it! She said in his head.

Amana turned his eyes to the Ya-Seti. One of them seemed dazed for a moment but looked over her shoulder. She tapped her partner, who also took a glance. Then they dipped back into the safety of the shadows.

"Hey, the Chief says it's time to start," one of the approaching Bajok warriors said.

"You all go ahead. We'll check the rest of these out."

"All right, but don't take too long."

They all pounded their chests and parted ways.

"We should tail them," Amana said, already moving to pursue them.

"There's no time." Ikenna grabbed his arm. "If the meeting is starting, we have to be there for the other villagers."

"But Emeka and the others ..."

"You have to trust your soldiers. You say you were some captain. Didn't you have to trust your crew?"

It was true—Amana had put trust in his crew. But those were individuals he had personally vetted for years before he could trust them. The men and women who fought under his direction now, he barely knew. But he knew that the villagers would need their help, and there wasn't much he could do now.

"All right, all right," Amana conceded. "Let's move on. Esi, you might have company, two Bajok headed in your direction."

Thanks! Emeka won't like that. He's really getting into it over here.

Amana smiled, following behind Ikenna, who had already regrouped with the Ya-Seti.

"All right, this is where we'll all break into pairs," Amana said when he finally caught up. "Everyone take a position around the festival grounds. Our best course of action is to surprise them. Once they know an ambush is happening, they'll come at us straight away. If we can take out one for each of us, that'll help us even the odds a bit."

"That hawk-shifter give a head count on the demons?" one of the Ya-Seti archers asked.

"He could only confirm the ones who were outside the main hut. And there were at least a dozen. So, we should expect more. Just be ready for the way they'll make you feel. They don't just fight with their teeth. Keep your wits about you. They'll try pulling at your emotions. Stay true, and you'll do fine."

"Nothing can break a Ya-Seti," said the same archer—more of that Ya-Seti confidence. Amana hoped it would do them well against the kishi. He looked over their heads. He could see more people shifting towards the center of the village. "All right, we don't have much time; let's head out, everyone."

They all went their own ways, keeping to the shadows. Amana led the way with Ikenna close to his back. They found a spot just next to the big hut. Many of the villagers were huddled in the festival grounds, far fewer than there should have been. That was good; the fewer in the cross-fire, the better.

But there was no sign of either Baako or Yemi.

"Are you sure Kojo got the message to Yemi?" Amana asked

"I don't see why not."

The villagers looked at the warriors that surrounded them with shifty eyes. How many of them had already known they were now controlled by a band of kishi? Some must have suspected. Many of the warriors that stood guard around the festival grounds were unshaven, shadows coloring the bottom of their eyes. The feeling was so unlike the festival that had been held only a moon-cycle ago. The silence was chilling.

"This is awkward," Ikenna whispered. "Where's the damn Chief?"

"Don't do anything rash," Amana warned. He almost had

forgotten that Ikenna had a personal vendetta against Baako, the kishi, who he believed had killed his would-be lover.

"You worry about yourself," Ikenna said, that defiant gleam in his eye back again. It was clear then why he was so keen on being here instead of backtracking. He wanted Baako for himself. And he wanted him now.

"There they are." Amana patted Ikenna on the back. From the threshold of the great hut came Baako and his Chief-Guard—Yemi and Nanga among them.

I don't see the kishi you mentioned, they might have turned back. Emeka said he only needs a half-hour more. Keep doing what you all are doing, Esi's disembodied voice said.

"People of Bajok!" Baako raised his hands. He wore an elaborate robe of jewels and silvers, the garb of his Chief-Father. "As most of you know, there has been a change of power. My father was faltering. He was not protecting the village as he swore he would do. Enemies came into our home and took from us which we hold most dear. When Elder Uzoma went missing, he made no effort to pursue, too afraid of the Black Rocks and the dangers that were there. As some of you know, I went there myself to pursue this threat, to stop it despite my father's denial."

Some of the villagers nodded their heads in agreement.

"So, I challenged my father to Ugara's Dance, which is the right for any of us here. And I was victorious. Unfortunately, he would not yield, and I had to end him." Baako gestured to one of his guards. The guard went into the great-hut and brought out the dead Chief Oba, laying him on the dirt. "This is the tradition of our people. We may only be ruled by the strong."

"Good riddance!" One of the villagers said.

Amana raised his eyebrows at that. Some of the villagers, including Ime, didn't like the Chief, but to see him dead, like this … Shouldn't there have been more remorse?

"You feel that?" Ikenna asked. Amana turned to him, then felt inward. The kishi were influencing the villagers, pacifying them.

"Not many cared for the Chief. They would have been more shocked, but the kishi are pushing their feelings in the direction they want."

It wasn't working for all of the villagers, though. Some of them had some loyalty to the Chief who had ruled over them their entire lives.

"Where are the Ya-Seti?" one of the women in the crowd shouted.

"They left because of my father. They thought him too weak," Baako lied. "Because of my father's indecision, they thought it best to take their alliance elsewhere."

"But what about their daughter? Why would they leave her?"

Baako clenched his jaw, his nostrils flaring. Amana could feel his empathic abilities push out towards the woman. But he wasn't doing it correctly. Instead of massaging her feelings, he tried to dominate them like a puppeteer.

"Your Great-Chief speaks." Yemi stepped forward. "You should not interrupt him."

Listen to Yemi, he's trying to save you, Amana thought.

What's that? What's happening? Esi thought back at him.

"Oh, sorry," Amana whispered. "Nothing, nothing. Keep Emeka working at the ritual."

"What are those marks on his neck?" one of the Bajok shouted from the crowd. Baako's lapse had let a few other villagers slip out of the kishi influence. Amana gripped his sword tight. The Ya-Seti tucked away in the shadows drew their bows.

"There is another confession I need to make." Baako raised his hands to the crowd. "But one more outburst and I will have to take action. You see, this village needs a strong hand to lead it back to the glory it once had. Bajok and the other villages need to bring back the dignity of the Golah Empire. But we can only do that from a seat of power. *I* will be that power."

Baako turned around, showing the back of his head. Now

Amana could see that his birthmark was no ordinary one. It was the crease of the hyena-head he could not fully suppress.

The birthmark protruded into a snout, eyes, and fur sprouted from his back as his body contorted in unnatural angles. Next to Amana, Ikenna started to change, too, ready for his time to strike. There were gasps from the crowd.

Nanga's knuckles went white around his spear, not sure whether to attack or hold his ground.

One brave—or entirely stupid—man made a dash for Baako, picking up a stone along the way. He was still twenty yards away from Baako when a spear was thrown through his neck. A woman screamed as the man fell on top of her, dead.

"We said we wouldn't kill anyone!" Nanga shouted, pointing his spear at Baako, a bit too close.

"Nanga ..." Yemi shook his head on Baako's other side. "Not now ..."

Nanga's face scrunched up in thin lines, but he let himself relax. Reluctantly, he let his spear settle back down to his side.

Baako stood to his full height. "I do not wish to kill anyone in this village." His voice was deep and animalistic now, nearly a growl. "I wish you all to survive under my rule. But there will be conditions."

Many of the villagers were too horror-stricken to do anything at all, plastered to the ground. Ikenna was trembling, though not from fear. The young man would not be able to contain himself any longer.

"Hey, remember that stuff you were telling me," Amana said. "Don't let your enemy conquer you."

"Shut up, Amana," Ikenna said through gritted teeth. His body twitched against itself. It seemed it was taking everything in Ikenna to hold himself back.

"We will be as powerful as the Ya-Seti and the other Great Nations with my power. But to ensure our line is strong, we cannot rule with the men we have. The first condition of my new rule is that all men of Bajok must submit their wives to the kishi, where they will breed with strong men," Baako said with a clenched fist.

That was the last straw for nearly all the men in the crowd—the kishi influence be damned.

"They didn't like that," Ikenna said, though Amana could make that out for himself.

"I'll die before I let you take my wife," one man spat. The fear that was once etched on the men's faces were now eradicated by bold-faced bravery. Other men came to the leader's side, bracing for a fight.

"Tell Emeka to hurry up," Amana said to Esi. "A fight's about to break out."

Almost there. Keep them busy. He needs ten more minutes.

Ikenna didn't need to wait for orders. He bounded into the crowd, barrelling straight for Baako.

"NOW!" Amana shouted.

Though there were only six Ya-Seti hidden, at least a dozen arrows flew from the shadows. Of those arrows, ten struck Bajok warriors. The rest of the arrows met their targets but were blocked by kishi-hides. The Ya-Seti continued to shoot two arrows at a time.

Amana chased after Ikenna, barking orders.

"To your left, Ikenna!" Amana shouted. Ikenna adjusted, avoiding a lunging strike from a kishi. He rolled away from the tackle but used that momentum to strike back. The kishi-hide was strong, but it was no match for another kishi's bite. Ikenna went right for the other beast's throat, stopping its movement quickly.

Wait. There's a problem. The kishi, they are here. They were waiting.

"Check your back!" Amana shouted again, but his directive was too late—Esi's voice threw him off. A pair of kishi converged on Ikenna, protecting their leader. Amana pushed forward with sword in hand, aiming for the closer one's human heart.

Stab!

The first kishi went down. That got the attention of his partner, who turned to Amana. Amana raised his sword in a defensive posture, letting his sight guide him. What he saw was Ikenna's jaw wrapped around the other kishi's neck. All Amana had to do was distract the kishi, so that his sight would come true. Easy enough. He only needed to dip into the spirit dance, avoiding the kishi's ferocious strikes. After a bit of bobbing and weaving, just as Amana saw, Ikenna's hyena-head sunk his teeth into the kishi's throat.

"Let's go!" Ikenna snarled.

"Wait, Esi called to me," Amana grabbed Ikenna's arm. "They're in trouble."

"We are already here. If we get Baako this is all over anyway," Ikenna said. "Trust them, Amana. They'll protect the shaman."

There was no one else between them and the stage where Baako waited. He was ready, hyena-head already growling. Amana didn't turn to see how the villagers or the Ya-Seti were doing. He could only hope they were at least surviving.

"Come, Yemi!" Baako shouted. "Help me!"

Yemi didn't move. Baako looked over his shoulder. Nanga pointed his spear from Baako to Ikenna, unsure who he should attack.

"You are War-Chief!" Baako said. "What are you doing? You, Nanga, help!"

Nanga's spear quivered, still pointing side-to-side.

Yemi only shrugged. "You should handle them fine, *Great-Chief*. Just like you did with your father."

"Traitor!" Baako lunged for Yemi, hitting him in the gut. Yemi flew back into the throng of fighting villagers and kishi. Ikenna tackled Baako, pushing him away from Yemi and the others. Nanga still was not sure who to attack.

"Nanga, go help Yemi!" Amana ordered.

Nanga nodded his head and jumped into the fray of battle, where a fire had broken out.

"I've been waiting for this a long time," Ikenna said with menace. Baako swiped at Ikenna but missed wide. "Why did you do it, Baako? Why her?"

Amana, those two kishi, they're here. They got most of the boys. Emeka is making a run for it. I tried to stop him but…

Esi's voice stopped suddenly. Amana turned his head south, but the battle was already raging. There was no way he could get back to them. Not now. Ikenna was right—the fight would have to end here.

Ikenna shuffled close to Baako, snapping at his throat.

"I didn't touch the girl." Baako bit back at Ikenna's leg. He drew blood. "Father told you to stay away from that girl. She had no magic, no benefit to our family."

"So, it was father that killed her, then?" Ikenna was the one who got wild, biting at nothing but air.

"You wouldn't listen," Baako said. "Women are distractions, remember what father said. It's good now that she's gone."

"Ikenna, he's baiting you!" Amana shouted, but his words fell on deaf ears. Baako was manipulating the fight as he saw fit, pushing his influence over Ikenna.

"Go to hell!" Ikenna spat as he overextended himself into the path of Baako's jawline.

Amana jumped to Ikenna's defense, using his sword as a shield. Baako's bite did not find Ikenna's flesh, but instead, found Amana's steel. Amana pulled his blade out, slicing through the hyena-head's lips. Baako cried out—though the wound was shallow. In defense, Baako lashed out with hand. Even Amana's sight wasn't fast enough to see the hyena's paw come down across his face.

The blow was hard, throwing Amana back several paces. Ikenna and Baako continued their fight.

Amana hoped Yemi was okay as he stood himself back up. Yemi must have been fighting amongst the others, or perhaps he was among the dead. The festival grounds were a bloody mess.

Amana could not distinguish between villager and kishi. And the fire that had started was spreading across the other huts and their straw-roofs.

If Yemi was there, Amana could not see him, dead or alive. The villagers were putting up a better fight than Amana could have hoped for. The kishi were winning, but it was not the slaughter Amana had envisioned.

"We could use Emeka's help right now, Esi," Amana said.

There was no answer.

"Esi, can you hear me?" Amana repeated.

Esi? He thought to himself. Maybe she would hear him better that way?

Still, there was nothing.

Ikenna was losing his fight with Baako, but the new Chief was winded. All Amana needed, was one strike through Baako's human heart, and he could end this. Baako was slow enough now that Amana could see him even without his sight. Amana turned to one of the dead Bajok warriors, taking his spear from his dead hands.

Baako was on top of Ikenna now, snapping at his throat. All it would take was one true bite, and Ikenna would be done for. Amana stretched out his arm, aiming for the Baako's human-head. But before he could throw his spear, an arrow struck Baako through the eye. Then a second. Then a third through his human heart. Baako fell off Ikenna, who was too exhausted to stand.

Amana followed the path of the arrows. He expected to find one of the Ya-Seti—but it was Yemi.

"Esi, are you there?" Amana whispered to himself. "Baako's dead. You all can move up now. Finish the ritual."

"Calling that telepath of yours?" Yemi said. "She won't answer you."

Yemi let another arrow loose. At first, Amana thought he wanted to make sure the job with Baako was done. But the arrow sunk deep into Ikenna's side. The young man gave out a small cry. Then, he didn't move.

"You of all people should know, Amana." Yemi stepped onto the stage. "My kind are very cunning and deceptive. Well, the ones who are worth a damn." Yemi kicked at Baako. He wasn't moving anymore, either. "You fail over and over again because you are too trusting, Amana."

Amana couldn't believe it. What was happening? Why was Yemi doing this?

"First, with Uzoma, now with me," Yemi said.

Esi, where the hell are you? Amana thought.

"Kishi of Bajok!" Yemi shouted. "Head to the northern walls. The Ya-Seti hide with their elephants in the tall grass. Show them a proper welcome. You four, go down by the river. The others should have captured the telepath and the shaman already. Bring them to me."

From the corner of his eye, Amana saw Nanga among the living. The man crouched low, unseen by the kishi. Once Yemi gave the order, Nanga shuffled toward the northern wall. Was he going to warn the Ya-Seti?

"No," Amana whispered. He could not believe that everything was betrayed. Yemi knew everything. He knew the location of the Ya-Seti, the location of the others. Amana had to do something. He had to fight back. "No!"

Amana shot up, letting his sight guide him, unabated.

"You will die!" Amana jumped high in the air, two hands held around his sword. He was going to kill Yemi. He was going to save his friends. No one would ever betray him again.

CHAPTER 23

THE CHIEF KISHI

THE FIGHT WAS ALL TOO EASY FOR YEMI. HE TOOK A SIDE-STEP and slammed the back of Amana's head with his bow. Amana's strike was entirely too predictable. He fell face first, eating dirt instead of victory.

There were a few defeated villagers left, but most were dead among the flames. Women and children lay mangled across the festival grounds. Amana had failed them.

There were only two Ya-Seti archers among the dead. Where the rest were, Amana could only guess. Perhaps, trying to warn the other Ya-Seti or saving the others.

"No," Amana resolved. He stood back up and attacked Yemi again. This time he stepped into the sway, thinking of what Kojo had told him about balance and the spirits. Though he did better, it wasn't enough. He managed to avoid two of Yemi's strikes, but he could not match the third. Again, he found himself face-first in the dirt.

"Why are you in such a rush to die, Amana?" Yemi smiled. "Don't you want to see your friends?"

"We trusted you!" Amana shouted through a bloody mouth.

He rolled onto his back. "It doesn't make sense, it doesn't make sense," he kept repeating to himself.

"It doesn't? I suppose this is the point where I tell you everything that happened and why it happened." Yemi knelt down next to Amana. Amana tried to swing his sword at Yemi's ankle, but the strike was feeble. Yemi kicked it away without effort. "You're a smart man, *Captain Lekkun*. You should figure it out."

"How did you ..." Amana said. It didn't really matter now, did it?

"I know, I know," Yemi said. "Betrayal is a hard thing to swallow. Captain Zuberi was a confidante of yours, was he not? I was betrayed, too. Trust me, I know how it feels. To see all those you've known most of your life just taken away in such a short time."

Amana didn't even consider how Yemi knew all of this. It didn't really matter in the end. "... Baako never killed that girl, did he?" Amana asked.

"No, he did not."

"Nor his father?"

"Nor his father. The transfer of power had to be legitimate before I could become Chief myself. Once the Chief falls in combat, the War-Chief takes his place."

"I don't understand. Why kill the girl?"

"Simple," Yemi said. He stabbed Amana in the arm. Amana yelled out in pain. He was going to die here, in this village, out in the Westerlands where he was never meant to be. "If I caused conflict between the sons of the Great and Mighty Uzoma, they would be less effective against a true enemy—me."

Amana turned his head to Baako and Ikenna's unmoving bodies.

"I suppose I should thank you, though." Yemi lifted himself from his squat. "I didn't actually think you would kill Uzoma. Thought that was impossible, honestly. I only meant for you to tire him."

"The kishi that attacked us," Amana said. "The ones that guarded us at the top of the Black Rocks—"

"Were all mine, yes."

Amana stood up again, though the pain in his arm and neck were debilitating.

"I'll show you how impossible it was to kill that old man." But Amana could not move. He could not bring himself to strike Yemi. The best he could hope for was to fall to his knees.

"You heard the story of this place, I'm sure," Yemi said. "About the heroes of Bajok: Chief Oba and the Great and Mighty Uzoma. The Bajok say they killed the kishi, forced them back into the rocks. But that wasn't true. They didn't kill *me*."

"Save me the story," Amana winced. His vision was blurred. "You'll die here today."

"I don't think so, Amana," Yemi said. "You and all your friends have no hope here. Oh, look. Here they are now."

Amana turned to the southern end of the festival grounds. From between the huts came Kojo, Emeka, and ... Nya. Why was Nya with them? Where was Esi? Nya should have been north of the wall with the other Ya-Seti.

"Before you die, I need to conduct a little test." Yemi walked over to the group. "I need to know how you defeated Uzoma. If there are others like you, I'll need to know how to fight them, as well."

"Where's Esi?" Amana ignored Yemi, asking the group.

None of them looked his way. Emeka only shook his head.

"I'm sorry, Amana," he said. "It almost worked, but they came from across the river. We couldn't hear them. You're right. They can walk on water."

"What happened to Esi?" Amana knew the answer, but he needed to hear it to be sure.

"Where *is* the telepath?" Yemi asked his men. "Bring her here."

One of the kishi went back through the huts. When he

returned, he had Esi between his jaws. She was slumped over, her neck bobbing freely. The kishi dropped Esi right at Amana's feet. Amana hoped it had been quick.

"Who did it?" Yemi asked peacefully, though there was a sharp undertone in his voice. "I told you not to kill the telepath. Do you know how useful they are?"

The kishi that had laid Esi down held his head low. Yemi was so close to him, just above his neck.

"I didn't tear her throat out … just hit her the one time," the man said, his hyena-head whimpering. "She was doing funny stuff to our heads. I just wanted to make the voices stop."

Yemi pressed his fingers into the bridge of his nose. "That's one thing I won't look forward to as a leader. I've always hated delegation. But you can't do everything yourself, can you?" Yemi patted the side of the other kishi's head. "It's okay, it's okay."

In the next instance, Yemi had transformed into his kishi form, snapping his subordinate's neck like a twig.

Amana had underestimated these kishi, had underestimated Yemi. He clenched his jaw, looking away from Esi. She would never get to leave this place. He could never get to show her the Sapphire Isles. It was Imani all over again. But now, he knew who to blame. It was Yemi he needed to direct his energy toward.

"Good," Yemi closed his eyes, sniffing the air around him. He pulled a piece of cloth and cleaned the blood from his hyena-head, letting it sink beneath his head once more. "It's anger that drives you. I thought that much would be the case."

And then Esi coughed, rubbing the backside of her head. She was alive!

"Damnit!" Yemi growled, kicking at the kishi he had just killed. "The fool knocked her out, was all. You two, make sure she doesn't play any funny mind games. Keep her suppressed."

A pair of kishi nodded their heads, throwing out their influence over Esi. She was still rubbing the back of her head, regaining her purchase when her eyes rolled back into her head.

It was the same look she had whenever she was around Uzoma. Yemi snapped his fingers. Three kishi surrounded Amana.

"I want to test you," Yemi said. "But don't get too excited."

From the north came the sound of an elephant war cry.

"Looks like we've found the Ya-Seti." Yemi smiled. "All right, Amana. So, it's anger that drives you. But that still isn't enough. Even now, your strength would not do much for you. There is something more. I need to push you further."

Yemi turned to the group.

"Which of you is most important to Amana? From least important to most."

None of them looked at Yemi. Emeka was breathing hard, wide-eyed and shaking his head. Kojo and Nya were warriors through and through. Neither of them gave anything up. But Amana knew that the both of them were in danger. He just couldn't let Yemi know that; he needed to suppress his emotion.

"No one?" Yemi said. "No one has an idea of who here is most important to Amana? I have a few ideas. I've been watching Amana closely since he came here."

Yemi stood next to Emeka. "This man helped clear Amana's name when he first arrived." Yemi turned his head to Amana. "To think some of the villagers thought *you* a kishi." Yemi laughed at that, examining Amana's reaction. There was none. "But no, Emeka isn't the one. No, not at all. He was vital to your plans here today, but he could have been lost. You only know this man as an acquaintance at best."

Yemi moved to Kojo. "Now this man. He stood up for Amana! Even got the whole village behind him. Were it not for him, perhaps Chief Oba would have killed Amana on the spot without going forward with the moonsbeam ritual. And I've noticed how Kojo and Amana train together, how they broke bread together. Yes, they became fast friends. What do you say, Kojo, is Amana your friend?"

Yemi touched Kojo's forehead with thumb and forefinger.

Kojo tried to fight the influence, but the kishi's power was too great.

"Yes," Kojo spat out. The veins in his neck and forehead were throbbing.

"Ah, I think we have a winner!" Yemi exclaimed, removing his hand from Kojo's forehead. Kojo fell to the ground, panting.

"Oh, but wait, we can't forget about Nya." Yemi turned to her. Amana bit his tongue. "Nya is interesting. When Kojo told me about your plans, she was to be with the Ya-Seti north of the wall, was she not?"

Yemi turned to Amana for confirmation. Amana gave him nothing but a scowl.

"My men found her trying to help Emeka as he attempted his feeble ritual. My assumption is that she came running when the telepath was no longer communicating. But still, why would Nya be so far from the battle when she is such an effective fighter?" Yemi pinched his lips. "When my men found her, I thought it an obvious answer. She no longer had a hand!" Yemi squeezed Nya at the cheeks. She jerked her head away defiantly. "Let me guess, that was Uzoma's doing? Judging by your faces, I would say it was Uzoma's doing. She would be of no use to the fight if she could no longer use her brilliant archery skills. But then, I had to remind myself about Nya. She holds more power than the ability to sling arrows from a string, that same power she is trying to use now."

Yemi took a side step as a mound of dirt came straight for his face. As Yemi spun from his dodge, he kicked Nya across the face in one fluid motion. His hands rested peacefully behind his back. Nya fell to the floor, face-to-face with Kojo. Amana almost jumped but held firm. Nya wasn't in danger—at least, not yet. Amana couldn't let on what Yemi wanted to know.

"So, if Nya could still use her magic," Yemi continued, letting Nya eat dirt. "Why would she be held back? So I reminded myself again of Amana and his time with Nya. You two had grown quite close. I didn't need my abilities to sense that. The kishi that guarded you told me all about the night you shared with one another. Didn't think you had it in you, Amana. You claimed to be a man of virtue. Tsk, tsk, the monks would never approve."

Amana spat at Yemi's feet. "Considering it was Amana who led this band of rogues, I suppose it was his decision to make sure Nya was out of harm's way. And why would he do that?" Yemi turned to Amana with a confident smile. Amana couldn't contain himself for much longer. He could feel his heart beating furiously against his chest. Yemi must have felt it too.

"Ah, that's it," Yemi said. "So, after my little examination it would seem that Nya is the most important." Yemi stepped over Nya. "And then Kojo." Yemi walked over Kojo. "And sorry, Emeka, it looks like you're the third wheel here ... Or maybe I should congratulate you? You see, I still need to test Amana, and since you would be no help with my evaluation, you will survive. It's sort of brilliant, really. The two who are already laid out on the ground are my two best subjects."

Yemi snapped his fingers again. The kishi pinned Nya and Kojo on the ground. One of the Bajok warriors gave Yemi a spear. Amana needed to break free somehow. But three kishi were more than he could handle. He needed to dig deep; there was no other option. But would he be able to control himself with his friends so close to his enemy?

"We'll start with Kojo." Yemi lifted his spear. "I don't want Amana too riled up. Kojo, do you have any last words?"

"Aya, Great Power Divine," Kojo lifted his chin, looking straight into Amana's eyes. *"Whose currents cleanse our spirit—I ask forgiveness for this one. They have failed you in life, may they fare better in death. Absolve their sins of the flesh and spirit. Let them serve you in your anointed stream, where they may be renewed in your image."*

Yemi was tapping his foot. "Is that it?"

"Amana," Kojo said. "Tell my family—"

Thunk!

Yemi's spear went straight through Kojo from pate to chin. Yemi was right about one thing. It did rile Amana up. Without conscious thought, Amana swept the kishi with his foot, behind their knees. The power behind it sent them all to the ground.

"Amazing!" Yemi knelt close to Nya. "See how focused he is, how powerful. Oh yes, I can see how Uzoma could be challenged by someone like that. But killed by him ...unlikely."

Amana could see the ghostly images of the kishi countering him, but he was four steps ahead, deep into his sight. Dodging them was too easy, killing them was easier.

"I don't have an hourglass on me, but that looked like Amana got through the lot in thirty seconds," Yemi smiled. "What do you say, Nya? Thirty seconds? Maybe twenty? Those kishi couldn't even control Amana's emotions. My, oh my."

Amana couldn't stand to listen to Yemi any longer. He ran straight for him. How dare he be so close to Nya? How dare he touch her and whisper in her ear? How dare he kill his friend?

As Amana ran toward Yemi, the Bajok warriors that remained shot arrows at him. Amana could see the arrows easily, pinpoint their targets and trajectory. Some would have hit him, most went wide. Amana focused on the ones that would do him the most damage, ducking and diving.

"My goodness!" Yemi clapped. "All right, I think I've seen enough."

Yemi lifted his spear above Nya's head. Amana redoubled his efforts. His sight showed him the quickest path to Yemi. But it would mean he'd have to take a few arrows to his side, non-lethal but painful, nonetheless.

The decision wasn't hard.

Amana sprang out towards Yemi, three arrows plunging into his side and chest. With an open hand, Amana swatted the spear aside, and with his shoulder, he drove into Yemi's chest. Both men flew back several paces into the middle of the village huts. Yemi was the first to get up.

"Brilliant!" Yemi transformed into his full kishi form. "Now it's time to end this thing."

The other kishi rushed to Yemi's side.

"No closer, no closer," Yemi said with an outstretched hand. "This is what I wanted, after all. Let me size him up, see what we could be dealing with."

The other kishi stood back, giving Yemi enough room to face Amana alone.

"Not a smart move. You don't want me alone," Amana said through a clenched jaw. Yemi's hyena-head snapped at Amana's injured arm, drawing more blood from Amana's shoulder.

"I like my chances," Yemi said as he bounced on all fours. "You're a marvelous talent, Amana." Yemi circled the injured man. Amana stood his ground, unwavering. "You could have killed me like you did Uzoma. But you're too injured now, and your magic—as powerful as it is—is finite."

It was true. When Amana had faced Uzoma, it was only a brief moment, no more than a minute, as Yemi had discerned. Amana's power drained quickly now. The black edges around his sight darkened; the ghostly images of Yemi's actions were fading.

"You're a good man, Amana," Yemi said. "It's always sad to see good people leave this world, no matter how necessary it may be."

Yemi was looking for a break in Amana's stance, a slack shoulder or a wobbling leg. When Amana gave into his fatigue, forcing himself to adjust his balance, Yemi went in for his final attack, pouncing like the hyena he was.

But then, the Ya-Seti arrived.

One of the elephants stomped through the huts. A lone archer on its perch shot an arrow at Yemi. The arrow lodged itself into Yemi's side, forcing the hyena-man to spring away. With Nanga in the lead, the Ya-Seti had turned the tides of the battle. But their attack was focused on the festival grounds, flanking the remaining kishi. None looked to the darkened huts where Amana and Yemi were laid out.

"The Ya-Seti are more resourceful than you think," Amana laughed with one knee on the ground. It was too much to stand.

"Go! Fight them!" Yemi shouted to the other kishi.

"War-Chief! Ikenna, he's alive." One of the kishi nodded to the festival grounds. Kor Mosai stood next to Ikenna with his guard close to his side. Was that Shanaki next to him, as well? Amana couldn't see what the Kor was doing, but Ikenna rose back to his feet.

"Go, finish the job, then!" Yemi shooed them away with a few bites. They all rushed towards the renewed battle. "It doesn't matter." Yemi turned to Amana. "Most of these kishi were Uzoma's. I'll find more."

"Not if I can help it." Amana would have stood, but his legs would not answer his call.

"And how will you do that?" Yemi laughed.

"I won't do it alone," Amana said as he crawled backward. The river wasn't far behind. If he could just …

"Your band of friends is gone. The Ya-Seti won't help you in time," Yemi said as he followed Amana. "They're too busy with the other kishi. I'll kill you before then."

"You misunderstand me." Amana still looked for strength in his legs. He just needed to stand up, he just needed to find his sway. "Dead or alive, they'll always be with me. The lessons they impart, the way they made me feel. They all have value."

"These are all just words," Yemi said. "You can't even stand now."

What had Ikenna told him before the fight? Uzoma had conquered Amana, had latched onto Amana's spirit even though he was dead. The same should be true for the others, as well. Kojo was gone, but he imparted himself onto Amana. He taught him how to listen to the spirits and the ancestors.

Amana placed a hand on his knee. The river was only a few paces away now.

Amana had limited himself because he used only the power within, his own anger, his own fear. But his magic was beyond that. It was the bridge between two worlds, a bridge between people—and how they connected through predicted movement. All Amana had to do was make that connection, find that contact. It was like the ritual at the festival. What had Emeka done? He got the whole crowd involved, used all their energy in unison. Not because Emeka was individually powerful, but because he understood the power of the collective.

Amana lifted off his knee. The river was only a few strides away now.

Uzoma was right. Amana could learn much from the people of Bajok. But there was one thing he had left out. There was also much to be learned from compassion. It was what drove Amana to this place. It was what kept him moving, kept him persevering. But Amana had betrayed the memory of his wife and daughter. He let Zuberi conquer him when he should have thought of them. He could not defeat Yemi now because he only saw Yemi.

Amana reached his feet. Finally, he felt the water around his skin.

Amana had allowed himself to hate Yemi. He allowed Yemi to cloud his sight. Amana hadn't seen it because he hadn't considered Yemi's motivations. But now, he saw Yemi in his horrid figure. Amana did not want to end him because he was angry. He wanted to end him because he had to. It was the way of things. Sometimes, a fight was just a fight. Sometimes, conflict was inevitable. And Amana had to meet the call.

Amana drew back into the sway, using not only his power but also the power that rested in the village grounds, and the power that flowed through the river. He started reciting words that made sense to him.

"I do not speak words of war," Amana rocked from left to right.

"What is this?" Yemi hunched his back, stalking Amana.

"I do not commit acts of war," Amana bounced forward and back.

Yemi attacked, but Amana stepped with the flow, letting Yemi push forward into the river.

"I do not deny anger nor compassion. I do not deny my strength nor my weakness." Amana continued his sway, letting the water lap around his ankles.

Yemi attacked again. Amana could see his action through his sight. The image was no longer ghostly and elusive, but thick and full. Amana pivoted away from Yemi, then brought his hand down on Yemi's human nose.

Crack!

Yemi went down hard, his body splashing into the river, his nose dislodged from its usual straight angle.

"The Spirits and Gods flow through my veins," Amana continued to chant. He was not sure where the words were coming from. "I am made in their image. And I will be their guardian in this world."

Amana did not attack, still flowing with the sway. He could feel energy course through him. His wounds were forgotten, his fatigue, nullified.

"You are not welcome here, demon," Amana said as Yemi climbed back on all fours. His growls were coupled with a salivating jaw. "You have lost your path, Yemi."

"To hell with you!" Yemi's voice was deep and chilling.

"For your actions against our world, I commit you to death."

"*I'm* the one who's going to kill *you*." Yemi slashed with his paws left and right. Amana rolled his shoulder side-to-side, countering with an open palm. He pushed out straight to the hyena's snout, connecting hard. Yemi flew back into the river, but he did not sink. Instead, he fell atop it as if it were solid. Amana picked up a sword from the ground. Yemi picked himself back up, standing atop the water.

"How are you doing this?" Yemi said. "How are you not dead?"

"I've been dead for years." Amana still flowed with the spirit dance, the water around his legs glowing a bright blue. His feet were light and weightless. It wasn't his own power carrying him on. "But this place, these people. They have shown me life, for all that it offers and takes away. It's not one or the other, but a conduit of energy. Don't you feel it, kishi?"

Yemi snarled, then hurled himself toward Amana. But the fight was already over. Amana had seen it while he spoke. Yemi would try to bait Amana to the left but use his hind legs to strike Amana across his wounded chest, then swivel back around to sweep Amana off his feet. But Amana already shifted to the left, letting Yemi get in close. Amana jumped over the kishi, slicing his sword through its human neck. Amana tucked into a ball in mid-air, coming out of it when he landed in the river.

Yemi was dead, though his hyena head took a few seconds to catch on, still snapping at the water before it ceased. Amana stepped close to Yemi's body, leaning over him as though in prayer, like Kojo's dancers.

"Aya, I ask forgiveness for this one. They have failed you in life, may they fare better in death." Amana could not remember the whole prayer, but he hoped that would be enough. After a moment, he collapsed, feeling all the pain and fatigue at once. "May the Gods forgive you for your sins, Yemi. And may they forgive me for mine."

CHAPTER 24

THE SENDING

AMANA DREAMED OF FIRE. HE SAT ON A RAFT THAT FLOATED ON water, but he was surrounded by an inferno. The fire painted the ocean's waters red, like a pool of blood. The flames painted pictures of his wife and daughter. They were angry specters, chiding him for his failure. Amana tried to convince them he couldn't have known, but they wouldn't have it.

Amana stopped making excuses and admitted his fault.

He was the sole reason for their demise. He was too confident of his hold over the Sapphire Isles. Amana should have seen it, he could have. But his thoughts then had been self-absorbed.

No, they weren't, Amana thought. *Asha and Sanaa would never think that of me.*

The flames dipped back into the water. The red sky drifted back to blue. Amana's raft careened to a small island, stopping only when it hit the sandbar. Amana fell on his back, letting the cool breeze drift across his pain.

The sky was clear, save for two clouds. The smaller one could have looked like Sanaa if he squinted hard enough. The larger one could have been Asha.

They looked happy up in the blue sky, even as the ocean winds split them apart and they drifted away.

"IT'S A MIRACLE YOU'RE STILL ALIVE," A VOICE SAID. "THE arrows in your side missed your vitals, but you lost more blood than I thought possible. Your back was brutalized. That may never heal the same, but there are still methods I can try. Your arm healed the fastest. The cut wasn't too deep."

"The kishi?" Amana asked through blurred eyes.

"Dead or ran away," the voice said. "Elder Chika, go tell the others Amana is awake."

"Yes, High-Chief." Amana could hear small footsteps leaving the room. The sounds of straw parting let him know that he was in a hut. Was he still in Bajok?

"I'm sure that's not the last we've seen of the kishi. But I've protected us against any new attacks. This time, it should hold. I've been teaching the methods to the younger ones."

Amana finally put a name to the voice.

"Shaman Emeka?" Amana's voice was hoarse.

"Yes and no," Emeka replied. "I'm now High-Chief Emeka, though I still do a lot of the shaman duties. You were an inspiration that night, Amana. I've never seen anyone manifest the spirits to their aid like that, not without a village full of supporters. Some of us heard what you said about not being alone. Thank you, for reminding us about the power of community—oh no, don't get up."

Amana's eyes cleared. He was in a small hut with a skylight shining down on Emeka's workstation. He lay in a bed of thick blankets. Emeka was right. He shouldn't have moved. His entire body ached.

"I think you're right about that," Amana laid back down with a thud.

"Like I was saying." Emeka turned back to his station. He had a fire going under a pot. "We had lost our way here in Bajok, too focused on reclaiming the glory of our old empire. We tried to fool ourselves that we could be like the Ya-Seti or the other Great Nations, a marriage of power. But we already had that power here amongst us all. We just needed to join forces.

"As you know, many in our village can touch magic, though no *one* individual is quite as powerful as the binaries in the Great Nations. We believed in a communal power when I was younger —that changed, of course, with the kishi. We thought we needed one great person to get rid of them all."

"How did the Ya-Seti fight back?"

"Well, I must admit, that Shanaki of theirs is pretty good." Emeka brought Amana some hot peanut soup and fufu. "She helped us fight the kishi back by nullifying their powers. And her father, I thought he could only regenerate himself—that's why he lived so long, you see."

Amana had already been familiar with Kor Mosai's powers when he was a pirate—but Emeka was so fascinated by it—Amana did not want to sully his re-telling.

"He was also pushing his magic out, healing soldiers that had fallen. It was mad!" Emeka started flinging around an imaginary sword. "I saw a Ya-Seti get taken out by a kishi, and the next moment, she stood right back up like nothing happened. Her wound was gone. Mosai was there on that elephant with Shanaki, healing everyone as he went. He couldn't save everyone, of course, but he did a great job, nonetheless.

"That's the reason your arm healed up so quickly, I think. He was dead tired after the fight, though. It took a lot out of him. I've had our own healers try to tend to him. He's still knocked out, just a few huts down."

Emeka said all this really fast, excited by his own recollection of the fight. Amana would have smiled if it didn't hurt so much.

"Esi?" was all he could ask.

"She's safe ... alive. But no one will speak with her. It's like they think they'll be cursed by the kishi. I tried to explain to them how it works—how the kishi are birthed—but they'd rather believe in their superstitions." Emeka shook his head. "I would talk to her myself, but I've been so busy tending to the wounded."

"Kojo ..." Amana whispered.

"He didn't make it." Emeka frowned. "We gathered all the dead. Baako, Nanga ... some of the Ya-Seti too.

"Nanga?" Amana strained himself. "But he was okay when I saw him. He was leading the Ya-Seti."

"The Ya-Seti owe a lot to him. He let them know the kishi were coming." Emeka nodded. "But he sacrificed himself for Nya, in the end. A kishi ripped him to shreds. No coming back from that ... We'll have the sending tomorrow. I'll be doing the ritual for the dead. The boys Kojo trained will do a special ritual for him. I heard his son and daughter will lead the ceremony. It should be beautiful."

Emeka finally fed some of the soup to Amana. It burned, but it was a welcome treat. Amana didn't realize how dry his throat had been.

"Ikenna made it, though," Emeka perked up. "But when the villagers saw he was a kishi, they didn't want anything to do with him. We tried to explain, but they wouldn't have it. So he ran off. Said he needed to hunt the other kishi down anyway."

Elder Chika returned to the hut. Emeka welcomed her in.

"She's here," Chika said.

"Let her in," Emeka replied.

Chika opened the door far enough to let in their guest. It was Nya. She looked beautiful, and healed, though the scar across her face remained. She wore loose, light-brown clothing now instead of her tighter armor slats. One long sleeve hung over her arm, hiding her stub.

"Chika, let's go check on the Kor, shall we?" Emeka sat up, leading Chika out.

"Thank you, Amana," Elder Chika said before she was shuffled out. "Thank you for what you did for our village."

Nya stood at the hut's entrance for a long while, taking all of Amana in.

"You'll be getting that a lot now," she finally said. "The people in the village adore you for what you did."

"I didn't do much."

"You did something that awoke those spirits. They weren't just working through you, they worked through the whole village."

"It was the Ya-Seti that gave me a second wind," Amana said. "Yemi had me before they showed up."

"You didn't see it." Nya sat next to him, taking on the duty of feeding him soup. "But we were losing. There was only one elephant left that pushed through. It took the kishi off guard, but they were winning. Until the spirits started sprouting from the fires. When I saw you fighting Yemi, you were glowing the brightest."

"So, it was the spirits that saved me then …" Amana frowned.

"Give yourself some credit, Mana," Nya said. Amana finally smiled. He liked it when Nya called him that. "The Elders say you had to be the vessel to call the spirits. They worked through you, yes, but you had to call them, to begin with. The power was in you, and you motivated everyone else. You know how the kishi use their powers to make us all feel like crap, right? Well, the spirits sort of counteracted that. Where hope seemed lost, they restored it. *You* restored it."

Amana wasn't sure what he could say to all that. He had never been a hero or savior before. What did heroes do when they saved people? When celebrating a successful raid with his crew, he just threw them all a feast. But that somehow did not feel appropriate for this situation.

"It was you, really," Amana finally said. "You helped me get through it."

"No, I compromised you." Nya turned away.

"You liberated me," Amana cut in. "Were it not for you, who knows what would have become of me. Maybe I'd be working for Uzoma now, or maybe I would have tried my hand at Zuberi again. But you changed that. I don't feel that hate anymore. It no longer clutches at me."

"But what about the mountain monks?" Nya fed Amana more soup. Amana took a big gulp before talking again.

"I don't think they'll have me," Amana said. "And they shouldn't. I'm no monk."

"Then back to pirating?"

"I don't think that works for me either."

"Then what?"

"I'm not sure, really." Amana hadn't considered it. He thought himself dead. His next journey, he thought, was to meet the Gods. "But I can't deny I'm a decent fighter."

"Well," Nya gave him a small smirk, "the Ya-Seti are offering. Shanaki needs to rebuild her guard."

"They asked you to speak to me?"

"No," Nya said slowly. Amana raised an eyebrow. "Well yes, but they didn't force me to—it was my idea first. We need someone like you."

Amana, a Royal Guard to the Great Nation of Ya-Seti? Amana of the Kor'de-guard. It had a nice ring to it, he could admit that much. It might even be decent, honest work. Amana had never known that before.

"Would it be okay if I thought it over on the way back?" Amana asked.

"For me, yes," Nya said. "But like I said before, if Shanaki thinks she can't have you, she'll let the Kor know who you really are."

"I think Kor'de Neema already knows," Amana said.

"Then you'll have two reasons to accept." Nya laughed.

"I suppose so." Amana took another gulp of soup.

Nya laid her hand on his forehead. "And what about us?" she asked. "I mean, you're not pledging yourself to the monks anymore."

"Won't I have to swear off marriage if I bow to the Royal Guard?"

"Yes." Nya moved one of Amana's locs from his face. "But who said anything about marriage? Remember, I told you. I'm not looking for love, just a lot of money. And the Kor'de pays well."

"But me and you ..." Amana was confused.

"Can have our own arrangements," Nya smirked.

"Is that not against your rules?"

"Ah, so you will take the job then?" Nya raised her eyebrows.

"No, well ..." Amana trailed off. "... It's one of my better options."

"I'm just playing with you." Nya chuckled. "If there was something between us, marriage or no, we'd have to keep it secret."

"Well, I'm pretty good at keeping those." Amana finally finished the last of his soup with the help of Nya.

"I'll let you get your rest," Nya said. "After the sending, we'll be leaving."

"Good to see you," Amana said, holding her hand.

"Good seeing you too, Mana," she said. "Let's keep it that way."

THE SENDING WAS JUST AS BEAUTIFUL AS EMEKA SAID IT would be.

The dead were buried just outside the village, close to the northeast wall which was now fallen, trampled by one of the Ya-Seti elephants.

Emeka started the ceremony with a delicate dance. It was much different from his first performance. During the festival, he had needed to gather hype to manifest the ancestral spirits. That night he had stomped the ground hard and shouted at the top of his lungs.

Now, he needed to quiet the dead souls so that they might find peace in the spiritual plane. His dance steps were soft and light-footed. He turned around in spirals with a smooth ebb and flow. It was not unlike the spirit dance, though far less threatening.

Amana watched silently, leaning on a walking stick. Emeka had explained to Amana that each person had their own spiritual alignment. When they died, they attached themselves to these spirits, whether it was Deh'ala of the gates or Aya of the rivers.

But the dead needed guidance, a map to help them find their way. Most spirits found their way just fine with time, but others needed a helping hand. Those who still held contempt—and were not sent—remained among the living. They created what Emeka likened to the "bad moods" of Elders or the "restlessness" of children.

When the ritual was over, Emeka placed his staff in the dirt, turning in circles until the dust cloud enveloped him completely. The dust lit up as it rose into the sky, letting the new spirits drift amongst the winds and clouds. Amana could have sworn two of the clouds looked familiar.

Next was the special sending of Kojo's spirit dancers. His children led the dance, shadow-fighting one another as the others clapped their hands and pounded small drums. Their necklaces with the spiral charm clinked atop their chests as they swayed left and right.

"They may love you, but I will never forgive you," a voice whispered behind Amana. He was surprised to find Ime behind him. "He trusted you. *I* trusted you. And you let him die. You saved that *foreign* girl, but you let *him* die."

"You're right. I couldn't keep my word. But—"

"Save it for someone who'll take that sorry story," Ime fired back. "Just know that my husband admired you. And you let him down. You should be ashamed of yourself."

"Listen," Amana turned slowly with his walking stick. "He was like my brother—"

Ime slapped him across the face, hard.

"Don't you dare call him a brother!" she shouted.

The spiritual dance stopped. Everyone turned to Amana and Ime. One of the villagers stepped forward to restrain Ime.

"No, no." Amana raised a hand. "I'll go."

Amana limped back into the village. The remaining Ya-Seti and villagers spoke to one another silently. When Amana made it near the markets, Nya had caught up.

"Hey, what was that all about?" she asked.

"She's right, you know." Amana clenched his fist. "I froze up when it came to Kojo. I could have saved him."

"There was no way; you had three kishi on you."

"And that didn't stop me getting to you." Amana shot back. He hadn't meant it to come out so harsh. But it was said, and it was the truth. Nya didn't have a reply, only frowned. "If I couldn't bring myself to save Kojo, how can I expect to protect anyone else?"

"You're not being fair to yourself," Nya said.

"It's more than just about me. I have to be better than that."

"Come on, let's go," Nya said. "You wouldn't be like this if that woman hadn't gotten you riled up."

"Maybe that's a good thing," Amana said. "Maybe she woke me up. I can never make it up to Kojo."

"That's stupid, and you know it." Nya stood full in front of him. "You make it up to him each day. You're making it up to him now. You can't let a black cloud like that stay over your head."

"How will protecting Shanaki or the Kor'de help any of that?" Amana said. "I'll be wasting my days in a palace. At best, I'll take down an assassin or two; at worst I'll spend my days arresting petty criminals."

"Petty criminals like you once were?" Nya crossed her arms.

Amana knew she hadn't meant her words harshly, but her tone was fierce.

"I don't think I'll take that job," Amana finally said. "Tell the Kor'de—"

"Tell her yourself," Nya sucked her teeth and stomped back to the ceremony. For a moment, Amana sat there, thinking it would be best to just let her walk away but …

"Wait!" he shouted with an outstretched hand. Nya stopped but did not turn her head. The drums still thumped outside the walls.

"We weren't going to work out," Amana said first.

"Yeah, I know …" Nya replied, her head still not facing him.

"And not just us, I mean the Ya-Seti—"

"I know."

"I have to find my own way in all this—"

"I get it, okay." Nya's voice cracked.

The drums outside the walls stopped. All that was left now was the chirping of birds and the wind passing through the high-grass.

"What will you do now?" Nya turned but did not approach him.

"I don't know, find another village to save." Amana cracked a smile.

"That'll be hard with …" Nya pointed to his walking stick, a smirk betraying her lips, as well. "We'll see each other again. I know it."

"We will," Amana said. He believed it, too.

"I'll give you an hour," Nya said. "But after that, I'm telling Shanaki."

"Thank you." Amana nodded.

"Get out of here, Mana." Nya crossed her arms. She leaned forward as though to approach Amana, but she held her ground. Then she shook her head, turned on her heel, and walked back to the sending.

For a long moment, Amana sat there. Ime was right after all. He could have done better for Kojo. And still could now. Going off to work for the Ya-Seti wasn't going to make up for Kojo's death. No, he would have to find his own way.

Does your offer still stand? The voice came loud in Amana's head. He looked over his shoulders but saw no one.

"Only if you promise to stop doing that," Amana said. "Where are you?"

Esi stepped out from behind a hut. She gave Amana a meek wave.

"So, you're leaving, then?" she asked.

"How much did you hear?"

"Just about everything."

Amana shook his head but couldn't help smiling. "Yes, I suppose my offer still stands, if you do still want to see Esowon outside of Bajok."

"Like I told you," Esi said, "I'm not accepted here. Plus, you look like you could use help getting out of here." She pointed down to Amana's walking stick. "How did you expect to get out of here?"

"I hadn't really thought of that," Amana admitted, looking down to his bruised legs.

"Oh, I almost forgot," Esi said. "I meant to give it to you when you woke up. But I was out in the farmlands, didn't want all the stares I usually get—or any of the thoughts, either."

Esi pulled out a necklace, a spiral charm at the bottom, the same one Kojo wore.

"He wanted you to have this, in case ..." Esi frowned.

"Ime would never let me have it—"

"It's not up to her. *Kojo* wanted *you* to have it." Esi stretched out her hand to Amana, open palm, holding the gift. Amana sighed but took the necklace, examining the spiral closely.

"What does it mean?" Amana asked. "I've seen Kojo, and the other dancers wear them."

"He said it represents the flow of Aya, the flow of life, of all energy, of a'bara."

Amana smiled, tying the necklace around his neck. "Thank you, Esi."

"Of course," she nodded, looking past Amana to the funeral ceremony. "Nya said she'd give you an hour, right?"

"In Nya-talk that's probably only a half-hour." Amana laughed.

"So, let's get going," Esi said, assisting Amana toward the river docks, stopping only for his travel pack—now equipped with a sword and shield.

Esi heaved Amana into one of the boats, using a paddle to push the pair of them into the water's current. After a while, Amana helped, though his arms ached. Emeka was right. His arm was the most healed part of his body.

Part of Amana thought he would be followed. Nya could have changed her mind at any time.

Though his upper body was healed, he was still raw. The boat moved slowly with his feeble paddling, though Esi helped whenever she saw his arms strain—or heard the fatigue in his internal voice. Luckily, the current was in their favor, but that didn't stop Amana from looking over his shoulder every few minutes.

After an hour, Amana knew they were free to travel as they pleased. No one was coming after them. Perhaps Kor Mosai thought it too much an effort to chase down a man half-broken. Amana was sure the Kor would love to head back to the comforts of his palace.

Amana wasn't sure where he would go with Esi first, letting the currents take him to the next natural destination. But Ikenna was right. There were still kishi out there that needed to be repressed.

Somewhere.

Amana

Thank you for reading my debut novel. I'll be honest with you. It was never my intention to write it.

I simply wanted to see an African-based fantasy in the same way I've experienced mythology and folklore from other cultures.

Instead of waiting on my hands for another author to write the story, I did it myself. And I'm glad I did.

If you enjoyed *The Kishi,* please leave a review with your favorite retailer or on social media to help others discover the story.

MORE TALES FROM ESOWON

Demon's, Monks, and Lovers is a collection from the *Lost Tales from Esowon*, a series of standalone stories expanding on the world and story presented in *Tales from Esowon: The Kishi.*

Inside, you'll find dastardly beasts, tortured monks, and unexpected lovers in a set of tales that'll transport you to lands lost to time.

The collection includes:

Last of My Kind
A Servant's Work
Hearts in the Dark

Visit this link to learn more:
antoinebandele.com/lost-tales-from-esowon

ALSO BY ANTOINE BANDELE

AN ESOWON STORY

The Man With No Name

The Kishi

Demons, Monks, and Lovers

Stoneskin

By Sea & Sky

TJ YOUNG & THE ORISHAS

The Gatekeeper's Staff

CHRONICLES OF UNDERREALM

The Legend of Cabrus

ABOUT THE AUTHOR

Antoine lives in Los Angeles, CA with his girlfriend. He is a YouTuber, producing work for his own channel and others, such as JustKiddingFilms, Fanalysis, and more. He enjoys napping, eating pasta, and creating. Whenever he has the time he's writing his debut series: *An Esowon Story*.

antoinebandele.com

GLOSSARY

Terms and Locations from Esowon

- **A'bara:** The word for "magic" in the Bajok Tongue and those who follow the Old Way.
- **Ajowan:** The birthplace of Amana. One of the seven islands on what is known as the Sapphire Isles.
- **Akeem:** One of the Great Cities which holds one of the most sacred religious sites in Esowon.
- **Aktah:** One of the Great Nations, just north of Ya-Seti lands.
- **Aya:** The Bajok God of the Rivers.
- **Baba:** The word for "father" in the Bajok Tongue.
- **Bajok:** A farming village once belonging to the Golah Empire.
- **Boism:** Also known as the "Balance of the Five." It is a discipline of the Junga Monks.
- **Chana:** Slang used for female pirates of the Sapphire Isles.
- **Deh'ala:** The Bajok God of Gates and Thresholds.

- **Eke:** The Bajok God of Harvest.
- **Fufu:** A dough-like starch eaten by the Bajok.
- **Golah:** The former Empire which stretched from Bajok in the south to Imtubo in the north.
- **Golden Lords:** The ruling Pirate Nation of the Sapphire Isles.
- **Gomesi:** A colorful floor-length dress popular in the Westerlands of Esowon.
- **Guela:** Another farming village once belonging to the Golah Empire.
- **Imtubo:** One of the Great Cities which holds three of the most prestigious academies in literature and arts, science and mathematics, and theology.
- **Ipe:** The Great River that runs from Aktah in the north all the way to Jultia in the south.
- **Jultia:** One of the Great Nations, just south of Ya-Seti.
- **Junga:** Also known as "mountain monks" from the Far East. They are named after the mountain where they reside.
- **Kanzu:** A cream-colored robe worn by Bajok men, mostly the devout oni'baro.
- **Kishi:** A hyena-demon that shares a body with a human male.
- **Kor:** The primary ruler of the Ya-Seti people.
- **Kor'de:** Spouse to the ruler of the Ya-Seti people.
- **Nyoka:** A river that borders the south of Bajok.
- **Ogó'ala:** The Supreme Bajok God.
- **Oni'baro:** Religious devotees to the spirit-religion of the Bajok.
- **Ugara:** The Bajok God of War.
- **Ula:** The Bajok God of the Cosmos and Foretelling.
- **Kijana:** Slang used for male pirates of the Sapphire Isles.

- **Sapphire Isles:** Seven Islands that cut between the nations of Aktah, Ya-Seti, Jultia, and Vaaj.
- **Ya-Seti:** One of the Great Nations. Known for their skilled archers and lavish palaces.
- **Yem:** The Bajok God of the Oceans.
- **Vaaj:** One of the Great Nations, just east of the Sapphire Isles.

www.ingramcontent.com/pod-product-compliance
Lightning Source LLC
Chambersburg PA
CBHW020605310726
48979CB00008B/1357/J

* 9 7 8 0 9 9 9 8 4 8 3 2 6 *